The Bends

The Bends

by

Leah Devlin

www.penmorepress.com

The Bends by Leah Devlin

Copyright © 2016 Leah Devlin
All rights reserved. No part of this book may be used or reproduced by any means without the written permission of the publisher except in the case of brief quotation embodied in critical articles and reviews.

ISBN-13: 978-1-942756-46-0(Paperback)
ISBN -978-1-942756-47-7(e-book)

BISAC Subject Headings:
FIC014000 Fiction / Historical
FIC008000 Fiction / General
FIC031010 Fiction/ Thrillers / Crime

Cover work by Christine Horner
Editor: Chris Wozney

Address all correspondence to:

Penmore Press LLC
920 N Javelina Pl
Tucson. AZ 85748

Or visit our website at:
www.penmorepress.com

Dedication

For Jeremy

Author's Note

Woods Hole is a real village on the southwest corner of Cape Cod. However, all characters in this novel are purely fictional. Their resemblance to persons alive or dead is coincidental.

Chapter 1

Thirty Feet Down

The *Jack Rackham* floated silently in the shadow of a cliff. The mural on its transom was painted in graphic and gruesome detail; bright splashes of color depicted the pirate, Calico Jack, dangling off a gibbet in Port Royale, Jamaica. In the verdant background of palmettos was a small prison where, from behind barred windows, two women gazed at the decaying body of their captain. The strawberry blonde pirate, Anne Bonny, had a look of smug contempt, while Mary Read's face was wracked with despair.

The jagged spire of rock that loomed over the trawler lacked the lush, tropical vegetation of the painting. The only inhabitants of the grey pinnacle were seabirds nestled along the narrow ledges and invertebrates clinging to the slick rock wall below the surface. The seclusion of the island was what attracted the artist of the pirate mural to this location. The art student, Maggie May-Nolan, loved secluded places.

The unseasonably warm October evening permitted a rare late season dive. Thirty feet down, Maggie and her dive partner, Lily Tate, hung off the rock wall on the opposite side of the spire to the *Jack Rackham*. Beyond the cones of light from their dive helmets all was an impenetrable black.

Maggie held an underwater camera over a patch of coral, positioning it for a perfect shot, while Lily waved a piece of fried chicken in front of a crevice. Odorants from the soggy chicken wafted into the crack, rousing the lobster within. The crustacean inched forward from its hiding place, the temptation too great to ignore. Two lobsters already writhed in Lily's mesh dive bag. If she could capture a third, it was time for a seafood feast on the *Jack Rackham*. The lobster's antennae poked curiously outward; next emerged the chelipeds, the pincher and crusher claws; quivering antennules followed; and finally the cephalothorax. "Just a little further," whispered Lily. She moved the chicken teasingly out of grasp, coaxing the animal out of the crack. The net swept silently behind the lobster's tail, the telson. *Swoosh!* The furious lobster flailed and twisted in the net.

"Dinner time!" Lily declared triumphantly into a speaker inside her dive helmet.

From within her own helmet Maggie said, "Just one more shot." Her camera paused over an orange coral. The tentacles swayed, searching for suspended food particles in the slow current. In a blast of light the pulsating tentacles were captured in digitized form. Back at the art college, images from the dive camera would become bursts of color on canvas. The paintings of marine invertebrates and underwater landscapes by the emerging young artist were attracting attention at local art exhibitions and auctions. The canvases were large and vibrant, and resembled, said one Cape Cod art critic, the paintings of Georgia O'Keefe.

Maggie tucked the camera into her dive bag. "I'm hungry."

"You're always hungry. How can you eat all the time and never gain a pound? That's why I hate you," Lily complained. She checked the bag to ensure no lobsters had escaped.

As usual, Maggie didn't comment. She seldom did. Besides, Lily was happy to do the talking for the both of them. Maggie's opinions were expressed by a nod or shake of the head, and her moods indicated by the speed and direction she blew cigarette smoke from her lungs. Fast skyward smoke meant anger or vexation, while a languorous downward stream expressed contentment.

"Did you hear that?" Maggie asked suddenly.

"Yeah," Lily said warily. "It sounds like a motorboat."

"Dim your head lamp. Who the hell would be out here at this time of night?"

"Besides us, you mean? Whoever it is, I hope they don't spot the *Jack Rackham*. What if they're pirates? What if they steal the boat and kidnap Kyle!"

"No one would bother kidnapping Kyle, he's too useless, but we'd still be screwed. We'd have to hold onto the rocks until Lindsey motors out to get us, which could take hours—"

"By then our legs might be chewed off by sharks," Lily interrupted anxiously.

"And then Lindsey will bitch and moan for the next few eternities about us diving at night." Maggie paused. "That boat's definitely getting closer. Hug the wall and turn off your light completely."

Lily shut off her helmet's lamp. "Hold my hand, so we don't lose each other in the dark," she said, her voice quavering.

The two divers hovered in the gently swirling blackness, staring upward. Their air tanks and helmets scraped against the rock wall, and bubbles trickled from their regulators in the cool silence. They strained to slow their breathing, lest the rising bubbles reveal their presence below.

The motorboat approached and stopped directly above them. Lily's grip tightened on Maggie's glove. The engine idled. To their submerged view the boat was silhouetted against a clear, moonlit sky. It appeared to be a rigid hull inflatable with an outboard engine. It was unusual for such a small boat to be so far out at sea, thought Maggie.

Clink... clink... clink...

"Weird," Maggie whispered, "it sounds like hammering."

Clink... clink...

"I hope they're not tethering their boat to the rock. Let's swim to the other side and make a run for it!"

"*Jack* can't outrun a motorized boat, not even a raft," Maggie countered. "Listen! The hammering's stopped."

The black silence was broken by a *splash!*

An oblong object drifted toward them. They gasped into their speakers and their locked hands tightened. Above, the boat revved its engine and sped away. The object continued to sink, teetering back and forth in descent.

"I'm gonna turn on my headlamp," Maggie whispered nervously.

"Me, too," Lily whispered back.

"Oh my... my... God...." Maggie stuttered.

A body, shrouded in white linen and rope, was visible only for an instant, before it disappeared into the blackness.

Chapter 2

Two Years Earlier
Woods Hole

Her entire life was punctuated by tragedy and missed opportunity! Maggie lit a cigarette, inhaled deeply, and blew a jet of smoke into the chandelier of the old beach house. When a high school senior, she'd received offers to attend the Rhode Island School of Design (RISD), Yale, and the Art Institute of Chicago, but in a state of temporary insanity and delusion, she'd declined them all. Instead, she'd opted to stay at home and attend art courses at the community college. All because of a fucking man!

Worse yet, Lindsey Nolan had been right—again. Her adopted mother and guardian had warned her that the limited selection of introductory art courses at the community college would quickly become boring. "Go to Yale, Maggie," Lindsey had urged at the time. "I could visit you and my friends in the Engineering Department."

Maggie had grimaced. Every decision Lindsey ever made was somehow connected to her work.

Now, just as Lindsey had predicted, in only three semesters she'd completed all the art courses the community college had to offer. She gnawed at her fingernail. Perhaps she could reapply to Yale or RISD? Bad idea. Horrible idea. That would mean leaving Woods Hole, and even though Connecticut and Rhode Island were not that far from the Cape, the thought of traveling still caused surges of panic. Another stream of smoke jetted upward. Besides, there was that new art institute—the Newbury College of Art—just up the road. Why hadn't she thought of this sooner? It certainly didn't have the same name recognition and prestige as RISD or Yale, but it might be a real possibility. But if she visited the campus, no way was she going on a scheduled tour. She hated guided tours.

"College websites tell you basically nothing," Lindsey pointed out, when Maggie brought up the topic. "You'll get detailed information if you go on a tour and can ask questions. Don't you want to know about Newbury's painting courses?"

"Right," Maggie muttered sarcastically, "like I'm really going to ask questions to some chirpy tour guide." Her teeth raked the side of her thumbnail.

"Chirpy tour guides can be very informative," Lindsey countered in a know-it-all tone.

Maggie's thumbnail started to bleed. She crammed her hand into her pocket before Lindsey commented on the nail biting. This tedious conversation, Maggie decided, could be terminated if she focused her attention out the window. Light streamed through the warped panes, and the grey bay beyond made for an interesting scene to paint, but the idea was quickly nixed for lack of originality. Countless artists had already painted seascapes through windows.

"...and find out about the credentials of the art faculty," Lindsey rambled on as background noise. "We could go together. I'd love to find out more about the college."

Maggie remained obstinately silent and fixed her gaze on the intricate geometric patterns in the ceiling tiles. She blew more cigarette smoke into the cloud encircling the dusty chandelier. Enough blather. With a non-negotiable "No," she dashed out the back door.

Perhaps streaming old episodes of *Game of Thrones* in the solitude of her cottage would obliterate all thoughts of a campus tour? A scheduled tour would mean an irretrievable hour (or more) of cheery babble from some admissions staff in a khaki skirt and loafers, with an undergraduate in tow nodding in obsequious agreement that everything on campus was ideal. Why couldn't the admissions people just tell the truth? *The cafeteria food sucks, the Internet's sporadic, and the professors are self-important windbags.*

Truth or nonsense, Maggie would hear none of it. Reruns could wait. Instead, she grabbed her wallet and car keys. She would conduct a campus tour on her own.

Maggie had passed the sign for the Newbury College of Art countless times, as it was located on the main road that led to her hometown of Woods Hole, but the campus could not be seen from the main road. She turned her Jeep onto College Avenue, passed through a dense forest and crossed a covered bridge to reach the campus. The trees parted to reveal a grassy field dotted with large metal and cement sculptures. Three grey buildings and a maintenance outbuilding sat in the distance. Down a hill, just like at her home, were a rocky beach and rickety dock.

Toward the left was a three-story dormitory constructed of cheap, modern materials. Its artificial façade lacked the charm of the stone buildings, which she guessed had been built during the Victorian era. A hedge of boxwoods circled the dorm, and the adjacent parking lot was filled with the battered compact cars of poor art students and the glistening BMWs and Audis of trust fund babies. Maggie found an empty parking spot in the commuter lot. She exited the Jeep and headed toward the dorm, but her entry was prevented because the door required a swipe card. A sidewalk led her around the building.

It was a warm day, so many of the rooms on the first floor were visible through opened windows. One room was painted black and decorated in Wiccan images and posters of Goth bands. Another room belonged to dance enthusiasts, as the walls were covered with prints of Edgar Degas paintings and the New York Ballet. Another room had a pyramid of beer cans on the windowsill, while another clearly belonged to Salvador Dali freaks, with prints of melting clocks, lobster telephones, and surreal religious paintings covering the walls. She rounded the corner to the back of the building.

Shirtless guys tapped a ball over a net on a beach volleyball court. The patio area clearly had Wi-Fi, as students were hunched over laptops at the picnic tables. Next to the woods was a white gazebo. It was unoccupied, so she walked over to it. She pulled a smartphone from her skinny jeans, sat down on a bench and read some tweets, but they were all were mind-numbingly boring. She gazed into the forest. The trees had a complicated crosshatched pattern of vertical trunks and diagonal branches that might make for an intriguing painting in hues of blue and green. The wooden beams of the gazebo's roof were draped with cobwebs and speckled with bird droppings, but the roof appeared leak-proof, so it would be possible to paint even in the rain without having the canvas ruined.

She crossed to the opposite side of the campus. The Administration Cottage was a stone building that looked like it had once been the residence of a gardener or chauffer. A notice board inside the door listed the offices that occupied the cottage: Admissions, Bursars, Business Office, Dean of Academics, Development, Registrar, Student Life.... From what she could see, a once charming turn-of-the-century cottage had been carved up into a honeycomb of cluttered offices. She scanned the list again. Visitors Registration. She darted back outside, fearing that an office drone might call campus security to toss her off the premises, since she hadn't registered for a visitor's pass. At least expulsion from the campus would be preferable to being signed up for the next campus tour.

Maggie headed quickly toward the last unexplored building. The Gripp Art Center looked like most mansions of New England. Forming the centerpiece of the campus, the small castle was surrounded by a large porch with stone arches. Dramatic turrets pointed skyward from a steep roof of dark slate. Impish gargoyles crouched along the eaves and watched the tiny mortals below. The grand building must have been constructed in the late 1800s.

She climbed the porch steps and passed under a massive stone archway. She gasped with awe, transported back to medieval times. The foyer and two adjacent rooms, an expansive library and elegant reception area, were paneled in a beautiful, deep mahogany. Intricate carved beams and bosses traversed lofty ceilings. Heavy stone walls in the passageways created a dungeon-like atmosphere; a knight or hooded executioner might lumber around the corner at any moment.

Her wonderment evaporated as she proceeded inward to discover that that rest of the majestic mansion had been gutted and remodeled in modern materials. The first floor was compartmentalized into art studios for painting, printmaking, ceramics, sculpture, and computer graphics. The air was rich with inspiring scents of clay, paint, plaster, and wood.

The studios caused her pause; their shape was odd, dictated by weight-bearing walls constructed of the same grey stone and mortar that composed the mansion's exterior. The central gallery also was bordered by unusually thick stone walls. White panels fixed to the walls were covered with paintings, and the hardwood floors were dotted with classical and modern sculptures. From white metal girders spanning the heights aerial sculptures gently swayed in the currents from the air ducts.

Winding her way through the second and third floors of the mansion, she found faculty offices, a small art library, a computer room, student study rooms, classrooms, and a conference room.

A picture on the wall of the foyer caught her eye as she exited. She leaned toward it. The image was of the same mansion in which she stood, but the cars in the circular driveway were from the 1970s. She read the plaque under the photo. The enchanting stone mansion had never been a domicile of some old patrician family, but had once been the headquarters for Gripp Architecture and Construction. The modest cottage had not been occupied by a gardener or chauffeur; it had been the home of the founder and CEO, Edward Gripp himself. The mansion had not been constructed during the Victorian era after all; it was built in 1970, when Edward Gripp was thirty-one.

Months later in Cos Cob, Connecticut

Jean Tate loomed over Lily, demanding her daughter's password to the student web portal of the Newbury College of Art. The email sent from the Admissions Office contained vital information: the name of Lily's prospective roommate for the upcoming academic year. Earlier that afternoon, Lily had emailed the girl, friended her on Facebook, and linked to her Twitter account. Her daughter's impulsiveness was so aggravating! Before the two girls bonded, it was absolutely imperative to check that the student would be an appropriate companion for her daughter. Upon receiving Lily's text about the email, Jean had immediately ordered her secretary to cancel all remaining afternoon appointments, scurried along a salad bar at the grocery store for three healthy dinners – there was no time to cook—and rushed home.

"Passwords are supposed to be confidential. Even the orientation leaders at Newbury told us never to reveal our passwords to anyone," Lily complained.

"Except mothers!" Jean insisted.

"Mom!" Lily implored.

Jean spun on the polished floor of her daughter's bedroom and headed toward the modem in the hallway. "I'm shutting down the Internet for a week," she called over her shoulder.

In a panic, Lily grabbed a pencil off the desk, scribbled down the password, and ran from her bedroom. "Here," she panted, her hand outstretched.

Jean stared at the paper. Her daughter's passwords were always baffling. What could slampiece69 possibly mean? "Thank you. Remember, you have violin lessons tonight."

"Do I have to go?" Lily whimpered. "I'm so tired. I just want to sleep."

"I'm spending a lot of money on those lessons and your recital is next week. You won last year. You must win again this year."

Lily retreated listlessly to her bedroom. "Whatever."

Jean entered her home office and delicately placed her navy blue blazer over the back of her leather office chair. She frowned again. A bit of lint was on the blazer's sleeve. With a sigh of consternation, she dropped the lint into a wastebasket. She moved to the laptop on her desk. Lily's password allowed her access to the email from the Housing Coordinator. She intently studied her desk calendar. Should the student not prove suitable, there would still be time to contact the Director of Admissions and request a roommate reassignment.

She typed the student's name into the search box of Facebook. Frustratingly, the posts on the girl's Facebook page were not visible. She enlarged the image on the touchscreen. The landscape photograph was clearly taken from a boat and showed a coastal property with a small beach and a grey clapboard house atop a hill. A glittery cigar boat and a trawler were tied up at a long dock. If this was the roommate's home, the square footage of the beach house certainly exceeded that of her own executive home in the Polo Springs development. She smiled to herself. So far, so good.

She scrutinized the roommate's face. It was the face of a serious, diligent student, she concluded. The girl was of mixed Caucasian and African descendent. Her ash blonde hair was cut very close to her head in an androgynous style, and her skin was mocha brown. Alternating blue and green studs outlined the girl's ears. Her eyes were large, blue, and alert.

Her own daughter was also of mixed race, diluted by the Caucasian blood of her husband. Compromises have to be made in life, Jean reminded herself. Marrying Evan Tate had been a clever and expedient means to obtain citizenship in the United States of America.

A painting—a vibrant interpretation of undersea life, embedded into a landscape photo—was alive with color. Jean fretted. This student might be an impediment to Lily's winning of Newbury's prestigious Windsor Award. But that was a problem to worry about later, so she returned to her immediate task. Another photo showed the girl in a wetsuit on a boat. "Wonderful!" she murmured, "Lily also scuba dives." The photo was a reminder to sign Lily up for her next specialty course, Advanced Open Water Diving.

Jean bent toward the computer screen, inspecting a photo of the roommate's family. The roommate and a tiny sister were in lovely gowns; the younger brother wore a black tuxedo. The parents—perhaps in their late-thirties—seemed a bit young to have a college-aged child. The father, also in a classic tuxedo, was tall and dashing. The mother wore an elegant silver evening gown.

Where had she seen this photo, she wondered, tapping her manicured fingernails on her desk. It was so familiar. Then it dawned on her—it was not this exact photograph that she recognized, but a similar one taken at the same gala. The parents had been photographed with the discoverer of the Viking wreck in Buzzards Bay, Jessie McCabe, at the opening of the Vinland Viking Museum. For weeks these photos had been all over the news.

Yes, now she remembered. The father, Derick Briggs, whose grandmother's philanthropic trust underwrote the museum, was an heir to the Briggs Tobacco fortune. His wife was that Cape Cod Nobel laureate, Lindsey Nolan.

In ecstatic relief, Jean dropped back into her chair. There would be no need to contact the Director of Admissions at the Newbury College of Art. The student, Maggie May-Nolan would be a suitable roommate for her exceptionally talented daughter.

Chapter 3

Spire Rock, the Present

The dishwashing detergent commercial had to be over, Kyle Monroe figured, so he aimed the clicker at the high definition TV and switched back to women's wrestling. *Life is good.* He belched with pleased deliberation, a Budweiser burp. For the past hour, he'd stretched himself across a sofa in the *Jack Rackham*, waiting for two babes in tight wetsuits to appear from the depths with lobsters for dinner. Not bad for a boy from Indiana. Both Lily and Maggie were hot in their own distinctive ways, but neither eclipsed the tangled, glistening wrestlers on TV, two full-grown women with poofy hair, clad only in black leather thongs and bras. How cool would it be to find some cougar—like the dean's gorgeous secretary, Doreen Best—to tumble around with?

He checked his cell phone for the time and rose with a groan from the cushions. Lily had told him that by the time they surfaced he had to have set the table, melted the butter, and made a green salad. Instead he'd chugged down three Buds, munched on Doritos, and alternated between chick wrestling and a replay of last weekend's Bengals-Bills game. He exited the salon and peered over the transom. Through the black water the two dive lamps appeared like yellow fog. Shit, the girls were ascending!

He bolted to the galley and jerked open the drawers, searching for silverware. He set three places, then flung open the refrigerator door and tossed two sticks of butter into a frying pan on the stove. He returned to the fridge, staring helplessly at the vegetables. How in the hell does one make a green salad? He glanced, discouraged, at his own belly. He was only twenty-one and a beer gut hung over his belt. If he had a ripped body like Curt Fredrickson, the chicks would be all over him, even Doreen. His mother, he recalled, first washed the vegetables when making a salad, so he held the lettuce, carrots, and cucumbers under a tap. The butter began to smoke and spatter, so he quickly slid the pan away from the heat.

It would be impossible to watch the girls peel off their wetsuits from the galley, so he carried the vegetables and cutting board to the table where there was a direct view to the deck. Lily and Maggie, in the futuristic high vis yellow dive helmets, finally appeared on the dive platform. They removed the helmets, detached the regulators, and hefted the air tanks onto a tank rack. Their conversation was emphatic and energetic.

Maggie stepped out of her wetsuit first and flung it toward the dive lockers. She was significantly smaller than Lily, weighing not much more than a hundred pounds. Her skinny body was like that of a teenager just entering adolescence. Standing in a red bikini, she gesticulated wildly, demanding something of Lily. Lily, who'd inherited her size from her tall American father, was holding her ground. She stood hands on hips, scowling and resolutely shaking her head. Looking up from dicing the cucumbers, he eagerly waited for Lily to strip off her wetsuit, as she was muscular and curvaceous, like the wrestlers on TV. Shivering, Maggie wrapped herself in a towel and stared seaward. Lily tugged off her wetsuit and strode wordlessly through the salon and galley, toward a hot shower in a cabin below.

*****

Kyle looked longingly at Lily's lobster tail; his dinner plate was wiped clean. Maggie's lobster was untouched. She impatiently flicked an unlit cigarette between her fingers; smoking was not permitted inside Lindsey Nolan's boats.

"We cannot talk to the police about the dead body," Lily argued vehemently. She took a large swallow of white wine. "What if it was a mafia hit? The mafia has moles all through the police force. Then the mole finds out we reported it, and some hit man comes after us!"

Kyle remained doubtful of the story told by his overwrought dinner companions; he'd seen no sign of an inflatable boat carrying a dead body. But the girls had been diving on the south side of the rock, on the opposite side from where the *Jack Rackham* was tethered. Still, he felt compelled to propose a theory of his own. "Maybe the body was a woman?" He cracked open another can of beer. "Like a mother who was selling drugs from her home in suburbia and a competing drug dealer knocked her off? If we reported it, at least her children would know that their mother was dead."

"Shut up, Kyle!" Lily cried. "Then the drug dealer would come after us! Drug dealers are violent, you know."

"The guys I buy weed from aren't violent," he mentioned casually.

Maggie shuddered imperceptibly. She didn't want to return to that place... to drugs... and drug dealers. It always resulted in nightmares and night sweats. The thought of losing her guardian, Lindsey, was equally distressing, especially since she'd already lost Rob, her adopted father and Lindsey's former partner. Deep in thought, she drew geometrical patterns in the perspiration on her can of Coke. "Kyle has a point," she said. "The family of whoever it was would at least have closure. When Rob died a few years ago, it really sucked. And it still does. But at least I know where his grave is, so I can visit him. Not to know would be the absolute worst."

"I bet it was a woman," Kyle mused aloud. "Maybe a man and his mistress killed his wife, and then dumped the body since she wouldn't grant him a divorce. Maybe the dead woman was an heiress, and the husband and mistress wanted the inheritance or insurance money."

Maggie nodded in agreement. "Whoever dumped the body was loaded. The yacht that the inflatable sped off to was a million dollar boat. I know everything about boats, and that one cost megabucks."

"We can sit here all night and speculate about the body, but we are never going to know, because we are never going to tell," insisted Lily. "None of us must ever tell!"

Chapter 4

Cape Cod

Detective Bill Bleach leaned out of his chair and peered down the corridor. His partner, Ray, was still—thankfully— at the coffee machine, yacking to their ever-patient police captain about the two sole interests in his small-minded world: the Boston Bruins and the bartender at the corner pub, whom he'd been hitting on unsuccessfully for the past year. The bartender clearly had some taste. Bill had a moment's peace. His attention returned to a website on reptilian diseases. His Chinese water dragon, Dr. Watson, was lethargic and losing too much weight; yet, frustratingly, Watson's symptoms didn't match any diseases on the Internet. Maybe if he replaced the crickets with a more substantial, high-protein meal, like goldfish, then Watson might regain his appetite? But what if it wasn't a dietary issue at all? What if Watson had some rare infectious disease, one that might decimate his entire family of lizards, anoles, and snakes? He could take no chances, so he'd spent the previous evening worriedly lugging the terraria of Dalgliesh, Miss Marple, Sherlock, Olivia Benson, and Jethro Gibbs into the dining room of his small apartment. A doleful

Dr. Watson had been quarantined in the living room, left in solitary confinement.

Bill craned his head and squinted once again between the slats of the venetian blinds at the young woman on the bench outside. What was up with her? She'd smoked numerous cigarettes, walked circles around the front entrance, and crossed the street to buy a cup of coffee, only to return to the bench to smoke another cigarette. What was there to fear about entering a police station? He shut down the reptilian diseases site and thought for a moment. Should he ask his captain how to proceed with the restless woman? But if he brought up the matter in front of Ray, the oaf would strut outside, insult her with some asinine or chauvinistic comment and cause her to flee. "Initiative, Bleach, you need to take more initiative," the captain had told him during his last performance review. And Ray endlessly chided him about dithering where females were concerned. Bill turned off his computer and headed outside.

"Um, can I help you with something?" he asked, shifting his weight from foot to foot. "You've been here for a while."

The young woman looked up from her cell phone and gazed skeptically at him. "Who are you?"

"Ur, Bill, Detective Bleach," he said uncomfortably. His name almost always elicited a jest, and, sure enough, a wrinkle of amusement appeared at the corners of her eyes. Compounding his dreadful name was skin so fair that he almost glowed in the dark. Worse still, he lived on Cape Cod, where five minutes on the beautiful beaches turned him beet red unless he slathered himself with industrial grade sunscreen.

She fidgeted again. "I think I want to file a report," she said cautiously.

"Sure. I can help you with that," he replied genially. "Let's go inside."

"No!" She fumbled for another cigarette. "Can we talk out here? Anyway, I'm not sure what I saw. Maybe it was nothing." She took a deep, thoughtful drag. "No, it was something. Definitely something."

Bill studied her face. Something had frightened her. He dropped onto the bench next to her, and pulled a pen and pad from his pocket. "Do you mind if I take notes? Otherwise I'll forget the details. I'm working on a lot of cases. And I'm a little distracted right now. Something's wrong with one of my lizards."

"A pet?"

"Yes." Already he'd strayed off-task. *Focus, Bleach, focus.* "What's your name?"

She jerked upright. "Why do you have to know that? Can't I just tell you what I saw?"

"Okay, we can start there," he replied. If he first gained her trust, he might be able to get her name and address later. Rule number one: Establish trust.

"I wasn't supposed to be there," she confided somewhat guiltily.

"Where?"

"At Spire Rock, night diving. Suddenly I heard a boat on the surface directly over me. Then there was this weird hammering on the rocks. I thought the boat was being tethered to the rock, but it wasn't. Then someone dumped a body into the water. The body drifted to the bottom right in front of me. I only turned on my dive light for a second, but I saw it."

"Are you sure it was a body?" he asked, intrigued.

She leaned forward, elbows on knees, and stared down at her high-top sneakers that were speckled with paint. She eventually faced him. "Yeah, I think so. It was about six feet long and in a white sheet wrapped with rope. When I came to the surface, I saw an inflatable heading out to a large motor sailor. It was dark, so I couldn't determine the make of the boat, but it had a single mast and was probably seventy or eighty feet in length. It was a transoceanic yacht of some sort."

"Was anyone with you? Can they corroborate this?"

Her eyes flashed again and she readied herself to leave. "I've said enough."

"No, wait. Please. I need more information so we can check this out. Where is Spire Rock? I've never heard of it."

"Most people don't know the place, since it's pretty far out at sea. I can show you." She rummaged in a frayed jean bag and pulled out a tablet. The alternating green and blue polish on her chewed-up nails matched the tiny green and blue stones piercing her ears. She wore baggy grey sweat pants and a long-sleeved grey T-shirt, both flecked with paint. The flecks were fluorescent reds, greens, and blues, not the muted colors used commonly by house painters for home interiors. The young woman was an artist. She pressed a button on the tablet and "Welcome back, Maggie" appeared at the top of the screen. She clicked on a Map app.

"There," she said, pointing. "Spire Rock."

The place was between Martha's Vineyard and the Elizabeth Islands. She expanded the image. "My boat was moored here on the northwest side of the rock, but I was diving there." She pointed again. "That's where the body was dumped, on the southeast side of the rock. I thought that the police might want to check it out in case you have a missing person that you can't find."

"When did you see this happen?"

"Last night."

"I'll search our missing persons database and see what comes up. Now, if you'll just give me your name, address, and phone number in case there are more questions...."

There was a stubborn silence. "No." She slid the tablet back in her bag and rose abruptly. She snuffed her cigarette into the pavement with her sneaker. "I've gotta go."

"How did you get here?"

"There." She glanced toward the parking lot.

"I'll walk you to your car."

They walked wordlessly around the building to where she stopped next to a rundown Jeep. She momentarily studied his tie. "I like that color combination," she said, pointing at his chest.

He smiled at the elaborate pattern of sea turtles. "I love this tie. My sister gave it to me for my birthday. Every summer vacation I volunteer at this sea turtle conservation project in Georgia where we monitor egg-laying —" He stopped himself. Focus, focus, focus.

"You're very young to be a detective," she commented, searching the bag for her keys.

"I'm the youngest detective on the force. I have a number of degrees and had some lucky breaks, so they promoted me early."

"Degrees in what?"

"Criminal justice and history."

She pushed her key into the lock and then hesitated. "When you're interviewing a person, say a murderer... or rapist, is there something about them, a look in their eyes, a gesture... something... that tells you they're guilty? Is that something they teach you guys at the police academy?" she asked uneasily.

"I wish it were that easy," he blurted with an awkward laugh.

Her face remained impassive. "I hope your lizard's okay," she said with genuine concern. She got in the Jeep and drove off.

The Jeep had told him loads. Hanging off the rearview mirror was a parking pass to the student parking lot at the Newbury College of Art. A faded old WH bumper sticker indicated that she was likely a resident of Woods Hole. Another bumper sticker read, ironically, that she was *A Friend of Bill*, and another one read *Just For Today*. She was a clean and sober girl. But the most valuable bit of information was the license plate that would tell him the last name and address of the art student named Maggie.

*****

A nicotine craving woke Maggie in the middle of the night. She groped around her headboard for her phone. It read 3:28 a.m. She rose silently so as not to wake Lily. Atop her desk, she located her lighter, cigarettes, and dorm swipe card, which she stuffed into a pocket of her pajama pants. She pulled on a leather jacket, shoved her bare feet into combat boots, and made her way down the empty hallway to the exit. The night air was moist and salty, and the lawn glistened with dew. She stepped into the gazebo and lit a cigarette.

Fog had crept up the hill from the bay, shrouding the college in a silvery gloom. The administration cottage and

Gripp Art Center were invisible across the vast lawn. For a moment she imagined herself the sole survivor on an abandoned fog planet in an otherwise empty cosmos. Just perceptible through the fog was the dorm where the black windows looked like those of a burnt-out crack house. It was strange living in a dorm again, especially when her own cottage on her family's property was only a five-minute drive away. The dorms of her youth, in orphanages and detention centers, had served their purpose, transient rest stops to acquire food and clean clothes before heading back on the road. Then, by the grace of her Higher Power, she'd wound up in a dorm room at a drug and alcohol rehab with a drunken bioengineer called, in AAspeak, Lindsey N. Eight years ago, when she'd been thirteen. In eight years, so much had been gained and lost. Gained: her sobriety, a home and family, her health, an education. Lost: Brian, her inseparable boyfriend and best friend. What she'd done, he'd raged, was unforgivable. Maybe it was... maybe it was. But it was done.

Holding a cigarette between her lips, she rubbed her hands together for warmth. She would never get used to the cold, for she was a creature of the desert. That much she knew of her past. Her transient mother, the story went, had abandoned her in a trailer somewhere in the Sonoran desert. She, a nameless two-year-old at the time, had been found by a parole officer, who'd named her after a favorite song. Who in the world is named after a Rod Stewart song? And from ancient times—1971. Mothering had not been in her mother's bloodlines, nor was it in hers. At least, mercifully, another unwanted child had not been brought into this world. Then Lindsey'd had to butt into her business and take Brian's side in the matter. "Mrs. McLeod and I could have taken care of the child. I would love to have another child in the family. Maggie, how could you have done this?"

For over a year Brian had assiduously avoided at her Narcotics Anonymous (NA) meetings, and the art college had been a welcome refuge from the cottage where they'd lived together. Too many memories lingered there. Lily and Kyle chattered too much, but there was always the painting studio, the dock, or the gazebo to escape to.

Her cigarette butt arced like a meteor and hissed into the wet grass. The dampness caused her to zip the jacket around her neck, and she whispered a prayer of thanks to her Higher Power for the warm clothes. Lindsey was also to thank, she conceded; the woman had taken her in after their stint in rehab, when they'd had no one else in the world but each other. The air was cold enough to see one's breath. The cold air reminded her of that unspeakable winter in Minnesota. Maggie shuddered.

*****

At four in the morning Bill Bleach wandered into his living room, the way lit by the glow of terraria lamps. He bent over Dr. Watson's terrarium. The goldfish that he'd picked up at the pet store that afternoon was gone. So that was it. The lizard simply wanted a change in diet, from insects to fish. Pleased, Bill swished a net through the new fish bowl and scooped up another goldfish. He slid the screen lid off the terrarium and dropped the squirming fish into a shallow reservoir of freshwater. Dr. Watson opened his bulging, amber eyes and crawled along a branch, while Bill pulled up a chair and watched through the glass.

The conversation with Maggie had distracted him all day. After she'd driven off, he'd returned to his office to find his partner standing at the window.

Ray had bellowed, "A girlfriend, Bleach?" to inform the whole office that he'd been talking to a young female.

"No. She was filing a report," he'd responded flatly, then plopped into his chair and turned on his computer.

"A looker! But me, I like something beefier to grab."

Bill had searched his desk drawer for his headphones and music. "I need to review some missing persons files." It was only a matter of time before Ray said something completely outrageous and that new, no-nonsense cop, Detective Murphy, who was twice the size of Ray, stormed in here with her nightstick. Oh, he couldn't wait until that day.

Ray had gulped his coffee and dragged his sleeve across his mouth. "Anyway, she looked too wild for you."

"Don't you have something to do?" he'd snapped, pulling the headphones onto his head.

Ray had thudded into his chair. "I know you prefer your women with forked tongues and green scales."

Bill had pretended not to hear as he logged onto the Massachusetts Motor Vehicles Administration database. The Jeep was not registered to a person named Maggie. Nor was it listed as stolen. He'd stared in disbelief at the name of the Jeep's owner. Dr. Lindsey Nolan was a periodic guest on one of his favorite shows on the Science Channel, *Guts and Gears*. He dug deeper into her file. One thing was clear. At one time, Nolan had had a drinking problem, as indicated by the DUIs, but those arrests had stopped over eight years ago. The AA bumper stickers on the Jeep now made sense. He continued to read. Years earlier, she'd been present at a drug bust in Provincetown, but she'd been found in another room in the house, with no apparent knowledge of the coke party in the boathouse. No charges had been filed against her. Later on she'd been investigated by Interpol for a case of art theft, but in the end she was found not to be involved, but anyone with a computer or smartphone had seen the infamous boat photos that had gone viral. Dr. Nolan had a knack for being in the wrong place at the wrong time.

The Nolan family was comprised an odd amalgamation of characters. Serving as security for the estate was her father-in-law from her first marriage, a retired captain of the Fredericksburg, Virginia police force, George McLeod. McLeod had married Nolan's housekeeper, Emily Richardson. The old couple resided on the grounds. Then there was Nolan's new husband, Derick Briggs, an immunologist and physician. Ava, an eight year old, was Nolan's biological daughter with the deceased Red Sox outfielder Robert Jenkins. Upon Robert's death, she'd adopted his son Daniel Jenkins, as the boy's biological mother had died when he was little more than an infant. Nolan had also adopted her roommate from rehab—a thirteen-year-old runaway from Arizona named Maggie May.

Bill had then opened Wikipedia. Nolan was an inventor of biomedical instruments and had won a Nobel Prize at the incredible age of thirty-five. She was currently employed at a marine lab in Woods Hole with her longtime lab associate and co-recipient of the Nobel Prize, Sara Kauni. The two women had recently started up a side business, NK (Nolan-Kauni) Dive Technologies, after the unexpected success of their C-trax underwater GPS device. The new company developed high tech dive helmets and recreational submersibles.

He'd closed the files on Nolan and begun a search in the police database for a person named Maggie May. May's file was shorter than Nolan's. His mood plummeted as he read on. At nine, the orphan had fled from a girls' home in Phoenix after reporting that a man in the kitchen had been harassing her. Between the ages of nine and twelve there were brief, intermittent appearances at detention centers. There were four arrests in total, two for shoplifting food at grocery stores in Texas and Florida, and two for prostitution in Wisconsin and Oregon. Curiously, for one year, between the ages of twelve and thirteen, the girl had disappeared. He had a very bad feeling about this. Young girls don't just vanish... not for good reasons, anyway. Out of nowhere, May, thirteen and a drug addict, had resurfaced from the netherworld; police officers had found her passed out in a crack house in Providence, Rhode Island. Then she'd been sent by Child Services to a rehab in Newport. There her luck had changed.

Bill had tried to convince his captain to send out a boat of police divers to Spire Rock. His boss had reviewed May's file. She was not credible, the man had stated gruffly, especially since she'd refused to leave her name, or divulge the names of the persons she'd been diving with. Moreover, budgets were tight, the captain had reminded him. Divers, boats, and gasoline were costly. But his boss had not said no. He would think on it, the man had promised.

From the branch spanning the terrarium, Dr. Watson eyed the goldfish before striking. In an instant the fish was devoured. All fine with the Chinese dragon's appetite, Bill wandered to his bedroom. As he drifted off to sleep, May's words lingered in his thoughts...

"When you're interviewing a person, say a murderer... or rapist, is there something about them, a look in their eyes, a gesture... something... that tells you they're guilty? Is that something they teach you guys at the police academy?"

Did these questions have anything to do with Maggie May's lost year?

Chapter 5

Woods Hole

Professor Tinkman's still life assignment in Advanced Drawing II was worth fifty total points, Maggie recalled from his syllabus. A maximum of forty points could be earned for an effective use of light and shadow, and the remaining ten points were for originality and arrangement of the objects in the piece. The title of the assignment was "From Conception to Middle Age", indicating that the work had to portray the evolution of some particular object to its current state. Lily Tate's still life had a phone theme and included a crank phone, old landlines with dials and push buttons, and a range of newer cell phones. Kyle Monroe's still life showed the development of music players, starting with an old gramophone, then an LP record player, a boom box, an eight-track player, and culminating with an iPod with ear buds.

Maggie had arranged her still life next to the window, because the most interesting shadows were created by natural light; plus she preferred space away from the distracting banter of the other students. Her arrangement had a nautical theme. From Lindsey's library she had "borrowed" a copper and brass 1850s dive helmet and an antique sextant; the modern evolution was Nolan's prototype NK dive helmet and an NK C-trax waterproof GPS.

The prototype dive helmet had worked remarkably well the other night at Spire Rock. The single lamp switched on and off reliably, the sound through the speakers had surprisingly little static, and the seal around the neck did not leak. She glanced across the studio to Lily and Kyle, who were gossiping in a corner. It had been the right thing to tell Detective Bleach about the body—it had lifted a load from her conscience. Some loved one would now have closure about their missing relative. Lily's outright refusal to go to the police was baffling. She would never, ever tell either Lily or Kyle about her visit to the police station. It had been a private conversation strictly between her and that peculiar cop, Bill Bleach.

"We're all chipping in for cases of beer and vodka," Kyle called to her from across the studio. "It's going to be a great party."

"I'll pass," Maggie answered.

"You never come drinking with us," Lily remarked.

"I have plans."

"What plans?" Lily pried.

"Plans," she repeated, refusing to elaborate. Dread had already caused her to chew off half of her thumbnail. Her avoidance of Brian would end this Friday when she asked him to remove the remainder of his junk from the cottage: his surfboard, clothes and DVDs. They had not lived together —or spoken—in over a year. She had been rehearsing what to say to him, "Emily McLeod, the housekeeper, will let you into the cottage. I will not be there."

Lily turned coyly to Kyle. "If I didn't know better, I'd say that Maggie has a secret lover somewhere."

"I have no time for men," Maggie said. "Besides, I'm a virgin."

"Right," Lily laughed disbelievingly.

"I volunteer my de-virginizing services anytime," Kyle offered optimistically.

"Thanks, Kyle. I'll remember that," Maggie said tonelessly.

A cell phone vibrated in Lily's still life and she read the text. "Bummer."

"Who is it?" Kyle tried to read it over her shoulder.

"My mother, of course. Who else texts me every five minutes? She's coming to the Halloween ball this weekend," Lily groaned. "That means I have to go. She was here just two weekends ago for Fall Fest. Why can't she give me space? She writes a big check every year, just so she can go to this party. She's fixated on old man Gripp. She hangs all over him. It's so frickin' embarrassing."

"I'd kill Lindsey if she came to a campus event," muttered Maggie. "Fortunately, she's too preoccupied with work to notice anything else."

"My parents never come," Kyle lamented. "My father hasn't found a job in two years. Who's going to hire a fifty-five-year-old computer technician when a thirty-year-old will do the job for half the salary and has newer skills? It's going to take me forever to pay off my student loans." He said in afterthought, "The Halloween party sounds fun. Lily, do you need a date? I'd love to go. Please take me."

"Well... okay," Lily agreed less than enthusiastically, "as long as you realize that it's a friends date and not a romantic date, and you don't drink too much or do anything idiotic. And you'll need to wear a costume."

"It's a deal. Thank you." He paused. "What are you going to be?"

"Maybe the Cat Woman. It's easy to do. Maggie, can I borrow one of your black shirts?"

"Okay."

"Great. So I'll wear a black shirt, my black spandex workout pants, and buy a black mask, cat ears and a tail at a Halloween store."

"What should I be?" he asked. "It needs to be done on the cheap. I'm broke." He wandered across to Maggie's still life and lifted the antique dive helmet.

"Put that back! I'll never get it back in the same position. The light's perfect right now. Kyle, move," Maggie ordered. "You're blocking the light."

"Sorry," he mumbled sheepishly. "Can I borrow this helmet? I'll be a scuba diver."

"No, I need to sneak it back into Lin's house as soon as I'm done. Besides, it's too heavy to wear all night. Your head and shoulders would ache."

He pointed to the yellow prototype dive helmet. "How about that one? I could be a space alien."

"No way," Maggie said quickly. "No one's supposed to have seen this yet. I need to return it to the *Jack Rackham* before Lin notices that it's gone. She's so obsessive-compulsive about all of her new gadgets. She thinks that corporate spies are lurking around every bend, waiting to steal her stuff. But I can lend you a mask, snorkel, and fins, if you want."

"Okay, perfect," he said.

"And you can use my lobster net," Lily offered, crossing the studio. "That helmet's so amazing, Kyle. Do you know that it has speakers in it? The whole time we were diving, Maggie and I were having a conversation. And the lamp means that you don't need to hold a dive light. It's hands-free diving. And, best of all, your whole head stays dry, so I didn't have to redo my hair after we dove."

Maggie pointed to a console attached to the back of the helmet. "And that's a tiny computer that does other shit, like measure oxygen and carbon dioxide inside the helmet."

"When do I get to meet Lindsey?" Lily asked with a whine.

"Never," Maggie answered firmly.

"We've been roommates for almost two years and I've never met her," Lily griped.

"I don't want my family anywhere near my life," Maggie said, turning her attention back to her sketch.

"Can you at least get me her autograph? My mother keeps bothering me about it. And how about the autograph of her friend, Jessie McCabe, who found the Viking wreck?" Lily added excitedly. "Can you get me that one also?"

"Me, too," Kyle interjected. "Maybe I can sell them on eBay to make some extra cash."

"Okay," Maggie acquiesced. "Now can we get back to work?"

*****

The Minotaur double-checked to ensure that the office door was locked. He shuffled across his office toward a storage closet and opened its door. A sturdy metal shelf against the closet's back wall held reams of paper, rolls of tape, a box of manila envelopes, a box of staples, an old coffee pot, stacks of post-it notes, and other assorted office supplies. His knotted fingers pulled on the shelf and the wall panel to which it was bolted swung silently open. None of the objects on the shelf fell out of place, as all had been glued carefully together years before. His heart was aflutter.

Passing behind the mobile wall panel, the Minotaur lowered himself gingerly onto a stool behind the office wall. With a dull pain in his hip, he bent to unlace his patent leather dress shoes and slid his gnarled feet into a well-worn pair of moccasins. He sighed; the old slippers offered temporary relief from his bunions. He lifted himself from the chair and patted his pants' pocket—extra AA batteries in case his headlamp went dim. He removed the headlamp from a hook in the wall, pulled its elastic strap around his scabby, bald head, switched it on and closed the wall panel securely behind him.

A cone of light broke the darkness. The labyrinth seemed to beckon, promising insight and pleasure. In an earlier day, his moccasins would have carried him in lithe silence down the stone stairway, but nowadays he descended cautiously, grasping rope handholds. The first part of the labyrinth was a straight underground passageway, leading him from his office in the administration cottage to the Edward Gripp Art Center. His hands grazed the walls, the texture and contours of each stone as familiar as a lover's body. He savored this part of the labyrinth where the rocks seeped a rich, earthy sweat.

He passed a wooden door that lead to an egress tunnel into the woods beyond, an emergency escape route should the walls collapse. But over the decades the stone walls had remained as firm as on the day of their construction. A stone stairway rose in front of him, and he dragged himself upward. Here the labyrinth climbed from the subterranean to ground level, and a cascade of new sensations bombarded him.

Outside, he knew, the autumn sky was a cloudless blue and the trees were a stunning mosaic of reds, oranges, and yellows. The sunlight of late afternoon blazed through the numerous windows of the ground floor, warming the rooms along the perimeter of the Gripp Art Center.

Yellow light diffused through minute cracks in the stone walls. The Minotaur clicked off the headlamp and let it dangle around his neck. Here the labyrinth forked, forming right and left passageways. If he traveled to the right, he would pass by the library and the ceramics, painting, and printmaking studios; to the left were the reception room, studios for sculpture and drawing, and a computer graphics lab. It was impossible to travel both passageways in one afternoon, as he tired easily these days. One direction would have to do. He checked his watch; it was imperative to be on the second floor by 5:15.

The cracks between mortar and stone were strategically located at various levels so that all activity in rooms beyond the labyrinth walls could be observed. He decided on the left direction and peered through a crack into the reception room. The printmaking major Olivia Moreno sat by a bay window, typing into a laptop. He'd seen her around campus over the past few years. The gloomy, clunky girl was a bit of a misfit. There was nothing particularly titillating about her, so he moved on.

A class was in session in the sculpture studio. At the moment, a new professor hired from California was discussing the Ron Mueck sculpture, *In Bed*, which was projected onto a screen. The Minotaur trudged on. Class was over in the drawing studio, but three students remained to work on their still life projects. The fit, black-haired girl he knew very well, as her pushy mother and timid father attended all of the donor receptions. And everyone knew Kyle Monroe because he hovered around any tolerating group of female students or secretaries. The boy's sculptures of ocean waves were breathtaking, and the Minotaur hoped to purchase one for his motor yacht at the next student art sale. Equally stunning were the paintings of marine animals created by the third student in the room.

Everyone knew of Maggie's guardian, who had an appetite for seducing men on her boats. Photos of Lindsey Nolan in romantic entanglements, with a Boston Red Sox player, and another time with a Scandinavian cop, had been all over the *Cape Cod Daily* and the Internet. A smile spread across the Minotaur's dry, thin lips. The dean's administrative assistant, Doreen Best, had told him that Nolan would be attending the Halloween reception that upcoming weekend. She would be fascinating to watch through the cracks in the labyrinth walls. It was going to be a marvelous party!

He checked his watch and moved silently on his way. He paused briefly to check out activities in the computer graphics lab. Nothing interesting there, only students working at computer terminals, though at the corner cubicle was that pretty student, Kristin Pucci, and her handsome boyfriend, Curt Fredrickson. How disappointing that there was no labyrinth in the student dormitory!

Another stairway led to the second floor. He had placed a chair behind the wall of the conference room some time ago. He gratefully eased himself down and leaned toward a crack in the wall, his filmy, opalescent eyes gazing with intensity. The committee meeting was chaired by Dr. John Sanders, a silver-haired ceramics professor from Philadelphia.

"The last agenda item is to collect the names of the nominees for the Windsor Award. Did each of you have a chance to consult with your colleagues in your respective disciplines?" Sanders asked, peering over his bifocals.

The faculty around the table responded with nods and yeses.

"Very good," Sanders said pleasantly. "Who's the nominee from printmaking?"

"Olivia Moreno," answered a balding man with thick glasses and sagging shoulders.

Sanders typed the name into his laptop. He looked across the table. "And from painting?"

"Hands down, Maggie May-Nolan," asserted Dr. June Perkins, a slim woman in yoga attire. The Minotaur smiled and checked his watch again.

Sanders glanced down the table. "From sculpture?"

"Ditto on the hands down: Kyle Monroe," replied a young man in a dress shirt and purple vest.

"I love Kyle's work," interjected the balding professor from the printmaking department.

Sanders nodded. "I do, too. And from photography?"

A grey-haired woman with cold, seen-it-all eyes proclaimed, "Amy Jacobsen."

Sanders turned toward his right. "How about from computer graphics?"

"This was a very tough decision," replied a wizened professor with a thinning goatee. "It was neck and neck between Liza Norris and Curt Fredrickson, but we finally decided on Curt."

"And from ceramics, we chose Lily Tate," Sanders announced. "So let me read through the list, in case I've forgotten someone. Olivia Moreno, Maggie May-Nolan, Kyle Monroe, Amy Jacobsen, Curt Fredrickson, and Lily Tate."

"You got it, John," the old graphics professor confirmed.

"Is there anything in the Award guidelines about financial need, or is the award based solely on artistic merit?" asked June Perkins. "I know that Curt and Kyle could sure use the money."

"The Windsor is awarded purely on creativity," the steely-eyed photographer answered in an imperious tone. "I chaired the Awards Committee for eons before John volunteered."

"That's correct. That's what's stated in the guidelines," Sanders agreed. "I guess the next step is for me to send the nominees an email to see if they'll give us three of their best pieces to evaluate. That's how we did it last year. Is everyone okay with doing that again?"

The faculty members nodded again. Such consensus was rare from a bunch of contrarian professors and temperamental artists, the Minotaur thought, but it was nearing five o'clock and they were impatient to leave.

Sanders glanced around the table one last time as the art professors headed for the door. "Let's meet next week at the same time. I'll see some of you at the Halloween party."

"I hope no one notices if I wear the same costume as last year," the sculptor in the purple vest said, lingering in the doorway. "I don't have time to make a new one."

"I'm not sure if I'm going to make it at all," Perkins said, collecting her folders. "It all depends on if Conrad gets home in time to take Denise to her Girl Scout Halloween party. There are too many activities at this time of year."

"I hope I'll see you there, Dr. Perkins," Sanders replied casually, closing his laptop.

The Minotaur struggled to his feet and shuffled along the labyrinth. His heart now raced with anticipation. Behind the wall of John Sanders' office, he dropped into another chair. His pocket watch read 5:13 p.m. His forehead pressed against the stone wall and he gazed through a peephole. Sanders was already there, and he popped a breath mint into his mouth. He shut off his computer and closed the blinds. At 5:14 there was a quiet tap at his door. June Perkins entered wordlessly; John walked silently to his door and locked the knob, then wedged a chair under the doorknob. June shimmied out of her yoga pants, and John rapidly peeled down his khakis and boxers. The two professors fell in a grasping heap onto the sofa. Delighted, the Minotaur checked his watch again. It was 5:15 and the Viagra was just kicking in.

*****

Maggie slammed on the brakes and the Jeep skidded to a stop in front of the garage. Derick Briggs looked up from the carburetor of an antique Norton motorcycle. Maggie had nothing against Derick. He largely kept to himself, working on his motorcycle restoration projects. In general he stayed out of her business. But Derick was not Rob.

All had changed that cursed summer three years before, when the family still lived at Dave's Marina in the three houseboats. Lindsey's partner then had been Rob Jenkins. Carefree Rob, who wandered the dock, chatting with the other boaters. Who raced jet skis with her along the coastline, supervised softball and kickball games for the children, and took the family to Fenway Park. Maggie's thoughts darkened. Rob, who'd had an affair with Sheila... who'd started drinking again... who'd died during a drinking binge in the woods. The same cursed summer that Jessie and Lindsey had been injured by Adrian Arrano... and she'd become pregnant. How had that happened? She *always* used birth control. She'd terminated the pregnancy and Brian had split.

Maggie slammed the car door and stomped toward the house, across the stone patio and porch, and pushed through the back door. Women's laughter from the living room arrested her steps.

"Shit," she muttered to herself, "chick flick night."

The living room was dark except for the glow of the TV and the burning logs in the fireplace. Sara Kauni—Maggie's least favorite person in the world—was sprawled across the sectional sofa with her on-again-off-again partner, Jessie McCabe—Maggie's most favorite person in the world. From the position of their tangled limbs Sara and Jessie were currently "on." What Jessie ever saw in Sara was one of the great unsolvable mysteries of all time. Lindsey was tilted back in a recliner with a bowl of popcorn in her lap.

"What the hell is this?" Maggie threw a wad of paper at Lindsey.

"What? Calm down." Lindsey unfolded the paper.

"It was in my school mailbox." Maggie crossed the room, stepped over the old coonhound, and dropped her forehead onto the mantle. She stared despondently into the fire.

Lindsey scanned the paper. "Oh, right. I got an invitation also. The Newbury Development Office contacted Derick and me, asking if we'd make a donation for new kilns in the ceramics studio."

Maggie spun in her high top sneakers. "You didn't, did you?"

"We did."

"I'm not going!"

"Then don't go. But Derick and I are. We already RSVP'd."

Sara pointed a clicker at the TV, suspending the movie at the exact moment Dr. Strangelove's artificial hand clamped onto his neck. "What is it, Lin?"

"A Halloween party at the art college. It's supposed to have amazing decorations made by the art students," Lindsey explained.

"I don't want you talking to my professors," Maggie snarled.

"I have no clue who your professors even are, since you tell me nothing about school. My sole purpose in your life seems to be paying for your data plan, car insurance, and tuition. Could we at least have lunch, or a cup of coffee some time so I know how you're doing?"

Stung, Maggie fell silent. She fumbled in her jacket for her cigarettes.

"You can smoke outside on the porch," Lindsey said.

"Shit," she grumbled, stuffing the pack into her pocket.

"You can't fight in here," Sara boomed in a mock, masculine voice, imitating a line from the movie. "This is the War Room."

Maggie glared at the three women.

"Sit down and join us, Maggie," Jessie said in a conciliatory tone. "This movie's hysterical. Why don't you join us for movie night? It's only once a month. We have so much fun."

Maggie grimaced at the TV screen. "I've seen this film before. Kubrick's too weird."

"So, what are you and Derick going to go as?" Sara asked Lindsey.

"Maybe we'll be Darth Vader and Princess Leia," Lindsey said. "But we haven't decided yet."

"You should wear the Princess Leia slave outfit that wears she wears in Jabba the Hutt's fortress in in *The Return of the Jedi*," Jessie suggested, bursting into laughter.

"Lin, you could definitely pull it off," Sara giggled.

"Nooo…." Maggie moaned. "Please, no!"

"It would be way too cold. And that's all I'd need," Lindsey said ironically, "more photos on the Internet."

"How about you two be the Vikings, Eric the Red and Freydis?" Jessie suggested.

"Or Andrew and Rebecca Stanton?" Sara ventured.

Jessie turned toward Sara, perplexed. "Who are they?"

"You never heard about Lindsey's ghosts?" Sara said incredulously.

"The whole story's ridiculous," Lindsey broke in. "Jess, there are no ghosts here."

"Local legend has it," Sara continued stubbornly, "that Andrew Stanton, a one-legged whaler, lived on these grounds. His beloved Rebecca was washed off the dock and out to sea during the Great Gale of 1812. People see his apparition waiting for her on Lin's widow's walk around this time of year."

"I've lived in this house for three years and have never seen or heard the ghost. The dock was put up in the 1980s, and this house wasn't built until 1910. None of it's true."

"It's a cool legend, anyway," Sara tossed off.

"Next year you two should make a donation to the art college and we could all go," Lindsey said.

Maggie frowned. "You three are worse than sorority girls. I'm outta here."

"Bring on those frat boys," Jessie laughed.

Maggie dashed out of the house, waiting until she was in the car to scream.

Chapter 6

It was an ideal evening for a Halloween party, Maggie conceded a few days later. All afternoon it had drizzled, but by nightfall the clouds had blown out to sea, and the fields and trees around campus glistened in the glow of distant stars. As she was leaving for her NA meeting at the Methodist Church, the dorm buzzed with activity. Lily, Kyle, and Amy Jacobsen had cluttered her dorm room with wire cat ears and a furry tail, snorkeling gear, and pieces of a Marge Simpson costume. Lily and Amy primped in front of a make-up mirror, while Kyle stretched across a beanbag chair, sipping a beer and belching loudly. Eager to clear out of the chaotic, tight space, Maggie grabbed her car keys off the desk.

She paused at the room next to hers, where two sculpture majors had constructed astonishingly authentic costumes of Jigsaw from the movie *Saw* and Hannibal Lecter from *Silence of the Lambs*.

"Way cool, guys."

"Do a bong with us, Maggie."

"I'll take a pass. Have fun tonight."

"You, too," the other said.

She stopped in the lobby to send a text. Lindsey might be wearing something mortifying; she had to prepare herself. The text back from Lindsey read that Derick was going as the pirate, Jack Rackham, and Lindsey as Anne Bonny. No slave Princess Leia... what a relief.

She slowed the Jeep and unrolled the window as she passed the Gripp Art Center. Purple and green spotlights on the front lawn cast eerie shadows across the building. Music from *Thriller* played on loud speakers. Styrofoam tombstones and creepy scarecrows lined a walkway to the front entrance. Ghosts and cobwebs hung from the stone arches of the porch. Students dressed as mummies, vampires, and witches were setting up extra chairs on the porch. She strained to see what was inside, but the foyer was lit by black lights. It looked tremendously fun, and for a moment she thought about quickly constructing some costume. But her sobriety and NA meetings came first. She pushed on the gas pedal. Had she gone to the party, she too would have chosen to be a pirate, but Mary Read, never Anne Bonny, who was a slut and adulteress. Mary Read had a higher moral character.

*****

After a meal at a diner with her sponsor, Maggie arrived at the NA meeting in Falmouth early, as it was her responsibility to make the coffee. This had been her home group since she was thirteen—she had eight years of sobriety —when she'd hitchhiked out to Cape Cod to find her roommate from the rehab, and been beaten up by those two inebriated a-holes... who didn't even pay her. Lindsey had patched her up and offered her a place to stay. But AA meetings with Lindsey were dreadful, populated by grey-haired old men, equally prehistoric divorcées, and assorted oddballs whose brains were so marinated with alcohol that they belonged in asylums. Besides, she'd never been drunk in her life, a fact that mystified Lindsey. It was the drugs that had gotten her, drugs used to numb herself from her horrible job... the only job that an uneducated girl could get.

In NA, not AA, she'd found her spiritual home. The addicts at NA meetings were closer to her age and had the same issues. There she'd met her sponsor, Tory, an old Dead Head with decades of sobriety, who'd become her mentor. And there she'd met Brian Cooper. For years she and Brian had sat together at this meeting and worked the Twelve Steps. But all had changed. "This is your group also, Maggie," Tory reminded her. "Keep coming." Tory was right. Brian's presence across the room would not dissuade her from attending meetings of her home NA group. Now he sat with a newcomer, Lisa, and that slippery landscaper, Frankie MacDonald. Maggie didn't trust him and kept her mouth shut when he was around.

While Manny, a lobsterman and recovering heroin addict, shared about the loss of his children in a custody battle, she rallied the courage to send Brian a text.

"can we set up a time for you to pick up ur stuff?" From the corner of her eye, she watched him sense a vibration in his pocket and pull out his cell phone.

Without looking over at her, he typed, "talk @ sea wall eel pond after mtg at 8?"

She typed into her cell phone, "Ill b there."

Finally, a small step forward. At least there was a response. The conversation on the seawall would be brief. She would state her rehearsed line: "I won't even be there. Mrs. McLeod will let you in." Her absence while he removed his things would spare them both an awkward, tenuous sadness. Soon all nagging reminders of him would be gone from the cottage. Perhaps a total redecoration was in order? What was it that Virginia Woolf had written? "A room of one's own," though not to write; to paint.

*****

Maggie checked the time on her cell phone. 8:05 p.m. There was something pacifying about sitting on the seawall at Eel Pond at night. A few lingering sailboats floated in a stagnant mist. The air was now cooler than the water. She zipped up her jacket, pulled her head into the collar like a tortoise, and occupied herself by thinking of ways to paint mist. Her legs dangled over the black water where Jessie's dive boat, *Mermaid*, was tied up. Strange... this was the exact spot where she'd met Jessie years before, when the marine biologist, a broke, skittish nobody, had arrived in Woods Hole. And then Jessie had found that Viking wreck in Buzzards Bay. Now the name Jessie McCabe was in American history books; her face had been on the covers of *Time, Newsweek, People,* and *National Geographic.* All summer long, tourists, Viking groupies, and other gawkers streamed by *Mermaid,* snapping selfies with the boat in the background.

Across Eel Pond was Sara Kauni's house, where Jessie lived when not traveling on a lecture tour or giving interviews. Sara and Jessie must be home, relaxing on a Friday night, as the windows were hazy gold rectangles through the mist.

Maggie checked the time again—8:20—and lit another cigarette. At this time of the year, the village of Woods Hole was a windblown, rain-beaten ghost town. The tourist shops were closed for the season, though muted music drifted from the Captain Kidd bar. In the summer the Kidd was jammed with tourists and summer scientists from the marine lab, but now only locals were slumped along the bar watching the World Series. Sadly, the Red Sox hadn't made the play-offs, but the Bruins and Celtics were both starting up their seasons. She checked a Boston sports app on her phone. The Celts were winning, the Bruins losing.

Perhaps Brian couldn't spot her because she was sitting down amidst the boats? She rose and started to pace the seawall. Her ears strained for the rattle of his pickup truck, but the only noises she heard were an occasional car swishing along the damp pavement of Water Street, the gentle tug of boats on their mooring lines, and the distant moan of the Nobska Point lighthouse.

She wandered over to the collecting trawlers owned by the marine lab. Brian had once worked on the large green one. Through the NA grapevine she'd heard that he'd quit his job on the trawler, which was surprising because it was a job he loved. She checked her smartphone again. It was 8:33.

She bit her fingernail. "That bastard's standing me up."

After Friday evening NA meetings, the two of them used to pick up some fast food, watch a DVD, and roll around in bed until well after midnight. Now he was screwing that newcomer Lisa. "Homo sapiens is not a monogamous species," Lindsey had once said. "Only some species of birds, prairie voles, and worms are monogamous. Humans are not." Why did Lindsey always tell her such random, irrelevant bullshit? Prairie voles? What the hell are they anyway? Only a dork would know about the sex lives of prairie voles!

Maggie seethed. Her time had been wasted. Worse, she'd been made a fool of. Her cigarette butt hit the pond with a sizzle. If Brian would not remove his shit from the cottage, she would remove it for him.

*****

Two pirates cooled off on a dark porch corner of the Gripp Art Center, their coats draped across a wooden railing. Lindsey tipped back a plastic cup of coke and ice. "I must have sweated off five pounds on the dance floor," she said, crunching on an ice cube.

Derick glanced downward. "I can't dance in these boots. I'm ready to call it a night."

"How about a soak in the hot tub?" she suggested playfully.

His wife's intent was obvious and he smiled into her clear green eyes. "That sounds wonderful."

She fanned herself with a program. "Before we leave, let's walk through the studios and see if we can find any of Maggie's pieces. It sure would be a lot easier if we knew what courses she was taking."

"She's definitely taking a painting course; Dr. Perkins said that she had Maggie in her class."

"That woman looks like she lives at the gym."

"Her Cleopatra costume was pretty nice," he admitted.

She grinned, as she well knew her husband's tastes. "I thought you'd like that one."

He looked appreciatively down his wife's low-cut peasant blouse. "But nothing comes close to that blouse."

She looked toward the doorway and lowered her voice. "You're wearing sailor pants. I undo those six buttons and I make you a very happy man." She whispered, "Maybe we could sneak upstairs and find a quiet —"

"No," he interrupted. "This is Maggie's college. We can wait."

"But I'm sure we can find an empty classroom, or..." she whispered, tugging insistently on his sleeve.

"No," he repeated adamantly. "You're not getting caught in any more compromising... photo opportunities. Not on my watch."

"You're right, but give me a kiss."

"Gladly." He pulled her into his white, billowing shirt with laces across the chest, and gave her a long kiss.

"All right," she said, mollified. "Let's go see some art."

"Maggie likes to draw, so let's check out that studio after we see her paintings."

"Let's slip in the back door to avoid being accosted again by the clingy dean and Lily's tiger mom." She slung a red velvet coat over her shoulder.

He lifted his calico coat from the railing. "Her husband, Evan, wants to be anywhere but here. He's been checking the Knicks' scores on his cell phone all night."

She consulted the program, which included a map to the various studios in the Gripp building. "The painting and drawing studios are right there." She pointed down a hallway.

After admiring Maggie's unique underwater paintings, the couple entered the drawing studio, which was well lit by fluorescent panels in the ceiling. They strolled leisurely from display to display. It was clear that the students were working on still life projects, the arrangements consisting of old and new shoes, hats, phones, music players, books, writing devices, and cameras. They studied the drawings tacked to some of the easels.

"Not that I know anything about art, but there's a staggering amount of talent at this school," Lindsey commented. Approaching the window, she grabbed Derick's hand. "Unbelievable! Do you see that?"

He laughed quietly. "I was wondering when you were going to notice."

She stared at the antique brass and copper dive helmet. "I was wondering who'd removed it from the library! I thought that Danny or Ava might be playing with it."

"Is it worth anything?"

She shook her head. "No. It's just a replica. I picked it up at a flea market years ago. The sextant is also a replica."

"And the C-trax device?"

"It's an old model. Completely worthless and obsolete."

"I wonder what Maggie had in this space." Derick pointed to a gap in the objects. He looked toward the easel next to the nautical still life for a clue, but it was empty of paper.

"God only knows," Lindsey remarked with a small laugh.

*****

Maggie decided that the exorcism of Brian Cooper from her cottage and her life would start in the kitchen. She bent under the sink for the industrial strength garbage bags. She opened the kitchen cabinets first, snatching his favorite hot sauce, crunchy peanut butter, and vile freeze-dried coffee, and heaved them into the plastic bag. They landed with a satisfying crash. His Bruins mug went next, shattering as it hit the bottle of hot sauce. His collection of tacky magnets of

Cape Cod tourist attractions she removed from the refrigerator with one gratifying swipe. She inspected the refrigerator, but it appeared as though the housekeeper, Emily McLeod, had already removed the long expired food. Only condiments and cans of soda remained in the door, but those were hers.

In the living room she pondered the rack of DVDs that she and Brian had watched together over the years. They might bring in a couple hundred dollars on eBay. But why prolong the misery? She spilled the entire rack into the trash bag on top of the broken glass and food. His raincoat was wadded into a ball and tossed; next went the snow boots. The stuffed bear that he'd won for her at a carnival made her pause. This was no time for sentimentality and nostalgia. Definitely heave.

She tugged on the trash bag but it was too heavy to lug upstairs, so she returned to the kitchen for a new one. She dashed up the stairs. In the bathroom she tossed all his toiletries. In the bedroom... everything went: the blue sheets, pillowcases, his T-shirts, boxers, and cargo shorts. Posters of his favorite rock bands were torn off the walls and shredded. Gone! She circled the upstairs, looking for any lingering traces of him, but she'd done a thorough job. She stepped carefully down the stairs, the trash bag thudding behind her. She dragged both bags outside and lugged them into the back of the Jeep. Next stop, the dumpsters behind the marina lab. But first, one last scan of the cottage.

She stopped in front of the surfboard by the front door. The surfboard was way too big to be loaded into the Jeep, since the car's roof was on for the cold weather. She pulled on her leather jacket and dragged the surfboard across the damp lawn, passing the sundial and Adirondack chairs. It then thumped behind her, along the splintery boards of the dock. Standing on the last plank she gnawed at the cuticle on her thumb. It had taken Brian two paychecks to buy the surfboard. He was joyous when he rode the waves at Nobska Beach. But he hadn't contacted her in over a year about it, so it couldn't mean that much to him. Besides, he'd had his chance tonight, at eight o'clock.

Maggie lifted the surfboard and heaved it into the darkness. Yards below, frothy water swirled around the pilings. The surfboard hit the water with a resounding splat. She peered over the tips of her soggy high-top sneakers. The surfboard, a white oblong in the black water, had landed fins side down. She pulled a cigarette from her jacket to calm herself. By the time she finished her smoke, the surfboard had disappeared in the mist.

*****

The psychology of Halloween fascinated the Minotaur. The choice of one's costume, he believed, reflected a desire for a more compelling identity. Nerds and weaklings would dress as super heroes, repressed virgins would dress as vamps, policewomen with handcuffs, or short-skirted nurses. Often the costume revealed some inner demon lurking in the dream world... a bloody surgeon, Hannibal Lecter, the Headless Horseman. Perhaps the macabre costumes also revealed one's subliminal—or conscious—lust for the blood of another?

As an old man, the Minotaur was exempt from wearing a silly costume and had dressed in his usual tuxedo. He wandered the reception with a plastic cup of sour red wine in hand, chit-chatting with the dean, his administrative assistant, Doreen Best, the Director of Development, Kate Taylor, and some faculty members. His head began to ache.

Why did they insist on playing that jarring music so ridiculously loud at all of these events? One had to scream to have a conversation. By evening's end his throat would be on fire. And it wasn't music, only pure cacophony. Nor was the "singer" carrying a tune. It was hostile, obscene chanting to pounding drums and strident guitars.

He glanced fearfully across the room. As at previous donor events, groups that included Jean and Evan Tate were to be avoided. Invariably the mother would dominate all conversations, steering all topics back to her wonderful daughter.

Lily was dressed as a black cat or cat burglar, he wasn't sure which, and was followed faithfully around by Kyle Monroe. Kyle's costume must have been put together in five minutes. It consisted of a surfer bathing suit, tropical shirt, a dab of sunscreen on his nose, and a scuba mask and snorkel on his head. The costume of Olivia Moreno was particularly disturbing. Papers pinned to her black clothes had the faces of right-wing Republicans—some of them his cronies—in the center of bloody bull's-eyes. Olivia had miraculously found a date for the evening. His face was concealed all evening by the leering mask of the character "V," from *V for Vendetta*.

The Minotaur turned toward the parquet dance floor. His conversation with the Nobel laureate and her husband was disappointingly brief, as the couple seemed eager to get onto the dance floor. Those two would be best watched from the labyrinth. Who knows what Lindsey Nolan might do? He felt his heart skip a beat. He turned toward the foyer where June Perkins was chatting with colleagues. She looked absolutely edible. His heart leapt for a second time in minutes. John Sanders had been exchanging glances with her all evening. No doubt they would put the professor's sofa to use some time later, and the Minotaur needed to be ready.

After dumping the disgusting wine into a plant box, he slunk out the back door and wandered over to his office in the administration cottage.

Behind the solid walls of the labyrinth the horrid music was dampened, and the Minotaur's headache faded. He walked the tunnel, reminiscing. There was one singular reason that Gripp Architecture and Construction had been the most successful architectural firm on the Cape, and that reason was the labyrinth. He'd been aware when his accountant had begun to skim monies from various accounts, when his secretary had started an affair with the intern, and when his structural engineer had begun to show signs of Alzheimer's, among other bits of vital information. The information was essential for gauging the productivity of his workforce, assisting him in the annual performance reviews, and if need be, making personnel changes. The Gripp Corporation had long ago been sold, the new firm relocated to Boston, and the extensive grounds and buildings donated to establish an art college on the Cape. All that Edward Gripp had requested in exchange for the property was the use of a small office in the cottage that was to serve as the administrative building.

The information gleaned now from the labyrinth had the same themes as before: lust, greed, power, changing alliances, and a desire for more vacation time and money. Only the players had changed. Without a doubt, the lust relationships were the most interesting, all the rest rather pedestrian. Years earlier, he'd been shocked by the skills of his mousy, punctual secretary and the staying power of the young intern. He could barely be in the same room with her without breaking into an uncomfortable, yet enthralling sweat. June Perkins elicited the same effect. Yes, it was definitely his secretary, Miss Wilkinson, who'd kindled his obsession for watching. He turned up the listening device in his ear that was required when loud music played. Tonight he was confronted by the delightful dilemma of watching both June Perkins and Lindsey Nolan.

The fetishes of Professors Sanders and Perkins were already familiar ground, so he focused his attention on Drs. Nolan and Briggs. He watched the couple on the dance floor, then followed them behind the studio walls as they looked for Maggie's artwork. From the snippets of conversation he managed to overhear, Nolan was quite emphatic about getting her husband, a robust pirate, into some hot tub as fast as possible. The Minotaur's spirits dropped—just as her murmurs became thrillingly graphic, the aroused husband grabbed her hand and shuttled her out the back door.

That entertainment gone, he scuffled behind the walls, searching for June Perkins amidst the donors. His mood rapidly improved. What timing! June approached John Sanders, who was dressed as Davy Crockett. She was holding a book; she opened it and pointed, as if consulting about a professional or artistic matter. Sanders nodded, lines of contemplation creasing his brow. The couple would soon make haste to the second floor. The Minotaur scurried to the stairway.

Any minute now, June would be appearing. The Minotaur silently repositioned the chair and sat down. It was impossible to restrain his excited breathing. He leaned forward, peering through the crack with the optimal view of John Sanders' sofa. Suddenly he sat upright and turned toward the dark passage. Had he heard movement? All was quiet now. It was nothing, he told himself, perhaps a breeze whistling from the eaves in the attic. Then he heard it again. Please, God, no rodents! In all the decades of traveling the labyrinth, he'd never spotted a single mouse, squirrel, or vole. Whatever it was, it was now closer. Then silence. His imagination was getting the better of him. It was only the wind. He leaned back toward the crack.

The alluring Egyptian Queen entered Sanders' office. Tantalizingly slowly, she reached for her shoulder clasps, coiled golden asps holding up the diaphanous gown. The white fabric slid down her body like river water. She stood teasingly in a lacy, transparent thong. Davy Crockett quickly reached boiling point, flung off his coonskin cap and fringed leather jacket, and—

The Minotaur gasped. A creature loomed over him, its blazing cyclopean eye blinding him. His forearm jerked to his face to shield his eyes from the relentless beam. A single question raced through his mind as he clawed the stones, struggling to his feet. *Who had found the labyrinth?* He squinted from below his arm, but the details of the body were indiscernible in the darkness. Which partygoer, he wondered wildly, was dressed as a spaceman in a yellow helmet?

A breeze that raised goose bumps passed over him as a heavily gloved hand descended. The first blow cracked his sternum and ribs and forced a bellow of air from his collapsing lungs. He staggered back against the chair, knocking it into the wall. The chair scraped and bumped along the stonework before falling to the dusty floor. A second blow snapped his head against the stones and mortar of the wall. He heard another crack of bone and pain surged through his brain. His head bumped from stone to stone, a trail of blood like red paint marking his descent. He felt another gust of wind just before a heavy boot crunched down on the cartilage in his throat. Footsteps thudded away into the blackness as he lay twitching with shock, struggling desperately to breathe through a crushed windpipe.

As blood seeped from a gash in the Minotaur's skull, the last sound he heard was June Perkins' distressed whisper. "I'm so not in the mood. There are rats behind these walls."

Chapter 7

Detective Bill Bleach stepped tentatively along the dock of the Falmouth marina; the planks were slick under his running shoes. He was not a strong swimmer, so boats, docks, beaches—water in general—made him queasy. It was another of life's ironies, like his ridiculous name and matching pale skin, that he lived and worked on a peninsula surrounded by a terrifying sea. A dense fog had rolled in from the Vineyard Sound, so the few remaining boats in the slips were barely visible. As it started to drizzle, Bill zipped up his new L. L. Bean raincoat that he'd gotten for free by collecting ten-dollar credit card coupons. He pulled down the visor of his UMass Track & Field ball cap and took a fortifying gulp of coffee before stepping onto the rocking boat. It was not yet 9:00 and already the morning had taken a series of bizarre turns.

He'd awoken around 5:30 as usual, showered, fed his reptiles, done his morning Sudoku, and proceeded through the drive-through for a breakfast sandwich and coffee. Headquarters had been unusually quiet upon his arrival, and he'd found himself the object of speculative stares. He'd entered his office to find that the work area of his partner, Raymond Parks, had been cleared. Gone were the Hooters calendar, the Boston Bruins pendant, and the laptop. Also absent was the stack of case files that they'd been working on together.

Then his circumspect police chief had stepped into Bill's tiny office.

"Mornin', Bleach. Parks has been discharged from duties pending an investigation. I've assigned Detective Murphy to work with you until further notice. She'll start next week."

Bill had nodded solemnly, suppressing a shout of elation. Sandra Murphy was a giantess of a woman and a former Marine who had served in Afghanistan and Iraq. She was fairly new to the unit but already had a reputation for honesty and incorruptibility. He could not believe his good luck.

Then his chief had handed him a folder. "A missing persons report that I want you to check out this morning. An old millionaire never came home to his boat last night."

"Speaking of boats," Bill had inquired, "did you ever decide to send a boat out to Spire Rock to check out the alleged body that the scuba diver saw?"

"Yes. They'll go out when the seas calms down," his boss had answered. He'd departed, revealing nothing more about the dismissal of Raymond Parks.

Bill had booted up his computer. He'd worked recently on two missing persons cases, both elderly individuals. One man had wandered from his nursing home, hopped the first bus that passed by, and been located in the food court of a mall in the suburbs of Boston. No problem. But tragically the old woman had fallen into the Cape Cod Canal and drowned. The new case, he guessed, was probably another elderly person with some form of dementia.

There were many hits when Bill typed the name Edward Gripp into a search engine, as the man was apparently an architect of some renown. His designs were modeled on summer estates from the Victorian era. The wiki entry revealed that his company had built numerous beachfront mansions around New England. Gripp was a generous benefactor to architectural schools around the Boston area and had served on various accreditation boards. Student scholarships had been created in his name, and he'd generously supported student internship programs during the firm's heyday. The property and buildings of his former company had since been given over to create the Newbury College of Art, where Gripp maintained a position on the Board. He currently lived alone on a motor yacht that was kept at a marina in Falmouth. Gripp had never married, nor had children. All of Gripp's wealth upon his death was to be left in trust to the art college.

Bill had clicked on Google images. Gripp appeared like most men in their mid-seventies, bald and slightly stooped. There was an overt pugnacity to his face and stance. He had small, furtive eyes, a spreading nose, and thin, unsmiling lips. Gripp's face was shrewd and alert. His was not the aimless look of a man with Alzheimer's disease.

Gripp's cook had filed a missing persons report that morning. Gripp's bed had not been slept in, nor was his car in the marina parking lot. The cook had sought out the marina's security guard, who'd last seen Gripp the evening before dressed in a tuxedo, heading out to a party. No one at the marina had seen him since.

Now, with a growing sense of dread, Bill peered over the edge of the dock into the water. Perhaps the old man had drunk too much at a party, a friend had driven him home, and he'd fallen into the water? That would explain the absence of a car. He scanned the rest of the slips, most of which were vacated for the fall and winter. The boats were stored on tall, metal racks in the parking lot. The water was a quiet, murky green-brown. Maybe after the divers checked out Spire Rock, they could take some exploratory dives around the marina. He shuddered at the thought of leaping into that water, so cold and dark. It would be hard to see anything down there.

A single-mast motor yacht emerged from the fog, and Bill hesitated. The only boats he'd ever been on were rowboats, trout fishing with his father in the lakes of Vermont. Even then, he'd only agreed to the trip if tightly secured in a flotation vest, and if his father promised to stay within feet of the shoreline. Bill inched forward, and a name on the transom appeared through the thick air. Bill's jaw dropped. The yacht *Minotaur* was spectacular.

An anxious man in a toque and white double-breasted jacket paced the deck and waved Bill onboard. Bill cautiously climbed up a plastic stairway bolted onto the dock. Taking in a deep breath, he leapt across the gap between the dock and boat. He hit the solid deck with a gasp of gratitude and relief.

Struggling to appear composed, he fumbled through his raincoat pockets for his ID. "Um—I'm Detective Bleach."

"I'm Lawrence Fontaine. I've been Mr. Gripp's cook for eight years. He would have told me if he was going to travel. He never goes away without telling me," the cook babbled worriedly. "Today was his day to have eggs Florentine. Saturday's the day Mr. Gripp likes this specific breakfast. But Mr. Gripp prefers it when I shred Romano cheese over the Mornay sauce, instead of using Gruyere and—"

"Mr. Fontaine, do you mind if I have a look around before we talk?" Bill cut in politely.

Fontaine paused, slighted at the interruption. "Of course. Please come in." He gestured Bill into the salon. "Would you like some coffee? It's a dismal morning. I just brewed a pot of Sumatran."

Bill extended his coffee cup from the drive-through. "That would be fine. I'm nearly out."

Fontaine's face contorted. "Fine coffee is served in glass coffee mugs, Detective. Let me throw that away for you." He reached reprovingly for the Styrofoam cup.

Bill pulled a small note pad from his pocket and circled the salon. The wealth on display was staggering. The walls were made of the finest cherry wood. Oriental carpets covered the floors. The lush sofas and recliners were of soft black leather. Artwork and bookshelves covered nearly every inch of wall space. The shelves held volumes of books on art and architecture: Greek, Roman, Egyptian, Japanese, Georgian, Gothic, Romanesque, Baroque, Renaissance, Victorian, and more. Another whole wall was dedicated to books on Greek mythology, especially pertaining to King Minos, the Cretans, the architect Daedalus, Theseus, and, not surprisingly, the Minotaur.

"How do you take your coffee?" Fontaine called from the pristine galley.

"Cream and sugar, please," the detective replied, stepping down a short stairway to the staterooms.

"Half and half, or heavy cream? White sugar or turbinado sugar?

"I have no clue what turbinado sugar is, so surprise me," he shouted up the stairs.

"I don't do surprises," Fontaine answered irritably.

"I'll live dangerously this morning and try heavy cream and turbinado sugar."

"Excellent choice. I picked up fresh spinach and shallots early this morning for Mr. Gripp's eggs Florentine. These ingredients need to be used by today. Shall I make *you* breakfast?"

Breakfast sandwiches never filled him up and Bill's stomach growled at the mention of food. He paused before answering, his imagination running amuck. What if the cook was a poisoner? What if he had knocked off his boss, Gripp, weighted the body down with anchors, and sent it to the bottom of the marina? Bill reined in his imagination. Highly unlikely. Poisoners were usually women. The old bachelor was probably sleeping off a hangover at a friend's house. "Eggs Florentine sounds great," he called, unsure what the egg dish even was. In the off chance he were poisoned, at least Dr. Blane, the medical examiner, would find from his stomach contents that his last meal had been a fine one.

The yacht had three staterooms, a laundry room, and an engine room down the stairs. All of the staterooms were meticulously clean and sparse, each with its own bathroom, a crisply made bed with nautical bedspreads, books along a wall shelf, and a high definition TV. The master stateroom, clearly Gripp's bedroom, also had an adjoining office. Bill dropped into a leather office chair and lifted the lid of Gripp's laptop. The screen-saver consisted of changing images of the Cretan archeological ruins at Knossos. Astonishingly, the laptop was not password protected and all of Gripp's folders appeared on the screen. A person's computer history always gave the detective an idea of the individual's interests. The top name on the list meant nothing to him. June Perkins. Bill googled the name.

Dr. June Perkins was a professor who taught painting courses at Newbury College. Bill found her webpage and found her to be a very good-looking woman, though her artwork was nothing short of hideous. Her painting style was abstract expressionism, which he recalled from Art History

101, taken to fulfill an art requirement in college, and which he had barely passed. Her works looked like random splashes of paint on a canvas. Was Dr. Perkins Gripp's girlfriend? It wouldn't be the first time that a rich old man had attracted a young lover, as money and power were potent aphrodisiacs to some. Certainly their paths would have crossed many times, as they both had ties to the same campus. Perhaps Gripp had gone home with her?

"Your breakfast is ready," Fontaine called down the stairs.

"I'll be right there." Another name on Gripp's history list caused Bill to lose his appetite. It was the second time in days that he'd come across the name Lindsey Nolan. And she was the guardian of an art student at the same college, named Maggie.

*****

It had been years since she had awoken in the same clothes that she'd fallen asleep in, Maggie remembered. But back then her clothes would have been damp, cold, torn, filthy, and sometimes sopping wet. This morning her clothes were rumpled, yet warm and dry. The night before, after heaving trash bags into a dumpster behind the marine lab, she'd decided to return to the cottage rather than confront the Friday night antics in the dormitory: loud music blaring from the rooms, marijuana smoke sifting down the hall, and bursts of hysterical laughter coming from games of beer pong.

Before she'd left for the dumpsters, she'd heard car doors slam next to the garage. Lindsey and Derick, in pirate costumes, had exited the car and hurried upstairs to the apartment over the garage. They slept there on date nights.

Shortly after they were married, the once grungy, mildewed apartment had been rejuvenated. The bathroom had been gutted and an elaborate hot tub with assorted jets and spigots installed. A king-sized bed had also been delivered.

Upon returning to the cottage after the run to the dumpster, Maggie had regretted tossing the bedding, so she'd turned up the thermostat and lain on the living room sofa, appreciating the solitude and watching shadows shift across the walls. A breeze rustled the autumn leaves outside, and small waves pulsed against the beach. It was cathartic to have unburdened herself of all of Brian's belongings. The cottage was now a blank canvas to decorate as she desired.

Too wide awake to sleep, she'd uncurled herself and wandered into the kitchen, searching for her cigarettes. She'd lit one and looked out a window toward the garage apartment. An orange light glowed from behind the blinds. Perhaps the newlyweds had lit a Halloween candle and were acting out some pirate fantasy. Lindsey was weirdly turned on by pirates. Maggie turned away in disinterest. In her former life, there wasn't a lot that she hadn't done or seen. Nothing surprised her; little excited her. She'd been celibate for almost two years and relished the sanctity of her body. Besides, in that horrid, former lifetime she'd contracted HIV. She should not be producing HIV-positive children. She'd finished her cigarette, returned to the sofa, and dropped into a deep, contented sleep.

The next morning she awoke in her clothes. A thick fog from the bay had crept up the lawn during the night. Barely visible through the grey mist were the garage and sundial. Her stomach rumbled loudly, but there were only condiments left in the refrigerator. She trudged upstairs for a hot shower and then over to the beach house, with hopes of finding a hot breakfast and cup of coffee.

The Bends

*****

Over breakfast Lawrence Fontaine explained to Bill Bleach that his only task for Edward Gripp was to prepare him breakfast. For the remainder of the day the cook ran a small catering business. What Gripp did for the rest of the day, or for other meals, was unknown to him. Rarely did Gripp travel, but when he did, Fontaine was notified of the dates. Bill recalled that Maggie had reported seeing a large motor sailor near Spire Rock, so he asked if the boat ever left the marina. Never, Fontaine answered with certainty. In all of his years of cooking for Gripp, the boat had been at the marina every morning. In fact, Fontaine doubted that Gripp had any knowledge of piloting a boat. *Minotaur* was merely a convenient and picturesque place to live.

While Fontaine cleaned up the dishes, Bill inspected the deck outside. There was no sign of an inflatable boat, or a winch with which to lift one. It was unlikely that this was the same boat that Maggie had seen at Spire Rock. He needed to check one more thing, however. As he hurried through the galley, he thanked the cook for the gourmet breakfast.

"Ingredients, Detective," Fontaine said energetically. "It's all about fresh ingredients and not overcooking the vegetables. Don't let me forget to give you my card before I go. I cater both large and small events. Whatever you need."

"Yes, wonderful," he said distractedly, running downstairs to Gripp's office. He sat down in the office chair and began to sort through a stack of papers. Most were medical records for a recent hip replacement surgery, glossy brochures for new Jaguars, and a party invitation. At last—a lead. Gripp had been invited to a Halloween gala at the Newbury College of Art held the previous evening.

Before leaving the marina, Bill stopped by the security booth. Jim Delaney, the security guard, corroborated what Bill had read in the original report, that Gripp had been seen driving from the marina around seven o'clock. Never did the old man return from any event later than midnight, Delaney explained. Gripp meticulously organized his time, like every other aspect of his life, so far as he had observed.

"Any visitors to the boat?" Bill asked.

"No," Delaney answered.

In all the years that the guard had worked at the marina, Edward Gripp had never had a single visitor.

*****

The drive to the art college took less than ten minutes, and Bill parked in the visitors' lot next to a small administration building. As it was a Saturday, the cottage was locked. He located the college's website on his smartphone and found the name of the dean. Charles Shoemacher's number was listed in the e-yellow pages, and Bill gave the man a call, explaining that a missing persons report had been filed. The Dean agreed to meet him at the college. He lived less than a mile away; he could be there in a few minutes.

Bill's stroll around the grounds didn't take long, as it was a small campus. He passed by a dormitory and walked over to a maintenance building. The forest parted, revealing a rocky beach. The morning sun had begun to sear away the fog, and there were glimpses of blue sky. The air was heavy, so he removed his raincoat and slung it over his shoulder. A gravel trail led him down to the beach, where he weaved around clumps of seaweed and stones toward a swaybacked dock. A number of boats, from half-sunken rowboats to a rugged motor trawler, were tethered at cleats. A rash of sweat broke across his forehead as he eyed the dock. Under no circumstances would he walk across such a death trap of warped and creaky planking. He looked to see what was painted along the transom of the trawler: *Jack Rackham.* Creepy—a dead pirate swaying from a gibbet.

"Detective Bleach?" a man called.

Bill knew that he'd be easy to spot. Who else would be wearing a grey suit and tie on a Saturday morning? He waved to the fifty-something man striding down the hill. The dean was stocky and wore jeans and an Icelandic wool sweater. "Charlie Shoemacher," the man introduced himself in a thick Boston accent.

Shoemacher, Bill decided, could have been from central casting for a sprightly New England sea captain. His thick, unruly hair and walrus mustache were as white as clouds. A perpetual smile was carved deeply into a ruddy face.

"Let's talk in my office. I thought it was a bit peculiar that Edward's car was still here when I left the party last night," the dean said with concern, as they climbed the hill. "I figured that he might have gone out for a bite or a nightcap with one of the other donors or faculty members. But I see it's still here this morning."

"Can you show me the car?"

"Of course. It's right up there," Shoemacher pointed. "The white sports car."

Bill circled the car. The two doors were locked. He peered through the windows. There was nothing on the two leather seats or the dashboard. The car was immaculately clean, both inside and out. He jimmied open the trunk, but it only contained a spare tire and flares. Gripp's license plate read MNTR 70.

"Do you remember what time he arrived last night?" he asked the dean, as they walked toward the administration building.

Shoemacher pressed some buttons on a keypad and held the front door open for him. "Yes. Edward's a most punctual man. He arrives at all of our events on time. The party was a donors' reception that started at seven, and we greeted guests together. The donors were primarily parents and art aficionados from around the area."

"Did Edward seem ill or fatigued last night?" the detective asked carefully. "Or mentally out of it?"

"Edward? You have to be joking," the dean replied with a guffaw. "He's as sharp as a tack and quite gregarious. He never misses a campus party. Edward's not a young man, so he tires easily. He slips away from most events early to take a catnap in his office. There's a recliner there. A recent surgery has slowed him down a bit. Would you like some tea or coffee?" The dean pulled a key from his pocket and opened his office door.

"No, thank you."

"Here, have a seat, Detective." Shoemacher gestured toward a chair.

"Thank you." Bill pulled his notepad from his jacket pocket, vexed at his lack of preparation. His writing pad was low on paper and he'd forgotten to bring a spare. He scrawled some notes to himself on the remaining sheets. "Did he bring a date?"

"I've never seen Edward with a date. I know little of Edward's personal life, but I don't believe he's ever been married. He's left everything in his will to the college, so I assume that there's no girlfriend or children. He loves art students. He's been a wonderful benefactor to the college."

"Does he have any close friends on the staff or faculty that he might have gone home with? Does he drink a lot?"

"Certainly not. Edward might have one glass of wine all night. He's definitely not a drinker."

"Who did he spend most of the evening talking to?"

"Me; our Development Director, Kate Taylor; and my assistant, Doreen Best. He was chased around for a while by one of our—how should I put it—more *eager* parents, Jean Tate. Kate introduced him to Lindsey Nolan and her husband, Derick Briggs; they chatted for a bit before the couple headed onto the dance floor. And he talked with a few faculty members. I don't recall him spending any long period of time with anyone in particular, but I wasn't really paying attention, since I was entertaining parents."

"Dr. Nolan was there?" he asked, surprised.

"Yes, she's a new donor. Kate's thrilled. On a first ask, Dr. Nolan agreed to pay for new kilns. Nolan's ward, Maggie, is a student here. Check out her work in the painting studio before you leave. Her pieces are quite beautiful. They're all underwater scenes." Shoemacher pointed out the window. "All of the studios are in the Gripp Art Center over there, the big stone building."

"I will. Was Maggie at the party last night?"

The dean was silent for a moment, and then shook his head. "No. I'm sure I didn't see her there."

"I'd like to have a look at Gripp's office, if I may?"

"Of course." The dean moved from behind his desk. "It's this way."

Shoemacher led Bill down a short hallway.

"Edward occupies this corner office. It's a bit spartan, just a desk and recliner," explained Shoemacher, opening a door. "Would you mind if I checked my email while you look around? It's been a hectic weekend with all of the parents about, and we still have a formal dinner tonight at the Yacht Club with the Blue Ribbon donors."

"No problem." In fact, it was preferable to have a look on his own.

Shoemacher started down the hall.

"Can you print me out a guest list from last night's party?" Bill called after him.

The dean's voice boomed down the hallway. "Sure."

Bill stepped into Gripp's office. Shoemacher was right. There was nothing much to see. A metal desk contained a drawer with letterhead stationery and envelopes; all of the other drawers were empty. A black metal bookshelf had a few coffee table books on painting and sculpture. Only a blotter and mug of pencils and pens were on the desktop. There was no laptop or printer to be seen. The blinds were drawn. There were no posters or paintings on the walls. A single recliner was positioned in front of a closet, but it had recently been moved, as seen from impressions in the carpet. He slid behind the chair and opened the closet door. Just a heavy metal shelf with office supplies. He turned and closed the closet door.

For some reason, Gripp had been googling both June Perkins and Lindsey Nolan. Shoemacher had not mentioned Gripp spending any time with Perkins at the party, but the list of attendees would confirm if she had been there or not. He still needed to interview Perkins, and he was almost out of paper.

The Bends

He opened the closet again, searching for a small pad of lined paper. He was partial to 5 by 7 note pads, but there only seemed to be reams of 8 by 11 sheets of white paper. Post-it-notes would have to do. He reached to pull a post-it note pad from the stack, but they seemed to be stuck together. He attempted to insert his fingernail between the colorful pads; they would not give. He then reached for the box of staples. It too was stuck to the metal shelf. And so were the dusty coffee pot, rolls of tape, and reams of paper. All of the objects had been glued to the shelf. His face heated and a flush of red traveled up his neck, as it always did when something was amiss.

He rapped quietly on the wall behind the shelf. It certainly sounded like a solid wall, and there was no hinge to be seen. He pulled on the shelf and—the wall swung open! He shuddered as a cool draft of rich, organic air swept over him. After settling himself, he turned his body sidewise and slid through the narrow gap. Behind the wall panel was a tiny space containing an old stool and a box of AA batteries. There was an empty hook on the wall, and on the floor, neatly placed side by side, were a pair of black patent leather dress shoes. There was no electricity in the small chamber, only ambient light from the office. Bill peered ahead. A stairway descended into the darkness.

Chapter 8

"Well, look what the cat dragged in," George McLeod said in his slow Virginia accent. "Give me a hug, sweetheart." Maggie bent toward the old man and gave him a squeeze.

"Hug me, too!" squealed Ava, outstretching her small arms from a seat at the breakfast table.

Maggie obliged, kissed Ava on the head, and dropped into a vacant chair.

"What can I get you to eat?" asked Emily McLeod from the stove. "We have bacon, scrambled eggs, and pancakes."

"All of them?" Maggie asked hopefully.

"You have an appetite, little girl," George said heartily.

Lindsey wandered into the kitchen, her hands warming around a mug of coffee. "I thought I heard Maggie. What did you do last night?" She pulled up a chair at the table. "You missed quite a party."

"I went to my usual NA group with Tory, and then came back here and cleaned Brian's shit out once and for all. I want to turn the cottage into a painting studio."

Ava turned toward Lindsey. "Mom, when can I say 'shit', like Maggie?"

"Shit, shit, shit," Maggie gloated with a laugh.

"You're in high spirits this morning," Lindsey said, amused.

"When?" Ava persisted.

"Never," her mother answered swiftly.

"That's not fair!" the girl protested.

"When you're twenty-one, like Maggie," Lindsey relented.

Ava silently pouted.

"I want to repaint the cottage walls downstairs, move the sofa against the wall, throw down tarps, and set up an easel," Maggie explained. "Create a room of my own."

"Who coined that phrase? Gertrude Stein?"

"Stein? Virginia Woolf!" Maggie said, exasperated.

Mrs. McLeod handed Maggie a plate piled with food. "Here you go."

"I'm ravenous. Thank you," Maggie said gratefully to the old woman. She turned again toward Lindsey. "So, which faculty members did you embarrass me in front of last night?"

"Only Dr. Perkins. She was the only one who introduced herself to us. She said that you were nominated for the Windsor Award. What's that?"

"Who knows? I received some email about it, but I haven't read it yet. Why don't they send us information in tweets? Who reads email?"

"Old people," George answered from behind the *Boston Globe*.

"I think it's some award that they give every year," Maggie said around a mouth full of bacon and eggs. "Olivia Moreno should win. Her prints are amazing. They resemble the Matisse cutouts, but better."

"Congratulations on the nomination," Lindsey said proudly. "Be sure to add this to your résumé."

"Right," Maggie mumbled sarcastically. "I'll do that first thing."

"Derick and I saw your paintings in the painting studio. I'd love to have the blue painting of the tunicates for the dining room. I can't imagine how you can paint transparent objects like that. How do you do that? It's brilliant."

"It's a trade secret," Maggie answered.

"Well—can I have it for the dining room?"

"I'll sell it to you."

"You won't give it to me?" Lindsey said in disbelief.

"I don't see you giving away your electrode or C-trax GPS designs. I'm a businesswoman, just like you. I work for profit."

"Fair enough. How much do you want for it?" Lindsey inquired, while George hid a smile behind his coffee cup.

"I'll think of a fair price, and maybe give you a discount, since we're family." Maggie smiled slyly. "And give you a second discount because I have a big favor to ask you."

Lindsey tightened. "What's that?"

"I have some annoying friends who are dying to meet Jessie McCabe, and you also. The only way they'll stop pestering me is if they meet you two and get your autographs."

Lindsey relaxed. "I'm happy to meet your friends. They're welcome here anytime. You know that."

"They really want to meet Jessie."

"Your timing is good. Jessie's agreed to be the spokeswoman for the dive company. She'll be at the dive lab later this week for a photo shoot with some of our products.

The prototype of the submersible is almost ready for depth tests, so I need you to bring back *Jack* so we can get back and forth to the platform in the bay. The pier at the dive lab is too shallow for depth tests."

"How about I motor *Jack* over this afternoon?" Maggie suggested. "Will you drive me back to the college?"

"That sounds like a perfect plan," Lindsey agreed.

*****

"Did you find anything that might tell us where Edward has run off to?" Shoemacher asked, looking up from his laptop.

Bill's face revealed nothing. "You were right. It's just an austere office. I shut off the light and locked the door behind me when I left. I appreciate you coming in to talk to me on a weekend."

"I'm happy to help. I work many weekends during homecoming, recruiting, and fundraising events. I checked the guest list for the dinner tonight. Edward should be coming. I'll give you a call when he shows up," the dean offered.

"That would be really helpful." Bill opened his wallet and pulled out a business card. "Here's my card, with my cell number." He extended his hand toward the dean. "This is an interesting old building. Has it been here for a while?"

"It used to be Edward's home. When he donated the property to the college, it was divided into administrative offices. He insisted on an office on the first floor so he didn't have to do steps. What is now the Gripp Art Center was a series of offices for his architects and engineers. Here's the guest list from last night."

Bill scanned the alphabetized list of names... M, N, O... P. Perkins, June had been in attendance.

*****

"What a freaking lucky break!" Maggie laughed aloud as she drove back to the art college. Lindsey and Derick had walked through the painting studio to see her works the night before, but fortunately had bypassed the drawing studio. "How could I be so spacey and forget to remove the nautical objects from my still life before the party? Lindsey would have flipped out if she'd seen her new dive helmet out on display to the world." Her apprehension about meeting with Brian after all this time had been a distraction for the past few weeks, but that was all in the past. Now she could give her full attention to her classes again.

Maggie pressed on the gas pedal and sped up Woods Hole Road, cranking up a Pink tune on the radio. She would bolt to the drawing studio, retrieve the helmet, and stow it back in the dive locker on the *Jack Rackham*, next to the second one. Lindsey would never know that it had been removed from the boat. She made the turn, passed through the forest and crossed the covered bridge. The plastic tombstones, fake ravens, and leering scarecrows in front of the Gripp building had lost their eeriness in the daylight. The damp grey stones of the building glistened in the sunlight now that the fog had burned away. It was a bright, crisp day.

Her plan was to change into fresh clothes and then retrieve the helmet. She parked the Jeep in the student lot and entered the dormitory, using her swipe card. The door to her room was already open, and Kyle, Olivia, and Lily sat on Lily's bed, huddled around a laptop. They burst into laughter. Maggie peered at the screen and grinned. That episode of Tosh.O was insanely funny.

The dorm room had clearly been used for a party the night before. A trashcan was full of beer cans, and ashtrays overflowed with cigarettes butts; there was a pervasive smell of smoke and beer. The cottage had been a good choice for a quiet respite and a sound night's sleep.

"What went on in here last night?" Maggie asked.

"Oh, the party was supposed to be in Kyle's room, but his roommate wanted to study, so we moved it down here. We played beer pong and Twister," Lily answered.

"Twister sounds X-rated," she said, smiling.

"You should talk about X-rated. You're wearing the same clothes as last evening," Lily observed. "Who were you with?"

"Myself." She stepped behind a colorful tapestry that separated the desks from the beds. She unlaced her sneakers and pulled off the wrinkled clothes. "Don't even think about looking, Kyle."

"I'm sooooo hung-over," he moaned. "I'm not capable of seeing anything this morning."

"Every Friday evening, like clockwork, you disappear. And this morning you show up in the same clothes as yesterday," Lily said insinuatingly.

"I went home to clean out my cottage. I'm setting it up as my painting studio."

"You're so full of crap. Cleaning on a Friday night? Right. Come on, Maggie, tell us who he is," Lily pleaded.

"Is it a chick?" Kyle asked. "That would be hot."

"Kyle, shut up," Maggie muttered tiredly. She pulled on fresh underwear and clothes. Closing her eyes, she gave herself a quick spritz of lavender body spray.

"It's her business," Olivia said, shutting down the interrogation. "I love being alone."

Maggie bent down to lace her high tops. "Thank you, Olivia," she said appreciatively. She removed the keys to the *Jack Rackham* from a bowl on her desk. "I'm going to the studio to work. Later."

Skipping a step at a time, she dashed up the front steps of the Gripp building. Cobwebs, plastic spiders, and ghosts still hung from the stone arches. Giant stereo speakers were still on the front porch. Tables were still set up in the library and reception room. Empty coffee machines and teapots remained on the table, and the room smelled faintly of stale wine and food. She headed toward the drawing studio, passing some students and parents milling around in the central galley.

Each art studio had its own distinct scent, and the drawing studio was among her favorites. There was something ineffable and wonderfully inspiring about the scent of paper, charcoals, chalk, and pastels. She was looking forward to finishing the nautical still life, and then locking the dive helmet safely away. Perhaps if the drawing turned out well, she could have it framed and give it to Lindsey for her birthday, since she loved nautical objects. By that time, the prototype dive helmet would be out on the market and no longer a great mystery. And she wouldn't charge Lindsey much for the blue tunicate painting, either—just enough to buy tarps, an easel, paint, and blank canvases for the cottage studio. Besides, it was her job in life to tease Lindsey N. at every possible opportunity.

The drawing studio door was open. She had the entire glorious place to herself. Sunlight streamed in through the windows, so there was no need to turn on the ceiling lights.

She wound her way between the easels and still life displays, careful not to disturb anyone's work. Her secluded drawing area by the window was bathed in the light of late morning. She stared, and froze in her tracks. "I'm fucking dead."

*****

Bill entered through the back door of the Gripp Art Center and sought out the painting studio, as Dean Shoemacher had suggested. Displayed on the walls were portraits, nudes, still lifes, and baffling abstract art, but the paintings of Maggie May-Nolan were inimitable. Any one of them could be studied for hours. The works were realism, but with abstract elements as well. There was an intriguing translucent tunicate on a blue piling, another showed the writhing purple tube feet of a starfish, and the third one depicted the orange and red tentacles of a coral searching the currents for tiny particles of food.

Her paintings were a temporary distraction from the ominous passageway, which still unnerved him. No way was he going down that black stairway without a flashlight. No way. Anyway it was probably nothing. Many building complexes in cold climates have underground corridors that lead from one building to the next, to prevent staggering through snowdrifts in the winter months. But little things didn't add up. First, the recliner that Edward Gripp allegedly napped in appeared as if it had never been used. There were no worn areas on the headrest, armrests, or footrest. The black dress shoes that might be worn with a tux were equally disconcerting. And what had been on the hook? And the AA batteries? For a lamp of some sort? If the passageway was a route to pass from building to building during inclement weather, then why no electricity?

And why hadn't Shoemacher told him that the passageway existed? There were two possible answers to that question: either the dean was not aware of it or didn't want him to know about it.

And why did Gripp insist on maintaining an office on campus, that particular corner office, when the man had a perfectly functional office with a laptop and printer on his boat?

Bill checked the time on his cellphone. He still needed to talk to June Perkins. He poked his head into the ceramics studio but found it occupied by students and parents. It was the same situation in the printmaking room. The computer graphics room was simply a room filled with cubicles and laptops, with a commercial printer for making posters. He followed the campus map that Shoemacher had given him to the drawing studio.

*****

Maggie's knees faltered and she collapsed onto a stool. Nearly hyperventilating, she stared at the empty space where the NK prototype dive helmet had stood. Countless parents, staff, and students had wandered through these studios over the past two days. Anyone could have grabbed it! Would Lindsey throw her out, as Lindsey's mother, Miriam, had done to her when she was eighteen? And what about Sara? The NK dive helmet was her project too, and Sara was a bitch most of the time. No, all of the time. Yes, Sara would certainly convince Lindsey to disown her and cast her back onto the streets. Maggie pressed her hoodie into her eyes. Living rough again meant dirty, wet clothes, sleeping on cold cement floors of abandoned buildings, subways, and storm drains, and eating filth from trashcans and dumpsters... and making money by... no, she would never do that again. She would kill herself first.

But Lindsey would never throw her out; she was nothing like Miriam Nolan. Her imagination was running wild and trouncing over any remaining bits of rational thinking, Maggie tried to convince herself. The serenity prayer, the serenity prayer... repeat the serenity prayer. *God grant me the serenity to accept the things I cannot change, courage to change the things I can, and the wisdom to know the difference.* Lindsey was kind, generous, and calm, most of the time. But she would be pissed, and Sara would be ballistic. They would have to be told, and the sooner the better. And the blue tunicate painting was Lindsey's for free, Maggie decided, and she'd paint anything else Lin wanted, and do work around the house, anything. And not say shit or fuck in front of Ava and Danny—anything to make amends.

Maybe someone at the party had drunk too much and had worn it around as a joke. Maybe it was just sitting in someone's dorm room while they slept off a hangover. Lily, Kyle and Olivia were loyal friends; they would help to pass the word around the dorm to search for it.

"Ur, hello, Maggie."

Maggie jumped to her feet, knocking over the stool.

"Sorry to have startled you," Bill said, surprised at the alarmed response. "Were you concentrating on your work?" He picked up the stool.

She stood rigidly as if caught in some illicit act. "Uh—yes."

Wide-eyed, she searched the room, but no one else was about. She leaned forward slightly. "Did you come to tell me what you found at Spire Rock?" she whispered in a frantic tone.

He shook his head. "My captain hasn't sent divers out yet. The seas have been too rough. But hopefully we'll have some news soon."

"You know my name." She looked warily at him. "You tricked me by walking me to my car that day. That way you found me from the license plate. How stupid am I?"

He smiled. "And from your tablet. 'Welcome back, Maggie.'"

"Shit. Plain stupid." She groped her pocket. "I need a cigarette badly."

Wordlessly, he followed her down the hall and onto the back porch. She lit a cigarette, inhaled deeply, and worriedly scanned the area for other students.

"So you know who I am... then I guess you saw that I have a police record," she said in a hushed voice.

He nodded. "Those things occurred before you were eighteen, so your record's expunged."

She was silent for some time. "But they're always part of me, aren't they?" she said mournfully.

"Only if you let them be." He went on optimistically, to improve her mood, "You seem to have landed on your feet."

"Some of us are cats. We have many lives. That's one life I don't want to return to." She chewed on her finger. "If you're not here to tell me about the body at Spire Rock, then why are you here?"

"I'm investigating a missing person."

"Who's missing?"

"Edward Gripp. He was here at the party last night and never made it home. Do you know him?"

"Everyone knows him. He's impossible to miss. He's an old man who hobbles around the campus all the time."

"Have you ever spoken with him?"

She smirked. "No, I avoid adults at every turn."

"Do you know June Perkins?"

"Yeah. She's my professor in Painting III. I also had her for Painting II and Painting Workshop. She's an excellent prof."

"Is she friends with Edward Gripp?"

"Who knows? Why are you asking about Dr. Perkins?"

"I want to talk to faculty who were here last night, so I can figure out when Gripp might have left. Lindsey Nolan was here last night also."

"I know. We had breakfast together this morning. She said that it was a fun party."

"Do you live at home or in the dorm?"

"In the dorm, but last night I slept at home because I was clearing out space to convert my cottage into a painting studio."

"Your works are beautiful. Are any of them for sale?"

"Yes. All of them, except the blue tunicate piece."

"Do you ever paint reptiles?"

"So far, no. I only paint what I see. I haven't seen sea turtles this far north. Thankfully, I haven't ever seen sea snakes. Most are poisonous."

"But *Hydrophiinae* are quite shy and docile. They only live in the IndoPacific."

"Is your lizard better?"

"Yes. Thanks for asking. Watson just needed a change of diet."

She smoked, deep in thought. "So you're going to be walking around campus interviewing people about Edward Gripp?"

"Yes." He pulled the guest list from his blazer pocket. "Here are the guests from the Halloween party. It will take me forever to go through the list," he uttered in frustration. "I'm hoping that Gripp shows up for another party tonight, so that I can move onto more interesting cases, like homicides. If I was in a large city like Boston or New York, I could be on a unit that only deals with homicides. Here I get assigned any random thing," he complained wistfully. "Missing person cases are invariably old, forgetful people wandering off somewhere."

"I'm going to make you an offer, detective."

He was taken aback and drew in a breath. There was a wily glint in her blue-grey eyes. "What?" he asked, unsettled.

"I've lost something, or something's been stolen, I don't know which. It was part of my still life in the drawing studio, and now it's gone. It's... it's the Nolan-Kauni dive helmet. If you'll keep an eye out for it as you walk the campus conducting your interviews, I'll paint one of your lizards for you. I'm desperate to find this dive helmet. Lindsey and Sara Kauni, her business partner, will kill me if they know I've lost it. Then you'll have a real homicide on your hands," she added ironically.

Perspiration formed on his nose. "Ur, would you have to paint in my apartment?... It's small... and has terraria all over..."

She broke in quickly, "Hell no! No way I'm going to your apartment. Just email me some JPEGs of your lizards, and we'll go from there."

He mulled over the offer. His apartment had magazine photographs of Galapagos tortoises, king cobras, poison dart frogs, and Komodo dragons tapped to the walls, but no original artwork. The walls were monotonously beige. A painting would perk things up. Maggie's paintings were brilliant, and one day might be worth something. But it wasn't a fair exchange. He'd look out for the dive helmet for nothing. That was no big deal. She was a young artist; she should be paid for her work. And there was finally money accumulating in his bank account, now that his student loans were paid off. "No, I can't have you do it gratis. I'd like to pay you for a reptile painting."

Her face wrinkled with worry. "I'm not exchanging money with a cop. I'm not that stupid." She turned to leave.

"Maggie, wait!" he called, taking quick strides to catch up. "I'll look for the helmet for nothing."

"I don't like to be indebted to people," she replied hotly over her shoulder. "It has to be an even exchange, a barter."

"Okay, I'll send you JPEGs," he panted, trying to keep up. "I agree to the terms."

Her eyes brimmed with tears. "Thank you. If I can't find this helmet, I'm screwed. It's really unique, a prototype. It has speakers, and oxygen and carbon dioxide sensors, and I think depth sensors, and probably other gizmos that I don't know about. It hasn't gone to market yet. Lindsey and Sara are still working on it. The design's worth a fortune. Can I show you what it looks like? There's another one on the boat. It's just down at the dock on the *Jack Rackham*." She pointed toward Buzzards Bay.

Another terrifying dock, another terrifying boat. "Sure," he responded weakly.

She talked nervously as they walked down the stony beach trail. "I saw the helmet yesterday morning during drawing class, around eleven in the morning. In the afternoon, the building was crazy loud and chaotic with caterers setting up for the party, so I stayed clear. I took off in the late afternoon to have dinner with some friends, then went to my Narcotics Anonymous meeting. I do that every Friday evening. I've been clean since I was thirteen. For over eight years."

"That's impressive," he mumbled, eyeing the frothy water.

She stepped onto the dock. "I didn't know that it was missing until I returned to campus this morning."

His steps faltered at the first plank. "Did you paint the transom?"

"Yeah, during my blue period. I think that everyone has a blue period at some point in their life. I was having a bad time with a boyfriend at the time," she answered candidly. "I was imagining that it was his body swinging on the gallows. Morbid, isn't it?"

He inched fearfully forward, trying not to obsess over all the cracks and fracture points. Should the planks buckle under him, he'd plunge into a dark cauldron of churning water. "It's certainly vivid."

She halted next to the trawler. Her hands clutched the hair on her head. She bent over the gunwale into the boat. "Look at that sand and mud!" She furiously pointed at a cleat. "I never tie the lines like that. Some assholes were joyriding in my boat!"

*****

Out of the corner of his eye, Jim Delaney detected movement outside the security booth. He looked up from a black and white TV and poked his head out the door. "Excuse me," he called sternly. "May I ask where you're going?"

"Yes, of course," the blonde woman said pleasantly. "I'm delivering these flowers to Edward Gripp's boat."

"Edward?" Delaney asked in surprise. "He's been found?"

"Found?" she said with a lovely laugh. "Was he ever lost? Edward has had quite the weekend." She smiled widely from behind a bouquet of lush flowers.

"Have the police been notified?"

"Yes, yes, everyone's been notified," she replied reassuringly. "Edward met up with an old flame at a party this weekend. Apparently she was his first love, many decades ago," she added in a breathless voice. "He's been at her home in Boston. He's bringing her down to his boat and wanted my shop to deliver these flowers before she arrived."

Delaney studied the woman for a moment. The congenial florist in the large sunglasses wore an apron and gardening gloves. From a shoulder bag projected a trowel, bottle of plant vitamins, and potting soil.

"Alright," he conceded, heading toward a secure metal box with boat keys. "I'll open it for you." He glanced briefly at the ball game on the TV screen. The bases were loaded.

"There's no need to move from your post, officer. Edward had a spare set of keys forwarded to my flower shop." Shifting the bouquet onto her hip, she reached into the apron and revealed a set of boat keys. "He wants everything to be just right for his lady friend."

"Edward's a stickler for details," Delaney agreed. He pointed down the dock. "It's the motor yacht on pier three called *Minotaur*."

"You are most helpful. Edward should be an inspiration to all of us. It's never too late to fall in love!" exclaimed the florist as she strode toward the dock.

*****

Back in his apartment, Bill Bleach zipped his smartphone into the pocket of his running pants to ensure it was handy. At any moment Dean Charlie Shoemacher might call him to say that Edward Gripp had showed up at the Yacht Club for a dinner of scallops, lobster tail, and champagne. Sidestepping down the row of terraria, he scrutinized each reptile. Dalgliesh, a Thayer's king snake, would make a handsome model for Maggie's painting because of his stunning coloration, beige with alternating rust-colored bands that were outlined with a hint of black. Plus, there was an interesting, rust-colored "V" right behind his eyes. The yellow-bellied slider, Miss Marple, was also photogenic, but she refused to pop her head out of her shell. At the moment it was impossible to photograph the lovely yellow and green stripes on her neck. And Sherlock, a Cuban knight anole, was a spectacular bright green. Too many choices. Do not rush the decision, he told himself. He put the digital camera next to the terraria, so that when a pet was in a particularly good pose, he could snap a picture of it. Then, when there was a complete folder of each animal, he'd email everything to Maggie and let her decide.

The microwave in the kitchen beeped. He answered the summons and scraped vegetable lasagna onto a plate, then reached into the refrigerator for a soda. For dessert... a butterscotch sundae with whipped cream and cashews. Lasagna with extra cheese and vegetables was the perfect meal before tomorrow's 5K race. Some carbs, plus protein and fat for a slow energy burn. Just once, he lamented, could he beat that marine sergeant who entered all of the same races? It was the story of his life: to always come in second place.

He placed his plate and soda onto a coffee table in the living room and reached for the clicker. Hopefully the baseball playoffs would distract him from all of the jumbled, disjointed information from earlier in the day now floating around in his head. A missing old man who seemed to have a fascination with two thirty-something women, a stolen dive helmet, a mysterious passageway. Did any of these things have any relation to any other?

It's Saturday night, he reminded himself. Down time. Work can wait. Focus on the race tomorrow. The old man's probably popping hors d'oeurves into his mouth at this very moment.

A muted rustling in one of the terraria alerted him, so he vaulted over the back of the sofa. Grabbing the camera, he directed it at Jethro Gibbs, an everglades rat snake who had roused himself from the crackly fall leaves, and coiled himself around a branch. Bill moved swiftly along the front of the terrarium, snapping photos of Jethro from different angles.

He leapt back over the sofa and landed in the cushions. Still zero-zero in the third inning. The game was a snooze. He reached for his laptop and opened Facebook. Weird—his old girlfriend from the police academy had sent him a friend request. It appeared as though she'd transferred from Brockton to the police force in Dennis. What was that all about? His finger hung tentatively over the "Confirm" button. Wait on this... wait. That relationship had ended badly, when he'd found out that she was two-timing him with the guy graduating Number One in their recruit class at the Massachusetts State Police Academy. No, do not Friend her.

He shut the laptop with resolve. There was no time for women at this critical stage in his career.

Rarely did he interview beautiful women, but that day he'd spoken with two, Maggie May-Nolan and June Perkins. The Perkins house was not too far from his apartment in East Falmouth, so he'd swung by on his way home. The one-story house was covered in grey clapboards, like every other house on Cape Cod, and it needed a new roof. It was located on a cul-de-sac and had typical domestic clutter in the driveway: a Big Wheel and a small pink bicycle. He was met by June's husband, Conrad, who emerged cautiously from the garage where he was bolting a child's seat onto the back of a ten-speed bike. A young girl in a pink bike helmet hovered around her father. Conrad was roughly thirty-five, had a long blond ponytail, and a two-day beard. He called in through the front door for June. A curt female voice responded that she was busy. "It's the police," Conrad had added with controlled dread.

There was a delay, followed by, "Okay, I'll be right there." June had appeared quickly, a toddler held protectively in her arms. She was wearing skintight black workout pants, wool socks, Birkenstock sandals, and a bulky sweater. A pleasant but nervous smile was pulled tightly across her full, pink lips. She was more attractive in person than in her photograph on the college website. Her eyes were green, and her thick auburn hair was the hue of autumn leaves.

He had flashed his ID and explained that he was inquiring about a missing person. Edward Gripp.

At the news, June had been visibly relieved. "Of course I know Edward," she'd said in a helpful, eager tone. "He attends all of the campus events. He's been quite generous with funds for the painting program."

"Did you talk to him last night at the party?"

"No. In fact, I've never had a full conversation with him. I thanked him once for the art supplies, and another time for buying one of my paintings at a student-faculty art auction. He just says, 'You're welcome,' and seems too busy to talk. He rushes away."

"Do you remember him spending any time talking to anyone in particular?"

She shifted the toddler onto her other hip. "I remember that he was the only person not in costume. He wore a tuxedo. He was near the front door for a while with Charlie Shoemacher, Kate Taylor, Doreen Best, and the Tates."

Conrad had listened carefully to his wife's words, his hands jammed deep into his jeans pockets.

Taking notes, he had next asked, "Do you remember when Edward might have left, or do you recall him leaving with anyone?

"Sorry," she'd answered, shaking her head. "I don't recall any of it. I wasn't really paying attention to Edward Gripp."

"If you do remember anything else," he'd said, reaching into his pocket, "will you please give me a call?"

She had retreated slightly as he'd stepped toward her with his business card, but "Of course," she'd answered pleasantly enough, and accepted it.

Departing, he'd asked over his shoulder, "Dr. Perkins, what were you dressed as?"

"Isis, the Egyptian goddess of motherhood," she answered with an engaging smile.

As his unmarked car pulled from the Perkinses house, Bill had glanced in his rearview mirror. The couple had been walking briskly toward the house in a hot exchange with one another. He'd laughed to himself. Conrad and June Perkins were clearly going to flush or hide their stash. Both parents reeked of marijuana.

The game still scoreless, Bill scrolled through the TV channels. He finally settled on *The Matrix*, even though he'd seen it twice. Marijuana should just be legalized, once and for all, he thought. Marijuana arrests were a time-drain when the police should be tracking down pedophiles, rapists, and murderers. Besides, he'd never seen anyone violent from the effects of marijuana, whereas alcohol made some individuals crazed and barbarous. It was impressive that Maggie had so many years of sobriety.

What a baffling temperament she had! At one moment she was making an erudite allusion to Picasso's blue period, and next she was stomping around her boat, cursing like a sailor. While he'd stood on the edge of the dock, rallying the courage to climb onto her boat, she'd leapt fearlessly onto the *Jack Rackham* and unlocked a dive locker. She'd handed him a glistening, yellow helmet and disappeared into the cabin. Seconds later, she'd returned with a broom and dustpan and meticulously swept up the flakes of mud and sand, all the while muttering to herself, "I'm going to kill those fuckers! Whoever the fuck they are!"

Relieved that he was not requested to climb down to the boat—smaller and more unstable than the *Minotaur*—he'd eyeballed the dive helmet. Minute sensors and consoles built into the helmet did gods-knew-what. The helmet was out of a sci-fi movie. After a furious rant around the deck, Maggie seemed to remember he was present. As she reached up for the dive helmet, she grasped his hand momentarily, as if sealing a deal. "Thank you again for helping me search for the missing one."

A flush of red started up his neck, and he tentatively pulled his hand away.

"I'm gonna paint you the most superlative reptile painting that's ever been painted," she'd called as he'd hurried off the dock.

*****

Maggie's few close friends from the dorm typically discussed sex, booze, and parties, topics that held little interest for her. On these subjects, she listened but remained unwaveringly silent, as though ignorant of all of it. It was best that her college friends consider her an innocent. No one must ever find out about her past. This was a deliberate strategy to keep a low profile at the art college. So, to go door to door through the dorm, holding up the image of the dive helmet from her cell phone, was a humiliating, excruciating experience. That meant conversing with people, everyone in fact! In the entire fucking dorm! On Monday, if the helmet was still missing, the same mortifying ordeal would have to be repeated, but this time with the faculty and staff in the Gripp building and administration cottage.

Lily had enthusiastically volunteered to tag along with her. For Lily it was an opportunity to introduce herself to guys that she didn't know. After covering all of the floors, they returned, empty-handed, to their dorm room. Maggie dropped despondently onto her bed, while Lily applied lipstick at her makeup mirror.

Without knocking, Jean Tate barged into the dorm room. A nametag was stuck to her pressed Oxford blouse. "Did you know that there's a donors' dinner tonight?" the mother asked, galled.

"No," Lily answered blandly.

"Well, apparently there is," she said indignantly. "A party at the Yacht Club for the Blue Ribbon Donors, and we were not invited! Were your parents invited, Maggie?"

"Not that I know of," she replied, gazing morosely into her smartphone.

The response seemed to placate Jean for the moment. "Are you ready to go, sweetheart?" Jean said to Lily.

"Yes," Lily replied. "Do you want to come, Maggie?"

She glanced up from the phone. "Where?"

"To dinner at the mall."

"Another time. I have to catch up on some reading."

"What a diligent student! See that, Lily? Maggie reads on a Saturday night."

"Maggie sneaks off with a secret boyfriend," Lily announced mischievously. "I finally saw him today."

Maggie sat erect. "What? Who?"

"The guy by your boat. The skinny guy in a suit and ball cap."

"He's definitely not my boyfriend. I hardly know him."

"Then who is he?"

"He was meeting with the dean. I just know him from around town."

"You and Maggie can discuss boys later," Jean cut in. "There will be a long wait at the restaurant if we don't go soon."

"Okay," Lily said. "See you later, Maggie."

"Yeah, later."

As they were departing, Maggie could hear Jean lamenting, "I wonder how much I'll have to donate to become a Blue Ribbon Donor."

Maggie checked the time. She hadn't eaten since Mrs. McLeod's breakfast that morning. She could find Olivia or Kyle and go to the dining hall with them, but she'd already talked far too much for one day. She pressed ear buds into her ears, found her favorite Pixies playlist on her iPod, and stepped toward the cube refrigerator. Popcorn, ginger ale, string cheese, and yogurt would be her dinner. She lifted her laptop onto her knees as the kernels started to pop in the microwave. A number of friends had recommended that she watch the old series, *Breaking Bad*, but she knew firsthand about meth dealers, and those horrible nightmares about Minnesota would resurface—she wouldn't sleep for days. Instead, she decided to stream re-runs of *Lost*.

Chapter 9

Bill opened a black briefcase and handed Sandra Murphy a heavy-duty flashlight. She walked back over to Edward Gripp's office door to make sure it was locked.

"So it's in this closet?" she asked, intrigued. She roughly shoved the recliner aside.

"Yes. Just pull on the metal shelf, and the wall will swing open. The whole supply closet look is a ruse."

She turned to Bill with a raised eyebrow. "Interesting."

Bill had taken an immediate liking to his new partner. Detective Murphy was alert and talkative, had a quirky sense of humor, and the uncanny trait that most women possessed: the ability to multi-task. In the short ride from headquarters to Woods Hole, they'd discussed the current case, strayed off on tangents—his 5K race, which he'd lost by 14 seconds; the Sunday afternoon cooking class that she was attending with her fiancé—only to return to the vital points of Gripp's disappearance. With his previous partner, Bill had to explain a case four or five times before Raymond absorbed the most rudimentary facts. All the while he'd be staring out the car window, interrupting with commentary on the plusses and minuses of the anatomy of a female standing at a bus stop or crossing a parking lot.

Sandra peered behind the wall panel. "It's very dark back here. I hope there are no bats. I'm not crazy about bats, or snakes."

"There are ten species of snakes on the Cape, none of which are venomous," he reassured her.

"That makes me feel so much better," she quipped.

"And none of them bite. They're all rather docile."

He moved into the tiny room, following her. She'd already moved down a short corridor. Her tan business suit and pink blouse were easy to spot in the dark. Under her suit jacket was a shoulder holster holding a Glock G30S sidearm. He rarely carried a gun.

"Watch your step, Bill. There are steep stairs here."

"Right," he replied hesitantly, grasping the rope handhold and starting down the steps. The passageway finally leveled off, and Sandra's flashlight beam flitted over the walls, revealing sturdy masonry and steel girders across the ceiling. "It would take an earthquake to bring down these walls."

"They're not coming down in our lifetime. I'm guessing that we're traveling under the parking lot in the direction of the art building," she called back.

His light was aimed directly at the dirt floor. "Whoever was down here last was wearing a smooth-soled shoe and shuffled."

"Yup, I noticed that too. So far, so good. No bats or snakes."

"If we do see a snake, I want to take it home. I don't have any local species. My pets are all from the South or other countries."

"Then I'll drive and you can hold the snake," she said adamantly, "because I'm not touching it."

"Snakes are not slimy like most people think. To me they feel like bendable candles. Warm and waxy."

"Warm and waxy, or not, I'm not touching it. There's a door up here. If we go straight, there's another stairway." She leaned forward. "It must go up into the Gripp building."

"Let's see what's behind the door first."

Sandra tugged, and the corroded hinges moaned as the door opened. Her flashlight beam broke the darkness of another passageway. "Whoever was walking down this passage was wearing hiking boots. It was probably a maintenance worker. But they're only partial prints. They're partly wiped out, as if something was being dragged."

For a few minutes they walked wordlessly down the straight tunnel, through cool, earthy air.

"We've been walking a while," he said apprehensively. "We're probably going to come out in the middle of Buzzards Bay."

"Then I wish I had my rain gear. There's another stairway up here, and a trap door." She thrust upward, and dirt and leaves showered down on her. "Jesus Christ! I just had this suit dry cleaned." She brushed the debris off her arms and ran her fingers through her military-style, ear-length hair. "Talk about a bad hair day." She turned around on the top step. "We're in the middle of a forest." Surrounding her was a soft cushion of red and yellow leaves.

Morning sunlight filtered down through a sparse orange canopy. "This is the forest next to the shore." He squinted between the tree trunks. "There's the dock."

"Someone's been back here. Look," she said, pointing. It was not a well-worn trail, but the weeds had been trampled to form a narrow path.

Bill studied the trap door. There were handles both inside and out, indicating that it could be opened from both the tunnel and the forest. "Shall we try the other stairway under the Gripp Center?"

She nodded. "This is probably an emergency egress. All burrowing animals have a backdoor."

They flipped the flashlights back on, and Bill closed the trap door over their heads. They retraced their steps down the straightaway and eventually passed through the old door, which they closed behind them. Another stairway rose in front of them, and they climbed to ground level.

A crosshatching of sunbeams sliced the grey air of the passageway, and the detectives looked at each other in tacit dread.

On either side of them, the massive stonewalls that formed the foyer of the Gripp Art Center were penetrated with tiny slits... peepholes.

"I have a very bad feeling about this," she whispered.

"Gripp's license plate was MNTR 70," he whispered back. "He constructed this building in 1970."

She shrugged. "I'm missing the point."

He continued in a hushed voice, "And his yacht is named *Minotaur*."

She grimaced. "So this is the Minotaur's labyrinth."

"It looks that way," he admitted sickly. He peered through one of the walls. The tables from the weekend's parties had been removed from the library, and all litter and trash bags had been carried away. He looked through another slit in the opposite wall. Reclining on the sofas in the reception room, students gazed into smartphones or tablets. On the sofa in the corner, Maggie napped, her head draped over an armrest.

After a moment, Sandra said, "Bill?"

"Hmm?" he replied vaguely.

"Do you know her?"

"Um—yes. That's Maggie, who reported the body at Spire Rock. I ran into her again on Saturday. She asked me to look out for a stolen dive helmet. She's in a panic. It's a prototype that hasn't gone into production yet. The helmet belongs to Lindsey Nolan and Sara Kauni."

"The Nobel laureates? Why did she have their dive helmet?"

"Nolan's her adopted parent."

She shook her head. "This morning's getting more bizarre by the minute."

Circling the labyrinth on the first floor, they observed that classes were in session in all of the studios. Most disturbing was the fact that there was not a square inch of any room that could not be spied from one of the peepholes. Also troubling were the small stools positioned with great deliberation at specific locations behind the wall.

They climbed in wary silence to the second floor. A computer room was occupied by students. A conference room was empty. Next were the faculty offices. One very old professor slept with his head across his desk. A woman professor reviewed a term paper with a student. The next teacher, clearly an art historian, was holding a review session for an upcoming exam on Greek art for three students. At the next office, Bill's eyes widened, and he signaled for Sandra to stop.

She tilted her head questioningly.

He typed into the memo pad of his smartphone. The name "June Perkins" glowed from the screen.

Sandra wordlessly nodded, remembering what Bill had told her, that Perkins' name was in Gripp's computer.

June Perkins was pacing the office of a silver-haired professor about ten years her senior. He sat behind his desk, fumbling with an unlit pipe. Then she dropped onto the sofa in a frustrated slump.

"John, can't we get a motel room somewhere? It doesn't feel right doing it here anymore. Especially after hearing rats in the walls on Friday night."

The two detectives stared at each other in surprise and sudden comprehension.

"But that would get so expensive, and I'm short of money right now. I'm paying so much to that divorce lawyer, but he's useless, an entire waste of money." John pressed his fingers into his temples. "I don't want to think about that right now."

June frowned in disappointment.

John scanned her athletic body. "You're on the wrong side of the desk, gorgeous." He grinned salaciously.

"I can't. I have class in five minutes."

"Then for four minutes?" he said in a needy whimper.

June sighed and pulled herself from the sofa. "Four minutes. I don't like to be late for class." She stepped behind John's desk and straddled his lap. She pressed her mouth onto his while he groped under her sweater.

Sandra shook her head and pointed forward. Bill nodded. They moved a few steps down the passageway and stopped abruptly. A stool had been knocked on its side. Bill knelt down on the floor and peered through the nearest peephole. It had a direct view to John's sofa. His heart began to pound. He motioned for Sandra to look, but she was oblivious to his gestures. Her flashlight beam twitched on a singular stone in the wall. She stared transfixed, her hand shaking. He rose and leaned hesitantly toward the wavering circle of light. A rosette of blood was splashed across a stone, and from it a maroon trail dripped down the wall and pooled in the dirt below.

*****

At the exact second that Gordon Franz of the Massachusetts State Police Underwater Recovery Team (URT) fell backwards over the side of the inflatable and hit the water, he regretted not wearing a dry suit. Despite all his years of diving, the first impact of hitting New England water was still a shock. Two weeks ago, when searching the bottom of the Cape Cod Canal for a stolen Lamborghini allegedly concealing a large stash of cocaine and cash, the water had still been warm enough to wear a wet suit. Distracted that morning by the tantrum of his fourteen-year-old daughter, he'd forgotten to factor into this dive at Spire Rock the depth, currents, distance from shore, and recent storms that had carried in cold water from the North Atlantic. Instead of packing his dry suit, he'd mistakenly thrown a wetsuit into his dive bag, which meant that icy water would be leaking in around his face, neck, wrists, and ankles for the entire dive.

Above Franz and his dive partner, the URT Zodiac inflatable bumped against the rock escarpment where it had been tied off. He was certain that they were diving in the right spot. The witness had described a metallic sound—like hammering—to Detective Bleach. Franz noticed that some sturdy metal hooks had been hammered into cracks well above the high water mark on the south side of the cliff. To one of these hooks Franz had tethered the inflatable.

The Bends

Seabirds lunged from the ledges above them, piercing the churning water for fish. Despite eddies swirling around the precipice, the visibility of the water was fairly good. The two divers crawled down the rock face, passing the usual inhabitants: barnacles, limpets, periwinkles, mussels, and starfish. The rock was covered with a slime of algae, and seaweed and kelp gently swayed in front of their masks. The occasional antennae of a lobster or the blunt snout of an eel poked curiously from crevices. Franz checked his depth meter. At fifty-eight feet the bottom was just coming into view. The natural light dimmed as they descended, so they turned on their dive lights. The bottom was sand with scattered fragments of rock that had eroded from the cliff. Schools of small fish darted between the rocks and clusters of seaweed.

Franz was alerted by his partner knocking on his tank, their system of getting the other's attention. His partner's eyes were wide in bafflement behind his dive mask, and he held up two fingers. Puzzled, Franz looked downward. The art student had reported seeing one body drop in front of her while she dove. But two bodies, shrouded in white sheets and wrapped in rope, lay in the sand.

*****

The labyrinth, peepholes, tilted stool, and blood-spattered masonry prompted the cops to search the forest and shoreline before notifying the dean and calling in the forensics unit.

"The man was a sicko," Sandra said disgustedly, as she scuffed through the leaves. "Maybe someone knew of Gripp's voyeuristic activities, and attacked him—if that's what that mess was."

Bill's eyes were also on the ground, searching the leaves for any bit of useful evidence. "Perhaps Gripp was blackmailing June Perkins and her colleague John?" he tossed out for purposes of discussion, though disbelieving his own words. They hadn't behaved like people under the shadow of blackmail. "But Gripp was worth significantly more than all of the faculty members' salaries combined, so it seems doubtful that he'd be blackmailing them for money."

"For sex?" she suggested, repulsed.

He groaned. "Gripp and June Perkins? It's too horrid."

"Maybe John was complicit, and knew Gripp was watching them? Or some jealous or self-righteous individual found out and wanted the whole business to stop?"

He visibly winced. "Who knows? Unfortunately, all I saw was his computer's history. We need to impound his laptop to get a closer look."

"Notice that we're both referring to Gripp in the past tense," she said gloomily.

"I noticed. Maybe Gripp, in his perverse excitement at watching June and John, tripped over the stool and hit his head against the stone wall? Then, disoriented, he wandered off somewhere, had a seizure or stroke, and died?"

"But there were the partial footprints in the egress tunnel and something being dragged. I'm guessing that we'll find Gripp's body stashed under leaves or bushes any second. With so many parents milling around at the various events over the weekend, it would have been pretty difficult to move a body. If he is dead, a body lying in damp forest for three days is going to be pretty horrible. Fresh corpses are bad enough, but this one will be bloated and putrefying... a Thanksgiving feast for maggots, insects, and assorted carnivores."

"Ugh—I'm bracing myself for the worst."

They walked the forest for nearly two hours, but just that morning chilly gusts off the bay had stripped the trees bare, covering the forest in dried leaves, and the forest was far too large for two individuals to search effectively. Dogs would have to be brought in, and this request, like everything else, would take time.

Well-trodden trails wound through the underbrush. It was clear that students frequented the woods. By an outcropping of boulders was a box of crushed beer cans. By another tree was an empty bottle of Jack Daniel's, and condom wrappers. Tree trunks were carved with lovers' initials. The detectives attempted a search of a salt marsh that bordered the forest and bay, but they sank into the muck and had to turn back. The marsh, like the forest, would have to be searched by dogs—and police in waders.

Two trails exited the forest by the beach, but numerous high tides since Friday night had washed away any trace of footprints. Bands of seaweed formed a wrack line in the otherwise smooth, damp sand. Bill peered through the underbrush at the rickety dock projecting out into the bay. The *Jack Rackham* was gone. He recalled Maggie's appalled words: "I never tie the lines like that. Some assholes have been joyriding in my boat!" The trawler, too, would have to be searched.

In mud-covered shoes and wet socks, the detectives slogged up the hill to the dean's office. They found Charles Shoemacher staring out a window. One's books told volumes about one's character, so Sandra scanned the contents of his bookshelf. Before entering college administration, the dean's academic career had been dedicated to Byzantine art, demonstrated by texts on the early Christian and Byzantine periods, written by C. P. Shoemacher. There was some poetry by Houseman and Elliot, and books on the whaling history of New Bedford. The office walls bore prints of mosaics and early religious paintings. Photographs of Shoemacher's white-haired, pudgy wife, adult children, and grandchildren lined the windowsills.

The dean turned toward the detectives. "Tough times. Very tough budgetary times," he said, desperation in his voice. "An old patroness decided to withdraw funding to the college because she was offended by one of the nudes displayed in the sculpture studio during the party. The artist was an eighteen-year old, I tried to explain to her. Of course some of the nudes would be in wishful-thinking poses."

He shook his head and politely addressed the concern that had brought the detectives to his campus. "Was there anything helpful in Edward's office?" he asked, changing the subject from the college's impending financial shortfall.

The dean's mood was about to worsen. "Ur, yes," Bill said bleakly.

They escorted Shoemacher back to Edward Gripp's office and locked the office door behind them. Sandra pulled out the closet wall panel.

"What is this?" Shoemacher asked, stepping cautiously into the black space. His face turned a ghastly white. "A secret tunnel?"

"You had no knowledge of this?" Sandra demanded.

Shoemacher shook his head, stunned. He fumbled through his suit jacket for a handkerchief and wiped perspiration from his brow. She stared at him doubtfully.

"We didn't find Gripp, but there's a considerable amount of blood directly behind the wall of a faculty member named John," Bill explained. "Do you know who John might be?"

The Bends

The dean dropped into the seldom-used recliner. "We have only one John on our faculty, John Sanders. He's one of our most popular faculty members, a very collegial man. He chairs many important college committees."

Sandra stepped out from the closet. "We need to send a forensics team in there. And we need to send dogs into the woods and marsh."

Alarmed, Shoemacher raked his fingers through his hair, which now stuck out in all directions, reminding Bill briefly of a hedgehog. "Oh, God, no. Can't this wait? Tonight and tomorrow night are the fall's biggest recruitment events! Police and dogs will certainly frighten away potential students. Do you know how hard it is to convince parents to send their child to an art college when they want them to go into IT, nursing, or business school? Especially in this economy!"

"It's not certain that it's a crime scene, since Gripp hasn't been located, but we do need to determine the source of the blood. It's necessary to send a forensics team through the labyrinth to check it out," Bill insisted.

Shoemacher's face sagged in confusion. "Labyrinth?"

"Yes, the series of tunnels. Gripp seems to have a fixation with the Minotaur legend. His yacht is called *Minotaur*, and his boat is full of books on Cretan archeology and the mythology of the Minotaur, King Minos, Theseus, Aegeus and the House of Athens. The labyrinth has a number of peepholes and stools. It seems that Gripp was watching activities in the art building. Do you want us to show you?"

Shoemacher was visibly nauseous. "This is such disturbing news." He again dabbed sweat from his brow and checked his watch. "I can't go in there. I'm terrified of tight spaces. I've always been claustrophobic."

"The tunnels must be keep confidential from faculty, staff, and students," Sandra emphasized, "so that we can conduct our investigation without distractions and interference."

"Yes, yes, I quite agree!" The anxious dean nodded wholeheartedly.

"And we'll need footage from your security cameras in the Gripp building from last Friday night," Bill added.

"Yes, of course. Ted Blanchard, our Director of Business Services and Maintenance, can get you that."

"And blueprints for the Gripp building and this one."

"Yes. Ted should have those, too. I'll get him on these things immediately." The dean levered himself out of the recliner.

Bill pulled his notepad from his suit pocket and flipped through the pages. He skimmed his notes from his earlier conversation with the dean on Saturday. "And we need to talk with Doreen Best and Kate Taylor."

Shoemacher led the detectives to Doreen Best's office and promised to send over Ted Blanchard. Best turned from her computer and reflexively offered to fetch coffees. Bill and Sandra declined. They needed to get the building blueprints and the camera footage and rush back to *Minotaur* for Gripp's laptop. Plus, it was imperative to get a team from forensics into the labyrinth as soon as possible.

Doreen Best was typical of many administrative assistants: reliable, officious, and cowed by the string of letters that followed her boss's name, despite the fact that her IQ probably eclipsed his. She was a perky blonde, around age forty, dressed in a tailored blouse, tight skirt, panty hose, and running shoes. Best's description of the Halloween party matched Shoemacher's almost to the letter.

"Edward helped us to greet parents, and then chatted with Kate and me about upcoming fundraisers. Edward was his usual self, pleasant and animated. Once or twice he complained about a lingering pain from a recent hip replacement surgery, and mentioned that he would need to sit down. Nothing was different from other campus events. Edward mingled with the guests and faculty, and then left early to rest his hip." Doreen then led them across the hall to the Development Office.

The news of the rich benefactress withdrawing support had hit the Director of Development, Kate Taylor, like an avalanche; the distance to reach her campaign goal was now multiplied exponentially. Taylor, an overweight, grey-haired woman, was fluttering frantically through papers atop her desk as the detectives entered. A red-lipsticked smile was pulled tightly across her preoccupied face throughout the interview. Her description of the Halloween party corroborated that of Shoemacher and Best. However, Taylor added that she and Edward had spoken alone for some minutes on the porch.

"Edward requested that we talk outside," Taylor explained.

"Why was that?" Bill asked.

"He complained that the music was too loud. He could hardly hear himself think, he said. I asked that the music be turned down, but I think that the student running the sound system turned it back up as soon as I left."

"What did Edward want to discuss?"

"He wanted to set up a meeting for later in the month to discuss the endowment of a new painting scholarship for a low-income student. Edward's wonderfully generous. And he was adamant that he be introduced to Dr. Nolan as soon as she arrived. He was quite anxious to meet her."

After interviewing Taylor, Bill and Sandra returned to Shoemacher's office. The Business Director, Ted Blanchard, had a flash drive with the camera footage of the party, and he unrolled the building blueprints across the dean's conference table. It was immediately obvious to the detectives that the blueprint of the Gripp building was bogus. The massive stone walls were shown as solid structures. There was no evidence at all of a system of tunnels. But if anyone would know about the tunnels, it would be the maintenance crew that routinely dealt with antiquated heating and cooling systems and the electrical problems so common in old structures. Bill watched Blanchard from the corner of his eye. A former Air Force materials manager, Blanchard stood erect while the blueprints were studied. He said little and seemed annoyed at the dean's request for camera footage and blueprints.

"Mr. Blanchard, were you at the Halloween party on Friday?" Bill asked.

"No."

"Where were you?"

"Bourne."

"Doing what in Bourne?"

"Watching hockey."

"Which hockey game?"

"My son's."

"How old is your son?"

"Which one?"

"How many do you have?"

"Four."

Bill was losing patience with Blanchard's passive aggressive non-cooperation. "Any plumbing or electrical problems with these old buildings?"

"No! Why would there be?" Blanchard said indignantly. "Everything's in excellent running order. I know how to do my job."

"Where did you get these blueprints from?" Bill asked nonchalantly.

"From Edward himself," Blanchard grumbled. "At the closing, when the property was signed over to the college."

*****

After a quick lunch at a drive-through in Falmouth, the two detectives proceeded to the marina. Bill extended his ID out the car window toward the security booth. Jim Delaney, the same security guard who'd been on duty the previous weekend, recognized Bill.

"Good news about Edward, eh?" Delaney announced cheerfully.

"What's that?" Bill asked uneasily through the car window.

"Meeting up with the old girlfriend."

Bill and Sandra glanced at one another.

"What girlfriend?" Bill asked.

"I thought you knew." The guard paused. "The florist said the police had been notified. Edward met up with some old love who lives in Boston. He's been at her place."

Sandra's head shook imperceptibly and said in a low voice, "Something's not right, Bill."

"This is the first I've heard about it," Bill confessed.

"Typical police," Delaney guffawed. "The left hand doesn't know what the right hand is doing."

Sandra leaned across the front seat. "When did a florist tell you this? What company did he work for? Did you get his name?"

"Edward ordered a bouquet to be placed on the boat before his lady friend and he arrived. The florist was a she, not a he. She made the delivery on Saturday afternoon. Edward had forwarded his boat key to the florist shop. "

"And have Edward and the lady friend shown up?" Bill asked.

"No, not yet. That's the odd thing," Delaney answered, his mouth pursed in puzzlement.

"I need a key to his boat," Bill said, "on police business."

Delaney stepped into the security booth and returned with a spare set. "Here you go. When the florist left, she said she'd left Edward's spare set of keys on the galley table."

"What florist company was she with?" Sandra asked again.

"I don't know. I didn't see a van. She walked in with the bouquet. She said that her partner was up the road making deliveries and was going to swing by and pick her up."

"Let's go, Bill," she whispered urgently.

"Thank you," Bill said, pushing on the accelerator as the security gate lifted.

He and Sandra parked the car as close to the water as they could and hurried across the dock. He was less fearful than on his previous visit. Should he fall into the water, his sturdy partner would surely pull him out. They climbed onto *Minotaur* and opened the door to the salon. The boat was, as before, immaculately clean. Lawrence Fontaine had left the granite counter tops and stainless steel appliances in the galley spotless. On the galley table was a bouquet of red roses. Dried petals littered the polished wood. Next to the bouquet was a set of boat keys.

Bill sprinted across the salon and jumped down the few stairs leading to the master stateroom. He halted in the doorway to the adjoining office.

"Sandra!" he choked.

"What?" she called, hurrying down the stairs.

Bill gazed morosely at Edward Gripp's desk. "No laptop."

*****

By midnight Bill's eyes were aflame from watching endless hours of the security footage obtained from Ted Blanchard. With a gesture of finality he closed his laptop and picked up his digital camera. The reptiles had been shot from every possible angle, which would give Maggie lots of material for the painting. The original plan had been that the JPEGs would be sent by email, but the file was now too large. Besides, in their mutual preoccupation, she with the missing helmet and muddy dive boat, he with the dangerously flimsy dock, they'd forgotten to exchange email addresses. Perhaps the JPEGs in his laptop might be displayed to her at some location where he could elaborate on the different traits of each reptile, so that its idiosyncratic personality might come through in the work.

After spending the day in damp running shoes and socks, he felt a cold coming on. He climbed into bed, the footage from both the Halloween party and the security booth at the marina twisting through his thoughts like his snakes. He'd studied the footage repeatedly; every frame felt imprinted permanently into his memory. The makeup and masks of the partygoers made it difficult to determine who was who, or decipher the nuances of facial expressions and body language. Most of the guests were unfamiliar, so he'd focused exclusively on Edward Gripp. Fortunately, Gripp's tuxedo made him easy to follow through the crowd. Gripp's actions were just as Shoemacher, Best, and Taylor had related, greeting guests and so on. On a few occasions a woman dressed as a 17th century French aristocrat, followed by her taciturn husband, one of the Three Musketeers, approached Gripp. The old man cordially chatted with the couple, and then politely begged off. The woman must be Jean Tate, the pushy donor whom the dean had mentioned. The last time Mrs. Tate approached Gripp, a black cat, presumably her daughter, was in tow. The Musketeer husband had long since retreated to the front porch, where he was engrossed by something in his cell phone. The mother and daughter pulled Gripp into a corner of the room and seemed quite anxious. Again, he nodded pleasantly, looked watchfully across the room, and seemed to make another excuse for a hasty escape.

June Perkins, an Egyptian goddess, arrived about a half an hour into the party. Gripp and John Sanders, dressed as Daniel Boone, both tracked her discreetly, following her movements with peripheral vision. Perkins spoke briefly with Shoemacher and Best before spending most of the evening with four other faculty members: a hobbit, Captain America, Count Dracula, and a woman dressed in the fabric of Vincent van Gogh's *Starry Night*. Not once did June Perkins speak with Edward Gripp during the entire party.

When Lindsey Nolan and Derick Briggs arrived, the dynamics of the party shifted. To the general populace, Lindsey Nolan was not a household name, however, to the science community and enthusiasts of the Science Channel she was as familiar as Stephen Hawking, Richard Attenborough, and the deceased Carl Sagan. Furthermore, in the Cape Cod and Boston regions, two photographs of her in romantic entanglements on her boats had generated quite a stir. Nolan's costume was not at all provocative. She wore black pants, black boots, and a wide black belt holding both a toy saber and a blunderbuss. Over a white peasant blouse she wore a bright red coat. The traditional plastic eye patch had been pushed up around her red bandana.

Nolan's husband was stocky, well over six feet tall, and towered over his petite wife. His costume was similar to hers, though he wore a baggy shirt with laces across the chest, sailor pants, a black pirate hat, and a calico coat. To pirate aficionados it was clear that they were Calico Jack Rackham and Anne Bonny.

As when celebrities enter a room, there was a hush followed by muted discussions, the partygoers repositioning themselves to watch the couple askance. The dean and Kate Taylor quickly descended upon the couple and gestured toward the wine and food, but the couple courteously declined. After a few minutes, Shoemacher returned to the front door to resume his role as greeter, while Taylor shuttled Nolan and Briggs around to various faculty circles. Mrs. Tate fluttered behind the couple, her skirts and petticoats furling and unfurling. Gripp, with an eager glint in his eyes, soon approached Taylor, requesting an introduction, and Nolan and Briggs chatted with Gripp for a few minutes before Nolan briefly grasped the old man's bony hand, politely excused herself, and pulled her swarthy husband off to the dance floor.

Bill had replayed this scene again and again. Gripp stood transfixed, smiling at the vacated place where Nolan had just stood. It was clear what had mesmerized him. It was impossible not to notice. Bill had witnessed such charisma and overt sexuality in some movie stars, but never in a person from the real world. He, like Gripp, found himself fleetingly falling in love.

After this, Gripp wandered the periphery of the dance floor, moving into and out of various circles of conversation, while simultaneously fixing on the positions of Perkins and Nolan. Later, when Nolan and Briggs left for the back porch, briefly out of Gripp's view, his face knotted in obvious consternation.

The cameras caught Nolan and Briggs again when they returned from the porch and strolled in and out of the art studios, likely searching for Maggie's artwork. Bill checked the time marker on the film footage. The couple had been at the party for roughly an hour when Briggs grabbed his wife's hand and hurried her out the back door.

A few minutes later, June Perkins approached John Sanders with a large, glossy art book. Gripp visibly perked up and departed out the back door in the general direction of the administration cottage. That was the last moment that Edward Gripp had been seen.

*****

A rustling downstairs in the kitchen roused Sandra Murphy at 3:16 a.m. She turned toward her fiancé, Lenny, as it had been his idea to buy the puppy, but his muffled snores were as rhythmic as the tides. She rummaged in the dark for her slippers and pulled on a faded USMC hoodie. Grasping the railing, she made her way carefully down the stairs. Until she stretched, her knee would be tight and achy. She'd been very lucky, only taking shrapnel in the knee. Sergeant Landy, just a few yards away from her when the mine blew, had lost both a leg and a hand.

She bent to open the dog crate in the kitchen. Lifting the puppy and carrying him directly outside would prevent him from peeing in the living room, where new carpeting had just been down. Who installs new carpeting throughout a house, and then days later goes out and buys a puppy? It was more of Lenny's anti-logic.

She opened the sliding glass door, crossed the patio, and placed the pug in the grass, where he gratefully peed. She dropped into a patio chair, flexing her knee to loosen it up. The yard of the townhouse was a cement slab and a small patch of grass, surrounded by a high wooden fence. Their townhouse in Mashpee, purchased with a VA loan, had been perfect. Though she'd loved the Marines—and had thought to stay in for the twenty—the close calls for both her and Lenny, who was infantry, had become too frequent. Their mutual decision to get out while body and sanity were still intact would never be regretted.

It was a beautiful, starry night and the fence blocked out the ocean wind that blew ceaselessly across the Cape. Still, she pulled the hood over her head and tugged on the drawstring. Cool, windy weather sure beat the hell out of the smothering heat of Iraq. Pugsly sniffed at the cooking utensils hanging off a propane grill. Could they have found a stupider dog? It was just their luck—out of five puppies to choose from, they had picked the dimmest one in the litter. The puppy obedience class that night had been a fiasco. Pugsly was weeks behind the other puppies, who had all mastered, at the very least, sitting. At every command from the instructor, Pugsly would roll on his back and beg for a belly rub. She and the dog must share telepathy, she thought, for at that very moment he waddled across the yard and climbed up her leg. She lifted the tiny dog onto her lap. "You're too damn cute," she said, rubbing his belly.

It had been a bizarre few days. It had all begun while working the nightshift. She and a senior officer, Mary Shields, had been on duty. She'd been filling her mug at the coffee machine and speaking with Shields when Raymond Parker lumbered unsteadily in. He reeked of scotch and was not supposed to be there; his shift was over. His smile was the usual: lecherous. He was already on notice for sexual harassment. His next move was a fatal one—he put his hand on Mary Shields' ass.

Sandra had felt her body tighten, readying to strike; but Shields had shook her head ever so slightly, gazed directly into Sandra's eyes for a moment, then said with determined calm, "I'll handle this." Shields had then downed the rest of her coffee, Parker's hand still cupped on her ass cheek.

"It's a shame to waste good coffee on a maggot." Shields suddenly spun, smashing her coffee mug into Parker's nose. Yowling, the man's hands shot to his face and he doubled over. Shields was not through. Her knee found his chin, which flung him backwards off his feet. Writhing like a fish on a dock, Parks was flipped over and cuffed. Each woman grabbed a kicking foot and together they dragged the cursing man to a holding cell. Such was the finale of Raymond Parker's inconsequential career in law enforcement. Sandra suspected that she might spot him next on a Segway, leering after teenage girls in the mall.

After that incident she'd been reassigned. Her new partner was a rising star in the department, unassuming, respectful, and dedicated. Bill Bleach had been promoted early for breaking that baffling cold case, capturing the Internet Killer, who'd been stalking lonely women on computer dating sites. It was probable that Mary Shields had had a hand in her fortuitous reassignment.

Their current case was equally bizarre, and all evening during puppy obedience school she'd mentally replayed the footage from the security booth at the marina. The so-called 'florist' was a slick one, completely befuddling the hapless security guard. Jim Delaney was putty in her conveniently gloved hands. The blonde woman did not have the same hairstyle or color as Doreen Best, Lindsey Nolan, or any of the other blondes at the Halloween party. But why did this person have to be a blonde? The florist could have been wearing a wig. It was Halloween season, after all. Wigs of all types could be bought at any of the costume stores that popped up seasonally during September and October. The sunglasses were oversized and resembled those worn in the 1970s. Her bulky jacket was covered over with a gardening apron, so details about body type were difficult to discern. In addition, the expensive bouquet was held in an intentionally concealing position.

The florist had obviously charmed Delaney, but dangling Gripp's boat key in front of him had sealed the deal. At that point, the guard had waved her through. It also ensured that he would not come with her to open the boat.

The key had to have been stolen at some time during the Halloween party. It had been a crowded party. Anyone in a jostling crowd might have lifted the key from Gripp's tuxedo pocket. But more likely the key had been in his raincoat, hung in his office. When Sandra had checked, all of the pockets had been empty—no keys, no wallet. Gripp's driver's license could have informed the so-called florist of his residence at the marina.

Gripp's campus office could be accessed through the hallway door or via the labyrinth. But only the dean, Doreen

Best, and Ted Blanchard had a master key that opened the office doors in the administration cottage. The camera footage confirmed that Shoemacher had positioned himself at the front door and in the reception room of the art center for the entire party. Four trips to the men's room suggested that the dean might have prostate problems, but he had always returned faithfully to his station near the foyer. Best, dressed as Minnie Mouse, had moved between the reception room, foyer, and library throughout the evening, except on three occasions when she had danced with Count Dracula. Best, like Nolan, had quite the dance moves. Blanchard had not been at the party at all that night, but had been coaching his son's ice hockey team in Bourne. It was plausible that the key and wallet could have been stolen from Gripp's office by someone entering from the labyrinth.

After reviewing camera footage that afternoon, she and Bill had spent the remainder of the time calling local florists about the recent purchase of two dozen red roses, and Halloween stores and wig stores for anyone purchasing a blonde wig. At one point Bill had turned from his desk and asked her a perplexing question: *"Why does the florist have to be a female?"*

Chapter 10

A call the next day from the Medical Examiner's office confirmed Bill's worst fears, but he insisted on talking to Dr. Blane in person.

Tracy Blane, Bill believed, was the most thorough forensic scientist on the east coast, but she'd chosen to supervise a small coroner's office on the Cape rather than that of a large city, as she was an avid sailor. She was wiry and athletic for a woman of sixty-one, with a haircut that was short and easy to manage while bent over a corpse or amidst the winds of the Vineyard Sound. In another lifetime, he imagined Blane, with her freckled skin, red-grey hair and clear blue eyes, slinging pints across a well-worn bar. But in this lifetime, she slung the findings from the labyrinth across a well-worn desk.

Blane's team had discreetly entered the labyrinth the evening before, after business hours, to obtain samples and photographs. She tonelessly read from a report on her laptop. "DNA from hair follicle cells and epidermal cells obtained from the stones at the impact point matched those collected in Gripp's bedroom and bathroom. Fingerprints on the various stools and chairs in the passageways and around Gripp's office were the same as throughout the yacht

Minotaur. Other than Gripp's, no other fingerprints were found in the tunnels. And the dried blood collected from the stones was of the same blood type, Rh factor and hemoglobin level as the blood assayed recently for Gripp's hip replacement surgery. The blood also contained the same cholesterol-lowering drug and a high blood pressure medication that had been prescribed by Gripp's physician. The black dress shoes behind the closet panel were the same size as the other shoes in the yacht, had the same wear patterns on the soles, and identical orthotics.

"From the type of hairs stuck to the blood spatter, it's probable that Gripp's head hit the wall, slid down the stone wall and bled out onto the floor. Blood was found nowhere else in the passages. From the point directly behind John Sanders' office to the trap door of the egress tunnel, however, fibers from a tarp and bits of acrylic paint in various colors were found along the ground. Most likely a tarp had been dragged along the passageway.

"In the dirt of the egress tunnel, some partial hiking boot prints could be obtained. But..." she said testily, peering over the edge of her desk at his and Sandra's feet, "someone's running shoes and day hikers had scuffed up most of the prints."

The pathologist rose from behind her desk, her stance indicating the meeting had concluded. "The files were sent to both of your computers."

Ignoring the cue, he planted himself in front of the photographs of rare birds and reptiles on the pathologist's wall.

"Bill," she said firmly, "we can talk about *Chelonoidis nigra* and *Conolophus subcristatus* another day."

"I'm not following," Sandra said.

"Dr. Blane worked with tortoises and iguanas in the Galapagos for a summer when she was a student intern," he explained reverently.

"And I promised you that we would have lunch one day to talk herps, but not today. I've been up all night analyzing your samples, and now I have two cold ones waiting for me." Tracy Blane shooed them out of her office and bustled toward the morgue.

*****

During the second visit to Doreen Best's office at the art college, both detectives gratefully accepted her offer of coffee. The warm fluid was soothing on Bill's scratchy throat, and Sandra needed a caffeine jolt after the late night with the puppy. Best's office was similar in décor and spirit to the Development Office. On a metal desk were the smiling cod fish mascot, a holder with the dean's business cards, and two photographs, one of a family reunion and the other of Best and a boyfriend on a catamaran off the coast of a tropical island.

"Where was this photo taken?" Sandra asked, bending over the boat photo. The island incited thoughts of honeymoon destinations.

"Barbados," Best answered. She waited for the faculty schedules of John Sanders and June Perkins to scroll from a printer.

"How did you like it?" Sandra asked.

"It was okay, but I liked Bermuda better. Bermuda's more expensive, but it's much easier to get to. It's only three and half hours from Boston and it's a direct flight."

Sandra continued to scan the photograph. "Hmm. I hadn't thought about Bermuda..."

The catamaran photo made Bill a bit ill, so he turned away. Best and her boyfriend were separated from the fathomless, swirling water by no more than a precariously thin canvas. There was no solid floor to the boat, or gunwales to hold them safety onboard should they hit a steep swell. It was incomprehensible to him that Best and her boyfriend were enjoying the ordeal and grinning like lunatics. He fumbled around in his pants pocket for another aspirin and inadvertently came upon the flash drive of reptile JPEGs for Maggie. "Ms. Best, I'll also need the email of a student named Maggie May-Nolan."

Sandra shot him a quizzical look.

"We'll have to take a look at her boat," he explained. "Maggie thought that someone had been joyriding in it on the night of the Halloween party."

"Oh, that reminds me," Best said, "another student reported that her boat had been tampered with sometime over the weekend."

"Really? I'll need her name and contact information also."

*****

Casey Genaurdi's Sunfish was in a row of other small boats that were light enough to be pulled onto the beach. Bill was hugely relieved: no walk across a rickety dock this morning. A short beach walk he could manage. He pulled his maroon U Mass. ball cap down over his eyes to protect himself from the sun and glare.

Genaurdi sat on the bow of her sailboat, texting, as the two detectives approached. She stood and paced worriedly as she spoke.

"My anchor was stolen sometime in the last few days. A friend and I sailed last Thursday afternoon. When I returned to my boat on Saturday afternoon, the anchor was gone! The boat," she explained in a doleful tone, "was my high school graduation gift from my father. He worked overtime to buy me this boat."

*****

The next stop was June Perkins' office, as the schedule from Doreen Best showed that her Painting II class had just finished. The nameplate on her office door read "June Perkins, MFA, PhD, Associate Professor, Painting." Her door was covered with glossy prints of famous and obscure paintings and a list of her office hours. When the detectives knocked, there was no response. A meticulously groomed man poked his head out of the next office—it was Count Dracula from the Halloween party. His nameplate read "Sherman Hayner, MFA, Assistant Professor, Sculpture."

"June doesn't have office hours at the moment," Hayner explained. "Tuesday's the day she paints in her studio between classes."

"Where's her studio?" Sandra asked.

"The faculty studios are adjacent to the teaching studios downstairs," the sculptor answered.

They found June Perkins in front of a canvas that was many feet taller than she was. The painting was no more than haphazard slashes of brown paint. Kindergarteners could produce the same effect if told to throw mud against a wall, Sandra decided. Perkins' looks far exceeded her artistic talent, and had taken her far. Sandra had seen it too many times: the cute girl in high school getting bumped from a C+ to B-; the pretty officer who looked trim in her uniform getting promoted from lieutenant to captain, passing over the dowdy officer who worked doggedly behind the scenes and ran the operation like clockwork.

Upon recognizing Bill, Perkins placed her paintbrush on a palette and tentatively crossed the studio. "Any word about Edward?"

"No. But we've been studying security footage from the Halloween party." He looked down at his notepad. "You were talking for some time with persons dressed as Captain America, a hobbit, Dracula, and a woman in a Starry Night print dress."

Perkins nervously scraped paint off her finger. "Are we all suspects in something?"

"We're trying to establish a timeline for Mr. Gripp and need to interview any persons that might have spoken with him, or who perhaps went out with him later, for a drink, for instance," he explained judiciously.

She seemed satisfied with his response. "Oh, okay." She sighed. "George Tussy was Captain America, Sherm Hayner was Dracula, Joy Carbini was wearing the van Gogh dress, and Jack Freeman was the hobbit."

Sandra circled the studio, examining the faculty paintings, good, bad and mediocre. "And who was the frontiersman?" she asked casually from across the room, though she knew the answer.

"That was Professor Sanders," Perkins said neutrally.

Sandra inwardly smiled. Perkins had used the distancing word "Professor"; of all her other colleagues she spoke familiarly, on a first name basis: George, Sherm, Joy, and Jack. Classic overcompensation. "And what was the book that you two were discussing?"

"The book? Oh, the book." Perkins nodded, smiling pleasantly. Stalling... nodding... stalling.... "Professor Sanders is an expert on the ceramics of the Renaissance period. I was asking him about Maiolica pottery. It's a brightly colored pottery of Moorish influence," she answered condescendingly.

"Did you discuss Maiolica pottery downstairs or upstairs?" Sandra prodded back.

"And this has to do with Edward Gripp how?" Perkins snapped.

She shrugged lightly. "Hey, I was just curious."

Perkins looked back and forth between the cops, her confusion growing. "Both downstairs and upstairs—as... as I was getting my coat to leave."

"At about what time?" Sandra persisted.

"Probably around 9:45," Perkins huffed. "I don't understand how any of this relates to Edward Gripp!"

"Just one other thing," Sandra said, stepping over to Perkins' painting. She pointed to the floor. "You're using newspaper. Under all of the other paintings are tarps."

"My tarp walked away over the weekend. This is really upsetting. We try to instill in our students a code of conduct. We leave the studios open 24-7, expecting everyone to respect other people's work and leave each others' supplies alone. In addition to encouraging the creative process," Perkins stated haughtily, "we encourage social values in our students."

"Values... good," Sandra said ironically.

Perkins scowled at her and returned to her palette and paintbrush.

The two detectives then hurried upstairs to the faculty offices, hoping to catch John Sanders before lunch hour.

Passing down the corridor, Sandra whispered to Bill, "Did you see the title of Perkins' painting?"

"No," he said, unsettled.

A smile twitched at the corners of her mouth. "It's called 'A Contemplation of Shit On Snow'."

"Really?"

"A joke, Bill."

"Um, oh, accurate title," he agreed with a gawkish grin.

The office door of John J. Sanders, MFA, PhD, Professor, Ceramics, was slightly ajar. The voices of a man and a woman could be heard as Bill tapped politely. "Come in," said the male voice.

The student in the office was the black cat from the Halloween party, the daughter of that overbearing French aristocrat, Jean Tate. As the cops entered, the student moved from behind Sanders' desk and lifted a backpack from a sofa.

"We can finish this discussion a bit later, Lily. Come back this afternoon when I have more time," Sanders said casually.

"I'll definitely be back, Professor," Lily promised. Unconcealed annoyance flash from from her eyes as she flounced from the room.

Sandra pushed the door closed behind Lily.

"John Sanders." The ceramics professor extended his hand to them. "Two detectives are reportedly inquiring about Edward Gripp. I assume it's you two."

"Correct. I'm Detective Bleach," Bill responded, presenting his badge. "This is my partner, Detective Murphy."

"Please," Sanders said amicably, gesturing toward the sofa, "have a seat."

Germs and STDs might still be contagious from that sofa, Sandra thought. "I'll stand, thank you."

The same thought had obviously occurred to Bill. "I'm fine. Our questions will be brief. We're trying to establish a timeline for Edward's activities. You two spoke briefly at the Halloween party. Did he mention where he might be going afterwards?"

Sanders dropped into a leather chair next to the sofa. He was a man of about fifty. There was a pleasant, relaxed expression on his face. "No. Frankly, I was hoping that he was going to inquire about one of my ceramics pieces. He occasionally buys faculty art. So far though, he hasn't bought any of my work. He typically purchases paintings. Instead, he asked me about the Windsor Award." He shrugged in puzzlement. "I thought this an odd question, so I asked him why. He was wondering when the pieces from the Windsor nominees were going to be displayed. My guess is that he was wanting to purchase one of them."

"What's the Windsor Award?" Sandra asked.

"It's the award we give out every year to a senior. It's our most prestigious award and comes with a five thousand dollar check. But more importantly, there's an exhibition of the winner's work at the Montaque Gallery in Boston. That event attracts art critics and collectors from all over the area. It's a huge coup for a young artist."

"Has the winner been selected yet?" Bill asked.

"No. The committee only recently selected the nominees. One student is nominated from each of the major disciplines: painting, ceramics, computer graphics, printmaking, photography, and sculpture."

"Do you have a list of the nominees?" Bill said.

"Sure," Sanders answered, pulling himself from the chair. "It's here somewhere. It's no longer a confidential list because emails were sent to all of the nominees last week." He searched through a pile of manila folders on a desk and eventually handed Bill a sheet of paper. The detectives perused the list, alphabetized by subject:

Ceramics, Lily Tate

Computer Graphics, Curt Frederickson

Painting, Maggie May-Nolan

Photography, Amy Jacobsen

Printmaking, Olivia Moreno

Sculpture, Kyle Monroe

"So what happens next?" Bill inquired.

"Now each student-nominee enters three pieces for the Awards Committee to evaluate. That's why Lily Tate was here this morning. She was requesting a change in the selection criteria, wanting the nominees to be able to enter more than three pieces for evaluation. Lily's never been one to shy away from expressing her opinions."

"And how's the winner selected?" Bill continued.

"The members of the Awards Committee vote by secret ballot."

"And what if there's a tie?" she asked.

"As long as I can remember there's never been a tie. But I've only been on the committee for the past couple of years, so my memory's not that long."

She persisted. "But in the hypothetical situation, what happens?"

"It's a scenario I don't want to even contemplate," the professor confessed. "It would be a decision between me, as the committee chairman, and Dean Shoemacher."

"Who counts the ballots?" Bill asked.

"Doreen Best and myself."

Bill couldn't resist the next question. "So who *do you think* is going to win?"

"I have no clue. The pool of talent this year is staggering."

"If you were a betting man...." Bill urged.

Sanders pondered the question for a moment, folding his arms across his green corduroy shirt. "The printmaker, Olivia Moreno, or the painter, Maggie May-Nolan. But Kyle Monroe's definitely in the running. He's a sculpture major. Of course I'm partial to Lily, since she's a ceramics major and my academic advisee." He thought for a moment longer. "But truly, I have no clue."

"Were Kyle and Olivia at the Halloween party?"

"Yes. Many of the nominees were there. Kyle was a tropical tourist. Amy was Marge Simpson, and Curt was a Chippendale's dancer. Olivia was hard to miss. She wore an outfit with bull's-eyes of Republicans all over her. Olivia has her dark moods, yet her art has amazing panache."

"Was she with V?" Sandra asked.

"Yes, that's her boyfriend, Ernst Hanson. He's a local. A fisherman, I believe. He's always around campus."

She glanced at the list of Windsor nominees once again. "You didn't mention Maggie May-Nolan."

"I didn't see her there," Sanders answered.

"We've strayed off-topic, Professor. We have a few more questions about the timeline of the Halloween party, and then we won't bother you any longer," Bill said. "From the camera footage, we noticed that you and Dr. Perkins were discussing a book together."

"Yes?" Sanders lifted his pipe from his desk. "Yes, yes... I remember now. Dr. Perkins had a question about Renaissance painters."

"In here?"

"Yes, briefly in my office, before we both went home."

"And what time was that?"

"I'm guessing it was between 9:30 and 10. Probably closer to 10. My wife gets home around 10:30, and we both pulled into the driveway at the same time."

"Did you see Edward up by the faculty offices around that time... or see, or hear, anything unusual?"

"No. I've never seen Edward on this floor, ever. Nor did I hear anything, except some rats or squirrels behind my wall. Ted Blanchard needs to call in an exterminator."

*****

Back at headquarters the two detectives huddled over Bill's laptop, studying camera footage for the hours following the Halloween party. Nothing in the images seemed particularly noteworthy. The party wound down around eleven. The last to depart were Charles Shoemacher, Doreen Best, Kate Taylor, some janitors, and the staff from Food Services. Around midnight two female students wandered up to the vacated front porch, passed a joint back and forth, and then walked off in the general direction of the dorm. The building was silent for a few more hours when... their view darted to the timestamp. Bill's hand leapt toward his notepad and scribbled "2:33 a.m." on the emerging timeline.

A figure slowly climbed the front porch steps. The building was dim, lit only by red exit signs. The person's gloved hand fumbled at his or her large, bulbous head. A blinding light switched on. A light from a yellow helmet! Body size and gender were impossible to determine, because the individual wore a long black cloak. They watched, transfixed, as the black figure and beam of light passed through the foyer, across the expansive art gallery, and toward the painting studio. The figure was briefly out of camera range. Then, at 2:41, the figure reemerged, returning through the gallery and foyer, disappearing down the front steps. A white tarp was nestled securely under its arm.

For a few minutes Bill wrote out all of the information into a chronology and turned toward Sandra. "Here's where we are so far." She rolled her chair across the small space between their two desks to read alongside.

<u>Friday, Oct 14</u>
? May-Nolan's dive helmet stolen from drawing studio after Friday morning drawing class
7:05 p.m. Gripp arrives at party
7:24 Perkins arrives
7:33 Nolan and Briggs arrive
8:25 Nolan and Briggs leave
9:11 Perkins approaches Sanders w/ book
9:11 Gripp leaves through back door
9:28 Perkins leaves for staircase to 2nd flr
9:32 Sanders leaves for staircase to 2nd flr
? 9:32—9:54 Perkins and Sanders hear something in the wall; Gripp watching Perkins and Sanders; Gripp falls/ attacked?
9:54 Perkins leaves bldg

9:58 Sanders leaves bldg

<u>Saturday, Oct 15</u>
2:33 a.m. *? enters bldg
2:42 a.m. *? leaves bldg w/tarp
1:13 p.m. florist arrives at Gripp's boat; steals laptop

"Have I missed anything?" Bill asked.

"Yeah. Some time between Thursday and Saturday, Casey Genaurdi's boat anchor was stolen. Three individuals were wearing black cloaks at the party. Dean Shoemacher as the Phantom of the Opera, Sherman Hayner as Dracula, and Ernst Hanson, as "V." We're going to need to check out those cloaks. On a different note, I checked the local court records. Our charming friend, Professor Sanders, never filed for divorce from his wife. There's no record of anything. He's stringing June along."

Bill frowned. "And his advisee, Lily Tate, was standing behind his desk. I have a bad feeling about that."

"I noticed that, too." Sandra laughed sardonically. "My favorite line of the day has to be from that paragon of virtue, Dr. Perkins. Quote: 'in addition to encouraging the creative process, we encourage social values in our students.'"

*****

Tiffany Carter was pleased by her own brilliance. Since the marsh was soggy, it had been smart to wear her flowered rain boots, rather than her Wonder Woman sneakers. She must have looked at the clock in her elementary school classroom a zillion times, waiting for three o'clock dismissal. When she arrived home from school, her father, Anthony, was waiting to take her to a wetland at Buzzards Bay. Though he now lived in Provincetown, he still visited her a lot. When she'd been smaller, a Brownie in the Girl Scouts, he'd helped her with the Hiker, Home Scientist, Bugs, and Computer Expert badges. Now that she was a Junior in the Girl Scouts, she hoped to complete both the Flowers and Animal Habitat badges before the end of the fall semester. Her goal in life was to have her entire sash covered with badges by the time she was a sixth grader and a Cadet. Goals were good, her doctor had told her. Dr. Michaels advised her to work on badges related to healthy snacks and exercise, which was annoying even to think about. He was referring to her diabetes and the fact that she was overweight.

"Computer games use your arms and hands," she'd argued.

"How about an afterschool sport like soccer?" Dr. Michaels had suggested.

"I earned the Hiker badge," she'd reminded him, miffed.

"Hiking's very good, Tiffany," the doctor had said encouragingly. "Hike as often as possible."

That afternoon Tiffany felt good about herself. "Walking through a marsh is hiking," she told her father.

As it was too late in the season to find flowers, Anthony suggested that they work on the Animal Habitats badge, before the snow fell. The Flower badge, he said, they could do at a gardening center that had a greenhouse, or at a florists' shop later that winter.

Her Girl Scout troop leader often talked about the different types of ecosystems. Tiffany didn't want to sound like a know-it-all, but she already knew everything about wetlands because the past summer she'd attended the Seashore Life, and the Woods, Ponds and Fields courses at the Children's School of Science in Woods Hole. Her mother said that next summer she could pick Marine Biology, Coastal Botany, or Oceanography. It would definitely be Marine Biology, because she was going to be a marine biologist like Jessie McCabe.

Her Barbie doll was dressed in a wet suit, except that it was pink and not blue like Jessie's wetsuit. Tiffany had cut Barbie's hair exactly like Jessie's and colored it brown with magic marker. Barbie's blue eyes were also colored brown. Now Barbie looked just like Jessie.

Jessie had visited her school during Women's History Month. Jessie had brought with her another scientist named Sara, who was an inventor who built stuff. Tiffany had pushed her way through a crowd of other excited girls and blurted, "Jessie, I know who Rachel Carson is!"

Jessie had said, "Awesome!" and given her a high-five. "Rachel Carson's my hero, and Sylvia Earle."

It had been the best moment of Tiffany's life. For the rest of that day, she'd whispered the name Sylvia Earle to herself, again and again, until she could get home to her computer. On wiki she found that Sylvia Earle built submersibles, just like Jessie's inventor friend, Sara.

A narrow trail though the tall grass ended at the shoreline, and Tiffany stopped. "Here, Dad. Can you carry Jessie?"

"Sure, sweetheart." Anthony placed the Barbie-Jessie hybrid in his camera bag and handed Tiffany his tablet. She tapped on the yellow Notes app. Blank lined paper appeared on the screen.

"Please be careful with that," he cautioned. "It won't work if it goes into the sand."

"I will. Maybe I should make one list for the animal and another list for its habitat."

He pulled binoculars from his bag. "That's a good idea." He squinted into the late afternoon haze. "I'm afraid I'm not going to see too many birds today. Most have migrated south for the winter."

"I'm already seeing tons of things," she said with aplomb. "I wonder if I should count dead things, like crab carapaces, and empty mollusk shells, or only count alive things?"

"Put them both down, and we can sort them later."

She weaved back and forth between the wrack line and the edge of the cord grass and pickle weed. "Barnacle—rock. Periwinkle-spartina grass and rock. Fiddler crab—hole in sand. Ant—hole in sand. Horseshoe crab shell—beach sand. Dead fish—bay water." She stopped in frustration. "Dad, I can't type as fast as I can talk. Can I talk while you type it in for me?"

"Alright. It's going to be dark soon." He accepted the tablet from his daughter and followed her meandering path along the sand, typing as she dictated.

"Scallop shell—bay water. Seagulls—everywhere. Clam shell—bay water and sand. Can we eat at Burger King tonight?"

"No. We're going to eat Chinese. Chinese food has vegetables and still tastes good."

She gave her father a disgruntled look. "Crab—sand on beach, clam worm—sand in bay...."

They rounded a spit of sand, and her father lurched to a stop.

"Tiff, come here, honey!"

"What?"

"I need a hug!" he said quickly. The tablet fell from his shaking hands into the sand. Her astonished face gazed up at his. He quickly pulled her to his chest.

"Dad, you dropped the tablet," her surprised, muffled voice came from his jacket. "And I can't breathe."

"Oh, sorry." He distractedly loosened his grip.

Thankfully, she hadn't spotted it. She'd been looking at the shoreline and inland, so she hadn't seen what he'd seen. The tide was out; and on a sandbar was a tattered white bundle; the rope binding it was loose and falling away... a hairless, eyeless head peeked out, grey and bloated... an arm in a black blazer reached out in a plaintive gesture for help... hungry crabs scurried in and out of the sleeve....

*****

From September to April the village of Woods Hole was desolate, occupied only by a small handful of residents plus year-round scientists and engineers from the marine lab and oceanographic institute, so Bill had his choice of parking spaces on Water Street. He chose one in front of the post office. No one else was on the dark road, except Maggie, who was illuminated under the front light of the café. His heart leapt in his chest. Her outfit was a rock fan's fantasy: black leather pants and jacket, a zebra-striped blouse, and black boots.

Classic rock music was Bill's passion, and his youth had been suffused with it. When his father had changed the oil in the car, Led Zeppelin, the Who, or the Rolling Stones had throbbed from a tape player in the garage. While preparing dinner, his mother would hum tunelessly to Peter Frampton, Pink Floyd, or Neil Young. And on every car trip one of his parents had invariably played "Truckin'," "Take It Easy," and "Ramblin' Man." It was a time before iPods and earbuds, when one listened—like it or not—to another persons' music.

He loved everything about rock music: blinding strobe lights, smashed guitars, big hair, crashing drums, and leather clothes.

He moved with forced nonchalance down the dark street, trying not to stare outright. No way the outfit was worn for his benefit. He wiped sweat from his forehead with his sleeve. Maggie clearly had a date later. It was hubris to even contemplate that such an outfit would have been chosen with him in mind. As he crossed the street and stepped onto the curb, she stomped out her cigarette and ground it into the pavement.

"Did you bring the flash drive?" she demanded by way of greeting. Her eyes, ringed with black eyeliner, glanced up at him.

"Um—yes," he said, swallowing. He held the door open for her and they entered the café. The place was nearly empty except for two other customers bent over their laptops. "I'm starving. I need to get something for dinner. Do you want something? My treat."

"I never refuse food," she responded in her low, gravelly voice—a smoker's voice.

They stood silently at a counter, pondering a limited menu of breakfast items written on a chalkboard.

"Are you going somewhere tonight?" he asked casually.

"No. Why?" she answered coolly, her eyes still on the menu.

He shrugged. "Just wondering. What do you want?"

"A kombucha and an everything bagel with jalapeño cream cheese."

"I'll have the same," he told the clerk behind the cash register. He fumbled in his coat pocket for his wallet and paid the bill. He scanned the café and pointed. "Let's sit over there, next to the outlet. My laptop battery's running low."

"Okay. I'll wait for the food."

He crossed the room, placed his coat over the back of a chair and stuffed his maroon ball cap in a coat pocket. He pulled his laptop from a carrying case and glanced once more at Maggie. "Way hot," he whispered to himself. Then he connected the charger to the wall, and his computer to the charger. He clicked on a folder called "reptile pics," to reveal the folders within: "Watson", "Dalgliesh", "Marple", "Sherlock", "Jethro Gibbs" and "Olivia Benson".

Maggie navigated the small tables, carrying a tray. She pulled a chair next to his and studied the screen for a while. A small, mischievous smile appeared on her face.

"Aren't you missing something?"

He shot her a questioning look.

"Folders for Hercule Poirot and Inspector Morse."

His eyes widened. "Strange you would say that! My next reptile's going to be called Hercule. Do you read murder mysteries?" he asked excitedly, his mind already searching for topics of future conversations.

"No," she said dryly. "George and Emily McLeod watch a lot of PBS. That's how I know about those detectives. Which pet is your favorite?"

"I love them all equally!" he said enthusiastically, then winced at his ridiculous outburst. Worse, she smiled uncertainly.

She reached for his laptop. "Let me just flip through the folders and see if I get some ideas." She turned the laptop for a better view, her hand hovering over the touch pad.

He ate his bagel, determined to say nothing awkward for the next few minutes.

She stretched her long legs out, resting her feet on a chair across the table. "I guess you didn't find the helmet, or you would have told me," she said sadly.

"No, not yet, but I'm not giving up." If he could identify the tarp thief, he might be able to locate the helmet, but the details of the Gripp case were not open for discussion.

"Thank you. I checked with everyone in the dorm. No one's seen it." She scrutinized the screen. "Some of your photos are quite good. I love this one. What beautiful colors!"

He craned his head toward the screen. "Yes, Dalgliesh is beautiful. He's a Thayer's king snake."

"Miss Marple's beautiful also."

He felt himself relax. "She's a yellow-bellied slider."

"How can you tell if they're boys or girls?"

"The usual way. By looking at their privates."

"That makes sense."

"Here's an interesting fact for you. The sex of many reptiles is determined by the temperature in which their eggs are incubated. It's called temperature-dependent sex determination."

"So all of the females live in Sweden and the males live in Africa," she giggled. "And they get together for wild weekends on Ibiza."

He laughed aloud; the unexpected humor from the sullen woman, albeit odd, was right on target. "That's right."

"That must be how I was conceived," she said with a smirk.

He smiled. "So that mystery's solved." His cell phone vibrated in his blazer pocket. "Excuse me, but I have to get this. Bleach here... Dr. Blane?" He listened intently, his face suddenly grim. "I'll be right there."

He rose, and disappointment sounded in his voice as he said, "Maggie, I'm so, so sorry, but I have to get back to Falmouth."

"Hey, whatever." She slid the laptop toward him.

"Um—could we have dinner another time?"

She seemed taken aback. "Yeah, okay," she finally said. "I already have some cool ideas for the painting. Don't forget to give me the flash drive before you go."

"Ur... right."

She'd said yes to dinner! His hands fumbled through his various pockets, fishing for the flash drive. There! He placed it on the table. Hurrying his laptop into its case, he knocked the flash drive onto the floor. "Sorry. I'll get it." He dropped to his knees and ducked under the table. The flash drive was under the chair where she rested her feet. His heart surged again, and his internal alert system switched on. A wave of red heat traveled up his neck. He stared. Maggie's black combat boots had hiking soles, and their edges were encrusted with sandy mud.

*****

When Bill had entered the medical examiner's office, Sandra Murphy was already waiting. She was muttering in irritation. The puppy had shat on the new carpeting, and worse, this summons meant she was missing "Dancing with the Stars." One of Blane's assistants, a medical student, led them past her office and down a waxy hallway toward the morgue. The chemical-necrotic flesh smell caused a swift upwelling in his stomach.

Dr. Tracy Blane stood, arms akimbo and stretching her lower back, next to a stainless steel table where the body was covered with a white cloth. Dark circles under her eyes were suggestive of a very long day, and her mouth was compressed into an uncharacteristic thin line. Just as she'd been leaving for her sailboat that afternoon, she said, her team had been called to a marsh where they'd raced the cold, rising water to get the body off a sandbar.

"I've only done a preliminary check tonight," Blane told the detectives, twisting her back once again. "Tomorrow we'll do a full examination." She pulled back the cover. Bill glanced briefly at the hollow orbits staring up at the ceiling and rushed to the sink, where he puked up bagel and kombucha. Ignoring his gagging and hyperventilation—she'd witnessed this before—Blane carried on. "There are three main points of trauma to the body. A single blow to the chest separated the costal cartilage of the rib cage from the sternum, numerous ribs were broken, and ribs four and five punctured the right lung. The cricoid and thyroid cartilage of the larynx were partially crushed, along with the top few C-rings of the trachea, apparently while the victim lay on the ground, to judge by the compression fractures. Gripp's head struck the wall, splitting the right squamous suture between the parietal and temporal bones of the skull. The head injury was the source of the blood."

Bill splashed water in his face. "How can you be sure it's him?" Sheepishly apologetic, he turned towards Sandra; she stared unflinchingly at the corpse.

"The gold engraved EG cuff links and tuxedo tipped me off," Blane replied with mild exasperation. "And this person's blood is identical to that found in the tunnel. A new scar indicates a recent hip replacement. Tomorrow we'll check his dental records. The body was wrapped in the same paint-spattered tarp that was dragged through the tunnel, and the tarp was bound with a standard boat line."

"But no anchor was attached?" Sandra asked. "An anchor was stolen from a Sunfish."

Blane shook her head and covered up the body. "If there was an anchor, it must have come untied. Bacterial gases inflating his body compartments brought him back to the surface. This is your missing person, Edward Gripp."

*****

The cough medicine for his burning throat should have knocked him out hours before, but at 1:18 a.m. Bill was still staring out his apartment window at the parking lot below. What his gut had intimated was now confirmed—the missing person case was in fact a homicide.

One more shot of cough medicine should provide the knockout blow, Bill hoped, returning to his medicine cabinet. He took a swig from the bottle, then collapsed onto the bed. Gripp's had been a brutal murder, the blows struck with ferocity. Females tended to murder by indirect methods, usually poisoning, whereas males tended toward direct contact: strangulation, stabbing, or beating. They now had a body, and they knew the location, time, and method of murder. Those were certainties. The investigation had gained significant momentum that day. But the two most important questions lingered: Who had done it, and why?

And thoughts of Maggie still ricocheted around his brain like billiard balls across green felt. During their time at the table, while she'd been gazing pensively at the images in his laptop, he'd been reordering her future with evenings at the rock club, movies, and candle-lit restaurants.

Then the sight of the black boots had doused ice water on his fantasies. Countless other students and staff members wore boots with hiking soles in the cold weather, he rationalized. Her boots were among a hundred others like them on that campus. She'd said that she'd attended an NA meeting the night of the Halloween party. That would be easy enough to corroborate. And the rest of her time had been spent cleaning out a cottage... with whom, where?

His eyes were closed. Maggie's face faded and was replaced by another, equally lovely. He shuddered and pulled a blanket around him. That face was eager and smiling, dimples forming parentheses around perfect pink lips and pearl-white teeth. Her soft brown eyes glistened at him as she said, "I'm happy to help, Detective Bleach." Her gentle touch grazed his sleeve as she chatted pleasantly, just as Maggie's had in the café when she reached for the laptop. Just as being with Maggie had conjured thoughts of entwined bodies and an entwined future, so had being near this young woman. Then there'd been a fleeting mention of an object in the last victim's car that only the police had known about. Ice shards had formed instantly in Bill's blood. For weeks his gut had been telling him that the Internet Killer must have had an accomplice for the systematical dismemberments, but he'd suspected the father or uncle. Never the sister.

Chapter 11

"The murder took place around 9:45 on Friday evening," Bill was telling a horrified Dean Shoemacher, "behind the wall of John Sanders' office. We believe that the perpetrator dressed in a stolen dive helmet and black cloak, then stole June Perkins' tarp around 2:40 a.m., probably reentered the labyrinth, dragged Gripp's body from the tunnel through the forest, stole a boat anchor, 'borrowed' a boat—possibly the *Jack Rackham*—and dumped the body down the coast in Buzzards Bay."

Shoemacher kneaded his fingers into his temples and slumped further into his chair. Bill had ruled out the dean as a suspect, for he was visible on the camera footage throughout the evening. But anyone could be an accomplice, like the deranged sister of the Internet Killer. The dean and Kate Taylor certainly had a motive: Gripp's generous bequest to the college upon his death made both of their jobs significantly easier at a very difficult time.

From either point of entry into the labyrinth, whether from the forest or Gripp's office, the perpetrator would have needed five to ten minutes, depending on their familiarity with the tunnels, to reach the passage behind Sanders' office. This meant that if the murderer were a partygoer they would have left the party by 9:30. But if the murderer was not a partygoer, a whole new series of complicating variables came into play.

"I need your cooperation in two matters," Bill stated. "First, the tunnel needs to be sealed."

"Yes, yes, I'll get Ted Blanchard on that immediately," Shoemacher agreed, his voice cracking.

"And second, I need to look at the black cloak you were wearing on Friday."

The dean's body went rigid with indignation. "My cloak! Surely you're not suspecting—"

"No, no," Bill broke in. "But the murderer stole a helmet, a tarp, and an anchor, and hijacked a boat. Who's to say that they didn't also steal the cloak?" And possibly a laptop from Gripp's boat.

"I see," Shoemacher mumbled. He rose and walked to a closet where his academic regalia and a London Fog raincoat hung. He opened a box and removed a black hat and cape. He presented the black cape to Bill. "Every year I'm a variation on the mysterious cloaked figure. Last year I was Zorro, this year the Phantom of the Opera. Who knows about next year?" he said glumly. "I'm worn out, Detective. It's all about finding money. That's not why I entered academic administration. And now this."

"Who has the key to your office?"

"Only Doreen and Ted. But Doreen was with me all night and Ted was off campus."

Bill studied the doorknob of the dean's office. There was no indication of tampering.

"I need to take this cape to our forensics lab," he informed the dean.

"Of course," Shoemacher said, closing up the box.

"And you'll get Mr. Blanchard to close up the tunnel as soon as possible," he pressed.

"No one besides Blanchard and I are to know about the tunnel—correct?" the dean asked.

"Correct. The less that the murderer knows of what we know, the better."

"Oh, thank God. The story on the news about Edward's body washing up in Buzzards Bay was vague and only obliquely mentioned a party at the college. I was grateful for that. Why do you think that Edward was behind John Sanders' office wall?"

Bill shook his head. "Your guess is as good as mine."

*****

The sculptures lining the windowsill of Sherman Hayner's office were clay or plastic replicas, mostly from the Greek, Roman, and Renaissance periods, and mostly of beautiful, muscular men. Bill's education in the arts was spotty at best; he could identify Rodin's *The Kiss*, Donatello's bronze *David*, *The Discus Thrower*, and Michelangelo's *David*, but all the other pieces on the windowsill were unfamiliar. Bill eyed the small replica of *The Kiss* from different angles. It was true what he'd read: the lover's lips never touched, but were instead separated by an ocean of longing and anticipation. The unconsummated kiss, he thought ironically to himself, symbolized the story of his own love life.

Bill placed *The Kiss* back on the windowsill and turned toward Hayner. As an assistant professor, the young sculptor was at the bottom of the academic pecking order and consequently had a tiny office with an unremarkable view of the faculty parking lot.

"So the name *The Kiss* is actually a misnomer," Bill commented.

"I'm impressed, detective," Hayner replied. "You must be an art dilettante."

"No, sadly I'm plebian in my art training, but I do know a lot about crime, both present and historical. This piece represents a prelude to a horrible crime of passion." He pointed toward the embracing nudes. "This is Francesca da Polenta and her brother-in-law, Paolo. At any moment, her husband, Giovanni Malatesta, is going to burst into the room, find them together, and murder them both with his bare hands."

"How wonderfully morbid!" Hayner said ebulliently. "You're not as plebian as you think. So, do tell why you're here. It's about Edward, isn't it? Everyone on campus is whispering about it, you know. He was murdered, wasn't he? That's what the *Cape Cod Daily* seemed to imply. He was a missing person for days, and then he turns up in Buzzards Bay, mysteriously dead. Was the murderer at the Halloween party? Ohhh, I wonder who it could be! Is that why you've been on campus these last few days? Tell, tell! It's so exciting, and so creepy!"

"The medical examiner still has the body," he replied noncommittally. "But, yes, we're trying to figure out what Edward did after he left the Halloween party. And a person of interest was seen in a black cloak walking through the art center in the middle of the night, which is why we're interested in examining your black cloak."

"A black cloak!" Hayner dashed over to a filing cabinet and pulled it open. He bent down and produced a pair of plastic fangs, a shiny red vest, and a red pendant with a metal bat. He then produced a large black cape and unfurled it with verve. Staring at the cape's back and front, he asked with fascination, "So you think someone broke into my office, stole this, and then returned it?"

"I don't know yet, but I'll have to take it with me."

The sculptor worriedly scanned his office. "I hope nothing else was stolen." He hesitated. "What if the person broke into my laptop and stole the manuscripts that I've been working on? I'm on the tenure track, and you know the drill... publish or perish."

"Well, it's an incentive to get your papers published as fast as possible."

"Don't you put a rosy spin on things? I have an idea," Hayner said cheerfully. "How about you and I have dinner together, to discuss another manuscript, one we might write together... on art and crime?"

*****

"You've watched too many horror movies," Sandra Murphy told herself. At the moment she wished that she and Bill were still conducting interviews together, but after their visit to the morgue the previous evening, the case had taken on a new urgency. For purposes of expediency they'd decided to split up. The Windwalker Motel was set off the highway in Hyannis, next to a miniature golf course, clam shack, and go-cart track. Motels in the offseason always seemed a bit forlorn and creepy, and this one was no exception: a cluster of tiny cottages with peeling, pink paint, built (and perhaps painted) in the 1950s, a swimming pool surrounded by a mesh fence, a rusty swing set, and a central office. A red sign read "Vacancy"... no surprise there. Twice she'd driven by the property, expecting the address obtained from the Massachusetts Motor Vehicle Administration to be a house or apartment building, not a hotel composed of no-tell cottages. She parked in a gravel parking lot next to the pool. There were no other cars on the premises, which gave her the willies. The Glock stowed in the shoulder holster under her raincoat provided a small sense of security.

She reluctantly left the warmth of the sedan. It was a blustery day, and a brisk wind swirled leaves across the parking lot. Her imagination continued to run wild. She opened the gate to the pool and peered downward. No floating body in the swimming pool. It had been drained and contained only a few feet of tan, leaf-stained water.

She pushed through the door to the office. Norman Bates did not greet her. Instead, the clerk was a frail old woman with an accent from somewhere in Eastern Europe.

"You want a room?" the woman asked in broken English. "You have pick of any nice cottage."

"No," Sandra replied warily. "I'm looking for Ernst Hanson. Does he live here?"

"Ernst is too big to live with me. His cottage is there." The old woman hobbled to a window and pointed to the far cottage next to a forest.

"Are you his mother?"

"His aunt. His mother die of leukemia four years ago."

Sandra pulled out her badge. "I need to speak with Ernst. Is he here?"

The old woman's blue-splotched hands nervously kneaded her cane. "Ernst good boy! He is always good boy. No problems ever with police!"

"I really need to talk to him. Where is he?"

"Ernst always good! Big help to me here at hotel. He help me with everything."

"Where is he now?" she repeated.

"You can't talk to him. He on fishing boat for many weeks. He go to George's Bank."

"When did he leave?"

The old woman struggled to remember. "Saturday... yes, Saturday."

"Did he spend the night before, Friday, at the art college?" she asked slowly and clearly.

"Yes, with girlfriend. He love Olivia. He marry her soon. He save money to buy house for them."

"I need to see his cottage. Will you let me into his cottage?"

"Yes, because Ernst good boy. Nothing to hide. I get my coat." The old woman disappeared into a back room and returned a moment later. A large ring of keys dangled from the hand not clutching the cane. There were metal braces attached to her heavy brown shoes. She hobbled her way across the parking lot. The lone seat of a swing set swayed in the wind, and leaves swished by the black windows of the empty cottages.

At Ernst's cottage, she handed a key to Sandra. "Too hard for me to go up stairs. I wait here." The front porch had enough room for one plastic lawn chair, and there the old woman sat. Sandra pulled open a screen door and jiggled the key in the lock. The cottage had one tiny room, which was clean and orderly, and a bathroom in the back corner. The single bed was made and covered with a wool blanket. A cube refrigerator contained a few bottles of ice tea. A bookshelf held books about or by John Locke, Confucius, Plato, Aristotle, Gandhi, Guy Fawkes, and Rob Roy. A laptop sat in a closed position on the bookshelf, along side of a hot plate, a saucepan, and cans of soups and beef stew.

Sandra inspected a narrow closet. T-shirts, men's boxers, socks, jeans, and flannel shirts were folded neatly in stacked milk cartons. In a dirty-clothes basket were white boxers, black socks, black jeans, and a black shirt, presumably those worn at the party. She flipped over the shoes, studying the tread. Neither the soles of the sneakers nor black dress shoes matched the hiking boot tread found in the tunnel. On a shelf in the closet sat the same black hat she'd seen in the camera footage, a wig with straight black hair, a white, grinning "V" mask, and a wide black belt. Missing from the costume was the long, black cape.

*****

After an excited call to Bill and a crawl down Route 28 East, Sandra made it back to campus by late morning. Bill was waiting for her at a coffee kiosk in the lobby of the dormitory. The students, as in other common areas around campus, were gazing into laptops, texting on smartphones, or snoozing in the chairs. Where were the textbooks? Did college students even read books anymore? The news of Edward Gripp's demise, both in the newspaper and on the local news, made the two cops the subjects of students' stares, whispers, and Tweets. One female student even aimed a smartphone at Bill, directed not at his face, but instead at his tie with the green snapping turtles.

"That'll be all over Facebook," Sandra chuckled.

"Ugh, let's get out of here."

The plan was to start the student interviews with Olivia Moreno, whose room was on the second floor, so they walked past vending machines, the offices of the campus nurse and housing supervisor, and a janitor's closet until they came upon a stairwell.

Moreno's door was slightly ajar, and when Bill knocked they were greeted by a surly, "Go away. I'm busy."

The cops entered cautiously. The dorm room was a single, furnished with a narrow bed, dresser, and desk. Barely an inch of the cinderblock wall space was left uncovered. There were posters of modern and classical sculpture, pottery, prints, art exhibitions in Paris and New York, Japanese temples and gardens, the Coliseum in Rome, Easter Island Moai, Stonehenge, and graffiti on the Berlin Wall. Like her boyfriend, Moreno was a neatnik. Her bed was made and ugly black shoes were lined up in a tidy row in a closet.

Moreno sat at her desk, painting her fingernails black. She was still in sleepwear: baggy pajama pants and a black tank top. Bill always noted the initial response of a potential suspect to his arrival: Defensiveness (June Perkins), Trepidation (Dean Shoemacher), Titillation (Sherman Hayner). After an initial flash of shock in her large, sparkling eyes, Moreno quickly composed herself and feigned Ennui.

"Go ahead, sit," she ordered, nodding toward the bed. She blew on her splayed nails for a moment, covertly eyeing them.

Bill pulled his identification badge from a suit pocket, but she interrupted him. "Don't waste your breath. I know who you are. This is a gossipy campus. Everyone knows everything about everyone. You want to ask me about Edward Gripp getting whacked."

Bill took in her striking appearance. Moreno's raven black hair, which fell to her waist, was separated by a razor-sharp part. Her eyes were white-blue, and her skin as ghostly white as his own. But most striking was the vast tattoo that covered her skin, starting at her sturdy wrists, traveling up her thick arms, across her broad shoulders and chest, and stopping at her jawline. The scene was spectacular in its beauty. Dashes of yellow and green spattered against a blue-black void: an aurora borealis on a polar night. Across her chest a string of icebergs floated in a milky Arctic sea. Down her arms were more icebergs and ice floes illuminated by northern nights. On one distant ice floe, a polar bear was bent over a splash of red, a devoured seal.

"We're inquiring about a black cloak," he began, struggling to focus on her face and not the extraordinary ink design. "We observed on camera footage an individual in the art center wearing a black cloak long after the party. We want to question this individual. We noticed that Ernst Hanson—"

Moreno bolted to her feet. "No way!" she cried, with astonishing forcefulness. "Ernst has nothing to do with this!" She shook her head violently. "You don't know Ernst. He's the world's gentlest guy. It's so fucking predictable that you cops would profile the immigrant! Just like Sacco and Vanzetti!"

"We're just looking for the cloak he was wearing during the Halloween party. It wasn't at his cottage," he explained calmly, hoping to defuse the burst of temper.

"You searched his cottage?" Moreno paced the small space. "While he's at sea? Are you allowed to do this?"

"Yes and yes," Sandra said decisively, her arms folded aggressively across her chest.

Moreno glanced at the formidable female cop and dropped listlessly into a chair at the desk. "Ernst was with me all night."

"And you don't remember him going anywhere, for even a brief time?" he inquired.

"No!" she fumed.

"You, Ernst, and a group of students left the party together at the same time. Around 8:30. Where'd you all go?" Sandra interjected.

"Everyone chipped in and bought a few cases of beer and bottles of vodka. We partied back in Lily's room."

"Lily Tate?" he asked.

"That's the only Lily I know."

"Who else was there?" he added.

"A lot of people. Kyle, Curt and Kristin, Amy, some other people from the dorm. And some people I didn't know. Any time there's free beer everyone in the world stops by."

"And what was everyone doing?" he continued.

"Drinking. What else does one do with beer? Everyone got really buzzed, and then we took off our shoes and socks and played Twister."

"Twister?" Sandra could barely suppress her laughter. "With the white plastic mat and colored dots?"

Moreno looked at her balefully. "Yes. The room got really hot with all the bodies packed in, so Ernst took off his hat, wig, and cape. Even with the window opened, it was too hot. People were getting really wasted and obnoxious, so we left."

"And where did you go?"

"Back here."

"And then what did you do?"

Moreno stared at him in disbelief. "Ernst was going to sea the next morning for three weeks. What do you think we were doing? How explicit do you want me to be?"

Bill's face reddened. "Not. And Ernst took the 'V' costume with him from Lily's room?"

"All except the cape."

"Why not the cape?" he asked excitedly.

"Kyle Monroe was wearing it. He was completely shitfaced, like at every party. He was going up to the girls, trying to bite their necks like a vampire, saying, 'I vant to suck your blood.'" Moreno scowled disgustedly. "That guy's such a lecher."

"And did you see the cape after that?"

"No. Ernst said that Kyle was probably going to barf all over it. The cape was a write-off as far as he was concerned."

"And do know what Kyle did with the cape?"

"No. I only heard that he passed out on Maggie's bed."

"Maggie May-Nolan?" Bill asked anxiously.

"Yes."

"She's the roommate of Lily Tate?"

Moreno nodded.

"And where was Maggie?" Sandra demanded. She was wondering if what Maggie had told Bill could be corroborated, maybe even verified.

"Who knows? She wasn't on campus on Friday night. She disappears every Friday night like clockwork around five o'clock, right before dinner, and then reappears around nine and goes right to bed. I think she's on some med that makes her sleep a lot. She doesn't party with the rest of us. She just works and sleeps all the time."

"Just to confirm, Olivia: you didn't see Maggie at all on Friday night?" he asked urgently.

"Nope, which was strange because she always sleeps in the dorm. The next morning when she appeared, Lily was haranguing her about having a secret boyfriend."

"Olivia," he exhaled, "this has been really helpful. Here's my card if you can think of anything else."

"I just want to repeat that Ernst had nothing to do with this," Moreno said emphatically. "He's had a tough few years. He was a philosophy major at Amherst and had to drop out when his mother got sick. He's a pacifist. He wouldn't harm a fly. If you want to find that cloak, ask Kyle. He's easy to find. You'll find him salivating over some group of girls."

*****

A quick phone call to Doreen Best sent the detectives to Kyle Monroe's room, which was 309; Lily and Maggie lived on the first floor, in 106. "There's no love lost between Kyle Monroe and Olivia Moreno," Bill said quietly, climbing to the third floor.

"Nope. Moreno was happy to throw him under the bus. Amazing tat. I bet she designed it herself," Sandra said. "And I thought mine was bold."

He turned. "I've never seen your tattoo."

"And you never will, partner," she laughed. "Lenny and I got matching tattoos of the Marine Corps Bulldog one night after having too much tequila."

He knocked on the door to room 309. A short male with thick glasses answered, but it was not the same student who'd been captured by the camera footage dressed in the garish tropical shirt, with a diving mask and snorkel dangling from his neck.

"We're looking for Kyle Monroe," Bill stated.

The student opened the door a bit wider. "Kyle, it's for you," he said over his shoulder, then retired to a desk.

Kyle Monroe was on his bed, a laptop across his legs. He pulled earbuds from his ears and greeted the detectives with a dull, "Oh."

The bookish roommate bent over a sketchpad, his head poised and listening.

"Kyle, let's talk outside," Bill said.

"Yeah, sure," Kyle said compliantly.

There was an unwieldy, oafish way about Monroe. His hair prematurely thinning and his torso gelatinous, he resembled a beaten-down forty year old who'd been sitting in an office cubicle for years, rather than a twenty-one year old art student. He slid his sockless feet into a pair of hiking boots and pulled a down vest from the closet.

It was a wordless walk along the hall, down three flights of stairs, and out a side door. The three stopped next to a hedge bordering the parking lot.

"We want to ask you some questions about the Halloween party last Friday night," Bill said, pulling out his notepad.

"Yeah, I was there. Lily invited me as her date. Otherwise, I'd never have been able to go. My parents are too poor."

"Lily and her mother spoke with Edward Gripp on one occasion. Do you know what they were talking about?"

"No, I wasn't there. All everyone was talking about all night was the Windsor Award. The list of nominees went out last week, so everyone was excited about that."

"And you're a nominee. Congratulations." Bill had memorized the list. All of the nominees had been at Lily's party—with the exception of Maggie.

"Thanks. I could sure use the money. And having an exhibition at the Montaque Gallery would be pretty cool."

"And then everyone went back to Lily's room to party," Bill remarked.

Kyle stuffed his hands deep in his vest pockets. "That's right."

"And what did everyone do?"

"My head throbs just thinking about that night," he said regretfully. "I did too many shots of vodka. But I'm over twenty-one, so it's legal."

"And everyone was playing Twister..." Sandra prompted.

"Yeah, but I wasn't. I'm not that coordinated. I wish I could have, though," he said dolefully, "because hot babes were playing."

"Then what?"

"I was just drinking some more, and changing the CDs in Maggie's CD player, and I put on Ernst's cape, pretending to be Dracula. I don't remember anything after that. By then I was in a blackout. Apparently Curt got pissed at me for hitting on his girlfriend and shoved me. I was told that I fell onto Maggie's bed and passed out. All I remember after that was waking in the middle of the night and going back to my own room, before Maggie returned. She'd be pissed at finding me in her bed. She has a wicked temper."

"Did Maggie return that night?"

"No, not until the next morning. And still in the same clothes that she'd left in the afternoon before," he added with an insinuating smirk.

"And when you returned to your room, what did you do with the cloak?"

"I don't know. I wasn't wearing it."

The Bends

*****

Room 106 was a corner room by the stairwell. After Bill's repeated knocking on the door, Lily Tate finally answered.

"Sorry," she apologized, opening the door. "I was changing. Come on in." She motioned the detectives inside. One of her running shoes was on, the other off.

The dorm room had a gloomy cast to it, since the venetian blinds were closed. The air was thick with incense smoke, causing Bill's throat to burn again. It was clear whose side of the room was whose. The wall over Maggie's bed was covered in pictures of boats and undersea life, while Lily's wall had large posters of the New York Philharmonic, the New York Marathon, and two famous impressionist paintings: Monet's *Water Lily Pond* and Renoir's *Luncheon of the Boating Party*.

"You were at the Halloween party last Friday," he said, by way of an opener.

Lily dropped onto the edge of her bed and pulled on her other running shoe. "That's right. With my parents. Who come to every college function possible, just to mortify me," she said in a dismal tone. She tied the laces.

"And your mother talked with Edward Gripp a few times that evening," he continued.

"I guess," she said indifferently.

"Do you have any idea what they were talking about?"

"I have no clue. My mom's the ultimate social climber. It could have been any inane topic."

"And then you, your mother, and Edward Gripp were talking briefly in the corner of the reception room. Do you remember that conversation?" Sandra put in.

"Yes, of course. My mother was completely bent out of shape that she wasn't invited to some banquet at some yacht club on Saturday night. She was asking Mr. Gripp about the criteria for becoming a Blue Ribbon donor. As I said, she's the ultimate social climber. She grew up abroad and had a horrible childhood working in some Malaysian sweatshop. All I heard growing up is that this is the place to seize the American dream."

"What did Mr. Gripp say to her?" he asked.

"He said that wasn't up to him and recommended that she ask Kate Taylor."

"Did she?"

"I don't know. As soon as The Nobel Laureate appeared, she forgot everything else and followed her around all night. Also mortifying," Lily groaned with a roll of her eyes.

"She'd never met Dr. Nolan before, even though you and Maggie are roommates?" he asked, perplexed. "How many years have you been roommates?"

"Only two. We're both transfer students. Maggie keeps her family far from the college. She was furious when she found out that Dr. Nolan donated money to the college and was coming to the Halloween party."

"Why was that?" he asked.

"Who knows? Maggie's shrouded in mystery."

"Where's Maggie right now?"

"I don't know. She's on and off campus all day in her Jeep. She never tells me where she's going. She just up and disappears."

"Let's return to the evening of October 14th," he suggested. "You had a party in your room."

"Yes. It got larger and rowdier than it was supposed to be."

"And what happened?"

"As usual everyone drank too much, and some people played Twister. And Curt Frederickson got angry at Kyle Monroe when he tried to bite Kristin Pucci's neck," she giggled.

"And Kristin Pucci is...?"

"Curt's girlfriend of a million years."

"Were they at the Halloween party?"

"Yes. He was the shirtless Chippendale's dancer with the great body, and she was a Playboy bunny."

Bill nodded. It was easy to recall that couple from the camera footage, as they were a handsome couple and scanty clothed. "And were you drunk?"

"A little buzzed. I was also panicking that my mother was going to show up, so I was clearing out beer cans all night."

"To where?" Sandra interrupted.

"The dumpster in the parking lot. We have the loudest room in the dorm, because it's by the door and the stairwell."

"And did your mother come by?" he asked.

"No, thankfully. The opportunity to schmooze with Edward Gripp, the dean, and the faculty was too tantalizing an opportunity for Jean Tate."

"And Kyle passed out on Maggie's bed, wearing Ernst's cape," Sandra said.

"Yes. He's a candidate for AA."

"And when did he leave?"

Sandra rose wordlessly as a thought suddenly occurred to her. She moved aside a large privacy curtain, separating the beds from the desks and dressers. Lily and Bill momentarily watched her wander the back of the room.

Lily's attention returned to Bill. "I have no idea. I went to bed and let him sleep it off. I was exhausted after a very long day with my parents, and I'm a very heavy sleeper."

"And Kyle was wearing the black cape when you went to bed?"

"I think so."

"Was he gone when you awoke the next morning?"

"Yes. That I do remember."

The grey-yellow light of early afternoon infused the room as Sandra lifted the venetian blind. Bill joined her at the window. Beyond the window was a hedge of groomed boxwoods, a sidewalk, and the student parking lot.

"Sucky view," Lily complained. "If we had a room on the other side of the dorm we'd have a scenic view of the forest."

"Thanks for talking to us, Lily," he said. "Here's my card, in case you can think of anything else that might be helpful to us." He glanced at her posters once again. "Do you run marathons?"

"I wish. I'm only up to 5K races. But my goal is to eventually qualify for the New York or Boston marathon."

"There are a ton of 5K races around the Cape. I run one almost every weekend."

"Really? How do you do?"

"I train all the time, but I never win."

Lily pulled down the venetian blind as the detectives made their way to the door. "I hate this room. We have to keep the blinds closed all the time. Maggie and I change back here. Any creep could be watching us from the parking lot."

The Bends

*****

After several futile minutes of searching the parking lot for the Jeep, the two cops concluded that Maggie's interview would have to wait.

"Let's get footage from the dorm," Bill suggested.

"Blanchard's office is in the Maintenance Building, I believe," Sandra replied.

They approached a large metal building with its garage doors open. Parked inside on a cement slab were lawn mowers, snowplows and a golf cart. The chilly space was lined with workbenches.

"Something doesn't add up; something's missing," she said quietly. "Kyle said he wasn't wearing the cloak when he went back to his room, and Lily said that he was wearing it when she went to sleep."

"But Lily didn't sound very certain. I'm wondering if someone else didn't take it off him while Lily was moving trash out to the dumpster. It sounded like a chaotic party with a lot of coming and going. And if everyone was drunk and impaired, it's hard to determine what actually happened."

"And where *was* Maggie all night? What if she came back and found Kyle in her bed and took the cloak? She would have been able to enter quietly; she has a key to the room. And Lily said that she's a deep sleeper."

Bill's blood pressure spiked at the mention of Maggie's possible involvement. "Or maybe it's not Ernst's cloak that we're looking for? What if it's someone from the outside, who was not at the party... that we haven't considered yet?"

Even as the words left his mouth, he realized all conversations invariably circled back to Maggie's absence that night. Caution, caution, he told himself again. Remember the charming sister of the Internet Killer. They had to verify Maggie's whereabouts last Friday night, and he dreaded the inevitable interview. There would be no reptile painting, no kombucha and bagels, no rock club, no beach walks.... As for romance... forget it.

*****

The Vinland Viking Museum never failed to astound Maggie. It was an architectural masterpiece. Massive stone arches like those of a medieval church rose out of a grassy field next to a salt marsh. The walls of the building were expansive panels of glass. Wood beams soared between the white arches reminiscent of the beams of Norse longhouses. Inside, in the center of the marvelous structure, sat a wreck of a mid-12th century Viking longboat, one end blackened by fire, the other end grey and unscathed. Along one wall were display cabinets containing artifacts brought up from the depths: coins, double-bladed swords, hand axes, and cutlery. Absent were spindles, brooches, combs, and pins; from all of the archeological evidence, or lack thereof, it seemed that the Vinland settlement had never been home to any Norse women. The Viking mariners had braved the wild swells of the Labrador Sea for the sake of timber, animal furs, and berries for wine.

The museum parking lot was lined with yellow school buses. After one last drag on her cigarette, Maggie tossed it out the window and maneuvered the Jeep into a spot allotted for cars. She'd been to the Viking museum once before, for the opening gala, when guests in gowns and tuxedos had been given a private tour before the opening to the public. For weeks, photos of the gala had been all over the TV news and Internet. Now the large central gallery swarmed with children, dashing from display to display case, or playing with the interactive touch screens. Another group of students shuffled impatiently at the entrance to the theater for the next viewing of "The Vikings of Cape Cod," narrated by Jessie McCabe. There was a frenetic buzz and energy among the children, for it was rumored that McCabe was present in the building that day.

Maggie passed the gift shop with the plastic horned helmets and shields, models of Viking ships, and Norwegian trolls, and made her way down a long corridor to the administrative offices. A pit bull-faced secretary seated behind a desk eyed her suspiciously.

"This area's not for the general public!" the secretary barked.

"I have a meeting with Jessie," Maggie said moodily. "I have a text in my phone to prove it." She tapped on her phone and pushed the phone across the desk. "See?"

"Have a seat," the secretary said grudgingly.

Unrolling the paper in her hand, Maggie sat and reviewed the document for typos. She then glanced out the window to the row of school buses. If she'd been on a field trip when in elementary school, memories of it were unsalvageable. No surprise there. She'd fled the orphanage after the first few weeks of fourth grade. Fortunately, her reading skills had been sufficient to understand road signs and navigate maps stolen from convenience stores.

Eventually a door opened and two middle-aged men in grey suits left the office—lawyers, accountants, or Jessie's agent, she presumed. Jessie stood in the doorway, her arms extended. "Hey, Homegirl!" Maggie rose from the chair, glared defiantly at the secretary, and embraced Jessie.

Once behind the closed office door, Jessie dropped onto a leather sofa and slid off her pumps and knee-high stockings. In Maggie's mind's eye Jessie would always be inextricably linked to the dive boat *Mermaid*, now as famous, though significantly less imposing in both size and legend, as Cousteau's *Calypso*. The elegance of the office decor clearly reflected Sara's touch, as Jessie was a philistine from a trailer park. At the moment Jessie seemed a fish out of water.

When they'd met three years before, Jessie had just motored up the Intercostal Waterway from a marine lab in St. Augustine, Florida. Taking a job at the marine lab in Woods Hole had been her chance to escape an arsonist brother (now in prison, along with his pastor accomplice) and a redneck fiancé. She'd tied up at the seawall on Eel Pond next to Maggie's Jet Ski. She'd been filthy from weeks at sea, diffident, hungry, and broke. In three years, so much had changed.

Maggie smirked. "Love the suit." The Floridian's usual attire was a tank top and cargo shorts, or a bathing suit.

Jessie glanced down at herself and smiled. "Ugh."

Maggie handed Jessie the scrolled piece of paper.

Jessie read the paper, perplexed. "I don't get it. You want me to edit your résumé?"

She grimaced. "Hell no. I want you to accept my résumé. This is a job interview."

"For what?" Jessie said, puzzled. "The museum's not advertising for any positions, as far as I know."

"Shit, I don't want to work *here*," Maggie replied brusquely. "I want to be your expedition artist. You know, like James John Wild on the *Challenger* Expedition, and Sydney Parkinson, the artist for James Cook on the

Endeavour. We've dived dozens of times together, so you know I can dive. When you start making your upcoming documentaries, you'll need someone to illustrate the underwater scenes and the flora and fauna, for posters, advertisements, books, and the like. What if you discover a new species? Who knows... like *Carcharodon mccabeus?*" She grinned. "I could draw it for you."

Jessie sat silently, taking it all in.

Desperate for some response, Maggie leaned forward on the sofa and extended her smartphone toward Jessie. "Here are some examples of my paintings." Her finger slid the images across the screen.

"Too fast, Maggie." Jessie reached for the phone and slowly moved the images, allowing herself time to study them. Her eyes widened. "Whoa!" She gazed at Maggie, reevaluating everything. "Lindsey told me you were good, but I had no idea...."

"I'm graduating in December. I can go after that, anywhere, at any time. I have nothing holding me here anymore."

"You told me once that you never wanted to leave Woods Hole... that you'd done more than enough traveling as a child."

"Things have changed," Maggie asserted. "I'm ready to see the world again."

Jessie nodded. Sara had told her about the break with Brian after the abortion, and Lindsey's sadness over Maggie's actions. "I'm going to ask you a question that I'm not legally allowed to ask, but I'm going to ask it anyway."

Maggie gnawed on her thumbnail. "Go ahead. Ask me anything."

"How's your health? Could you endure months at sea and lots of travel?"

Maggie took no offense to the question. Jessie was familiar with her health issues, as they'd once been neighbors at the marina, before Jessie's meteoric fame, when she'd rented one of Lindsey's houseboats. "Unequivocally, yes. The new HIV drug's working much better than the other one. My white blood cell count is now normal. I just won't be able to stay up and party with you and your crew. Remember, I'm a friend of Bill Wilson, so I don't party. I'll just need to go to bed early."

She looked questioningly at Jessie. "Well, what do you think, Jess? Am I hired?"

Jessie answered frankly, "I love the idea and your work's stunning, but I don't control the budgets. I'll need to run it by the producers."

"Producers?! Shit! Remember what Lin tells you all the time, that you're the boss of all of this, that you call the shots. Not the lawyers and agents and other poohbahs."

Jessie nodded again. "What does Lin say about your plan?"

"I'm twenty-one," Maggie cried, "I don't need her permission to do anything!"

"But it is a courtesy to let her know your plans," Jessie said calmly. "Besides, she'll probably love the idea. What is it she says all the time?"

"I know," Maggie muttered. "Her biggest regret is not traveling and seeing the world."

*****

The Bends

It has been a bad week, a very bad week. In my haste, my gloved hands didn't secure the anchor line tightly enough. Edward Gripp's body was never intended to ooze up from the bottom and wash ashore. He was supposed to simply fade from concern as a missing person. Who cares about the death of an old man, anyway? It was his time to die. But it would have been so much simpler if Edward Gripp had just "gotten lost." Now the campus is crawling with cops, and dogs sniff through the forest.

Then that freaky Ted Blanchard put a padlock on the trap door in the woods. Did he really think that would stop me getting back into the tunnel? The lock was a shock at first. I had to drive to Falmouth hardware stores, wasting almost an entire afternoon, until I could find an identical lock—that I have the key to—and bolt cutters. That was an inconvenient, but not an insurmountable, problem.

Then there was the annoyance of leaves falling away from the trapdoor every time I entered the tunnel, exposing the entryway. I had to completely camouflage the trapdoor, painting a glue-water mixture across the wood planks, then strew it with leaves and dirt.

Worst of all, last night I made one quick dash through the tunnel and obviously some CSI team had been taking samples. The blood's been cleaned away and the door to Edward Gripp's office had been nailed shut. If Ted Blanchard knows about the tunnel, who else knows? The dean? No matter now. As far as they're concerned, the tunnel's sealed.

At last—the tunnel's now for my exclusive use, not to be shared any more with Old Peeper Gripp!

Now I sit alone with my thoughts as the faculty members wander into the conference room. It's a shame that the police dogs found the garbage bag with the Nolan dive helmet. I liked using it, and as long as it was missing that was one more distraction for the police. But that, too, is ultimately trivial. That helmet has to have the fingerprints of every stray passerby visiting the drawing studio that week. Ha!—that has to be confounding the CSI team. And Edward Gripp's headlamp is perfectly adequate. Another clever thing was dumping the cloak in Buzzards Bay. I knew the cops would study footage from security cameras; all they'd be able to see was the cloak and helmet. I'm light years ahead of them, just like the other time. Our IQs are simply not comparable.

I squint through the peephole. The Awards Committee's now assembled. I turn on Edward Gripp's listening device. Thankfully the agenda is not a long one. A discussion of the Windsor Award, and then faculty travel grants, says the chairman.

"All of the student nominees for the Windsor Award were emailed," Sanders announces. "One student has requested that more than three pieces be entered in the competition. How does everyone feel about that?" Such a diplomat.

The faculty members mutter and moan.

Finally the icy photography professor speaks up: "The evaluation criteria should not be changed midstream in the competition, especially if the pieces are to be displayed by the deadline."

"Some nominees have already set up their three pieces," adds the computer graphics professor with the billy-goat beard. "This would mean that those students would have to go back and redesign their displays."

"Which students have set up their pieces?" Sherman Hayner asks. "I can't wait to have a look."

"When I checked earlier today it was Olivia Moreno, Curt Frederickson, and Amy Jacobsen," answers the old goat.

"We've drifted off on a bit of a tangent," Sanders says, bringing the faculty back on task. "Are there any more ideas on entering more than three pieces?"

"I concur that the criteria should not be changed at this late date. Perhaps we might re-evaluate them before next year's competition," remarks the professor with the thick glasses from the printmaking department.

"And remember that we currently have six disciplines, times three works. That means we're already assessing eighteen pieces of art," June Perkins objects. "Adding more pieces will add to our work load." Lazy bitch.

"Hmm... that is a consideration," chimes in the professor from printmaking. What a gonadless yes-man.

"Do we want to table the question until later in the year, and this year stick with three pieces?" Sanders asks.

There's a unanimous muttering of "Yes".

"Please encourage your colleagues from your respective disciplines to view the displays and give you their feedback," Sanders sums up. "We'll have a final vote at the next meeting. Now, let's move on to faculty travel grants."

I lean my head against the stone wall and close my eyes; there have been too many late nights recently. It's of no consequence to me if a photography professor gets funding to photograph glaciers in Greenland, or a sculptor is awarded funding to go to Prague. Who truly gives a shit?

Finally the faculty meeting disbands, and I rouse myself. I creep toward John Sanders' office and lean anxiously forward, no longer having to compete with Gripp for this chair. Now it's all mine. As usual, June Perkins sneaks in just after five o'clock. Recently their relationship has been strained. The Old Pervert's death has made everyone a bit testy, including June. She requests an update on John's divorce. He says (again) that these things take time... "Patience, June, honey... patience." I've heard that before. She grumbles that she's tired of fucking on a sofa, yet still peels off her yoga pants. John's always good-natured and eagerly climbs on. June's a wonderful fuck when her heart's in it. But today she simply fucks because she's there and it passes the time.

There's a lot to be learned from June Perkins.

Chapter 12

Maggie made it a point to stay clear away from the premises of Lindsey's new experimental business venture, NK Dive Technologies (NKDT), because she'd inevitably run into the co-owner, Sara Kauni. Lindsey and Sara had started up the dive business after the unexpected boom in the sales of their C-trax GPS. Due to a savvy marketing campaign, the waterproof tracking device that was originally designed for scuba divers was soon fixed to windsurfers, jet-skiers, kayakers, and the flotation vests of tour companies that ran snorkeling adventures around the tropics. With a portion of the GPS profits, the two women had bought a coastal property that had been on the market for over a year, on the same road as Nolan's own beach house.

According to Lindsey—who could talk of nothing but work—the house that was to form the offices of NKDT was bought on the cheap, as the electrical system was antiquated, part of the foundation was rotting, and with every torrential rain the basement flooded. To the lady in Texas, who'd never been east of the Mississippi River but had inherited the property from a distant aunt, it was a relief to unload the property after struggling to pay taxes on a home in which she would never live. What sold Lindsey on the property was not the house itself, which was obviously a money pit, but the long dock that projected out into Buzzards Bay, and the spacious boathouse that would form the basis of an engineering workshop. She and Sarah had hired three engineering post-docs from MIT; one worked on the sensors in the NK dive helmet while the other two built the recreational submersibles.

The only remotely interesting part of the dive enterprise was a fourth part-time employee who was to be the public face of the dive company. Jessie McCabe. Since discovering the Viking wreck in Cape Cod waters, Jessie had become a household name. Soon after the highly publicized find, she had appeared on *Oprah*, *Good Morning America*, and *Late Night with Stephen Colbert*. She'd been to the White House to lunch with President Elizabeth Warren, and was signed by the BBC to make a series of underwater documentaries, much in the same spirit as *The Undersea World of Jacques Cousteau*.

Maggie watched Jessie, in her trademark royal blue wetsuit, follow the instructions of a photographer and his assistant on the NKDT dock. First Jessie was photographed on a bollard, then on the bow of *Mermaid*; in each pose she was holding the high vis yellow dive helmet. On the dock, Olivia, Kyle, and Lily huddled in hushed excitement, while Maggie paced alone, lighting one cigarette off another. Every time she glanced at the helmet her anxiety skyrocketed. It had been so humiliating, and it had wasted so much of her time, spending days walking the floors of the dorm, then the faculty offices, hoping someone had found the missing second helmet, only to be answered with "don't knows," puzzled looks, and vague shrugs. That afternoon she would have to own up, and Lindsey and Sara would kill her.

The photo shoot was to continue at sea, so Maggie and the group piled aboard the *Jack Rackham* and set out for a sturdy platform floating in the swells. Bolted to the platform was a metal crane, and dangling from the crane by a thick cable was a futuristic, two-man submersible. It, like the helmet, was a high vis yellow. In addition, it had numerous bubble-like Plexiglas windows that resembled the bulging eyes of a fish, or Captain Nemo's *Nautilus*.

After fighting the wind and white caps in Buzzards Bay, Lindsey toggled the bow thruster and the *Jack Rackham* eased alongside the teetering platform. Maggie jumped off to secure the fore and aft lines and everyone spilled off the boat. It was a brisk day and waves splashed against the platform, causing the art students to secure their hats and coat zippers. Lindsey and Sara, meanwhile, consulted with the engineers and inspected the cable, while the photographer struggled to set up his tripod on the shifting planks.

Given the go-ahead that the photographer and Jessie were ready, Lindsey flipped a switch on an instrument panel. The crane and the cable squealed and groaned as the submersible descended and dropped into the frothy bay.

Jessie looked with misgivings at the submersible. "Lin, are you sure this thing's attached securely? It's a very cold day to be floating out into the North Atlantic."

"It's not going anywhere. Trust me," Lindsey said confidently.

"If you say so...." Jessie replied with a doubtful smile.

A clear, Plexiglas hatch opened and Jessie climbed cautiously into the submersible. She ducked her head into the interior. "Whoa, this is way cool. It has a touch screen control panel like a smartphone! But why aren't we testing this in St. Croix?" she asked facetiously.

Sara added her two cents. "St. Croix works for me."

"What works on this thing?" Jessie asked, studying the instrument panel.

"Only the lights," Lindsey said. "But it's water tight. Either I can control the submersion depth from up here with the switch, or you can do it from inside with the depth app."

Jessie pressed an app for the lights, and just below the surface, powerful beams of light cut through the green water. "The lights definitely work," she called up to the group peering over the edge of the platform.

The photographer shooed the observers away and scurried along the edge, shooting Jessie and the submersible from various angles: as she sat on the edge of the hatch, next with the hatch closed and locked, then looking up through the Plexiglas as it was submerged inches below the surface.

Threatening clouds began to darken the sky and the temperature plummeted, so the submersible was raised and Jessie climbed onto the platform. The submersible was maneuvered back to its resting place on blocks. Once all was secured on the platform, *Jack Rackham* carried the group back to the NKDT dock.

The photographer and his assistant departed, and Jessie hurried into the old beach house for a hot shower. Maggie followed her three companions to Olivia Moreno's dilapidated car, where she pulled a package from the trunk. She said a reluctant goodbye to her friends. With the autographs of a famous marine biologist and two Nobel laureates in hand, the other students headed toward the main road.

Hefting the package, Maggie walked in dread to the boathouse. Lindsey and Sara were at the coffee machine, talking to the engineers.

"Can I see you two?" she asked, urgency in her voice. She glanced toward a supply-room-turned office. "In there?"

"Sure," Lindsey replied uneasily. It was unusual for Maggie to initiate a conversation, and the more polite she was, the worse the problem usually was.

They stepped into the office and Maggie closed the door. She shoved the package at Lindsey. "Here. It's a gift. It's the least I can do."

Lindsey unwrapped the painting and held it out for Sara's view.

Sara's eyes flew wide in awe. "Maggie, that's incredible!"

"Isn't it amazing?" Lindsey said proudly to Sara. She then turned toward Maggie. "But I told you I'd pay you for it. As you said yourself, we're businesswomen. We work for profit."

"But I want you to have it. Take it," she muttered feebly, pulling a cigarette pack from her leather jacket. "Sara, I'll paint one for you too. Gratis."

"You can't smoke in here. There's too much oil and gasoline," Lindsey said automatically.

"Fuck it," Maggie mumbled, returning the pack to her jacket. She took a deep breath. *Higher Power, help me.* "I've done something really stupid."

"You're not using, are you?" Lindsey asked worriedly.

"No!" Maggie was incensed at the suggestion. She stalled for a moment, biting the skin around her thumbnail. Another deep breath. "I lost one of your dive helmets."

"What? Where?" Sara said hotly.

Maggie looked frantically from Lindsey to Sara and back. "It was part of a still life that I was drawing! Then it was gone! I think someone stole it during the party last Friday night. I've asked everyone if they've seen it. No one knows anything about it. I'm so, so sorry! I know that you guys have been working on it forever. I'll do anything to make amends."

There was a knock at the office door. Sara cracked it open.

An engineer peered in. "Someone's here to see Maggie."

"This is a really bad time," Sara said testily.

"But I think she needs to talk to him. It's the police...."

*****

The day before, the dogs had sniffed out a plastic bag in the forest on the art campus, a bag which most intentionally had been covered by a heap of autumn leaves. The helmet inside was the one that Maggie had reported stolen, and had surely been worn by the suspect dragging June Perkins' tarp in the wee hours of Saturday, October 15th. But Bill found the evidence from the helmet more confounding than helpful. The absence of hair samples or skin cells indicated that the user had worn a bandana or balaclava underneath, and a confusing mosaic of fingerprints smudged it. Some of the fingerprints could be identified from records of previous arrests: Lindsey Nolan's from her DWIs; Sara Kauni's from a gay rights rally in Mississippi; NKDT engineer Harry Cheng's, for marijuana possession in college; Kyle Monroe for under-aging drinking; and Olivia Moreno for civil disobedience (throwing eggs at Sarah Palin supporters at a rally in Boston). It might have been a red flag if any of these individuals had had a prior record for assault or domestic violence, but substance abuse and public protest were not, in Bill's mind, prerequisites to murder.

However, the majority of prints on the helmet were identical to those acquired from databases in the states of

Oregon and Wisconsin, taken almost ten years before, belonging to a child prostitute named Maggie May. There were also a smattering of unidentified prints presumably belonging to students and faculty who'd wandered through the drawing studio at some point during the still life assignment and felt compelled to examine the amazing helmet.

Despite a burning throat, Bill drove to the campus, intending to interview Maggie and inform her of the discovery of the helmet—now entered as evidence in the crime lab. Again, she was nowhere to be found, but a student in the next room said that she and some friends had gone to NK Dive Technologies for the afternoon. Chewing down another throat lozenge, Bill hurried to his car.

NK Dive Technologies was less than a ten-minute drive from the art college and was marked by a small, unobtrusive sign half covered by an azalea bush. The property was surrounded by a high metal fence on which were mounted numerous security cameras. Surprisingly, though, the front gate was open, probably to allow the passage of the students' car. A number of surveillance drones, certainly of Nolan and Kauni's design, circled the air space above the property. Other than the ominously silent and stealthy drones, the dive company looked unimpressive: a weathered, old beach house that sorely needed new shingles, a large dock, and a boathouse. Maggie's Jeep was not among the few cars in the parking lot, and Bill feared that she had already come and gone.

At the dock, however, he spotted the *Jack Rackham,* so he walked gingerly along the planks to inspect it. Toolboxes, tools, oilcans and greasy rags were strewn around the deck. Muddy footprints covered the deck, gunwales, and bow. The boat was now contaminated with sand, mud, oil and grease, so it was doubtful that any useful forensic evidence could be obtained. Still, Blane's team should conduct a luminal test to search for traces of Edward Gripp's blood.

A young Asian man strode toward Bill. "Can I help you?" he asked in a guarded tone.

Bill flashed the man his badge. "Detective Bleach, and you are?"

"Harry Cheng."

"I'm looking for Maggie May-Nolan. Is she here?"

"She's in the office. It's this way," Cheng said, gesturing toward the boathouse.

Externally, the boathouse was in the same state of disrepair as the beach house, yet it was watched over by more of the intimidating security cameras, and as he stepped inside, his steps faltered. All of the company's assets had clearly been invested in the equipment—astonishing high-end equipment—deteriorating exteriors being irrelevancies to the two owners. The old wood walls and beamed ceiling had been painted bright white, and large bright lights illuminated the cluttered space. Workbenches were covered with computers and state-of-the-art electronics. Dive tanks, gas cans, and spools of wire covered the cement floor. Space heaters attempted, to little avail, to heat the drafty space. Jazz music drifted from speakers through the salty, metallic air. Two engineers were bent over what appeared to be a motor and stainless steel propellers. Another workbench was covered with the new model of dive helmets in varying stages of assemblage. The sensors and components next to them were outside of Bill's scope of understanding.

Cheng knocked nervously on a door to a side office. The door cracked open. "Someone's here to see Maggie."

"This is a really bad time." It was not Maggie's low, raspy voice. This woman's words were irritated and clipped.

"But I think she needs to talk to him. It's the police...." Cheng added timidly.

"Let him in," a different voice commanded.

The door opened wide, and Bill stepped in. The door slammed behind him, almost drowning the sound of a muted gasp from someone in the room. Instantly he felt trapped, and that telltale wave of heat started up his neck despite the coolness of the air. Sara Kauni glowered, her arms folded across her chest. He'd seen photographs of the Polynesian woman before. Despite being dressed in a bulky down jacket and wool watch cap, Kauni was gorgeous beyond words. Lindsey Nolan flicked a pen against the thigh of her jeans, her striking green eyes boring into his as if to read his thoughts. Maggie slouched against a desk and stared down at the cement floor. She was dressed again in the black leather outfit and *the* black boots. He forced his eyes back to the two engineers. They stood wordless, fiercely poised like lionesses protecting a cub. At any moment, he feared, they might pounce and rip him to shreds.

He groped through his pockets for his badge. "Um-I'm-uh-Bill Bleach-um-Detective Bleach."

There was still no response from the women.

"Er... um... hello, Maggie," he assayed.

She whispered a dejected "Hey."

The familiarity in the cop's "Hello, Maggie" caused Lindsey to turn in astonishment. "Maggie, do you know Mr. Bleach?"

"Yeah," she replied quietly, still gazing downward.

Only the flicking pen was heard in the protracted silence. Lindsey glanced back at him. "Do you want to tell me from where?"

"Just fucking kill me now!" Maggie wailed in anguish. "I was night diving at Spire Rock and saw a dead body being dumped. So I reported it to the police. Detective Bleach took my report."

"Jesus!" Lindsey cried. "That's way out there! What were you doing at Spire Rock?"

"Catching lobsters. The underwater cliff's crawling with them. Big ones."

"And you can't buy lobster in a grocery store, if you want them?" Lindsey exclaimed. "Night diving's so dangerous, Maggie. No more night diving. Hopefully you weren't diving alone."

"I wasn't. Actually, I was doing underwater photography. It was my dive partner catching lobsters."

"And who was that?"

Maggie gnawed away at her cuticle.

Lindsey stared questioningly at her.

"I promised I wouldn't tell!" Maggie shouted.

Lindsey continued to frown. "Why the hell not?"

Maggie pulled a cigarette from a pack. "I really need a cigarette!"

"Not in here! Why did this person not want to report a dead body?"

"How do I know? This person doesn't know that I spoke to the police. I just thought that the family might be missing the dead person."

"Um, Maggie, you did the right thing in reporting it," he interrupted, hoping to change the tenor of the conversation.

"But it wasn't a body at all. It was someone dumping chemical waste. Someone has set up an illegal drug lab. We're not sure who, but we intend to find out."

Surprised relief passed across Maggie's face. "They're probably making meth."

He shook his head. "That's what we thought, too, but the waste was not the by-products of meth production. The primary reason I came by was to tell you that we found your helmet."

"Oh, thank God!" Sara cried.

"Where was it?" Lindsey demanded.

"In the forest by the art college. But I can't return it to you yet. It's still at the crime lab."

"Crime lab?" Lindsey exclaimed. "Why?"

"We believe that the person who murdered Edward Gripp was wearing it during the early hours of October 15th, the night of the Halloween party on campus."

Lindsey was aghast. "The murder occurred on the campus?!"

"Yes."

"Where?"

"That can't be disclosed yet."

Lindsey swiveled toward Maggie. "I want you to stay in your cottage until they catch the murderer. Just go to classes and come right home!"

"No way! All of my friends are on campus," Maggie argued.

A gloomy silence suffused the room again.

"The helmet's covered with the fingerprints of Dr. Nolan, Dr. Kauni, Harry Cheng, Maggie, and some other students," he mentioned reluctantly, "plus some other people we can't identify. They were probably from students or faculty wandering through the drawing studio where it was on display."

"Of course our prints would be on it. We built it," Sara said defensively.

"Who were the other students?" Maggie asked.

"Kyle Monroe and Olivia Moreno."

She shook her head vigorously. "That's bullshit. It wasn't either of them. They're both normal and nice. They're both in drawing class with me, so they could have touched it at any time."

Lindsey turned toward Sara. "At least the helmet's locked safely away and not in the hands of one of our competitors."

"I need to ask you three about your whereabouts on Friday, October 14th," he informed them, bracing for other outbursts. "And Harry Cheng. From roughly the time period of 9:30 to 10:30 p.m."

"You're kidding, right?" Sara erupted. "*We're* suspects? I've never even met the man. Why would I kill him?"

"This is just standard procedure," he replied wearily, searching his pocket for another throat lozenge.

"Un-fucking-believable," Sara fumed.

"Please, Dr. Kauni," he insisted.

Sara gave him a hard look, then said, "Harry and his wife, Lydia, were at my house. Jessie McCabe was there, too. We had wine and cheese fondue and then streamed a movie from Netflix. Harry's boy and my boy are the same age and were playing video games upstairs."

"And how about you, Dr. Nolan?"

"You know exactly where I was and what I was doing. The police have to be studying camera footage from the party."

He nodded. "What was Edward Gripp discussing with you?"

"We met that night for the first time. He invited my husband and me to dinner at his club to discuss potential scholarships for low-income students."

"And what did you say?"

"I said fine, but we didn't set a date. Things are very hectic at work right now."

"Was there anything else you remember talking about?"

"Yes. He congratulated me on Maggie's nomination for the Windsor Award. That's all everyone was talking about that night. Apparently the list of nominees had just gone out. The dean, June Perkins, and Jean Tate all mentioned Maggie's nomination to me."

He pulled his rumbled notepad from his pocket. "You left the party at 8:25. Where did you go from there?"

"Lin, your lawyers should really be here," Sara interjected.

"Every move I make is captured by some goddamn camera, Sara. This can be confirmed electronically." Lindsey turned toward him. "But I can promise you, Mr. Bleach, if there are *any* conversations after today, or *any* leaked images of me, my lawyers *will* be present. Derick called Luigi's Deli for a pizza, which you can confirm from the cell towers. I'm sure we were remembered in the pizza joint, as we were two adults in pirate costumes. Then we returned home. Maggie was also home, because her car was at the cottage. All of our comings and goings are recorded on my home security system and you're welcome to them."

The door pushed open.

"Lin, I'm loving this new jacket," Jessie McCabe announced cheerfully, stepping into the office. Her hair was wet and she had on a fleece jacket with the NKDT logo on the breast pocket.

The Jessie McCabe! Bill dropped his pen.

The tension in the air was palpable. Jessie obviously noticed. "Who's this? What's going on here?"

She looked at him cautiously as he shifted on his feet and his face heated. Then he remembered his pen at Lindsey's feet. The area was too confining, too smothering... the circle of women seemed to be closing in upon him. His face was covered with red splotches, he was sure of it. Worse, if he bent down for the pen, his face would be inches from Lindsey's.... He looked helplessly at her and began to bend his knees.

"Here," Lindsey said flatly, handing him her pen.

He blinked and focused his eyes on his notepad—anything not to stare outright at the superstar marine biologist. How stupid would he look if he asked for her autograph in the middle of a murder investigation? Still... he'd never get this chance again.

"This is Mr. Bleach, Jess. A cop," Sara said bitterly. "Apparently we're all murder suspects."

"What? Who was murdered?" she exclaimed.

"The old man they pulled out of the bay. Remember? We saw it on the news," Sara replied. "He was murdered on Maggie's campus."

Jessie grabbed Maggie's hand. "Thank God you're safe! Stay away from that place until they catch that person."

"Uh, er, no, no, you're not suspects," he sputtered. "I, I understand why your prints were on the helmet. I'm just trying to establish a timeline... trying to establish where everyone was."

"Can you tell the detective what Harry and I were doing last Friday night?" Sara said to Jessie.

Bill turned toward Jessie McCabe, readying himself to take notes. His hands shook uncontrollably. This time he dropped the notepad.

*****

Bill watched Lindsey stride angrily toward her SUV, a forlorn Maggie and a large blue painting in tow. He looked into his rearview mirror. The red splotches were still visible on his neck. With any luck the women hadn't noticed. Maybe the redness had never spread to his face at all? Oh, what did it matter at this point? The interviews had been a complete disaster! Could he have appeared more ridiculous? Perhaps if Sandra had been with him, he would not have felt so cowed and cowardly in the presence of the two Nobel laureates. There had been way too much estrogen in that suffocating office. Each one of the women was beautiful in her unique way. And then *Jessie McCabe*, of all people, appears and squeezes herself into the office. Adorable Jessie McCabe, with her adorable dimples and adorable doe-brown eyes. At that point he'd been completely befuddled. His notes were barely legible.

He turned the ignition and followed Lindsey's car out onto the main road. The solitude of his car gave him a chance to calm himself. He checked himself in the mirror again. Thankfully the splotches had almost disappeared. Both Jessie and Harry Cheng corroborated Sara's account of what they had all been doing on the night of October 14th, even down to the details of the wine (a dry California white), type of cheese fondue (gruyere and swiss) and movie watched (*Life of Pi*). Satisfied that Sara and Harry had been cleared from suspicion, Lindsey was adamant that he watch the footage from her home security system, "to put this matter to rest, once and for all." She'd insisted that he follow her and Maggie to her house right there and then. Sara and Jessie had hurried away before he'd had a chance to ask for autographs.

The Nolan beach house was only minutes from NK Dive Technologies and was fortified by a high stone wall. The single entry point was an iron gate watched over by two prominent security cameras. He followed the SUV through the gate, and then through a forest that opened up to a groomed lawn and circular drive. The home was a turn-of-the-century stone and clapboard house with a large porch, turrets, and widow's walk.

The second the SUV stopped, Maggie hopped out and dashed toward a cottage. Lindsey lugged the painting from the car and up the porch steps. On old wicker chairs by the front door were a skateboard, roller skates, and un-carved pumpkins. It was still too early in the day for children; they would be at school. A Halloween wreath hung on the front door. Lindsey placed her hand on one of her other inventions, the keyless doorknob, and the door swung open. Once in the house, she placed the painting on a dining room table.

"It's just me, George," she called down the hallway.

"You're home early, darlin'," a Southern accent boomed from a room that Bill presumed was a kitchen.

"Yup. I'll be up in my office for a while." She gestured for Bill to follow. They went up one flight of warped stairs to the second floor, and up a short flight to an attic that had been converted to a home office.

"I don't have time for this," she said to him. "I'm trying to make a really important deadline at work. I just don't have time for this. Sit."

He dropped obediently into a chair against the wall, his throat aflame and fever rising. She inserted a flash drive into a computer and her fingers flew across the keyboard. He felt sweaty and warmer by the second. The worktables were covered with three computers. A white board was covered with mathematical formulae.

She paused and watched him study the board. "Do you know what any of that means?"

"No. I could barely pass freshman algebra."

"Good," she said, returning her attention to the computer.

"What is it?"

She eyed him once again, her eyes lingering on his tie dotted with tree frogs. From his bumbling interviews in the boathouse, she'd certainly deemed him no threat to scooping her intellectual property. "I'm working on a theoretical model for the electrochemical basis of consciousness."

He nodded, a bit bewildered. "How's that going?"

"It's not, because of too many disruptions. Like policemen." She tilted the computer screen in his general direction. "Here it is—the footage from October 14th. Pull your chair over here."

He nodded obsequiously and repositioned the chair. His nervously bouncing knee was a mere inch from hers. She smelled like fresh cotton sheets. The two infamous boat images burst in vivid Technicolor into his mind's eye, one with the baseball player, the other with the Scandinavian cop. He glanced briefly at her breasts.

She noticed and ignored it. "Here." She handed him the flash drive, while he stuffed in his pocket.

"Thank you. I really appreciate your cooperation."

"I want to review this with you so you *clearly understand* that Maggie and I had nothing to do with Edward Gripp's death."

He pulled his notepad from his jacket and patted his pockets for a pen.

Her look was one of exasperation as she handed him a pen from the table. "As you can see from the camera at the front gate, Derick and I left to go to the party at 7:20." She scanned the timeline on his notepad. "When did we arrive and when did we leave the party?"

He flipped through the pages. "At 7:33 and 8:25. May I?" His hand reached for the mouse.

"Of course."

He fast-forwarded through the footage. "But you didn't return home until 9:20? It doesn't take that long to pick up a pizza and drive back here."

She hesitated. "We stopped at the beach for a few minutes before getting the pizza."

"And why was that?"

Again she paused.

"Why, Dr. Nolan? I need to know all of your movements that night."

"I bet you do," she said ironically.

"Why did you have to stop?" he repeated urgently.

"We stopped briefly to... talk."

Her SUV, he recalled, had tinted windows. He felt his neck flush and perspiration break out beneath his collar; he tugged on his tie. "Okay," he said quietly.

"Then we picked up a pizza at Luigi's and drove back here. You can see that Maggie came home at 8:43, while we were gone. I noticed her Jeep at the cottage when we returned. I was surprised, because she never sleeps here any more. She stays at the dorm."

Her clean sheets scent and her oblique reference to the beach stop had flustered him, and he struggled to focus on the footage. Suddenly it felt as if someone had kicked him in the stomach. Lindsey seemed to be experiencing the same sensation: she was silent, still, and wide-eyed. On the screen, the Jeep departed through the gates again at 9:25 p.m.

*****

In the doorway to Maggie's cottage, Bill's steps faltered for a second time that afternoon. Xeroxed pictures of Dalgliesh, Jethro, Sherlock... all of his reptiles... were taped to the kitchen island, backs of chairs, and lampshades. The living room floor was covered in tarps. Furniture had been shoved against the walls. A single easel was set up in the center of the room. Maggie sat on the edge of a sofa, elbows on knees, flicking ashes into an empty Coke can on the floor.

"You've been busy," Lindsey said with surprise.

"I need to talk to my sponsor," Maggie mumbled. "As soon as possible."

"What's a sponsor?" Bill asked.

"A person in a twelve-step program with a lot of clean time who mentors other addicts and alcoholics," Lindsey explained. She halted in front of the easel. "Marvelous!"

"I just need to see my sponsor," Maggie repeated with a frantic edge in her voice.

He joined Lindsey in front of the painting. He gasped

audibly and blinked sudden, welling moisture from his eyes. Then place and time evanesced as, in a trance, he crossed the room and dropped to his knees in front of Maggie. He reached for her hand. "That is pure genius," he whispered reverently.

Maggie looked baffled, as if she'd had no role in its creation. "It just came to me."

Astounded, Lindsey stared at Bill and Maggie, her eyes fixing once again on his tie. "Oh my god... you painted this for him."

Maggie' eyes, wide and stricken, flicked from Bill to Lindsey and back again. Suddenly she sprang to her feet and, dodging Lindsey and the paralyzed detective, fled across the lawn toward the garage, hopped into a pickup truck and drove off.

Once again Bill was left to confront the suspicious genius, whose green eyes moved like a pendulum between him and the painting.

He rose awkwardly to his feet and cleared his throat. "Dr. Nolan, I really need to talk to Maggie about what she did that night. Who is Maggie's sponsor? I need to talk to her also."

"A woman named Tory V. at her NA meetings. I don't know her and I don't know her last name. Last names don't exist in twelve-step programs. Only last initials." She gazed unnervingly into his face. "What time was the murder committed?"

"Around ten o'clock."

Lindsey had obviously constructed her own timeline. "And Maggie left here at 9:25 and returned here at 10:31. We both saw that on the camera footage. I expect you to look at every security camera between Woods Hole and Falmouth, check phone records, *everything* to determine where she was." There was a tinge of threat in her voice.

"I know how to do my job, Dr. Nolan," he replied defensively.

Any pretense of civility was gone. "You'd better."

He inhaled and decided to lay it all on the table. "We believe that Edward Gripp's body was transported into the bay on the *Jack Rackham*. Maggie told me that someone had been joyriding in the boat on the night of the Halloween party. That was no joyride."

Lindsey dropped onto the sofa.

"I'm glad you're sitting," he said bleakly. "Our forensic team is going to need to check out your boat. And the murderer was wearing shoes like Maggie's black combat boots."

Her head fell into her hands. "My head's going to explode."

"If I can just get her boots, it can exonerate...."

She sprang to her feet and sprinted up the stairs. He followed.

It was a bedroom in transition. Unopened paint cans were placed in a corner. A new bedspread sat unopened on a chair. The bed had been slept in and was unmade. Skinny jeans, the legs like accordions, were strewn on the floor, along with a thong and a lace bra.

She searched the closet. "They're not here."

"Didn't you notice? She's wearing them!" he said, his voice quavering.

His frantic voice exposed his feelings for Maggie and momentarily silenced Lindsey. She glanced down at the underwear on the floor. "You and Maggie?"

He tightened. "I'm a police officer, Dr. Nolan. I'm working on a case. I would never—" he replied indignantly.

"Right," she said sardonically.

*****

Three extra-strength aspirins had not make a dent in Maggie's headache, so she distracted herself by watching shadows crawl across the ceiling and walls. How to depict in paint the movement of light and shadow, she wondered. A small consolation in her miserable existence was that her room was the best in the whole dorm, because car headlights from the parking lot cast intriguing patterns of grey light through the blinds every evening. Another plus was the room's location on the corner of the building, next to the side door and a short walk from the gazebo. She burrowed farther under a blanket. The chill from an afternoon on the water was finally leaving her limbs. Lily's chatter from across the room was soothing. Her roommate was still excited by the visit to the dive company, so much so that she couldn't sleep.

The trip to the dock had gone well... at first. Before the photographers arrived, Jessie had talked with the art students in her usual easygoing manner. Sara was typical Sara, aloof and arrogant, until she noticed Olivia's tattoos. Then layers of jackets and sweaters were peeled off as Sara and Olivia showed their vast ink artwork to one another. And Lindsey was typical Lindsey, chatting politely for the absolute minimum socially acceptable period of time before disengaging at the first possible moment to get back to tinkering with equipment.

And then Detective Bleach had showed up. His news about the dive helmet may have saved her ass, she thought moodily, but why did he have to follow her to the cottage? Now, in addition to work, Lindsey would be obsessing about her dating a cop. Lindsey had a visceral aversion to police since her DWIs. Bleach would be more crap for Lindsey to nag her about.

Lily's head turned on her pillow. "What pieces are you going to enter in the Windsor competition?"

"Huh?" Maggie murmured.

"Where's you're head at? You've been out of it all night."

"What?"

"I *asked* you what pieces you're entering in the *competition*."

Maggie turned on her side and propped her head on her hand. "I don't know. Maybe I won't even participate. I have too many other things going."

"Like what?"

"Like trying to graduate by December. I asked Jessie for a job."

"Doing what?"

"Doing illustrations for her undersea documentaries."

"What did she say?"

"She was noncommittal. She said that she was going to ask the producers."

"Then you should definitely enter the Windsor competition in case the job falls through. Winning means an exhibition at the Montaque Gallery. That's huge."

"What pieces are you entering?"

"The Etruscan urns."

"Good choice. Those are beautiful. Maybe I can use the paintings of the starfish tube feet, and the feeding coral, since they're already on campus. But I don't have a third one that's good enough, since I gave Blue Tunicates to Lin."

"I can't believe you did that! That one would have sold for thousands of dollars."

"It's the least I could do after losing her dive helmet," Maggie said remorsefully. Lily, Kyle, Olivia, all of them, students and faculty alike, must never—ever—find out the visit by the police. Just like her past. No one could *ever* know. "I just had a crazy idea. I need to paint one more painting fast, before the Windsor Award deadline. Since it's getting too cold to dive, maybe I can go down in the submersible and try to photograph some interesting fish swimming by, and maybe paint one of those."

"And what if a fish doesn't swim by and you're sitting there for hours freezing your butt off?"

"I could put some bait in the water."

"That's a really bad plan. Some shark might come by and chew on the cable."

"I'm not talking about chum. Just some small bait. Besides, even a great white couldn't chew through that cable."

"I don't know," Lily said worriedly.

*****

"Twenty more pounds, just twenty more pounds," Sandra murmured as she started Mile Four on the treadmill. Shedding twenty pounds in four months was entirely doable. If she could burn five hundred calories a day between running and power walks, it would offset the fast food lunches with Bill (thankfully, salads were now available at drive-throughs), and she would be able to fit into the white lace gown that she'd purchased—and not look like a white whale floating down the aisle on her father's arm.

Nothing was happening on the ten o'clock news, so she aimed a remote at the TV and turned it off. She wiped her face with a towel and felt the treadmill move into an inclined position. She groaned aloud. Hills were the enemy. To distract herself from her burning calves, she forced her mind back to the case, the homicide of Edward Gripp, which had the same annoying features as military life: hurry up and wait. Brief flurries of activity and epiphanies were followed by hours, days of drudge work chasing down no—or irrelevant—information.

There was still no clear motive. They knew Gripp to be a pervert-voyeur, but in the public eye the old man was a respected, generous patron with no apparent nemeses. And why would someone steal his laptop? There'd been no headway in determining the identity of the computer thief. A woman in sunglasses had purchased the two dozen red roses on the morning of Saturday, October 15th at a florist shop in Falmouth, but she had paid in cash. The order had not been called in; the woman had seemed happy to wait for the bouquet to be assembled. No car had yet been identified as hers; the woman had either walked some distance to avoid detection by security cameras or taken public transportation. The detectives had tabled the idea of contacting every Halloween costume store and tracing the purchase of every blonde wig—for now. God, it might come to that. She groaned inwardly.

What if the murder had been committed to prevent, or put a stop to, blackmail, related to some incriminating information on Gripp's laptop? What was this person searching for?

Sandra took a long swig from a water bottle and slogged on. The inclination on the treadmill leveled out to a flat running surface once again, and the lactic acid burn in her legs subsided. Everything that could possibly go wrong with the case seemed to be going wrong. The perpetrator had covered his/her tracks too well, with wigs, gloves, cloaks, helmets and sunglasses. That struck her as... significant. The crimes, both murder and theft, were so perfectly conceived, so well executed, as to hardly be the work of an amateur. Could this person be linked to other crimes?

When Bill had headed back to campus that afternoon to interview the elusive Maggie, she'd remained at headquarters to review camera footage from the morning of the Halloween party. There were no cameras in the art studios, so she had no way of seeing who stole the dive helmet. Had the thief known that?

She'd then moved on to footage from the dorm on the evening of the party was studied. Olivia Moreno and Ernst Hanson arrived with a group of other partygoers around 8:30 p.m. At 7:36 a.m., they were seen embracing in the lobby before he departed. Without the "V" mask and wig on, Hanson appeared to be a serene-faced young man.

Kyle Monroe entered the dorm with the same group of students at 8:30 p.m; the camera showed him staggering queasily—without a cape—up to the third floor around 1:30 a.m. He did not leave the dorm again until the next morning at 11:39 a.m.

Lily Tate entered with the same students around 8:30 p.m., and was seen repeatedly dashing out of the side door of the dorm throughout the evening, emptying trashcans of empty beer bottles. At 11:39 a.m. on Saturday morning, she left the building with Kyle Monroe and Olivia Moreno.

Curt Fredrickson and Kristin Pucci entered the dorm with the rest of the group at 8:30 and didn't leave the dorm until the next afternoon, when they appeared to be going for a run. So far, the evidence matched what they'd heard in the interviews.

Another student, looking like photographs that Sandra had seen of Maggie, entered the dorm at 11:06 a.m. on Saturday morning, and left just minutes later, at 11:14, having changed into a different set of clothes. Maggie appeared to leave quite hastily in the direction of the Gripp building.

No student was seen leaving the dorm, from any of the exits, around 2:30 in the morning. Had the murderer come from off campus? It was an open campus with no security gate whatsoever. Anyone could have driven onto campus from the Woods Hole Road.

Bill had called to report that Maggie had been found, not on campus, but at NK Dive Technologies, and that he had conducted interviews with Sara Kauni and Lindsey Nolan—and with Jessie McCabe, of all people. The missed opportunity to meet Jessie McCabe was too painful to think about. Twice she and Lenny had been to the Vinland Viking museum. They'd even purchased matching his and hers *Cape Cod is for Vikings* T-shirts from the museum gift shop. While Bill was out meeting celebrities, she was chained to a computer, watching entitled millennials come and go from a dormitory. Then Bill had been invited to Lindsey Nolan's home to view footage from her security cameras. Oddly, he wasn't particularly conversational about that meeting. He was heading to a doctor on his way home, he'd said in a subdued tone, as his throat was on fire.

Her cell phone vibrated next to the water bottle, and Sandra lifted it to her ear and reflexively pressed the red

STOP button on the treadmill. News coming from headquarters at that time of night was not going to be good news.

*****

A physician at the Ten Minute Clinic found that William Wallace Bleach had strep throat and a fever, so she wrote him a prescription for antibiotics and ordered him home to rest. This was just another piece of bad news in an all-out-unsettling day, Bill concluded, as he swished antiseptic around his mouth at his bathroom sink. That whole incident at NKDT and Nolan's house, culminating with him prostrating himself at Maggie's feet, was beyond embarrassing and pathetic.

He dropped tiredly onto his sofa, aimed a remote at the television and stared at a Celtics-Heat game. Paul Pierce and Ray Allen were the heroes of his boyhood; since they'd left the Celtics, basketball had never been the same.

The Edward Gripp case was going nowhere. What was he missing? Was there something so obvious that it was being overlooked?

Repetitious beer and hot wings commercials made his stomach rumble, so he returned to the kitchen. The refrigerator was nearly empty. With a bag of trail mix in hand, he wandered by the terraria to see what the reptiles were up to, then slumped back onto the sofa. The Celtics were just no fun without Pierce and Allen. Of all teams, how could Allen allow himself to be traded to the Heat? The act was as traitorous as Johnny Damon and Jacoby Ellsbury leaving Boston to play ball for the Yankees.

Bill's ring tone—"Wild Thing"—sounded. It was headquarters. He rose quickly from the sofa and tugged on his pants, boots, and coat. He swallowed down two more antibiotic pills and headed out into the darkness. He punched the directions into the car's GPS and noticed that he had to go only four miles from his apartment. The destination was a small business on a remote road bound by a pine forest.

In the distance, the red and blue lights of police cruisers and emergency vehicles flashed. Bill pulled off the narrow, unlit highway onto a gravel parking lot. Sandra's car was not yet there. He squinted into the pulsating lights, zipped the coat around his neck, and apprehensively pushed into the cold.

An old compact car was parked next to a dumpster at the forest's edge. A parking pass hanging on the rearview mirror read *Newbury College, Faculty Parking*. The front door of the car was open and Dr. Blane was gesticulating orders to her staff.

Upon spotting him, Blane extracted herself from the CSI team and moved from the glow of searchlights. "You might want to take a Pepto-Bismol, or something, before seeing this one," she recommended.

"I haven't eaten much tonight. I'll be alright." He eyed the uniformed policemen shuffling like pack horses, heads huddled into shoulders, clouds of air streaming into the night from their low murmurs. His nickname among them, he was sure, was something like Barfing Bill. In high school, his nickname had been equally humiliating: Snow White. Tonight, he resolutely told himself, he would *not* get sick.

"Good luck," Dr. Blane said doubtfully, returning to the car.

He approached a one-floored, gray clapboard building. A large sign bordered with pink lotus flowers proclaimed it to be The Namaste Studio. The door was open and a weeping woman in purple stretch pants, Ugg boots, and a down parka was talking to a police officer. He peered inside. There was one large room with a mirror along one wall, and a ceiling-to-floor shelf holding mats, assorted cushions, and Pilates exercise balls. The other two rooms were a small business office and a restroom.

The woman blowing her nose into a tissue was the owner of the studio. Shuddering, she explained that she'd taught a class that evening to her advanced students, and that after they'd left she'd stayed on to finish up some bookkeeping. Locking up the building for the evening, she'd noticed a car in the distant end of the parking lot. At first the car had appeared empty. Then she'd looked into the front seat....

Dr. Blane watched Bill worriedly as he trudged stoically across the parking lot. The forensics technicians parted to let him through.

Bill kept his gaze focused on the ground and swallowed a few times and willed his stomach contents to stay put. He reached the car and raised his eyes to look at what was on the front seat. It took less than a second for the image to register. His stomach heaved and his eyes squeezed shut of their own accord, and he gripped the car door for balance. Hot air shot from his nostrils as he clenched his jaw shut.

A gentle hand rested on his shoulder. "Bill, you can't touch the car. It's evidence," said Blane.

He had no idea how he got there, but he found himself behind the dumpster, his hands splayed against the cold metal, his stomach somersaulting and erupting trail mix and antibiotic pills. His eyes were closed, but the image, in high definition, was engraved forever after in his memory.

It was death by garroting. The nearly severed head drooped onto the left shoulder like an unattended puppet. A waterfall of blood had cascading across shoulders and breasts, and then froze in the fabric of a wool coat. The victim's frantic, blue hand was tangled in the steering wheel. A desperate blare of the horn had gone unheard, for the garrotter had cut the wires in the steering column.

Chapter 13

There is standing room only at the memorial service for Dr. June Perkins. The only space on campus large enough to accommodate so many visitors is the central gallery. Sculptures and bench seats in the middle of the gallery have been pushed aside to make room for rows of folding metal chairs. I imagine myself floating above it all, among the hanging sculptures in the rafters, swooping down at brief times, to hover between the shoulders of the mourners, listening for whispers and snips of gossip. The gods of Mount Olympus must have observed mortal gatherings in the same way, as at the amphitheater of Epidaurus.

Dean Shoemacher drones on for too long, the vapid eulogy clearly derived from June Perkins' résumé, pulled from a filing cabinet in Doreen Best's office. His black suit looks hot and constricting; he has gained too much weight since its purchase. Deans eat well. It's amusing to watch his face redden throughout the monologue, like a teapot forgotten on a stove. June's doctoral dissertation title is an unintelligible jumble of words that he stumbles over twice. Everyone in the audience is looking uncomfortably askance, wondering who among us, faculty, staff, student, is The Killer.

And they are wondering how June Perkins met her fate. The police have been silent and cagey.

In the back of the gallery sit the two detectives: the brawny chick, and the anemic guy with the baby face. Both glance often at Maggie. She must be the prime suspect. They'd have to be morons not to have connected the dots to the dive helmet and the Jack Rackham.

Conrad Perkins sits with his fidgeting daughters and heavy-jowled mother-in-law. He weeps into a handkerchief, not so much over his wife's death as his angst over having to find a real job. There's not a lot of work in (bad) experimental music, but there are openings at the Home Depot. I bet he's thinking he won't miss June's nagging. Amazing what's learned from spousal phone conversations while I sit in the tunnel.

This is the first time I've seen John Sanders' wife. It's no wonder about the trysts with June. Mrs. Sanders looks like she could be John's shriveled mother. Rumor has it she is a high-octane attorney who reputedly eats light bulbs (and unfaithful husbands) for breakfast. No wonder John never suggested getting a divorce. Divorce would mean, God forbid, paying for his own housing, food, and insurance. John Sanders, like most academics, is cheap beyond words. Again, those oh so revealing spousal phone conversations.

Olivia Moreno and Amy Jacobsen sit together. Amy sniffs into a tissue, while Olivia gazes stone-faced into that undefined space just over the heads of the crowd. Her brain is wired like no other, her thoughts otherworldly. Perhaps she's thinking about Ernst at sea, or the rapacious one percent destroying the global economy, or right-wing extremists, or murderers. Kyle Monroe has already tossed down a few shots and chugged a beer to calm his nerves before the service. Maggie May-Nolan and Lily Tate are holding hands and pulling tissues from Amy Jacobsen's Kleenex box. Sniveling wimps.

My attention returns to the podium. Dean Shoemacher has stepped away from the microphone, and unbuttons his blazer with an ecstatic expression of relief. A faculty member from the painting department takes his place behind the microphone and reads some of June's favorite poems. Nothing interesting in the gallery. I elevate myself between the swaying aerial sculptures once again and float to a smaller gallery where the works for the Windsor Competition are displayed.

Olivia Moreno set up her display before the rest of the nominees, so her works are the first seen when one enters the room. Her three prints are abstract and breathtaking in color. Lily Tate's Etruscan vases, placed on pedestals near Olivia's works, are tan and black with elegant lines. The crashing wave sculptures of Kyle Monroe are next to a window, where the sunlight causes teal glints of light to jump from the glaze. No one sculpts water like Kyle. Amy Jacobsen's black and white photos are of the homeless in Boston; they are stark and somber, reminiscent of the photographs of Elliot Erwitt. The three computer mosaic images created by Curt Frederickson are of a faceless female nude in different positions, superimposed with the circuitry of a computer. That perfect, nebulous body certainly belongs to Curt's model, Kristin Pucci.

It is SO maddening that Maggie's display is still incomplete. Because she waited until the last minute, her pieces are placed in the worst location in the room. Two of the three pieces have been hung, but I've seen them before because they were in the painting studio during the donors' weekend: the starfish tube feet painting, and that of the feeding coral tentacles. Between them is a large gaping void of white wall. What's going into that space—the uncertainty of it—is driving me insane!

*****

From the corner of her eye, Sandra watched Bill tug at his tie. She was having grave doubts about her partner. It was not his vomiting at the sight of a corpse that was worrisome, for humans have varying sensitivities to gore and death, his being at the lowest end of the spectrum. But even the most seasoned of soldiers and corpsmen had that reaction on the battlefield. No, her fear was that Bill had lost objectivity.

He'd been on the Nolan property and obtained valuable information from Nolan's security system, but he hadn't collected any information from Maggie about her whereabouts on the evening of the Halloween party. How could he have let her slip away? Had he been so stunned by the celebrity status of Jessie McCabe, Lindsey Nolan and Sara Kauni that his reasoning was clouded?

As one of the painting professors read poetry at the podium, Sandra watched out of the corner of her eye as Bill fumbled through his dog-eared notepad, perhaps hoping that something, anything, might jump out at him. He yanked at his tie once again. Maybe his thinking was impaired by the strep and fever. His barking cough of the last few days had cleared up, but he still seemed preoccupied and listless. She needed him focused. The murder of June Perkins had escalated the panic across the campus—and the pressure at headquarters—to the nth degree. There were no limits to the savagery of this murderer, and what was downright terrifying was that the murderer was versatile. That told its own story, and in Sandra's experience the more competent and skillful a murderer was, then more practice they'd had. With June Perkins, a razor thin wire must have been used, and again in such a way as to leave no prints, hairs, or helpful DNA evidence. Of course, it might not be the same murderer; but methods are like signatures, and these two murders were similarly methodical.

Sandra decided to focus on her surroundings. The memorial service was the first time she'd seen Maggie in person. Maggie was a painting major, and June Perkins had been both Maggie's academic advisor and professor. At the moment Maggie and Lily were consoling each other. Maggie was dressed all in black like the other students. Black leather jacket, skirt, stockings. Black boots. Sandra craned her head. Boots with a hiking tread!

She nudged Bill. "Maggie's boots! We need to check them against the prints in the labyrinth."

Glum-faced, he turned slowly to look at the boots.

"Let's talk to her right after this, before she runs off again," she quietly urged.

He nodded despondently. "But let's wait for the crowd to disperse. So we don't call attention to her. She's very sensitive and volatile."

She looked impassively at her partner and said nothing.

The memorial service over, the mourning students wandered back to the dorm, anxiously speculating on the cause of June Perkins' death, which had not been revealed in the service, or the news. Sandra kept Maggie in her direct sights and the Jeep in her peripheral vision. Suddenly, Maggie broke away from the pack of students and headed around the side of the building, in the general direction of the forest.

"Now, Bill! Now's our chance to talk to her!" Sandra led the way at a jog. She did not want to lose sight of the girl. Once again Bill's actions were cause for grave concern: he lagged behind, slowing their pace to a brisk walk.

When they caught up, Maggie was sitting in a white gazebo at the edge of forest, blowing cigarette smoke into the rafters. Seeing the approaching cops, she sprang to her feet.

Bill and Sandra had developed an unspoken strategy for their interviews in the chaotic first week of their partnership. He steered the direction of the interview while she silently scanned the terrain, searching for any clues or evidence. It was her training as a soldier that made her focus on the contours and details of physical space. But instead of initiating an interview, her partner just repositioned his ball cap on his head and stared evasively into the forest.

That's three strikes, Sandra thought regretfully.

Sandra pulled her badge from her coat and stepped into the gazebo. He remained behind in the grass. "I'm Detective Murphy, Maggie. You already know Detective Bleach."

Maggie trembled slightly. Her exotic eyes were wide with fear and she wiped away mascara that had smeared during the memorial service.

"Please sit down. You know that we've been interviewing students about the night of Halloween party."

Maggie dropped tensely onto the edge of the bench, looking ready to bolt at any moment.

"Please tell us what you did that night," Sandra requested.

An uneasy silence loomed between them as Maggie smoked. "How early in the day do you want me to start?" she finally asked.

"As early as you think is important."

"I went to dinner with my NA sponsor and two NA friends. We've been doing that every Friday night for years. We eat at the Old Salt Diner."

"At what time?"

"At 4:45. Then I went to my NA meeting at the Methodist church at 6 to set up the coffee. My sponsor, Tory, and I are the coffeemakers. The meeting goes from 6:30 to 7:30. After the meeting I was supposed to meet my ex-boyfriend, Brian, at the seawall at Eel Pond, but the asshole stood me up."

"What time were you supposed to meet?"

"At 8:00. So I waited until about 8:30, I guess, and then left for my cottage."

"What were you two going to meet about?"

"We were supposed to set up a time for him to move his shit out of my cottage. It had been sitting there for two years and he never came to pick it up. I was pissed that he didn't show up, so I went back to the cottage and cleaned it out by myself."

"Is this cottage on the Nolan estate?"

"Yeah."

"And then you left Nolan's place at 9:25. Where'd you go?"

"To the dumpster behind the marine lab to dump Brian's stuff."

"You cleaned out an entire cottage from roughly 8:40 to 9:25?" Sandra said skeptically.

"I worked fast. I tossed his surfboard off the dock into Buzzards Bay because it wouldn't fit in the car. I just wanted his shit out once and for all. I've converted the cottage into my painting studio." She added hotly, "Detective Bleach can confirm that."

He nodded wordlessly.

"But then you didn't return back to Nolan's place until 10:31," Sandra said. "It doesn't take an hour to dump stuff in a dumpster. Nolan's house is five minutes from the marine lab. What were you doing until then?"

"I went to Stony Beach," Maggie said, her vexation growing.

"Where's that?"

"It's a beach in Woods Hole. Only locals go there."

"Were you with anyone?"

"No." Maggie wiped perspiration from her forehead.

"What were you doing there?"

"You think I killed Edward Gripp!"

"What were you doing there, Maggie?" Sandra repeated.

Maggie fidgeted on the bench. "Sitting on the jetty chain-smoking cigarettes. And praying to my Higher Power to remove my anger over Brian. Which you can clearly see has not fucking happened!"

Sandra eyed both her agitated partner and the smoldering student. Neither of them, during the entire conversation, had looked at the other. Could things get any worse? Something was definitely up with those two.

"Bill, do you have any questions for Maggie?" Sandra asked irritability.

"No, I'm okay," he said softly.

Sandra kept the irritation out of her voice, but it took an effort. "Maggie, I have two more questions, then we'll let you get on your way. Do you remember what shoes you were wearing that night?"

"My shoes?"

"Yes, shoes."

"My sneakers. I remember because they got wet when I dragged the surfboard across the lawn. My feet were cold for the rest of the night."

"So you weren't wearing these?" Sandra pointed to the black boots.

"No."

"Where were they?"

"In my room. Where else would they be?" Maggie answered flippantly.

"We're going to need to take them with us."

Galled, Maggie jumped to her feet. "Why?"

"Because we believe that boots like these might have been at the crime scene."

Maggie fumbled for another cigarette and glared at Sandra. "And where was that?"

"That's information we can't release."

Bill interrupted, "Maggie, maybe the boots weren't there at all. At least we'd be able to prove that."

There was no acknowledgement from Maggie that he'd said a word. She bent down and furiously unlaced her boots. She shoved them in Sandra's face. "I want these back! These are my favorite shoes and perfectly broken in. I know that you think I killed Edward Gripp, and you know that I don't have an alibi. These boots are going to prove my innocence!" She sprinted away in her stockinged feet.

"Wait!" Sandra shouted. "I haven't asked my other question."

Maggie spun, her stockings wet with the morning dew. A seething jet of cigarette smoke shot skyward. "What?"

"What did you do two nights ago?"

The implication was not lost on Maggie. "I was with my sponsor, and you can talk to my lawyers from this point on!" She turned abruptly and strode across the lawn, her middle finger held high in the air.

"Don't leave town, Maggie!" Sandra called in warning.

*****

"Fucking asshole cops!" Maggie wiped sweat from her forehead again. Her stockinged feet made a spattering of wet footprints on the slab by the door as she rummaged through her pockets to find her keycard. Her chest heaved and her heart pounded. Worse, she could barely steady her hand long enough to swipe the card through the keycard reader. The last fucking thing she wanted to do was talk to fucking lawyers! Besides, she didn't even have one.

If Lindsey found out about this conversation, she would be on her cell phone in nanoseconds, searching for the most ruthless defense team from Los Angeles to New York. This would be followed by months of interminable meetings with slick lawyers, and imprisonment behind the walls of the Nolan estate, shut out forever from contact with the outside world. This was all fucking Brian's fault! If he'd picked up his shit, she would not have cleaned out the cottage on her own, or dumped his stuff at the dumpster... or gone to Stony Beach... leaving herself with no alibi!

That bitch Detective Murphy was for sure convinced of her guilt. "Don't leave town, Maggie!" Why didn't she just come out and say it? "You're going to serve ten life sentences for the murders and never see the light of day."

Her door was open. Kyle and Lily sat on a bed, watching a YouTube video on a laptop. They noticed her shoeless feet and looked questioningly at her.

"Don't fucking ask!" Maggie yanked the privacy curtain to divide the room and began to strip. She wiggled out of the leather skirt and flung it fiercely onto the dresser, bottles of skin cream and perfume careening into the mirror. She pulled off the damp stockings, wadded them into a ball and hurled them at her desk. She jammed on a pair of clean jeans, a shirt, and dry socks. She tugged on her high-top sneakers and attempted to lace them, but her hands still jittered. She stuffed her car keys into her jacket pocket and grabbed her jean bag from the back of her chair.

"Are you okay?" Lily asked timidly. "Do you want to talk?"

"Thanks, but I'm FINE," Maggie retorted, moving through the door. In AA- and NA-speak, FINE translated to "Fucked Up, Insecure, Neurotic, and Emotional." Her response had been a truthful one.

Maggie floored the Jeep across the wide, grassy field where the large sculptures stood. The squealing tires swirled orange leaves into the autumn air. For June Perkins' sake, she was glad that the funeral was on a sunny day. It was horrible to think of those small girls being raised without a mother. But at least a father and grandmother were in the picture, which was more than she'd had.

Dr. Perkins had been a kind and fair-minded professor and advisor, and Maggie was going to miss her. But attending the burial at the cemetery was out of the question; there was a quiz and a review of sketchpads in Professor Tinkman's afternoon drawing class. Which of the painting faculty was going to step in to finish out the rest of the semester for Dr. Perkins? No one would be as good. She turned the wheel and the Jeep skidded onto the shoulder by the covered bridge.

Where the hell was she going? She had no idea. She'd hopped mindlessly into the Jeep without a destination. It was always comforting to talk to George McLeod, as he was a former police captain and might offer some consoling advice. But inevitably Lindsey would find out, and there would be a heated family discussion over the kitchen table, where she would be hovered over, buffeted by yacking adults, and just want to scream. She could confide in Derick, but he was at work, and he, too, would tell Lindsey. And her mentor Tory was irked at anyone interrupting her writing between the hours of 9 and 4.

Maggie turned off the ignition and stared in horror at her reflection in the rearview mirror. Mascara formed hazy black circles around her eyes. "Fucking strung-out panda bear," she cried aloud. With a napkin from a cup holder, she rubbed away the mess from her face. And Detective Bleach had left her dangling... just like Jack Rackham's body on the gibbet at Point Royal. Detective Murphy had clearly castrated him; he'd been worthless and pathetic during the entire interrogation. Earlier she had—erroneously—glimpsed compassion in him, and even had a fleeting, deranged idea to invite him to Rock Revival. He had a nerdy appeal, but he had to be married; that was why he didn't want her to go to his apartment to see his reptiles. No way was she going to invite him now! What the hell was she going to do with the second concert ticket? If she invited Lily, Kyle would be pissed. If she invited Kyle, Lily would be pissed, and Kyle would think it was a date and she'd have to shove him off all night. Fuck it, she just wouldn't go.

And why was she obsessing over concert tickets when her professor had just been murdered, and she was being accused of it? Unfortunately there was no death penalty in Massachusetts, which meant an insufferably long life rotting away in some prison cell. The logic of her Higher Power was unfathomable. It was just her fucking luck to be convicted for two murders she didn't commit, when she'd escaped being implicated in the other two... during that unspeakable winter in Minnesota. She couldn't help herself. She bent her face into the steering wheel and sobbed.

*****

Bill surreptitiously pulled a bottle of aspirin from his desk and swallowed down more tablets with a lukewarm coffee, though he wasn't sure why he bothered. The aspirin he'd choked down earlier hadn't touched his headache. Most of the time he enjoyed working with Sandra Murphy, but now he just wished she'd shut up. His partner had lost all objectivity. She was unwaveringly convinced of Maggie's involvement in these murders. She was searching the databases with the tenacity of a bloodhound, looking for some overlooked, incriminating fact about the runaway, Maggie May. "Two arrests for shoplifting and another two for prostitution," she reminded him over her shoulder. He struggled to block out her words, as blood pounded against his temples. The last thing he wanted to contemplate was the squalid existence of child prostitutes.

He preoccupied himself, with little success, by searching the local phone company's records for a woman named "Tory V." Frustratingly there were no hits for a Tory with a last name starting with a "V," but there was an unlisted number for a Victoria Valence. He googled the name and was directed to the Facebook page of a writer of romance fiction. He skimmed the brief synopses of Valence's eight novels, all of which were historical love stories that focused on burly sea captains and widow lighthouse keepers. His taste in literature tended toward the supernatural (H. P. Lovecraft) and sci-fi (Phillip K. Dick), so this author's name was unfamiliar to him. He turned his chair. "Have you ever heard of a writer named Victoria Valence?"

"I love her stuff!" Sandra said with alacrity. "I've read all of her novels. Sylvia Franklin, the lighthouse keeper, is one of my favorite characters. She's a bit lusty, and the sex scenes with Captain Sevilla border on pornography, but you can't put those books down."

"I think this woman's Maggie's sponsor," he said flatly, as he was in no mood to discuss sex. His chances of ever having as much as a cup of coffee with Maggie were up in smoke. And forget about ever glimpsing the amazing reptile painting again. That painting alone would thrust her into the spotlight of the art world and the arms of dashing, millionaire art collectors. Romance with Maggie... not.

"Her sponsor? As in AA?"

"NA, actually. She's some kind of mentor."

Sandra jumped from her chair. "Let's go! I'd love to meet her! I wonder if she's anything like that enthralling Sylvia!"

*****

Victoria Valence lived in a clapboard cottage at the end of a nondescript residential street in Woods Hole. Her low picket fence was overgrown with honeysuckle vines; it circled the cottage like a giant, green caterpillar. A water bowl for some pet lay next to the front door. The doorbell was covered over with a piece of peeling duct tape, so Bill used a lobster doorknocker to announce their presence. An old Subaru Baja sat in the driveway, so he assumed the writer was home; he persisted with the knocker at intervals until finally the door creaked open.

The woman at the door said with a disgruntled sigh, "I don't remember any interviews being scheduled for today." Bifocals were buried atop her wavy gray hair, and she barricaded the door with her stout body. "I don't give interviews unless they're scheduled, and never before four o'clock. If I don't keep to a strict writing regime, I won't make my publisher's deadline. You're going to have to make an appointment."

Bill flashed his badge. Her expression changed from weary irritation to wary interest.

"Are you Tory V.?"

The cranky woman eyed him. "Then you're not here to ask about my novels?"

"No, we're investigating two murders and hope that you might confirm someone's presence at an NA meeting at the Methodist church."

Tory V. opened the door. "Come in, then. I have all sorts of whack jobs showing up on my doorstep to see if I'm anything like Sylvia Franklin. Why do readers always assume that the author and the main character are one and the same?"

Sandra abashedly followed Bill inside. They passed through a tight foyer that was overburdened by coats, vests, and raingear, and into an open room that functioned as kitchen, dining room and living room. The air was redolent with the odor of cats. A wooden table was covered with a computer, reams of paper and a printer. A steep stairway climbed toward the rafters and a loft bedroom. Tory V. ushered the two cops to a sofa and scooted two obese cats off, then gestured for the cops to sit. She dropped gracelessly into an old recliner across the room, tilted her head, squinted, and lit a cigarette.

"Whose murders are you investigating?"

"Edward Gripp and June Perkins," Bill replied, pulling his notebook from a pocket.

Sandra recovered enough from her embarrassment to register that her partner was resuming his proper role in their team investigations.

Tory shrugged and shook her head. "Sorry. I don't know about them. When I'm working on a novel, I don't read the papers or the Internet. It blocks the creative flow. Who are they?"

"Edward Gripp was a renowned architect and philanthropist for the Newbury College of Art, and June Perkins was a painting professor there."

At the mention of the art college, Tory knew where the conversation was headed. Her face wrinkled in concern and she inhaled deeply.

"A student there, Maggie May-Nolan, mentioned that you were her sponsor," he explained.

"That's correct. I met Maggie that first day she came into the program, when she was just a girl of thirteen. She asked me to be her sponsor a few weeks after that."

"And what does a sponsor do?" Bill inquired.

"It varies from person to person. But Maggie and a few other women I sponsor meet for dinner each week before the meeting, and sometimes we get together do to other things. Our goal is to keep each other clean and sober. We meet to work through the twelve steps of AA. There's no one who wants to stay clean as bad as Maggie. I'm sure you're familiar with her past. More than anything, she does not want to go back there."

"Were you two together on the evening of Friday, October 14th?"

Tory thought for a moment and then nodded. "We're together every Friday evening, except when I'm on a book tour. We go to the Old Salt Diner in Falmouth, and get to the meeting early since we're the coffee makers. That night she rushed with the cleaning of the coffee kettles after the meeting; she was going to meet with Brian, who's also in our NA group. Since their breakup, I'm afraid he's fallen in with a slippery crowd. I pray for him. He's a nice boy. She was anxious for him to move his belongings from a cottage where they once lived together."

"Did they meet that night?" Bill asked, looking down at his notepad.

"No, he stood her up. She was pissed about that and I don't blame her. She wants closure from the whole relationship and hopes to move on."

"Is she seeing anyone now?" he asked nonchalantly.

"That's not my business. My concern is Maggie's sobriety, not her sex life."

Bill heard his partner choke back a snort and felt his neck redden.

"Have you seen her since then?" he managed to ask.

"She was here two nights ago."

"And what did you all do?"

"I made us some sandwiches and we talked. She's stressed about graduating early and getting a job. She wants to travel the world with Jessie McCabe and be the artist for a documentary series that Jessie's making with the BBC. She was friends and dive buddies with Jessie before Jessie McCabe became *The* Jessie McCabe. She's desperate to get out from under the rather conspicuous shadow of Lindsey Nolan. She's anxious to venture out on her own. And she's worried about some award."

"The Windsor Award?"

A calico cat slunk around the back of the recliner and jumped into Tory's lap. "That's the one."

"So, what's the problem?" he wondered.

Sandra stood and wandered toward the glass sliding door. For a moment she appeared to be watching birds on a bird feeder next to a grill. His partner, Bill noticed, always gravitated toward windows—Dean Shoemacher's window, Doreen Best's window, Maggie's dorm window.

"She doesn't give a shit about the competition, but she feels obligated to make a good showing," Tory stated. "And she's lacking a third work. She's rushing to finish something, anything at this point. She's feeling a lot of pressure from a lot of fronts right now, which is normal for a graduating senior."

Sandra bent to pet a black and white cat that had slunk by her legs.

"Don't touch that one!" Tory shouted at Sandra. "She bites. She's feral."

Sandra's hand jerked back. She straightened up and crossed the room to a wall covered with photographs.

"What time did she arrive here and what time did she leave?" Bill resumed the questioning.

Tory V. stubbed out the cigarette with disgust. "If you think that Maggie had anything to do with those murders, you're way off track, detective. There's not a malicious bone in her body."

"Please Ms. Valence," he pleaded, "we're trying to create a timeline that will hopefully eliminate her from a pool of suspects."

Tory noted the detective's imploring tone. "She arrived around 6 and she left around 9:30."

He raised an eyebrow. "You all talked for a long time."

"Besides talking, we also worked on Step Five."

"Which is?"

"*Admit to God, to ourselves, and to another human being the exact nature of our wrongs.* She does very well on the other twelve steps, but this one troubles her. It troubles her deeply. She hates this step and balks and whines when we cycle around to it. When she was a child and living on the road, I think she was involved in something really bad. Or witnessed something while she was hitching through Minnesota. I suggested that she talk to a psychologist about it, since I'm not a mental healthcare professional. I can offer advice on how to stay sober, but I'm not equipped to advise on some deeply rooted childhood trauma."

Sandra turned from the photos. "What does she say when you recommend this?"

"As I'm sure you're aware, Maggie has a vocabulary of roughly twenty words, most of them obscenities. Fuck it, she says, I'll deal with it later." Tory's face saddened. "But I wish she'd deal with it sooner. Whatever it is, it's an anchor on her soul."

His cell phone vibrated in Bill's pocket. "Excuse me," he said to Tory. He listened carefully. "Okay, we'll be there soon."

"Who was it?" Sandra asked.

"Dr. Blane." He stood and extended his card toward the writer. "Thank you for taking the time to talk to us. If you can think of anything else, please give us a call."

"Maggie's not involved in this," Tory reiterated forcefully.

He nodded hopefully and walked toward the wall of photographs. Many of the photographs were of a muscular boxer. One photograph caught his eye. The same man was with members of the Grateful Dead band, when they were all very young. The man slouched against a bus and stood directly next to Jerry Garcia, who was one of Bill father's favorite musicians. But conversations about the Dead would have to wait for another time. "Sandra, do you have any questions?"

"Yes, two." She turned in shy embarrassment toward Tory. "May I have your autograph? I've read all of your novels. I have to admit that I've had more than one Captain Sevilla fantasy."

An expression of ironic amusement flitted across Tory's face. "You and every other middle-aged woman in America." She twisted from the depths of the recliner, lumbered across the room, and scrawled a salutation on a piece of paper from the writing table.

"What's your other question?" she asked.

Sandra's view returned to the photos. "Who's that handsome boxer? Your brother?"

Tory V. stared incredulously at Sandra, her eyebrows raised. "You're kidding me, right?"

Sandra shrugged, confused. "What?"

Tory V. exhaled and said, "That's me in another lifetime."

*****

Bill squirmed as Dr. Blane enumerated the relevant facts of June Perkins' autopsy.

"The cause of death was obvious," Blane said matter-of-factly. "The garrote used was two narrow wires twisted together to prevent breakage. It hasn't yet been found. Perkins had had sexual intercourse sometime earlier in the day before the yoga class, and the DNA did not match that of her husband, Conrad. Her body exhibited previous surgical incisions from an appendectomy and a Caesarian section. Her blood indicated recent marijuana use. Marijuana ashes were found in the car's ashtray. A partially smoked joint and lighter were found on the front seat next to the victim. Metabolites of Valium were also in her bloodstream. The temperature readings taken from her body at the crime scene indicated a death around 9:45 p.m.

"Caroline from IT emailed us all the transcripts from a series of text messages between Perkins and Sanders. The advanced yoga class had run from 8:30 to 9:30. At 9:33 Perkins received a salacious text from Sanders. She responded in kind at 9:34. He answered seconds later. More texts, escalating in detail, on the same topic, bounced back and forth until 9:40.

"Both are vivid, imaginative writers," Blane commented dryly. "The details of their texts are in the report. Perkins finally texted that she was cold and wanted to end the conversation to get into her car. They agreed to an assignation the next day in his office. Then she deleted the thread of texts from her cell phone. In her car, she started to light a joint: flakes of marijuana were stuck to her bottom lip. The perpetrator was probably hiding in the back seat and rose up to wrap the wire around her throat. Her death would have been almost immediate from severe trauma and rapid blood loss. At around 10:18 the owner of the yoga studio locked up the building, found June Perkins, and called 911."

Bill flipped through his notepad and turned toward Sandra. "There's no way Maggie could have gotten from Tory's house in Woods Hole to East Falmouth in fifteen minutes, snuck into the car, disabled the horn, and murdered June Perkins by 9:45. Besides, another yoga student leaving class would have seen Maggie or her Jeep."

"And where did the cell signal from John Sanders' phone come from?" Sandra asked.

"I know what you're thinking," the pathologist said. "That it was Sanders' wife, Alice, using his phone to call from the backseat, distracting Perkins before she got in the car. Caroline already checked into that. Alice Sanders made a call to her daughter around that same time from Boston. And John Sanders' cell signal came from Boston as well. But you're going to need to verify the whereabouts of both John and Alice, and why those cell signals came from the city. And get a DNA sample from John. This was a carefully planned murder. In the trees behind the dumpster, the forest litter had been trampled, possibly for some time. We believe that the murderer might have been watching Perkins' activities over some weeks and was waiting for the right time to strike. The perp broke into the passenger's side door so that Perkins wouldn't notice a tampered lock, and then cut the wires to the horn. The killer was lying in wait in the back seat well before 9:30. And Perkins did herself no favors by parking at a distance from the other cars so she could get high before returning home."

Maggie could not be guilty of this crime! Bill wanted to shout the news to the world at the top of his lungs. Curbing his elation, he instead remarked, "Both Alice and Conrad have a motive here, but Conrad has been cleared. He was with his daughters at a neighbor's Halloween party that night."

Sandra checked her watch and rose from a chair. "I have to get home to let my dog out, or I'll be mopping up my kitchen floor tonight. Bill, we'll have to go back to the campus tomorrow to interview students and faculty again. We should enroll for art degrees for all the time we're spending there."

Dr. Blane stood and flexed her lower back. "We should be getting a lot of rain later. You two get home safely. By the way, those black boots you sent me are a positive match for those prints in the labyrinth."

*****

Maggie squeezed nearly an entire bottle of Visine into her red, puffy eyes to be presentable for drawing class, then rushed into the Gripp building just as Professor Tinkman was distributing the quizzes. Her desk and easel were by the window so she adjusted her chair toward the pane so that her eyes were not too conspicuous. Throughout the quiz she slipped a tissue from her pocket to blow her nose as quietly as possible.

"Time's up," Tinkman said imperiously, heading toward the students' desks.

Maggie handed in her quiz. If she hadn't been so distraught she might have earned a better score; she knew her answers to questions 11 and 15 were incorrect. The best she might score was a B. She glanced across the room. Olivia mouthed a concerned "Are you okay?" Lily made a sympathetic sad face, and Kyle too had had a look of curious worry.

The professor slid the quizzes into a folder on his desk. "Place your sketchpads on your easels. Hopefully you've read your syllabus and have completed all of your assignments. Today's another critique of your work."

One small break as her life spiraled into the abyss. Sketchpad review day meant that she didn't have to think. This was an advanced class of only eight seniors, so they would follow the professor from easel to easel while he commented on each student's drawings. They'd done this a number of times during the semester, so everyone was familiar with each other's drawing styles. She rose from her chair and hid at the back of the group as Tinkman chattered about line, shadow, negative space, and light. She didn't hear a word. *The boots will release me from blame*, she chanted to herself. *The boots will free me...* her favorite boots, the ones she'd bought at the mall with her paycheck from the pizzeria, the same afternoon that Brian had splurged and bought an expensive Tom Brady Number 12 football shirt. Then they'd had dinner at the food court and watched *Despicable Me 3* at the mall cinema. Those asshole cops better return those boots....

"Maggie," Tinkman said sternly.

"Hmm?"

"Your turn. Are you with us today?"

She nodded vaguely. As the professor had with the other students, he flipped through the pages of her sketchbook, commenting on line and space and...

"What's this?" Tinkman exclaimed.

All eyes swerved to fix on her.

"What assignment is this for?" The professor's voice rose

to a tenor pitch. "Which class?"

Maggie's face heated in embarrassment. "Uh... I'm sorry. I didn't have paper when I was designing a painting so I used my sketchpad." She stuttered, "It... it was all I had at the time. I'm sorry... I won't—"

"Where is this painting?" he interrupted. "In the painting studio?"

Her eyes glazed with tears. The day was a catastrophe in every way, and now this! "No. At... at my home," she explained lamely. "It's not for any painting assignment. It's just a gift for a friend. P—painted on my own time."

The professor's hand raked through his hair and he gazed for some time at the drawing. Finally he spoke. "I've never seen anything so astonishing... in all my years of teaching, not from a student, ever. Bravo, Maggie."

As the students disbanded, Professor Tinkman hurried back to Maggie's easel. "Please stay for a minute," he insisted. "We need to talk."

She shuffled confusedly and slid her materials into her frayed jean bag.

"The drawing's brilliant. But I'd love to see the painting. Will you bring it in so the faculty can see it? What inspired such a work?"

"A friend of mine took photos of his lizards and I just put them together in this montage."

"It looks like a hallucination, only not eerie, but wonderfully beautiful and primordial. Please don't give this to your friend. It should go into a gallery of modern art."

"It's not quite finished."

"When it is, will you promise me that you'll bring it in for us to see?"

She pulled on her jacket. "Yeah, sure."

Her nerves were still short-circuited so she rushed to the gazebo and wiggled a cigarette from the pack. Never, ever, had she been so desperate for a cigarette and never, ever, had a cigarette tasted so good. Friend, my ass, she thought. Bill Bleach is no friend. It had been vaguely sickening to use that term to describe him, though she couldn't very well tell the professor that the painting had been created for a duplicitous dickhead of a detective who'd come to her cottage all for the purposes of spying on his prime suspect. The reptile painting, she'd imagined earlier, was going to meet the same fate as the surfboard. But now she'd let the art faculty take a look at it. Maybe one of them might tip her off to a good auction house. Maybe the painting would fetch some money. Then she'd graduate and take off with Jessie on a thrilling voyage around the world, and never look back to asshole cops and asshole ex-boyfriends. In fact, never again would she have anything to do with men. And my boots will free me, she told herself again. Her stomach jolted from hunger; she had missed lunch while she wept into her steering wheel. She finished her smoke, hurried back to the dorm, dropped her jean bag in her room, and headed to the cafeteria.

Kyle waved at her from across the room of tables where he sat with Lily and Olivia. She gave him a slight nod and stopped at the condiments counter, where she slathered two cheeseburgers and a giant mound of french fries with catsup. Her tray was also laden with two monster pieces of cheesecake, she was that hungry. She navigated the maze of chairs and tables to join her friends.

"Kudos, Maggie!" Olivia said exuberantly. "That drawing was really special. Stink Man never compliments anyone or gives an "A." I've never seen him drool, until today."

"Is that the painting you're going to use for the Windsor Award competition?" Kyle asked. "If so, we're all cooked."

"You should, Maggie," Olivia encouraged.

"I just want to eat and not talk," Maggie said tersely, stacking a pickle on a french fry and stuffing it in her mouth.

"All of the pieces have to be displayed by the end of *this week* so that the judging can start," Lily reminded her in a patronizing tone.

"So use the reptile piece," Olivia urged again.

Maggie chewed pensively. "I don't know. The reptiles are terrestrial vertebrates. The starfish and coral are marine invertebrates. The reptiles just wouldn't go with the ocean theme of the other two."

"Then what are you going to do?" Lily asked, leaning forward across her tray.

"I already told you," Maggie said, her grumble muffled by cheeseburger. "Go down in Lindsey's submersible, get some photos, and paint something quickly this week."

Lily slouched back in her chair. "When are you going to have the time to do that?" she sighed. "I've never seen anyone procrastinate like you."

"It will get done," Maggie promised. The burger and fries were improving her mood. She no longer felt quite so testy.

"When?" Lily persisted.

"Tomorrow night. The seas are too rough tonight. Besides, it's movie night in the lounge."

"But promise me, Maggie, you're not putting chum in the water. That would attract sharks. No chum," Lily said adamantly.

"Chum, chum, lots of bloody chum." Maggie grinned playfully. Olivia and Kyle laughed.

"No!" Lily cried.

"Kidding, Lily," Maggie said drolly. "The lights on the submersible will attract the fish."

"Can I come with you?" Lily asked.

"No. I'll be there for a while, and it will be too cold for you to hang out on that platform at night. I don't want to feel rushed. I need to wait patiently for good shots." She grimaced. "Can I not talk anymore? I'm really trying to eat. I'm starving."

"You're always starving," Lily said. "What's the movie tonight?"

"An oldie and one of Spielberg's best," Olivia answered. "*Jaws.*"

*****

By the way, the black boots you sent me are a positive match for those prints in the labyrinth. Tracy Blane's words had affixed themselves like a leech to Bill's brain, sucking out all other thoughts. Twice a girl's voice coming through the speaker at the Taco King drive-through had to ask him for his order while he stared numbly at the glowing screen of menu items. *The boots are a positive match positive match positive match....*

At the incriminating words, he'd spun from the tortoise photos on Blane's office wall. "How can you be sure?" he'd nearly choked. Dr. Blane had hesitated, alerted by his agitated tone. Sandra, too, had paused in the doorway. He'd tried to feign a relaxed, disinterested stance while both women eyed him.

"There's no doubt, Bill," Blane had explained. "The boots are very worn; at some point the owner reattached the sole with Super Glue and a staple gun, which caused a buckling on the right side of the right shoe. You can see the same depression clearly in the prints. The shoe is a size seven. Same as the prints. And other wear patterns are identical to the prints in the labyrinth."

Bill thumbed through his wallet for some dollar bills and reached across the wet air toward the window of the drive-through. The teenage girl at the cash register took the money and handed him his change and a bag of Fuego tacos. He pushed on the gas pedal and headed onto the main road. A sudden and violent downpour made the road slippery and reduced visibility to almost nothing. He gripped the steering wheel to avoid being blown onto the shoulder. His windshield wipers, even slapping their fastest, were useless. The road ahead was a black blur. What a wretched night to be at sea! Ernst Hanson was somewhere off George's Bank, and Bill hoped the young fisherman was safe. Tomorrow would be a brutally long day interviewing the students and faculty—again. It was urgent that he talk to Maggie, if she would even give him the time of day. She was surly and hotheaded, but she was not stupid. Underneath the monosyllabic curses were glimmers of genius. The painting had revealed everything about her level of creativity. She was a lefty, with different brain wiring than ninety percent of the population. Dr. Nolan, too, he'd noticed, was left-handed. The artists Leonardo Da Vinci, Michelangelo Buonarroti, and Henri de Toulouse Lautrec were all lefties; actors Judy Garland, Charlie Chaplin, Marilyn Monroe, Angela Jolie and Brad Pitt... more lefties, as well as the musicians David Bowie, Kurt Cobain, Sting, and Jimi Hendrix.

No criminal would be so stupid as to use their own dive helmet and boots to commit a crime, and then use their own boat to dump the body. Maggie was being set up, plain and simple. But what if the intent was to so obviously implicate herself as to so steer the police off course, in pursuit of a putative framer who did not exist? Was she that devious, that cunning? But she couldn't have murdered June Perkins; she had an alibi. Unless she had an accomplice.... He was like a dog chasing its own tail.

Twice over the past few days his captain had called him in to his office, asking about his progress on the case.

"Do we have a serial murderer here, Bleach?"

"I don't know yet, sir." Could he have sounded like a bigger idiot?

"Let's wrap this up ASAP," the captain had said. "If these are serial killings, then the feds will move in and take over. Our lives will no longer be our own, and you and Murphy will be reassigned to the parking meters on Main Street."

Certainly the two murders were linked, but how and why? There was still no clear motive. Two murders, both savage, by two different techniques. Did that even matter? One pointed to Maggie, the other did not. She'd been with her sponsor in Woods Hole when June Perkins was killed. Did petite Maggie even have the muscle to drag Edward Gripp along the labyrinth, up the steps of the egress tunnel, through the forest, across a beach and dock, and into a boat? Impossible. She was simply too small. Could it have been two people? Doubtful. There were only prints from one individual in the tunnel.

He veered into the parking lot of his apartment building and turned off the engine. His head dropped miserably onto the steer wheel. It was he who had lost objectivity, not

Sandra; this was why the investigation was at an impasse. Essential clues were staring him in the face and he was blind to them. His heart was drowning in quicksand! All was hopeless. Besides, Maggie hated his guts. Dr. Nolan knew his feelings toward Maggie, and now Dr. Blane and Sandra Murphy knew also. Hopeless... hopeless... hopeless....

His apartment above was dark, and a plastic lawn chair sat alone on the balcony. Rain hammered the roof on his sedan. By the time he'd dashed across the parking lot and struggled with his keys, he and dinner would be sopping wet. Instead he turned up the car radio and immediately recognized the guitar riffs. He laughed plaintively. "Perfect," he lamented out loud. It was Eric Clapton singing "Layla." He would eat the tacos in the car, he decided, and contemplate his brief, brilliant career that was nearing its end.

Chapter 14

The first person on the list of campus interviews was John Sanders. Bill and Sandra found him reading a journal and puffing away at a pipe, stretched out in an expensive leather chair. Sanders rose, his body language making it clear that he would not be as convivial as during their earlier conversation. With June gone, he was not getting any. Unsmiling, he signaled the cops toward the sofa in his office; as before, they chose to stand.

There were a lot of people to interview that day and Bill had lost patience with over-privileged professors. He got right to the point. "Professor, in addition to Edward Gripp, we're now investigating the murder of June Perkins and would like to ask you some questions about your whereabouts on the night of her murder."

"Yes, a terrible thing about June. So I'm a suspect, am I?" he asked austerely.

"This is purely procedural, professor. We're interviewing all faculty members that were at the Halloween party, for a start."

"How would you describe your relationship with Dr. Perkins?" Sandra blurted.

"Dr. Perkins was in the painting department. I'm in ceramics, so our pathways did not cross often. However, over the years we were on various campus committees together. This year we were both serving on the Awards Committee."

"Which does what?" Bill inquired.

"It's a selection board for distributing faculty travel monies for conferences and research, awarding the Best Teacher and Researcher of the Year, and for selecting the Windsor Award winner, which we already discussed during our last chat," he said curtly.

"Yes, I remember," Bill replied. "Please tell us about your activities, and those of Alice, on the evening of Dr. Perkins' death."

"Alice?" The professor's voice rose in pitch. "What does she have to do with this? For that matter, what do *I* have to do with this?"

"Please, professor," Bill said firmly.

"I remember the night vividly, because I took Alice on her birthday to see the ballet at the Boston Opera House. Then we went to dinner afterwards, and we didn't get home until late. It was some time around midnight. Somewhere around this office I have the program." He searched his desk. "Here it is." He flung it onto the coffee table. "I understand that you two have been watching camera footage of the Halloween party. I'm sure that the opera house has similar cameras that will verify our presence there. And I have the receipt for the e-tickets somewhere in my computer."

"Yes, thank you. This is all very helpful. There was also evidence that Dr. Perkins had sex on the afternoon of her murder."

Sanders shrugged. "As far as I know she was a married woman. Why does that have any relevance?"

"Because the DNA from the semen did not match that of her husband."

A film of perspiration broke out across the professor's forehead.

"We'd like you to provide us with a DNA sample. Semen's not necessary. Saliva will do," Bill stated tonelessly.

Sandra thumbed through the program. "The ballet started and ended when?"

"Who knows?" the professor said caustically. "Maybe it started at 8 and ended around 10:30."

"With an intermission around 9:30?" she probed.

"That sounds about right."

"Back to the DNA...." Bill said.

"You'll get my DNA when my lawyers tell me to turn over my DNA, not before then!" Sanders snarled. "And there's no reason to talk to Alice about any of this. She and June didn't even know each other, you incompetent amateurs!"

Bill pulled from his coat pocket a transcript of the texts exchanged between Perkins and Sanders moments before the murder. "Perhaps texts such as this might have been motive for Alice. But we'll ask her."

John Sanders' eyes bulged as he read the texts. He wilted against his desk.

Sandra coldly eyed the professor. "June Perkins was killed around 9:45, Professor. These texts from 9:33 to 9:40 caused her to wait and respond, while the parking lot cleared of other cars. Your texts could not have come at a more fortuitous time for the murderer."

*****

The same two detectives are on campus again, no doubt asking questions about June Perkins. This morning they're making their way through the faculty offices. Later they'll visit the student dorms. As far as I can tell, they're making no headway in discovering the identity of Edward Gripp's murderer. Why they haven't arrested Maggie is baffling. Could they be so dim as to not have connected all of my clues? Maggie no longer wears her black boots. Presumably they're at some crime lab.

It's almost time for another trip into the tunnel. Were I to enter the forest from the small trail behind the dorm, I might be spotted by the students whose rooms face the woods. And Maggie visits the gazebo by the forest's edge a few times a day to smoke. But there's a small, well-disguised trail near the covered bridge where I enter the forest without detection and can access the tunnel. My visits have been sporadic since June's death. Sadly, there's nothing interesting to watch anymore, just tired old professors who nap in their offices all day. I want to be paid to do that.

AGAIN I check the gap on the gallery wall. Maggie STILL has not hung her final piece. The whole judging process is postponed because of this. The Awards Committee might not meet again for a week or more because of this infuriating delay. When all works are complete, I will camp out in the tunnel behind the small gallery so I don't miss a single comment from the faculty judges. Maggie's drawing continues to be at the center of every vexing conversation. I wandered by the drawing studio to have a look at her sketchbook for myself. The drawing's troubling in many ways. Her work has taken on a new level of complexity and insight. My blood boils when I hear that the elaborate reptile image is "pure genius," and will "seal the deal for the Windsor." It makes me want to break something. Instead I watch an episode of Gilligan's Island *on my tablet. I want to be as rich as Mr. and Mrs. Howell and live in a world where people wear tuxedos, feather boas, and smoke cigarettes from diamond-studded cigarette holders. If the police don't get rid of Maggie, I'll have to do the job myself.*

*****

Bill and Sandra discovered that on the night of June Perkins' murder, Sherman Hayner was visiting his mother in a hospital near Plymouth; the *Starry Night* professor was teaching an evening course on campus to twenty-three students; Captain America was at home helping his twins with math homework; and the hobbit was with his wife, shopping for living room curtains at the Cape Cod Mall. Ted Blanchard was again coaching his son's hockey team, though this time they were playing a team in Hyannis. They forwarded the information to headquarters, and the sergeant on desk duty had the task of corroborating these alibis. All of the stories checked out.

Bill and Sandra headed over to the administration cottage to find that Dean Shoemacher, Doreen Best, and Kate Taylor had been at an emergency dinner meeting with the Newbury College Board to discuss damage control. As they were wrapping up the interview with the dean, Shoemacher said gloomily, "Now the college's reputation is tainted forever. Support has fallen drastically, and fall applications are only dribbling in."

Bill checked the time on his cell phone. "Please excuse us. We need to move on to the dorm."

"Be sure to swing by the small gallery in the Gripp building," Shoemacher said. "I'm so proud of these Windsor students." The dean, amidst his despair, still showed a spark of optimism.

The gallery displaying the pieces from the Windsor nominees was unoccupied when the cops entered. Their muffled footsteps echoed across the polished wood floor and stark white walls as they studied the works, drifting apart as they lingered to study one display or another.

"Who's going to win?" Sandra wondered aloud.

The bright prints, photographs of the homeless, Etruscan vases, and crashing waves that he'd seen so far were all wondrous, and Bill shook his head uncertainly. "It's all excellent. I'm clueless. Maybe Olivia or Kyle?"

"Really? I was thinking Curt or Maggie. But who knows what the judges are looking for, and I know zero about art." She moved directly in front of a large white space between the starfish tube feet and coral tentacles paintings. "I wonder what's going here?"

"That's the question of the day," said a voice in the doorway. It was Kyle Monroe.

"I'm glad we ran into you, Kyle," Bill said. "We need to ask all of the students at the Halloween party about their whereabouts on the night of June Perkins' murder."

"Sure." Kyle leaned against the doorframe in a good-natured slouch. "I had an evening class with Dr. Johnson, and she takes attendance, which is a bummer because it means I have to show up. I hate evening lectures," he moaned. "It's three hours of droning babble on art theory once a week. I can barely stay awake, especially after a full day of classes."

"Did you ever have Dr. Perkins for any courses?" Sandra inquired.

"No, I had a different professor for Intro to Painting. I mainly do 3-D stuff like sculpture. I'm not so good at 2-D stuff like drawing and painting." He positioned himself in front of the starfish painting and admired the sweeping brush strokes. "I'm in awe of painters that can create the illusion of 3-dimensional objects on a 2-dimensional surface. The picture we saw in drawing class yesterday transcended 2-D *and* 3-D space. These reptiles were entwined with each other in some weird dream world, some solid, some transparent, some a combination of both, in a semi-solid state. It's impossible to describe. It was like nothing anyone had ever drawn before."

She raised an eyebrow. "Who drew it?"

"Maggie May-Nolan."

"And it's of reptiles?" She didn't need to look at Bill; his face glowed neon red. He'd moved silently to another side of the room and stopped in front of Curt Frederickson's computer nudes.

"Yep," Kyle answered, "which is really strange because up to now Maggie has only painted marine life. Apparently there's a painting of this drawing somewhere. Which we never hope to see. All of us in the competition are praying that she doesn't submit this painting, or it's all over for the rest of us." He glanced at his cell phone. "Oops, I'm late for class. Gotta go. By the way, I know who the killer is."

Bill turned instantly. "Who?"

"Professor Moriarty," Kyle said, with a theatrically diabolical chuckle.

Bill groaned.

"Not Professor Plum with the lead pipe in the study?" Sandra chimed in.

Kyle smiled. "Nope. Later." He disappeared around the corner.

"We need to interview Curt Frederickson," Bill remembered, stepping out onto the porch. "We never talked to him about the Halloween party or the party in Lily's room. And his girlfriend." He thumbed through his notepad. "Kristin Pucci." He looked around the room once more. "This building spooks me. It has ears."

"And eyes," she reminded him.

They moved down the porch stairs and across the lawn.

Abruptly, Bill halted and faced his partner. "I have to get this off my chest. I know you know this, but Maggie made that reptile painting for me," he said, a distraught expression contorting his features. "I met her at headquarters before these murders occurred, when I took the report about Spire Rock. When I came to campus looking for Edward Gripp, who was then only a missing person, I ran into her again. She was in the drawing studio, in tears over losing Nolan's dive helmet. She asked me to help her find the helmet. In exchange for my help she wanted to paint me a painting. I told her that that wasn't necessary, but she insisted. She told me to give her a flash drive of photos of my reptiles, so I met her at a coffee shop in Woods Hole and gave her a series of JPEGs. I didn't stay long, because that's when I got the call about Edward Gripp's body being found in the marsh.

"I saw the reptile painting when I interviewed Dr. Nolan at her beach house. I tried to talk to Maggie, with no luck. Nolan and I were stunned. The painting is breathtaking. What Kyle said was true. If Maggie enters that painting, she will win that award."

Sandra scanned the grounds. "I have a very bad feeling about this award."

"Everything about this case feels wrong! I feel like something's so obvious that we're missing it," he said in an anxious whisper.

"And then there's that goddamn laptop stolen from Gripp's boat," she said quietly. "I knew something was happening with Maggie. Be careful. She has edges, very sharp edges."

He found himself tighten. It was best not to argue.

She looked around once again to see if they were being watched. "I'm not sure Maggie committed Edward Gripp's murder," she conceded.

"Why not?"

"She's too small and scrawny to have moved Gripp's body. She never completely developed, probably due to malnourishment as a child. I've seen women with her same build in refugee camps where food was scarce." She thought to herself for a moment. "Firecrackers, Bill."

"Firecrackers?" The disjointed shift in topics was confusing, and he turned to look at her.

"They have a very short fuse. That's Maggie: spontaneous, harmless bursts of temper. She lacks forethought and deliberation. But that's not our murderer. Our murderer has a long fuse. The spark travels along it, slow, planned, and directed. Then it arrives at the dynamite. The blast's catastrophic, targeted, and intentional."

"You think it's one murderer," he whispered again. "Which means the person was in the tunnel around 10 on the night of the Halloween party, at the marina the next day around 1, and at the yoga studio around 9:45 a few days later."

"And the person is a paradox of both calm and impulsive. Imagine waiting week after week in the woods for June Perkins, and then one night climbing into her back seat and nearly removing her head. A normal brain cannot get around that." She shivered.

"This is not the work of an amateur," he whispered, "but someone who has probably killed before."

"A serial...."

"But if we let on, the FBI's going to take over and it's out of our hands."

"So we say nothing for the time being. And I think we finally found the motive."

They said it in unison. "The Windsor Award."

*****

The detectives located Curt Fredrickson and Kristin during the lunch break in a room full of workout equipment, exercise mats, and free weights. Curt had a crew cut and a cleanly shaven face. Kristin was a freckled blonde with glistening hazel eyes. At the approach of the two detectives, Curt dropped a barbell and Kristin stepped off a stair climber machine. They dropped side-by-side onto an exercise bench.

When asked about their activities on the evening of the Halloween party, Curt said, "Kristin and I are in training and weren't drinking. We remember everything."

Finally, reliable, sober witnesses!

"A bunch of us went from the Halloween party to Lily's room where everyone was drinking beer, doing shots of vodka, and playing Twister. More and more people packed into the room and it got ridiculously hot. Everyone started taking off their costumes. Ernst opened the window. He,

Olivia and Kyle were standing by the window when Milo and Nick came by and asked if they could climb in."

"Who are Milo and Nick?" Bill asked, exasperated. That's all they needed at this point, more potential suspects.

"Townies who wander by the dorm every few weekends, looking to score weed. Since they don't have a swipe card, they wanted to climb in the window."

"And where was Lily?" Sandra asked.

"She was in the middle of the Twister game with us. We were all tangled up. She called to Milo and Nick that it was okay, so Kyle handed Maggie's desk chair out the window. He placed Lily's chair inside. The townies climbed in, passed through the room, and disappeared down the hall. They never returned. I guess they found a room where they could get high."

"Then what?" Bill prodded.

Curt frowned. "Kyle was obnoxiously drunk, like every weekend. He put on Ernst's cape and then he pretended to be Dracula and kept trying to bite Kristin."

"That freak left a bruise on my shoulder! Look!" Kristin pointed to a purple mark. "You can still see it!"

"When Kristin shrieked, I lost my temper and shoved him onto Maggie's bed. He was too drunk to stand up, so he curled himself against the wall and went to sleep."

"Was he still wearing the cape?" Bill asked.

"Yes."

"When it got too crowded to play Twister, we left."

"When was that?"

Curt looked questioningly at Kristin and shrugged. "Maybe around 11."

Kristin nodded. "Yeah, I think so."

"Then what?"

"We went back to Kristin's room. She has a single room. I spent the night there. The next morning we ate breakfast together in the cafeteria. Then I went to lift weights and Kristin went back to bed."

"What did you two do in the afternoon? Around one o'clock?" Sandra broke in.

Curt paused to think. "Kristin and I met up after lunch and took a run down the Falmouth-Woods Hole bike trail. We try to run every weekend when the weather's nice."

"And what did you two do on the Tuesday evening of June Perkins' death?" Bill asked.

"Both of us are in Dr. Johnson's art theory course," Curt replied. "Dr. Perkins was a great professor. This whole thing's so messed up."

"Is Kyle in your art theory class?" Sandra said.

"Yes. He sits in the back row and sleeps the whole time," Kristin tattled.

"And Maggie May-Nolan, Lily Tate, and Olivia Moreno?" Sandra asked.

"No. They must have taken it last semester. It's a course you need to graduate," Curt clarified.

"I hear that you're a nominee for the Windsor Award," Bill said to Curt. "Congratulations."

"Thanks. I was really surprised to have been nominated."

"What are you going to do when you graduate? Be employed in the art field?"

Curt sadly shook his head. "I wish, but I'm not that good. I'm joining the army. I need a stable job to pay off my student loans. Both my father and grandfather were army officers, so that seems the logical way to go."

"So what do you plan to do in the army? I was a jarhead, military police," Sandra said.

"That's cool. I could never be a marine. It involves too much swimming," Curt admitted. "Hopefully I'll do something in arts and media, or with computers."

"But Curt's in good enough shape to be a Navy Seal," Kristin bragged.

"I'm not joining the Navy, Kristin," he reminded her with forced pleasantness. "We've had this discussion before."

"But the Seals are the coolest—" Kristin whimpered.

"I'm not going to be a Seal. I can barely swim," Curt said, losing patience.

"And how about you, Kristin?" Bill asked, attempting to diffuse the bickering.

"I'm undecided," she said, glowering at Curt.

"She's going to be an Army, not a Navy, wife," Curt said testily.

"One last question," Bill said. "During the party in Lily's room, do you remember anyone leaving for an extended period of time?"

Curt and Kristin looked blankly at one another. "It's impossible to tell," he finally replied. "The room got so hot that people started climbing out the window to cool off. People were handing beers out the window and drinking outside by the parking lot."

*****

"What?" Olivia Moreno snapped when the detectives tapped on her open door. A rerun of *I Love Lucy* was playing on her small TV. That day her arctic tattoo was covered by a long-sleeved black T-shirt that had an image of the Borg

Cube and read "Resistance is Futile". She pointed a clicker at the TV and muted the sound.

"In answer to your question, no, I did not kill June Perkins," Olivia stated preemptively. "I loved that woman. She was the best professor on this campus. And I hope you catch the prick that did it and string him up high. I was with Amy Jacobsen all night in the printmaking studio, trying to finish up a project that we're working on together. Our professor, Dr. King, was there all evening and can vouch for our presence. Besides, my piece of shit car is in the shop again, so I couldn't have gone off campus even if I'd wanted to."

"During Lily's party, do you remember anyone leaving for an extended period of time?" Bill asked.

"I don't remember. Ernst's and my costumes were so hot that we stood by the window for a while. The room got hotter and hotter, so people climbed out the window to drink outside. It got way too hot, so we left pretty early and cooled off by sneaking into the women's shower room before going to bed." She smiled brazenly at Bill.

*****

The last stop for the two detectives was the dorm room of Lily Tate and Maggie May-Nolan. The whereabouts of Maggie on the evening of June Perkins' death had already been confirmed by Tory V., so Lily was the remaining student to be questioned. Lily answered the door immediately, which was a relief, as it precluded the need for campus search. They stepped into the double room and hesitated; Maggie was asleep under a comforter.

"Don't worry. You won't wake her," Lily explained in normal decibels. "She sleeps like a log." She signaled them into the back, behind the privacy curtain. "She wants to paint tonight, so she's napping today. Chamomile tea knocks her right out."

Sandra made a beeline toward the window and peered outside. There was about two feet of space between the windowsill and the hedge, which meant that students could have climbed out the window with ease, sidestepped the space between the hedge and building, and lingered on the sidewalk next to the parking lot. A pair of binoculars was the sole object on the windowsill. She lifted them to her eyes. To the right was a clear view across the field, with the sculptures all the way to the covered bridge; to the left and across the student parking lot was a view to the front entrance of the Gripp Center. Directly across the circular driveway was the administration cottage, where the windows of Edward Gripp's corner office were curtained.

"Whose binoculars are these?" Sandra asked.

"Maggie's. Or maybe they're Lindsey Nolan's. We use them on the boat. Maggie drives while I watch for shoals. We've also spotted whales with them."

"Really? In Buzzards Bay? Whales come in that close to shore?" Bill asked curiously.

"No, they're out in deeper waters." Lily blinked back tears. "I know you're here to ask about Dr. Perkins. It's really horrible about her. We adored her. She was definitely one of our favorites."

"We're asking all of the students about their activities on the night of Dr. Perkins' death."

"Sure. No problem. I was at band practice that night. I play violin for the Lighthouse String Ensemble. We have a fall concert coming up, so we've been putting in very long hours. Our rehearsals on Tuesday nights go from 7 to 10, on some nights until 10:30." She opened a violin case on a desk. "Look at this beauty," she murmured reverently. "Of course, it's not a Stradivarius, but the sound is close." Her hand stroked the smooth, brown wood. "It was a birthday gift from my parents."

"I love music more than anything. I wish I could play the electric guitar," Bill said regretfully, "but I'm hopelessly tone deaf."

Lily closed the violin case and opened the bottom drawer of a desk. She rested the case inside gently, as if laying a baby in a cradle.

He stared at the desk where Lily had placed the violin. "Isn't this Maggie's desk?"

"No, why?" Lily asked in turn.

"The chamomile tea and the dive stickers on the desk. I know Maggie's specialty is painting underwater scenes."

"I'm a better diver," Lily boasted. "I have two advanced certifications, Advanced Open Water and Cave Diving, while Maggie's only done the basic course."

He pulled aside the privacy curtain. Maggie hadn't so much as stirred during the entire conversation. She was absolutely zonked. Suddenly, the memory of the heated exchange between Maggie and Lindsey Nolan resurfaced and struck a gong. Night diving. Lobsters. A dive partner:

"Night diving's so dangerous, Maggie. No more night diving. Hopefully you weren't diving alone."

"I wasn't. Actually I was doing underwater photography while my dive partner was catching lobsters."

"Lily," he asked innocently, "if I was to get dive certified, where's the best place around here to catch lobsters? I love lobster tail and melted butter."

Sandra looked inscrutably at him. Her partner was terrified of the water.

"Definitely this place called Spire Rock. That's out beyond the Vineyard," Lily said.

*****

Bill and Sandra swung by Doreen Best's office for the academic transcripts of the Windsor nominees in question. For the rest of the afternoon, they would focus primarily on the female suspects; although the degree of savagery was atypical for a woman, it would have been impossible for Kyle, Curt, or Ernst to fit into a female size-seven boot.

At the headquarters they filled their mugs with coffee and settled down for an afternoon at their computers. Kristin Pucci was added to the list of suspects, as a victory for Curt would be a vicarious victory for her, and her expectations and ambitions for her boyfriend were high. But a background check of Kristin Pucci from Orlando, Florida, revealed a stable nuclear family, no involvement with the police, no indications of violence—in short, nothing out of the ordinary.

Winning the Windsor Award would directly benefit Amy Jacobsen, Olivia Moreno, Lily Tate, and Maggie May-Nolan. But Amy Jacobsen, like Kristin Pucci, had nothing questionable in her past. She was the daughter of a stockbroker and an art dealer, and had grown up in an affluent neighborhood by Central Park. Olivia Moreno had had a prior arrest at a Sarah Palin rally, but had no other record of involvement with the police. She was one of a pair of twins from Amherst, Massachusetts, where her father was a political science professor and her mother an economist. She'd meet Ernst Hanson when they'd taken a summer school class together at Amherst College two years before. The twin sister was a journalism major at UCLA.

The academic transcripts of Lily and Maggie sat side by side on Bill's desk. Maggie had straight "A"s in all of the humanities courses, and "C"s and "D"s in college algebra, general chemistry, and introductory biology. Lily had "A"s and "A" minuses in all subjects. Yet it was Lily who had been unwilling to report the alleged body (now known to be hazardous chemical waste) to the police. Why? Lily had no police record at all. Maggie's police record was known to both detectives, and yet it was Maggie who'd filed the report with the police—albeit grudgingly.

Lily had alibis for the nights of both murders. But Maggie only had an alibi for the night of June Perkins' murder. And what if Tory V. had mistaken the time Maggie left her house? If Maggie had left at 8:30 instead of 9:30, then she could have made it to Falmouth in time.

Superficially, the two roommates had a lot in common. They both had upper middle-class families. Maggie's adopted mother/guardian was a bioengineer, and her adopted father, now deceased, the former Boston Red Sox player, Rob Jenkins. After Jenkins' death due to a respiratory tract infection, Nolan had married Derick Briggs, a microbiologist who worked at the marine laboratory in Woods Hole.

"How does a healthy athlete like Rob Jenkins suddenly die of a respiratory tract infection?" Sandra inquired from across their office. "And the next husband's conveniently an infectious diseases expert?" she pointed out suggestively. "That doesn't sit right. I'd like to know what Nolan was doing on Tuesday night. Maybe she fell in love with John Sanders and wanted June out of the way? She's certainly strong. And she's even blonde. How solid are her alibis?"

Bill remained wordless. From his visits to Dr. Nolan's dive business and home, she seemed a no-nonsense, type-A workaholic, too obsessed with work to contemplate anything like murder. Besides, from the camera footage at the Halloween party, she appeared quite enamored with her current husband. Did she even know John Sanders? There was no footage of them talking to one another at the party—but neither were John and June, with the exception of the brief encounter with the book.

"What if Nolan and Briggs created some super bug that killed Rob Jenkins, and they were the ones dumping chemical waste at Spire Rock," she expounded, as if this epiphany would unravel the case.

"You're making my thoughts reel," he said. "I'm trying to interpret this data from the IRS. God, I hate doing taxes!"

Lindsey Nolan's tax returns indicated that her yearly salary was paid from an NSF grant. Other income was generated from various patents and inventions. In total, her yearly earnings way exceeded a typical middle-class income, yet her family lived fairly modestly. She owned a SUV, an ancient pickup truck, and a Jeep; the old beach house, cluttered with books and nautical memorabilia, was a bit rundown. Nolan's extravagance seemed to be boats.

As for Lily, she had grown up in an exclusive gated community in Connecticut. Her father, Evan, was a CPA, and her mother, Jean, a small business owner. Evan and Jean drove a Lexus and a Corvette, respectively, and recently an addition on their home had been constructed that included an indoor lap-swimming pool.

That reminded him that both students were divers. Another commonality between the two roommates was that they were both transfer students and had lived together during both their junior and senior years. Maggie had always lived in the Woods Hole area (after age 13), and had attended a local community college during her freshman and sophomore years, despite having been accepted to the best art colleges in the country. That fact was puzzling. Certainly Nolan had the means to send Maggie to any of these schools. Why had Maggie opted to forego top art schools for a nameless community college with no art program?

Lily had attended an exceptional art and music college in the Midwest. Her grades there were excellent. Why, then, had she transferred?

Bill decided to find out and placed a call to the college's Office of Student Life. After a few minutes, he nudged Sandra and switched the call to speaker mode. They listened for over ten minutes. The director of Student Life was tremendously helpful. She remembered the incident as if it had been yesterday. Lily Tate had lived in a suite on the sixth floor in a high rise on campus. Three other girls were her roommates. There had been a particularly raucous party. Some time during the night, one of the roommates, Ellen Caruso, from Houston, Texas, fell from their balcony. A lethal combination of alcohol and sleeping pills were found in Caruso's bloodstream. Overwrought by the incident, Lily and another one of the roommates had transferred to other institutions. The administrator remembered quite clearly the heated conversations with the mother, Mrs. Tate, who aggressively accused "the slack supervision by the residential assistants and lax university alcohol policies." She'd threatened legal action. In the end, the university had refunded the Tate family two semesters' tuition and were relieved that they finally went away.

Bill and Sandra stared at each other. "Sleeping pills," he cried, leaping to his feet. "I need to talk to Maggie!"

"She was going somewhere to paint," Sandra reminded him. "I'll check the university and local police reports and newspapers about the Caruso accident. And I'm going to check on Mrs. Tate." She tore off her shoulder holster with its gun and handed it to him. "Take this. Just in case."

Bill paced in front of police headquarters, not knowing what to do next. He fumbled for his cell phone and pushed the button for Maggie's number. There was no answer.

He could barely calm his shaky voice. "Maggie, this is Detective Bleach. Bill Bleach. Please call me as soon as you get this message. It's urgent that we talk! Right now! Maggie, this cannot wait!"

His trembling fingers stumbled across the letters in attempt to send a text. "please txt me URGENT"

A response from Maggie indicated that she was no longer napping. "F O"

Bill: we need to talk about ur boots NOW URGENT

Bill: this CANT WAIT

Bill: NOW! THIS CANT WAIT!

Bill: where r u?

Bill: i think ur being framed

Maggie: ill b @ daves marina ocean rd green monster 10 min

Bill: on way

*****

Bill exhaled a giant sigh of relief. Across the parking lot the Jeep was parked next to a solitary houseboat. For the moment she was safe.

He'd driven by Dave's Marina countless times, although he avoided the marsh road in the summer months, when the intersection was invariably blocked by pickup trucks and boat trailers. He'd stopped at the marina once before, to use the restroom in the bathhouse and to buy a sandwich in the bait shop. All of the slips that day had been occupied by an assortment of watercraft, and he recalled waiting in a long line of customers for his sandwich. Scruffy boaters had wandered up and down the dock, while muted music (Jimmy Buffet) had played from a boat's stereo system. Another line of trucks and boats had been waiting their turn at the boat ramp.

The chronology of Maggie's life was finally falling into place. This was the marina where she and Lindsey Nolan had lived together after their release from rehab. Now the marina was desolate, all of the slips vacated except for the old houseboat, the *Green Monster*. The bait store was closed for the evening, and only two lights penetrated the grey dusk, one from an apartment above the bait store, the other from the *Green Monster*.

He climbed from the car and scanned the marina for any unusual movements. A cat circled a dumpster near the bathhouse; otherwise the marina was quiet. The crickets and insects of summer were long silent. He inhaled deeply, eyed the water with trepidation, and walked across the dock with his heart in his throat. The houseboat appeared low and stable, and he stepped quickly over the gap of water onto the deck.

Maggie flung open the door, a cigarette dangling from her lips, and he froze. "Don't just stand there. You're letting out the heat." The door slammed behind him. "What the hell does this mean?" She shoved her cell phone toward his face: "*i think ur being framed!*"

"Whose boat is this?" he asked, disregarding the phone. The *Green Monster* was nothing like Edward Gripp's boat. It had a homey, disheveled feel and was tacky with Red Sox trinkets and memorabilia.

"What does this *mean*?!" she ranted, cell phone extended. "Don't ignore me! *You* called this meeting. Now talk!"

"Please tell me whose boat this is. Where am I? Then we'll talk," he said, unmoved.

"I don't have a lot of time. I'm in a big hurry, actually. I'm supposed to be painting tonight."

"Whose boat is this?" he persevered.

She heaved her phone into the sofa cushions across the room. She dropped onto the edge of a chair and buried her face in her hand.

"Maggie..."

"It's where I cut up the bodies."

"That's not funny!"

"You've made me a basket case," she cried. "I have midterms and a painting to complete before the end of the week, and I'm getting nothing done. I did not commit those murders!"

"Whose boat?" he urged again.

She dropped to her knees and warmed one hand in front of a space heater, while the other held her lit cigarette. "It was Rob Jenkins' boat. Now it's Lin's. He left everything to her. But she never comes here. It's been sitting here for years. Lin's spooked by this place, but doesn't say why. But I can sense it."

"What happened here?"

"I don't know, but I think they had a big fight here that ended it all." She rose and flicked cigarette ashes into a sink in the galley.

"This place doesn't feel scary to me."

"Me, either. It's full of happy memories. All of us used to live here. In three houseboats in a row, *Anne Bonny*, *Mary Read*, and *Green Monster*." She wiped away a tear. "Then Rob fucked it all up. He started drinking again and had an affair with this bitch, Sheila, from the bait store. In one day, Lin packed us all up and moved the other boats to the beach house. It's all my fault. I'm the one who told her."

"And what happened to Rob?"

"He couldn't stop drinking. He had twelve years of sobriety before he took up with Sheila. Twelve! He was a member of AA and she *knew* that, and *still* she encouraged him to *drink* with her! Then he caught pneumonia or something while he was drinking out in the woods. I'll never forgive him for drinking or for that affair. Everything was perfect before that. Lin adored him and was good to him. She didn't deserve that. Men are fucking assholes."

He gazed out the window, again searching the parking lot of the marina. "Do any of your friends know of this place? Have you ever brought any of them here?"

She shook her head. "No. This is the first time I've been back in years. I don't understand your texts. What about my boots? How am I being framed?" The fierceness in her voice returned. "Or is this a ploy to get me to talk to you? I don't have a lot of time. I need to paint!"

He took another deep breath and crossed to the galley. "No, Maggie, tonight you're going to talk to me." He grabbed her shoulders, surprising the both of them. His eyes bore into hers. Red splotches dotted his cheeks. "I can't help you if I don't have information. The painting can wait. This is very important, in fact, much more important!"

She angrily shook him off, but he grabbed her hand. "Sit. Please!" He pulled them on to the carpeting by the space heater. "Your boots were at the place where Edward Gripp was killed. I need to know why. How."

She shuddered. "It... it couldn't be. It's a mistake. I... I was in Woods Hole, at the seawall, then at the cottage, and then at Stony Beach. I was wearing my high-tops. I didn't—"

"But someone took your boots from the party," he interrupted. "Does anyone ever borrow your clothing?"

"All of us borrow each other's clothes all the time."

"Was anyone borrowing your boots?"

"No. We don't lend each other shoes. Just shirts, scarves, and stuff."

"Olivia, Amy, Lily, Kristin?"

"Yes, we all wear each other's stuff all the time." She dabbed her eyes. "Why do you ask about them?"

"Because someone does not want you winning the Windsor Award."

"Why?" she asked plaintively. "Who gives a shit about that?"

"Somebody very much gives a shit about it. And who that is, is what I need to find out. Where do you keep your boat keys? When you had the *Jack Rackham* on campus, where did you keep those keys?"

"I have a bowl on my desk where I keep my swipe card, cigarettes, and keys."

He hesitated for a moment. "So here's what I believe happened, and this information *must remain* on this boat between you and me. Do you understand this?"

She nodded.

"Someone who was wearing your boots, your dive helmet, and Ernst Hanson's cape, stolen off a very drunk Kyle Monroe, killed Edward Gripp, then stole a tarp from the painting studio. In the middle of the night, the person dragged the corpse to the dock in the tarp, stole your boat, and dumped Gripp's body in Buzzards Bay."

"Where did the murder occur?"

"I can't answer that exactly, but it was in the Gripp building and it was very dark. The dive helmet not only concealed the identity from the cameras, it provided a light."

The hot filaments of the space heater cast orange light on Maggie's face. "I'm burning up." She stood, untangled her scarf and tugged off her jacket. "What's going to happen to me?"

"I don't know. But to me it's an obvious frame job." He stood also. "I'm ordering us a pizza. I'm starved. Do not try to escape," he ordered, zipping his coat.

"Yeah, right. Like I wanna swim across a freezing pond tonight," she grumbled, lighting another cigarette.

He stepped outside onto the deck of the houseboat to place the order. Then he called Sandra.

"You okay?" Sandra asked from her car. "And Maggie?"

"Both fine. What did you find out?"

"Nothing conclusive. Lily and the other roommates were questioned by both township and university police about Ellen Caruso's death, but it was ruled an accident. Especially when the toxicology report came back. But that Mrs. Tate's the helicopter-parent-from-hell. She gives me the creeps.

Earlier records from Lily's school district showed a number of letters and emails from the mother, insisting on Lily's admittance into the Gifted Student Program, even though her test scores were below the cut. Mrs. Tate claimed that the teacher administering the test had harassed Lily, causing her to feel flustered and intimidated and that that had resulted in low scores. The school district did not want to touch the allegation with a ten-foot pole and permitted Lily entrance to the program."

He hunched his coat up around his ears. The temperature was dropping rapidly on this lovely, starry night. "Anything more about the other students nominated for the Windsor?"

"Nothing yet. I'll continue first thing tomorrow morning. I'm heading home. I'm trying to have something called a life."

"Will you teach me how to do that?" he asked facetiously.

"Remind Maggie not to drink any tea unless she makes it."

"I will."

"Where's my gun?"

"Locked in the trunk."

"Be careful, my friend. Get home soon. And watch out for those edges."

"I don't see any," he said honestly.

"I was afraid you were going to say that. Edges aren't seen, they're felt."

*****

He should have ordered two pizzas, Bill realized. Maggie could eat. Between the two of them, the whole pie was devoured in minutes. "Why didn't you go to art school at RISD, or one of the others?" he asked, refilling cups of ginger ale at the galley table.

"I got pregnant. I have no clue how it happened, because I was using birth control," she answered, picking cheese off the box. "So the plan was that I'd have the baby, stay near the family, and go to school part-time. Everyone was thrilled: Brian, Lin, the McLeod's, Brian's family. Everyone except me. I was terrified and miserable. I have HIV, and the thought of putting a child through all of that, endless trips to the doctor's and changing meds, which may or may not work, or may or may not make the baby sick or tired... it didn't seem fair. And I don't have the parenting genes. I only do one thing well—paint. I'd be a horrible parent. I'm a complete scatterbrain." She stood and walked to the aft window. "So I opted out. Without consulting Brian, or anyone. Now I'm persona non grata in both our families." She changed the subject. "I'm still hungry. I wonder if Dave has ice cream."

"Who's Dave?"

She pointed to the apartment over the bait shop. "Dave who owns this marina. It was his wife, Sheila, who ran off with Rob, leaving Dave and Lin in the lurch."

"What's Brian's last name? Would he frame you to get back at you?"

"Brian? Impossible. He's a good guy, and I was a shit to him."

"But he stood you up, leaving you with no alibi."

She vigorously shook her head. "No way it's him."

"What's his last name?"

"I've already told you too much. My personal life's none of your goddamn business."

"Everything about your life is my business now. Two people from your college are dead and I don't want to deal with any more bodies, including yours."

"Let's get ice cream somewhere."

"You're stalling. His last name?"

"Cooper, but you're wasting your time."

Her cell phone vibrated from the sofa. She stared at the text for a moment. The salon was heavy in silence.

"Maggie?"

She leapt onto the sofa and bounced across the cushions like a delighted child. "Get your coat on, detective! You're taking Jessie McCabe's Expedition Artist out for ice cream!"

*****

Ted Blanchard is a complete stooge. "Mr. Blanchard," I asked in my most polite voice, "can I use the air pump to inflate my bicycle tire?" That was back in September. In his odd, morose way, he agreed and scurried back to his cluttered office in the Maintenance Building. He watches Stanley Cup replays all day and is annoyed when he's interrupted to do any part of his job. Next to the air pump were a series of building keys, including the key to the Maintenance Department's work skiff. I pedaled to a hardware store in Falmouth, copied the key, and pedaled back to campus. "Mr. Blanchard," I called again, "my back tire's also a little low." His arm flailed over his head in a dismissive wave and his eyes never left the hockey game. I returned the original key to the key rack and pretended to fill my rear tire. Then I pedaled on my way. After that, throughout the fall I snuck to the skiff at night, started the engine and topped off the gas. One never knows when one might need a boat… for dumping old perverts. How clever was I to toss wet sand around the Jack Rackham, stamp around leaving the telltale boot prints across the deck, and retie the boat lines to the cleats in a messy jumble, all to incriminate the wrong boat? Maggie always meticulously coils the boat lines on the dock in Flemish coils. She must have gone berserk. It's too funny.

Tonight the stars are neon in their intensity. The work skiff floats against the black fringe of a marsh, waiting and unseen. I check my cell phone again. Everything in life—and death—is timing. I pull my hood over a balaclava mask as a chilly breeze picks up and watch the platform in the bay. For some time, there's no sound. Then I hear it, the low murmur of the Jack Rackham. *It will take some time for Maggie to tie up the trawler at the platform and lower the submersible. Timing, timing, timing… it's all about perfect timing.*

I raise a monocular to my eye. Her slender silhouette climbs over the gunwale and ties off the fore and aft lines. For some minutes her black figure moves around the platform. A dim light's turned on and she hovers over the controls of the crane. Finally a cable squeals and the dangling submersible is lowered toward the water. At last, a gentle splash. She tosses something square in shape into the open hatch of the submersible. That's rough treatment of a bag with a sketchpad and camera. Then she climbs inside. The hatch shuts, and the submersible lights flash on, changing the black water to a murky pea green. The submersible then disappears in green bubbles.

The well-tended outboard of the skiff starts right up.

*****

In a corner booth of the ice cream shop, Maggie ordered a banana split, french fries, and a chocolate milk shake, while Bill asked for a butterscotch sundae and coffee. His eyes lingered on her. The contrasts were stunning: light hair, dark skin, light eyes, full, long eyelashes. It was just his luck. Just as she seemed to no longer hate him, he finds that she would be leaving in January to go on a round-the-world voyage, filming underwater documentaries with Jessie McCabe. Where handsome filmmakers and sailors would be all over her. In two months, Maggie wouldn't even remember him.

Focus, Bill, focus. You're a policeman, he reminded himself. She's still—the thought was unbearable—a suspect, and, more horrible still, a potential victim.

"There's an electric teapot in your dorm room," he said reluctantly.

"What about it?"

"Who drinks tea with you?"

"All of us drink it."

"Who's us?"

"Amy, Lily, Olivia, me, and sometimes Kyle, when he's trying to detox from the booze. We share different kinds of teas. Green tea, vanilla chai, pumpkin... we're trying to eat and drink healthy and avoid the chemicals in soda. Olivia insists that we not purchase food from transnational companies, so we try to buy local and organic."

"Who makes the tea?"

"It depends. I usually make it during the day, and Lily makes chamomile at night so we can sleep."

He leaned across the table. "Will you do me a favor?"

She frowned slightly. "You're a buzz kill. You're getting paranoid and spooky again."

"That's my business, to be paranoid and spooky." He smiled apologetically. She grimaced. He leaned further across the table. "It's really important," he repeated quietly. "Will you not drink anything that you have not made yourself? Promise me that?"

She made a throw away gesture. "You think one of my friends is going to poison me? That's preposterous."

"I want to you take every precaution and have your wits about you at all times. This killer's a complete savage and sicko. And very methodical."

The ominous warning sunk in and her breathing accelerated. It was a huge gamble, but he slid his hand across the table and covered hers. Hers was shaking imperceptibly. "Promise me, Maggie."

She looked uneasily at her covered hand. "Alright. There's no way I'm going to get a new painting started tonight, or get anything done this week. I'm going to have to use your reptile painting. You can have it after the competition's over." She pulled her hand back slowly and checked the time on her phone. "It's still early. Do you live with anyone? Is it okay to go to your place to see your pets?"

"Yes, no... ur, I mean no, yes!"

*****

I peer over the edge of the platform. The submersible's a few feet below the surface. The cable's taut and squeaks with each gust of wind. Maggie's head is covered in the same wool hat she wears every winter, the navy blue one with the red B for the Boston Red Sox. It's difficult to see what she's doing through the small Plexiglas hatch. She appears to be fidgeting near the control panel, probably positioning her camera against the front window for the best angle. I check the time. I have to work fast. American Idol's on in an hour.

My original plan was to cut the cable with heavy-duty wire cutters, but the cable's too thick. Instead, I pull a small blowtorch from my bag. I return once again to the platform's edge. Over the past days I've been doing extensive homework on small one- and two-manned submersibles. It's amazing what one can find on the Internet. This submersible is far from complete. There are no propellers at the rear of the craft, so the propulsive system has not yet been installed, nor are the oxygen tanks in the oxygen receptacles. Maggie's relying solely on oxygen that's trapped within the submersible. From my calculations, there's just enough oxygen for an hour's worth of work before resurfacing and replenishing the oxygen supply with atmospheric air. She's already been down for seventeen minutes.

But this submersible won't ever be resurfacing. I pull protective goggles over my balaclava and direct the butane blowtorch at a bracket that attaches the cable to a metal crane. Time to go to work. A blue flame leaps from the nozzle of the blowtorch. After a while I check the time again. This is taking longer than anticipated. Finally the bracket glows red, but I'm pissed off. I'll certainly miss the first ten minutes of my show, and one of the most amusing parts is the judges' opening remarks. Finally, the metal liquefies and stretches. The cable emits a low moan. Glowing metal is a lovely shade of orange. The cable continues its mournful sound. The pitch intensifies. I leap behind the instrument panel and curl myself into a ball. I peek around the edge.

SNAP! The cable rips along the metal crane and loops wildly in the air. It splats into the dark water.

The submersible rocks unfettered. Then I gaze in fascination at the green lights plummeting toward the depths. I dash back to the instrument panel and snip all wires and circuits. Who knows what emergency power systems these engineers might have installed? I can't take any chances. I peek over the edge of the platform once again. The green glow dims and finally disappears in a shroud of black. For ten more minutes I pace impatiently, but the waters around the platform remain still. Nothing's coming up off the frigid bottom tonight.

At the cleats, I unravel the lines to the Jack Rackham and shove the trawler off the platform. I climb back into the work skiff and start the outboard. Damn! By the time I get to shore, I'll have missed at least twenty minutes of American Idol.

Chapter 15

A clamor of cabinet doors in the kitchen woke Bill the next morning. He struggled out of bed and watched from the bedroom door. Maggie was helping herself to orange juice and powdered donuts, then she returned to the sofa where she'd fallen asleep the night before, after watching *American Idol* and some shows on Comedy Central. He'd covered her with a blanket, taken a shower *alone*, and fallen into bed *alone*, but his sleep had been a surprisingly contented one. For that evening, she was out of harm's way.

It would be a hectic day at headquarters, conducting searches on the Internet, making phone calls to confirm students' alibis, and reviewing camera footage. Something about the footage was nagging him, but he couldn't put his finger on what it was. He headed for the bathroom for a shower and shave, changed into his suit and tie, and hurried to the terraria to feed the reptiles. Maggie, bundled in her jacket, scarf, and Red Sox winter hat, waved from beyond the sliding glass door of the small balcony, where she'd absconded with the bag of donuts and her cigarettes.

They left his apartment and stopped at a drive-through, where he bought them breakfast sandwiches and coffees, and then headed toward Dave's marina. All activities with Maggie involved eating. It had been wonderful to have a woman around the apartment the night before; it was a first since he'd moved to take the job on the Cape. Should she ever live with him, his grocery bill would triple... he wished that he would have such a problem. His fantasies continued to swirl, while she flicked through new reptile photos on her smartphone, commenting on Jethro's and Olivia's patterns and colors. He stopped next to her Jeep. As she slid out of the front seat, he urged her again to be vigilant, and to avoid all food or drink prepared by students in the dorm. She agreed and closed the car door. As he was backing away, he heard a small tap next to his ear. He unrolled his window. She said nothing, instead she pressed her lips against his— tobacco and powdered sugar. Yes! This was not a sisterly kiss!

His euphoria was short-lived, as Sandra was waiting for him in front of headquarters. Car keys jangled in her hand.

"Let's go," she said bleakly. "Something's happened at NK Dive Technologies. Dr. Blane and her crew are waiting for us."

News vans lay in wait along the main road, and news helicopters circled the gray skies over Buzzards Bay. Uniformed policemen waved them through a roadblock at the entrance to the dive business. The NKDT pier was already a circus. A number of police cruisers, a CSI van, and —Bill's stomach lurched—an FBI sedan clustered around the boathouse-turned-engineering lab. The police appeared to be taking statements from the engineers, including Harry Cheng.

Bill squinted toward the bay. A Coast Guard emergency response boat was towing a pilotless *Jack Rackham* into the dock. A swarm of inflatables belonging to the Underwater

Recovery Team (URT) had cordoned off the waters around the platform. Worst of all, a solemn Dr. Blane was standing on a teetering police boat, gesturing for him and Sandra to climb aboard.

Bill climbed into the boat, hoping his hands didn't tremble. If he looked steadily at a single, stationary object on the boat, and completely ignored the water in his peripheral vision, he might not get sick. At least, he'd read that. His leg started jumping uncontrollably. He stared fixedly at Sandra's sturdy walking shoes. Thankfully, there'd been no time to eat his breakfast sandwich. He'd saved it to munch on while working on his computer. If only he could beam himself to his computer this very moment... but instead his stomach flip-flopped with every swell. Sandra and Dr. Blane sympathetically glanced his way, expecting him to retch over the side at any time. After a seeming eternity, the boat stopped, but now came the precarious bit of jumping over a moving gap between the boat and platform. He might as well be attempting a leap across the Grand Canyon, the chasm was that terrifying. He swallowed, hopped with a gulp, and landed on the wooden planks, but the rocking platform was no better than the rocking boat and he grabbed desperately for the instrument panel.

"Don't touch that, Bill," Dr. Blane scolded. "This is a crime scene."

Embarrassed, he stuffed his hands in his coat pocket and stood with his feet splayed wide, imagining for a moment that he was surfing, a sport for lunatics with a death wish. He struggled to listen to Blane's explanation of what had happened. She ducked her head under the instrument panel and pointed her white-gloved hand to a tangle of severed wires.

"All cut," Blane said.

"But no wire cutters were found onboard?" Sandra asked.

"No. Nor have they been located on the bottom. The perpetrator must have taken them with him or her."

"And the bracket here," Blane pointed again, "was melted with a hand-held butane or propane torch. Also taken off site. Our perp came with a very well-stocked bag of goodies."

A yellow high vis submersible hung on its side from a winch on a police boat, seawater drizzling into the bay. The open hatch was draped with seaweed.

He watched two more URT divers jump into the water and disappear into a surge of bubbles. "And no body found yet?"

"Not yet. The divers are combing the seafloor," Blane answered.

He craned his neck over the edge. "How deep's the water here?"

"About sixty feet. But our biggest concern's not depth, it's water temperature. No one could survive the night in this water. It's only 58 degrees. And that's not the worst of it. The divers are skittish. Two overly curious Makos sharks have been patrolling the area all morning. And those two fish are over ten feet long."

Another premeditated killing, he thought, as the police boat returned to the dock. Clearly the murderer knew that the victim would be working at the submersible platform at that particular time.

He was relieved to step back onto terra firma, but next was the dreadful task of interviewing the victim's family. Sara Kauni and Jessie McCabe dissolved into each other's arms, Kauni using a post on the porch to support herself. The three young engineers huddled in shock. The two children, Ava and Danny, had skipped school and were at the house with Emily McLeod, awaiting any hopeful news. At the end of the pier, George McLeod and Derick Briggs stood granite-faced, staring seaward toward the activities of the URT divers.

The case was more muddled than ever. Over the past few days, Bill had had a vague sense that a pattern was emerging, dominos finally clacking into sequence. Now it was as though a petulant child had upended the table, the pieces flung and suspended in mid-air. He scanned the dock. One individual was conspicuously absent. Why would one of the Windsor nominees—or anyone—want to kill the Nobel laureate, Lindsey Nolan?

*****

Maggie was mortified. What insane impulse had caused her to kiss a cop? "My god, you've truly lost it," she whispered to herself. And, while sleeping on his sofa, she'd had a fabulous sex dream—starring The Detective. First they were making love on the—no, one couldn't call it that, because there was nothing tender about it, it was an unrestrained, free-for-all-fuck-fest. It started on the sofa in her cottage where she was on her back, then somehow they were in the cabin of the *Jack Rackham* standing up against a bulkhead, and then, just as she was waking from the dream, she was straddling him in Lindsey's hot tub. She awoke from the dream ridiculously wet. Never had she had a dream of such passion.

She pulled into the student parking lot, deciding to heed Bill's warning. She would go to her classes and spend the rest of the time in her cottage, where she could prepare her own food or eat Emily McLeod's cooking, at least until they captured the murderer. Besides, the cottage was a quiet place to study and paint. Maybe if she really buckled down, she might bring the "A" minus in Professor Jasper's class up to an "A." How great would it be to graduate with a semester of all "A"s! To be followed by the best job in the world: artist and illustrator to the immortal Jessie McCabe!

Bill's reptile painting was almost complete, but she was eager to start a new one. An amazing idea had occurred to her. But first she'd need to review her JPEGs of marine fishes. The next painting would fuse fish images with those of the reptiles to create fantastical, hybrid creatures. The piece might be called *Metamorphia*, or, better yet, *Evolution*.

Maybe that hottie, Bill, might come to visit her at the cottage. And then they might sneak over to the hot tub in the garage apartment, aka the Nolan-Briggs Sex Cave. God, did Lindsey hate it when she called the apartment that! It was too funny. How many times had Lin pulled her aside, out of Ava or Danny's earshot, and insist that she not call the garage apartment "the Lust Loft" or "Nooky Nest"? It was impossible not to burst into laughter! She was put on God's green earth for the sole purpose of goading Lindsey Nolan.

Maggie was still giggling as she tossed the empty coffee cup and wrapper from the breakfast sandwich into a trashcan at the dorm. She entered the building with her keycard and walked to her room. The door was ajar so she pushed her way in.

Lily jumped to her feet. "Oh my god!"

Maggie laughed. "You're jumpy."

"I... I... just wasn't expecting anyone. You scared the hell out of me, Maggie!"

"Your face is as white as a sheet. Like you just saw a ghost," she grinned.

Lily stuffed her balled hands into the pocket of a Newbury College hoodie. "You're right. These murders have made me so jumpy," she admitted. She dropped onto the edge of her bed. "And where were you last night? This is the second time you've been out all night."

"I ran into an old friend from high school, so I spent the night at her place."

"I thought you were going to work on a painting. Did you get that done at all?"

"No, I had a change of plans."

"You're such a procrastinator. What are you going to submit to the competition?"

"Mythic Reptiles."

"The painting based on the drawing we saw?"

"Yeah. It doesn't go with the marine theme of the other two, but I'm hoping that the judges will overlook that."

"I can't wait to see —"

A sharp knock at the door caused them to turn their heads. Bill Bleach and a giant redheaded man stood in the doorway, looking dour. "Maggie, you need to come to headquarters with us," Bill said.

*****

Jean Tate was furious. Because of Lily's phone call, three appointments had to be cancelled that afternoon. And the room in the motel off of I-95 in Rhode Island for their meeting was filthy. There was hair in the sink, and she wouldn't even comment on the bathtub, it was that disgusting. Furthermore, her trip to the appliance store would have to be postponed, and she could not bear the white refrigerator, dishwasher, and stove at home. Only stainless steel would go with the new granite countertops.

Jean could barely contain her disappointment. On top of everything, Lily was letting herself go. The girl was clearly not taking her vitamins nor eating properly; her skin had broken out again. Make-up could not conceal the circles under her eyes. Lily was doing too much partying. To compound all of this, her daughter was wearing jeans and a hoodie. Good heavens! Just that August she'd purchased velour tracksuits in a whole spectrum of lovely colors for Lily. What could Lily possibly be thinking, wearing such gauche clothes, instead of the latest in designer tracksuits?

"Mom," Lily said despairingly, "I need to take some time off."

"In mid-semester?" Jean's eyes bulged in shock. "Do you know how much tuition at a private art college is? Do you realize how much money would be lost?"

"I know, a lot," her daughter sighed. "But if I could just take a leave of absence for the remainder of this semester, then I could take a heavy load in the spring and still graduate in May."

Lily's untenable suggestion rendered her speechless. Plus, her new Prada shoes were pinching, but she couldn't bring herself to sit on the bedspread. God only knows what people did on bedspreads in a hotel such as this. The vinyl chair by the grimy window would have to do. She dropped into the chair and reached for her daughter's hand. "Darling, you can confide in me. Tell me what's going on."

Lily gazed into Jean's perfect, smooth face and glimmering eyes. "Mom," she said meekly, "I'm worried about so many things. These murders are freaking me out."

"I talked to Dean Shoemacher numerous times this week. He assures me that full security measures are in place for the students. Undercover police are all over the campus. He's hopeful that the police will be making an arrest soon. Student safety is paramount, he has told me."

"There's just too much pressure on me right now. The fall concert's in two weeks and the practices are taking up too much time."

"It's imperative that you practice every day," Jean said uncompromisingly. "How else do you expect to make the New York Symphony?"

"And I'm afraid that I'm not going to win the Windsor competition—"

Jean interrupted. "Ridiculous, Lily! At the Halloween party I closely studied all of the student art. Your urns are so delicate and the lines so dainty. Most of the other art was simply garish, and some outright obscene. Isn't your mentor, Dr. Sanders, the chairman of the Awards Committee? He'll be in your corner during the deliberations. Please talk to him, Lily, so he understands how important this is for your career. My goodness, just think of it: an exhibition at the Montaque Gallery! I can't wait for that! I've been thinking about our matching gowns...." her voice trailed off dreamily.

"I'll talk to Dr. Sanders, but I don't know if it will do any good. Maggie has this painting. I haven't seen it yet, only a sketch of it, but it's wondrous. It's all everyone, including Professor Tinkman, is talking about."

Jean's fingernails clicked on the table. "Perhaps she might be convinced not to enter."

"How? She's already put up two pieces. The deadline's Friday."

"Computers, Lily. Remember what I told you about computers. One's computer is like one's brain. It holds all of one's secrets. Remember Darren O'Day. For him to even suggest that you might have been on that balcony... the nerve! All it took was a whisper of the contents in his computer for him to retract that outrageous allegation."

"And what did you find in Edward Gripp's computer?"

"Absolutely nothing," Jean huffed in frustration. "Only photos of his travels to Crete and Greece, financial records, and correspondence between him and architectural schools and accreditation boards. There was absolutely nothing of a negotiable nature. To the police, this will simply appear as a computer theft and nothing more." She paused. "Edward's obstinacy in not putting in a word for you regarding the Windsor Award was truly disturbing. He and I had become such good friends over the past two years. I thought that he would at least do that for us."

"And then someone kills him," Lily said bleakly.

"Yes, that was horrible. Does anyone know where or how it happened?"

"No, the police have said nothing."

"Back to computers, Lily," Jean said firmly, keeping her daughter on task. "Might there be something in Maggie's computer that might convince her to withdraw from the competition?"

"Doubtful," said Lily dismally. "I've seen Maggie's computer a thousand times when we watch videos together. Term papers, iTunes, and folders and folders of photos from her dives."

"Sex partners?"

Lily shook her head vehemently. "Maggie's completely asexual. I don't think she's ever had sex before. She never talks about it at all."

"You must find something, Lily. Everyone has a chink in their armor. If that painting is as wondrous as you say it is, Maggie must not enter that competition."

*****

All that terrible day, Detectives Bleach and Murphy, accompanied now by Special Agent Jack Harris from FBI Boston, gathered statements from the engineers, the Nolan clan, and Sara Kauni. Despite the distracting clamor from the press and gawkers outside of headquarters, by the end of the afternoon they had a clear picture of the events that spurred Lindsey Nolan to take the *Jack Rackham* out to the platform the night before.

Days ago, Nolan had received a call from a potential investor from California. He was a CEO at a deep-water salvage company. It was not the submersible as a whole unit he was interested in, but the revolutionary touch-screen control panel. He had business in the Boston area at the end of the week and could possibly squeeze in a visit to the Cape. The news threw Lindsey into a state of exhilarated panic.

Only the controls for the underwater lights, air flow and pressure, and the rear and aft cameras had been configured and tested. Lindsey had rushed with the engineers to finish and download the software that controlled the speed and direction of the propellers, but it would be impossible to install the entire propulsion system in time. Sara had agreed to oversee their experiments and supervise the graduate students and post-docs at their lab in Woods Hole, while Lindsey worked exclusively at the NKDT site.

The day before, Lindsey had left NKDT around 4:30 p.m. to see her family. The three engineers had stayed on until about 5:45, when two of them left for a happy hour at a bar in Hyannis and to see a retro punk band. Harry Cheng returned home to take his wife to a natural childbirth class at a women's clinic. This was a refresher course. Lydia was pregnant with child number two.

Lindsey had dinner with Derick, Ava, Danny, and George and Emily McLeod. After dinner she'd helped Ava construct a pair of antennae for a Martian Halloween costume and headed back to the dive business. *Never*, Derick had told the detectives, did she mention to him that she was taking out the *Jack Rackham* and descending in the submersible *alone* and *at night*. He'd assumed—erroneously—that she'd be working in the office. His vexation at her recklessness was apparent. After she left, Derick remained home all evening and helped Danny with his junior high pre-algebra, then Danny and George worked in the basement on the model trains. After Ava finished her homework, she watched TV with Mrs. McLeod before going to bed.

Derick went to bed around 10:30, after working on a motorcycle restoration project in the garage. Lindsey sometimes worked late, he explained, so he went to sleep without concern. When he awoke again at 3:30, he was alarmed that she was not yet home. He drove to her business and spotted her SUV, but she was not in her office. The boat house-laboratory was dark. He hurriedly searched the offices in the old house. The *Jack Rackham* was not at its slip, nor could he see it at the platform. At 4:20 am, his panic escalating, he called 911.

Sara Kauni confirmed the engineers' testimonies. Lindsey was stressed about the visit from the CEO and was rushing to install the software for the propulsion system.

"Once Lindsey got something in her head, there was no stopping her. She *was*," Sara sobbed at her use of the past tense, "the most single-minded workaholic on the planet."

When asked her whereabouts the night before, Sara jerked back in the chair. "You're kidding me, right? Lin was my best friend!"

"Please, Dr. Kauni, this is standard procedure, nothing more," Bill explained patiently. "We need a record of everyone's activities."

"The evening was a complete and utter disaster," Sara groaned, sniffing into a tissue. "Jessie wanted to come with me to Zephyr's back-to-school-night. She was accosted all night by aggravating parents seeking autographs. It's time for Jessie to hire a bodyguard. Our days of private life are gone. So you're welcome to check on my whereabouts with my son's five teachers, and a flock of intrusive parents who followed us around for the entire evening."

Bill and Sandra dreaded the last interview, as it would certainly warrant Bill's removal from the case. Special Agent Harris was overtly doubtful of their competency; he considered them yokels and ignoramuses at best. After all, it had been seven days and three murders, without a single arrest.

All day Maggie had waited in a chair next to the interview room, George McLeod beside her. Finally it was her turn. The three detectives sat across a narrow gray table, while she writhed and chewed her thumb. She avoided eye contact with Bill and stared longingly at her cigarette pack, next to which a growing pile of wadded tissues was mounting.

"I... I received texts to meet with Detective Bleach," she stammered. "We agreed to meet at Rob Jenkins' houseboat, the *Green Monster*, where I used to live. We discussed my boot-prints being found at Edward Gripp's crime scene, and speculated on who might have worn them. Detective Bleach urged me not drink or eat food prepared by other students. Then I received a text from Jessie McCabe, offering me a job upon graduation. I was thrilled and nagged the detective to have ice cream with me. After I nagged and nagged, he finally agreed. I then wanted to take photos of his reptiles for a future painting, so I invited myself to his apartment. Detective Bleach reluctantly said okay, but only after I had badgered him for a while." At this point, she pulled her smartphone from her jacket and showed them the reptile JPEGs and some paintings. "I've done a series of paintings of marine organisms, see? Now I'm expanding to reptiles."

Despite himself, Agent Harris was impressed by the images of her paintings. He was reluctantly inclined to give Maggie's story some credence.

She continued in a shaky voice, "It had been an exhausting day and my new meds cause fatigue. I fell asleep on the detective's sofa. The next morning, he dropped me off at the marina."

Bill listened in mute disbelief. It was certainly an interesting interpretation of the evening's events; her version managed to salvage his reputation. She was taking all onus onto herself, and he was overwhelmed with gratitude. Maggie was no scatterbrain. She was savvy and had street smarts.

Agent Harris seemed momentarily appeased. "Okay, Maggie, can you think of anything else?"

"There's one other thing," she mumbled. She burst into tears. "I killed Lindsey!"

"That's impossible, Maggie! We were together last night," Bill blurted in her defense.

Her face was tear-streaked and wretched. "I did. *I* was supposed to be in that submersible last night. That person meant to kill me!"

Her subsequent explanation took another hour. She was finally released to George McLeod, under strict advisement to remain at the Nolan estate, attend classes on the campus, and then go straight home. She willingly agreed. The interviews over, Sandra and Bill excused themselves and hurried back to their desks.

Sandra called the Midwest police department that had handled the investigation of the Ellen Caruso accident, and was referred to a retired detective, Pete Jones, now living in Tampa. Her call to Florida was answered by an affable, talkative man who was happy to talk shop if it helped an active case.

"I remember the case like it was yesterday," Jones said. "I especially recall this one obnoxious mother of one of the roommates. She was under foot at every turn. And there was another slimy character, a student named Darren O'Day. Early in the investigation, he'd reported seeing Caruso and another student on the balcony minutes before Caruso's body was found. He was well known to us for selling drugs in the dorm, and for a drunk and disorderly outside a nightclub. If my memory's serving me right, when O'Day was in high school, he'd been cited for harassing a small girl in his neighborhood. But when we questioned him for a second time about Caruso's death, he denied his previous statement about the alleged second student. He said that he'd been mistaken and too drunk to remember. In the end, O'Day's original testimony was dismissed as non-credible and a fabrication to stall the investigation, nothing more.

"A search of the girls' dorm," Jones continued, "revealed a plastic bag of sleeping pills in Ellen Caruso's instrument case. Caruso had not been prescribed the pills, but they'd been prescribed to one of the other girls living in the suite, who thought that some of her pills had gone missing. It looked like Caruso had stolen her roommate's pills."

"Do you remember the type of musical instrument that Caruso played?" Sandra asked.

"Sorry, I don't. Maybe a stringed instrument," he answered. "Here's the other odd thing. Months later, after the case was closed, an anonymous tip came into our Tip Line. The informant described Darren O'Day as distributing child pornography. You wouldn't believe the trash we found in that man's computer."

"Where's he now?"

"Serving time in a Nebraska state prison, and good riddance."

After ringing off with Detective Jones, Sandra surfed the web for Lily Tate's midwestern college. On the alumnae webpage was a link for old yearbooks. She located the.pdf of an e-yearbook from two years ago and scrolled to the music programs: marching band, jazz band, barber shop quartet, swing band, string ensemble. She located a photograph of the string ensemble. All of the males were in black pants and white dress shirts; the females were in floor length black skirts and white blouses. Ellen Caruso was a smiling girl in the front row, second to the left. Next to her was the driven face of Lily Tate.

Under the photograph was a list of names and instruments played. Cellos, violas, bass, violins....

"Bill, I think you'll want to see this," she said grimly over her shoulder. He swiveled his chair and she tapped a pencil tip against the computer screen.

Ellen Caruso... first violin

Lily Tate... second violin

*****

George McLeod had reprimanded Maggie countless times about texting while driving, and now he was breaking his own rule. At a red light in Falmouth, he checked his smartphone.

"Anything?" Maggie asked hopefully.

There was no word from Derick Briggs at the NKDT pier. "Nothing yet, darlin'."

She sobbed into her hands. "This is all my fault! I—"

"This is *not* your fault," George interrupted firmly. He handed her his handkerchief. "It's horrible, but not your fault in any way. And the person responsible for this will be caught."

She honked into the cloth. "And I'm going to kill the fucker personally when I find out who he is. I don't care if I spend my life in jail. At least I will have avenged Lindsey's death."

"No, you won't," he replied. "You're going to let the police do their job. I'm going to be your bodyguard to ensure that you're safe and that you don't do anything stupid and impulsive that you'll regret later."

"I was always such a jerk to Lin. I teased her every chance I could get."

"And I teased her, Derick teased her, all of us teased her. She was irresistibly tease-able. That's because we all loved her so much."

"But I never told her so!"

"But she knew."

"We're all talking about her in the past tense. It's so fucked up."

"I'm trying to be optimistic about this, but I am also a realist. It would be difficult to survive in such cold water for so long."

She sniffled into the handkerchief again. "I'm never going to forgive myself for this." She pointed toward the right. "Turn here. I need to get some things from my dorm room and let Lily know where I'll be."

"Okay, but I'm going with you. All the guys in the dorm will be really jealous when they see the handsome, older man in your life," he joked to lift her spirits.

She managed a small smile. "I don't know how I'm going to concentrate, or finish out the semester. Everything in the world sucks."

He gave her hand a squeeze. "You'll do it one day at a time, like every other day."

"I haven't had time to set up my third painting for the Windsor competition. Oh fuck it, I'm just going to withdraw. Are you sure I can't have a smoke? Under the circumstances?"

"You've already smoked a pack today. How your lungs are even functioning right now is beyond me. And Emily doesn't want the new car smelling like smoke."

"She's pussy-whipped you."

He guffawed, "Right." She looked at the giant man, an unflappable, fearless Scotsman. "Use the beautiful reptile painting that Lindsey told me about."

"I guess I could, but it's not quite finished."

"How much is left to do?"

"Maybe one percent."

"One percent? Would anyone notice but you?"

"Probably not."

"Use that as your third piece, then finish it later, after the competition. Be done with it, darlin', so it's not hanging over your head. How's this for an idea—if you win, you dedicate the award to Lindsey? That would be a wonderful tribute to her."

"I love that plan. Let's swing by the cottage and get the painting. I'll quickly hang it in the gallery, and then I'll get my things from my dorm room."

"Done," said Maggie's self-appointed bodyguard.

*****

There's a sudden commotion in the Gripp building. Students jog up the porch stairs, nearly knocking me down. A din of voices is coming from the small gallery. I quickly follow. Students and faculty members crowd against a wall. I feel like shoving them aside. I gasp. The white gap in the wall has been filled. I stand on tiptoe, stretching my head from side to side, but all I see is a wall of irritating bodies. Were I the grim reaper, my scythe would whack away the heads so that I might have a clear view. Someone mentions the title—Mythic Reptiles. There's an awed discussion about line, space, light, and color. I cringe; the words "superlative," "revolutionary," "transcendental," and "supernatural" assault my ears. Hands stretch upward with smartphones and tablets to click photos of the work and further obstruct my view. I hate the title, Mythic Reptiles.

My imaginary scythe whacks at the air. Severed arms and hands drop among the decapitated heads. Phones and tablets smash into blood pooling on the wood floor. Snippets of conversation run like a mad dog around my head (which is the only head intact): "Did you see the news?"... "Poor Maggie..."... "Will she be returning to school?"... "Why would anyone kill Lindsey Nolan?"... "A spurned wife?... a competing lab?... someone she scooped?"... "Sick, sick bastard..."

Idle chatter is of no consequence to me. I elevate myself above the infuriating crowd with their infuriating, small-minded thoughts. The scythe disappears from my hand and in its place appears a glistening, double-edged razor. I swoop downward like a Mythic Fury. My blade swipes wildly from side to side and Mythic Reptiles falls from the white wall in shreds.

*****

Bill returned to his desk with a third cup of burnt coffee from the pot at headquarters. His dinner of potato chips and pretzels from the vending machine congealed in his stomach, all because of Agent Harris's theory... that Maggie had committed the two murders and an avenging angel had tried to stop her killing spree, accidentally killing Lindsey Nolan instead. Harris waved away Maggie's alibi for the second murder, arguing that drug addicts would of course try to cover for each other. Harris had found in Maggie's records what the two detectives had already seen, arrests for shoplifting and prostitution, and the FBI agent saw the world in black and white. Once a thief, always a thief. Once a hooker, always a hooker. It was inconsequential to Harris that the thefts had been at grocery stores, for food, and that an eleven-year-old runaway had no other means to earn money… for food.

Worse, Bill's captain had invited Harris to set up his own computer in the captain's office, and chummy banter had sounded from the office all afternoon. The Captain and Special Agent Harris, it turned out, were "old buds": they had grown up in the same neighborhood in Quincy, and their sons had played on the same high school football team. That meant the captain would back Harris. The agent, for his part, directed suspicious glares at the two detectives every time he went to the men's room, which was frequently.

Bill checked his watch. It was nearly nine o'clock, nearly twenty-four hours since the attack on Lindsey Nolan, and her body had not been located. The divers had motored in for the evening and would try again in the morning, weather permitting.

He and Sandra were more convinced than ever that it was one of the Newbury students. Maggie had mentioned her plan to take photographs from the submersible to a bunch of the students in the cafeteria, information that could have been passed to any student in the dorm. Or what about Brian Cooper? He certainly had a motive to set Maggie up.

He searched his desk drawer for some antacids and grabbed his coat. "I'm going to swing by Brian Cooper's place on my way home. I want to know why he stood Maggie up on October 14th."

Sandra shut down her computer. "I'm going with you. I'll follow in my car and go home from there. I can't stand getting the hairy eyeball from Hair Ass a minute longer."

The detectives discussed Brian Cooper's background in a cell phone conversation on their drive to Cooper's apartment. He was twenty-eight—the same age as Bill—and born in Barnstable. He'd moved to Woods Hole when he was five and graduated from the local high school with mediocre grades. There was no indication of additional education. Directly after high school graduation, Cooper obtained a job on the collecting trawlers at the marine lab, and more recently had been employed on a fishing boat stationed in Hyannis harbor. He had no police record.

"He might know Ernst Hanson and Olivia Moreno," Sandra ventured. "Ernst's boat is also moored in Hyannis. If Cooper is the one, he might have learned that Maggie was to be on the submersible from Olivia."

"Maggie told me that she met Brian at an NA meeting when she was thirteen, when she got out of rehab and moved in with Lindsey. She and Brian began dating immediately, and were together until she was eighteen."

"When she was thirteen, he would have been nineteen. I believe they call that statutory rape."

"She loved him. It was consensual," he said, pulling into a parking lot. "We're here."

"You always defend her."

"Pathetic, isn't it?"

"Hey, I was Lenny's superior officer for a time. Like I can cast stones...."

They parked in front of a red brick, three-story building across from a strip mall and headed inside. The hallway reeked of a nauseating combination of odors from the apartments. Cooper's place was on the second floor at the top of the stairwell. Sandra knocked forcefully. A scurrying movement was heard behind the door. Someone was definitely there, perhaps looking through the peephole. The next time she pounded with her fist. The door cracked open as far as the security chain would permit.

"Who is it?" a male voice asked.

"Detectives Bleach and Murphy," Bill replied.

There was another susurration, then silence.

"Brian, we need to talk about Maggie," Bill insisted, leaning toward the crack. Using Maggie's name as bait worked; Brian unlocked the chain and stepped quickly into the hallway.

"Is she alright?" he asked anxiously, slamming the door behind him. "Is she alright? I saw the sad news about Lin."

The young man's face was wracked with worry. At one time he might have been a handsome man, but presently his eyes seeped and his nose was red and runny. He sniffed often and swayed slightly.

"We need to ask you some questions about the night of October 14th."

"What night was that? I don't remember it." He reached behind his head to scratch at his neck. "They all seem to bleed together."

There was a muted shuffling behind the neighbor's door. "Can we come in? This is of a confidential nature," Bill said.

"No, my place is a mess. We'll have to talk out here."

"No, Brian, inside," Sandra said firmly.

"It's too hot in here. Let's go outside."

Bill and Sandra glanced at one another. She reached into her coat for the Glock.

"Open the door, Brian," she ordered.

"I'm fucked," he said to himself.

The apartment was much like Bill's place in layout, with the kitchen, dining room, and living room merged into one space. A narrow hallway led to a bedroom and bathroom. But there the similarity ended. The place had a revolting smell of stale trash, smoke, and body odor. Counters and tables were covered with empty bottles and food containers. Brian dropped onto the sofa, his head falling into his hands. On a coffee table was a bong and a bag of weed. A mirror had a small piece of plastic straw, a razor blade, and lines of cocaine.

"Please don't tell Maggie about this!" Brian begged. "She'll never take me back if she finds out about this."

Sandra pulled the pistol from her shoulder holster. "You talk to Detective Bleach, and don't move from that place. Do you hear me? Don't move, Brian."

He nodded miserably.

She moved toward the kitchen counter. "Christ. Bill?" She pointed to baking soda, tea candles, and a burnt spoon.

Brian—or someone—was cooking crack.

"Sandra, call for backup." Bill's attention returned to the hunched man on the couch. "October 14th was a Friday night and the night of one of your NA meetings. Maggie texted you during the meeting. Do you remember the text?"

"Yeah. We were supposed to meet at the seawall in Woods Hole."

"At what time?"

"I think it was 8:00. The NA meeting always ends at 7:30."

"She waited for you. Why didn't you show up?"

Brian fingered an empty book of matches. "I got invited to a party, so my plans changed."

"With who, and where?"

He didn't answer.

"Brian, I'll check your phone and text messages tomorrow, but I'd appreciate the truth now. This information will help Maggie. I know you care about her."

I do! I still love—"

A thump sounded from the bedroom. Bill turned to look down the hallway. Sandra was in the kitchen, on the phone with headquarters. She rang off immediately. "Who's in the bedroom, Brian?" She strode into the living room. "Do not move." She pointed the pistol at his knee. "It's very difficult to haul fishing nets without knee caps. Who's in the bedroom?"

"My roommate." He wept into his hands. "Please don't tell Maggie about this!" he pleaded. "Everything fell apart when Maggie and I split."

Sandra disappeared down the hallway. "Come out with your hands up, or I'm coming in to get you," she called out. There was a protracted silence. "Okay, your choice," her exasperated voice echoed from the bedroom. "We'll do it your way, the hard way." There was a tinkling of coat hangers, then a crash and the shattering of glass.

"Owww, you bitch!" a voice yowled.

A gangly, ugly woman was led down the hallway, her arm pinned behind her back. Her other hand clutched at her nose. Blood seeped from between her fingers.

Sandra gestured the woman into a chair. "Sit and don't move."

The woman snarled, "I'm calling my lawyer. This is police brutality."

"You struck first. I was defending myself. It's called self-defense," Sandra responded tiredly.

"Then if I struck second and you struck first, it would be...?" she asked dully.

Sandra handed her a roll of paper towels. "Bill, we have a couple of Einsteins here."

"What's your name?" Bill asked.

"Lisa," she hissed.

"Lisa what?"

"Lisa-you-can-ask-my-fuckin'-lawyer."

"The longer we sit here, the harder it's going to be to reset your nose," Bill said coolly.

"Caffrey." Lisa Caffrey glowered at Brian. "Roommate! Since when am I just a roommate, fuck-head?" She turned to the detectives. "*I'm* his girlfriend now, not Maggie."

Her words seemed to stab at Brian; his expression was one of utter despair.

"Where did you go that night instead of to the seawall?" Bill asked him.

"Don't!" Lisa yelled.

"We're already fucked, Lisa! Can't you see that? We made a pickup offshore."

"What type of pickup?" Bill asked.

"Some coke."

"You went straight from an NA meeting to pick up drugs? That's insane," Bill said incredulously.

"I told you," Brian said dismally. "Everything fell apart after Maggie and I split up. We were so happy at the cottage. The Nolans... the McLeods... Ava and Dan were like my sister and brother. We were family. Then Maggie ended it." He pulled a cross from under his white undershirt. "My family doesn't believe in ending life."

"But it's okay to sell crack that could potentially end someone else's life. That makes a lot of sense, pal," Sandra said sarcastically.

Brian continued to weep. "Nothing makes sense anymore."

"What was the name of the boat?"

"Don't answer that!" Lisa snapped at Brian.

"*The Misty One* from New York City."

"What kind of boat is it?" Bill asked.

"Shut up, ass-hole!" Lisa shrieked. "You're digging our fuckin' graves!"

"You shut up! We're already dead!" It took a moment for Brian to compose himself. "It's a single-masted motorsailer."

Chapter 16

This was the third time in the entire two years of their rooming together that Lily had awoken to find Maggie's bed empty. On the first two occasions her explanations had been hard to believe. Staying a high school friend's place... yeah, right. Last night, though, Lily was sure Maggie was where she'd said she would be—at home, mourning with the rest of the Nolan family.

The morning news streamed on her laptop while Lily ruffled a towel through her wet hair. "It's a bright sunny day in Woods Hole, Massachusetts. There's been a sudden break in the weather, and a few days of Indian summer are forecast for the remainder of the week," the TV news reporter chirped optimistically. Then her tone turned ominous, "But the tiny seaside village is in a state of shock."

Lily knew just where the woman was standing, in her Cable News windbreaker, her hair whipping across her face as she spoke into the microphone. On the NK Dive Technologies pier. In the exact place where she'd stood with Olivia and Kyle. No way would she ever sell on eBay her McCabe, Kauni, and Nolan autographs, like Kyle intended to do. In the last twenty-four hours the Lindsey Nolan autograph had probably tripled in value. Lily studied herself in the mirror and wondered what her hair might look like if she cut it to shoulder length like the news reporter. But a short haircut would throw Mom into a conniption. It just wasn't worth the argument.

"The bright sun and calm waters today mean good visibility for the Underwater Recovery Team divers," the reporter added breathlessly.

"Duh," Lily commented aloud, "like anyone with half a brain doesn't know that." She scanned her bottles of perfume. Something seductive for today... hmm... how about Elizabeth Taylor's "White Diamonds"? Definitely. This was perfect for her current mood. How cool would it be to have violet eyes like Liz Taylor!

"Yesterday the divers reported seeing two large Makos sharks in the area, and today they'll be equipped with anti-shark stun guns and a repellent that's still undergoing some tests," the reporter continued in her throaty TV voice.

"Makos... I hate sharks," she muttered. Maggie had some brown eyeliner, she recalled. That would perfectly match the dab of rouge and peach-colored lipstick. No, the lipstick needed to be flavored. Only cherry would do for this morning. She checked her teeth in the mirror. They looked dazzling because last night she'd applied whitening strips. She wandered over to Maggie's dresser and searched amidst her roommate's trinkets. The two stoners in the room next door had reported that Maggie and a tall redheaded man had returned to the dorm yesterday afternoon, packed up some of her belongings, and left. The absent belongings, Lily noticed, were Maggie's laptop, tablet, keys, and, most frustratingly, her cosmetic bag containing the brown eyeliner. Her own light green eyeliner would have to do. While she was searching for the cherry lip-gloss, a knock sounded at the door.

"Come in."

"You look nice. What are you doing today?" Olivia asked.

"I feel horrid for Maggie," she said. "I'm just trying to perk myself up by putting on some makeup."

"What's the alluring perfume... Eau de Tear My Clothes Off?" Olivia asked with a kidding grin.

"Yes," she giggled.

"The police are following many leads and will not specify when an arrest will be made," the reporter continued. The remark chilled the levity and they turned toward the laptop. "Nor will they confirm if this incident is in any way linked to the Edward Gripp and June Perkins murders."

Olivia had a sly glint in her eye. "You know what I think?"

"What?"

"That it's one of us."

"What? Why do you say that?"

"Remember when Maggie was talking about the submersible in the cafeteria? Anyone at the other tables could have overheard her. It was a botched job. The murderer killed the wrong person."

"That's absurd."

Olivia shrugged indifferently. "It's just my hunch. But just in case, all I'm asking is that you watch your back."

"Now I'm really creeped out."

"Just be alert." Olivia opened an envelope. "I'm collecting money for flowers for Maggie and the Nolan family. Kyle collected money from his floor and I'm doing the other floors. My car's finally out of the shop, so I can run by the florist's later and drop them by the house this afternoon."

"I definitely want to contribute." Lily reached into a designer leather bag and handed Olivia a bill. "What a sweet idea! Thank you for doing this."

Olivia started for the door. "Yeah, no problem." She turned briefly. "Heed my words, girlfriend, watch your back."

*****

Bill gazed at the white board covered with photos of the murder suspects. One of the faces looking back at him had killed three people, he was sure of it. One singular face was taunting him, but which one was it? Most frustrating was that all of the alibis so far, for both students and faculty, were checking out.

He and his partner had earned some brownie points for locating a crack distribution house—albeit a small one—and linking the *Misty One* to a questionable chemical laboratory near New York City. But the drug bust had only reduced the number of distrusting glances Agent Harris directed at his and Sandra's office. By morning's end, the crack case was out of their hands and had been transferred to the drug unit.

Brian Cooper's alibi on the nights of Edward Gripp's murder had checked out. He, Lisa Caffrey and Frankie MacDonald had been seen by the harbormaster taking Frankie's boat from the marina around 8:30; the trio hadn't returned until 10:30. During June Perkins' murder, Cooper had been in Rhode Island at his grandmother's eightieth birthday party, and during the sabotage of Nolan's submersible he was swabbing a walk-in freezer with two other fishermen in Hyannis.

It had taken Sandra a morning of phone calls to the State of Nebraska Board of Corrections to obtain the various consents to have a conversation with Prisoner Darren O'Day. By eleven o'clock all permissions had been granted and O'Day's face in the granular pixels of Skype appeared on her laptop. In prison he'd fallen in with skinheads; his head was cleanly shaven and covered with swastika tattoos.

O'Day was desperate for someone to listen to his side of the Ellen Caruso incident, even two years later. "My dorm room was one floor above and one room over from Ellen Caruso's room, so my balcony had a direct view of her balcony. I knew that balcony well," he continued with a twisted smile, "because those chicks often sunbathed in their string bikinis."

"Just tell us about the night of the party," Sandra cut in.

"It was a crazy, crazy party. All sorts of crazy shit going on. Even before the party, those girls were goofing off and doing shots on the balcony. Later, the two of them, Caruso and Tate, were on the balcony arguing about something. I couldn't hear what, but Caruso was loaded and emotional, and Tate was pissed about something. Then my roommate called me inside, so I left. Later on, I heard a commotion, so I went outside to see. A bunch of students were in the parking lot, and Caruso's body was splattered across the sidewalk. It was fucking disgusting."

Sandra leaned toward her laptop. "And was anyone else on the balcony below?"

"No. It was empty." He stopped talking, and his face worked. Then he continued.

"I mentioned the argument to the police, but no one seemed to believe me. A day later I get this fucked up email from some Hotmail account. The email listed all of the files in my computer and said, 'You have seen absolutely nothing. If anything's reported to the police, all files will immediately be released to them.' My computer was filled with porn. What fucking choice did I have? I had to deny my earlier testimony." He was silent for a few moments. "At first I suspected Tate of getting into my room while I was at class. But when I asked about her whereabouts, she wasn't even on campus. She was at a band competition somewhere, maybe Chicago, for the week." He shook his head furiously. "To this day, I have no fucking clue who blackmailed me! And worse, just when I thought everything was over, the fucker released my files to the police anyway! That's how I landed in this shithole with a bunch of perverts!"

As Bill and Sandra terminated their conversation with O'Day, a secretary poked her head into their office and said that a student wanted to speak with them. Olivia Moreno, dressed in a long black dress in the general style of Morticia Addams, awaited them in the reception area.

There was no salutation. "I have a theory," Olivia said brashly.

Bill inwardly groaned... another theory. The Avenging Angel Theory was bad enough.

"That third murder was botched," she explained. "The murderer meant to kill Maggie. She was talking about the submersible in the cafeteria. Anyone could have heard her."

"Interesting theory, Olivia," he replied.

"And another thing. Maggie put up her third painting yesterday. It's called *Mythic Reptiles*. It's nothing short of brilliant. It's standing room only around that painting. Some of the faculty members have called in colleagues from other institutions and galleries to have a look at it, that's how good it is. No one can get near that painting."

"So this means that the judging for the Windsor competition can now begin?" Sandra inquired.

"Correct, but it's no competition now. I'm imploring you to protect Maggie. Don't let anything happen to her. We're witnessing the emergence of the best American artist of our generation. Arrest this psycho as soon as you can."

"That's our first priority," he assured her.

Olivia extended a bouquet of flowers toward the cops. "I know it's been a gruesome week for everyone. I was just at the florists. I had some money leftover. I thought you two might need a little cheering up."

He reached tentatively for the flowers. "Thank you. This is very thoughtful."

"Get him, please!" Olivia pivoted quickly on her clunky black shoes and departed.

"Here," he said, a bit dumfounded, handing the flowers to Sandra. "You can put them on your desk."

Sandra's hands remained unflinchingly at her sides. "No, you keep them. I'm never going to feel right about florists again. And Moreno's weird. I'm double-checking her alibis to see what she was doing when Gripp's computer was stolen. And I'm doing more homework on Mrs. Tate." She hurried back to her desk.

Bill watched Olivia disappear down the sidewalk. Agent Harris looked skeptically at the bouquet from his sentry post at the coffee pot. Bill's thoughts circled. Was Olivia's intent to throw him off Maggie's trail? What if Maggie and Olivia were partners in this? Olivia was large and strong; she could have helped Maggie move Gripp's body, and she seemed unusually protective of Maggie. Maggie had no alibi for the first murder, and the second alibi was solely based on the word of Tory V. No... it couldn't be Maggie. It just couldn't be. But still... if Tory was mistaken by just one hour, Maggie would have had time to get to the yoga studio in Falmouth.

Other than Tory's word, Maggie's actions could not be confirmed by either security cameras or witnesses.

Agent Harris still watched him from the coffee machine. Bill no longer cared about that nosey blowhard. He moved the bouquet to his nose and breathed in the wonderful fragrance, but it did nothing to lift his spirits. During his first meeting with Maggie, she'd asked him, "When you're interviewing a person, say a murderer... or rapist, is there something about them, a look in their eyes, a gesture... something... that tells you that they're guilty? Is that something they teach you guys at the police academy?"

With a churning stomach, Bill returned to his desk to check out cold cases in Minnesota.

*****

Lily Tate chewed up a breath mint and dropped a folder onto John Sanders' desk. "I just wanted you to sign off on my intent-to-graduate paperwork."

"Did you also bring your transcript?" the professor asked, searching his desk for his bifocals.

"Here it is."

Sanders pulled his glasses over his ears and reviewed the transcript for a moment. "Yes, you're ready to go. What a terrific GPA! Great job. What are your plans after graduation?"

"I'll probably try out for various symphony orchestras." She handed him a pen and the graduation form. "Sign here, please." She smiled widely to show off her dazzling white teeth.

He reflexively signed his name on the signature line. "Really? You're not sticking with art? Maybe get an MFA?"

"That will depend on the outcome of the Windsor Award, I guess. Have you seen Maggie's new work?"

"Yes. It vaguely reminds me of an M.C. Escher work with the changing dimensions, though most of Escher's works were in black and white. Her use of color is intriguing. Changing the subject, I did want to mention to you that I put your idea forward to the committee about entering more than three pieces; however, they felt that the guidelines shouldn't be changed in the middle of the competition. But they're considering an amendment of that policy for next year."

"Thank you for listening to my suggestion. I have another one, in light of the recent circumstances...." She closed his office door.

"What's that?" He removed his glasses and rubbed the bridge of his nose.

"That the judging and awards ceremony be postponed for a while. At least until Maggie can join us back on campus." She moved to an open window. A warm breeze fluttered the curtains. Boys in T-shirts and shorts were tossing a Frisbee in front of the dorm.

"How long do you expect that will be?"

"I have no clue. They still haven't found Dr. Nolan's body."

"I hate to be the pessimist, but everyone needs to prepare for the worst. She was probably swept away by some underwater current. Every day that goes by diminishes the chances of finding her."

"Worse than that," she said softly, "there have been reports of sharks in the area."

"I heard that, too."

She leaned across his desk. The low cut shirt had been a deliberate choice. "So I'm just requesting that you delay the process until Maggie returns."

"It's not a decision I can make independently. And the Montaque Gallery has been reserved for our Windsor exhibition over winter break. That date can't be changed, but I can email the Awards Committee and listen to their input about postponing the judging and campus ceremony, at least temporarily."

"Thank you. I know Maggie would appreciate it. I can't imagine what she's feeling. I'm devastated by the recent events. This semester's been so traumatizing."

"It's been truly horrid."

She whispered demurely, "Will you hug me?"

"Of course, Lily." Before he could stand, she'd slipped behind his desk, and dropped on to the lap of his khaki trousers. She wept softly into his shoulder, and then soft kisses swept across his neck and cheek. By the time they found his mouth, the kisses had lost their girlish innocence.

*****

Maggie moved to the window of the cottage again and checked the time on her smartphone. It had been over five hours, and Derick Briggs was still on the dock. Every so often he lifted a pair of binoculars to his eyes and scanned the bay. The platform in the distance was still surrounded by URT divers. Ava and Danny periodically wandered down to sit with him, only to return listlessly to the house. Danny was numb with shock; Ava was teary. For Danny, this would be the third parent lost: his biological mother, Paola Ruiz-Jenkins, in car wreck when he was a toddler, his father,

Robert Jenkins, by a mysterious respiratory infection, and now his adopted mother, Lindsey Nolan, while working on an experimental submersible. The kid was going to need some serious therapy, Maggie thought, gnawing her thumbnail.

After the two children had gone to bed the night before, Maggie, George, Emily, and Derick had gathered around the kitchen table and decided that if the body were not found by week's end, a memorial service would have to be held. If nothing else, it would provide a small sense of closure and pay tribute to Lindsey Nolan's short but extraordinary career of biomedical innovation. And it would not be the raucous media circus that Robert Jenkins' funeral had been, where baseball players and most of the population of south Boston had crowded into a stifling church. This would be a small ceremony—invitation only—for Lindsey's family, sponsor and closest AA friends, as well as her engineers from Woods Hole. In lieu of flowers, donations could be sent to a foundation researching Alzheimer's, the disease that had afflicted Lindsey's beloved mentor from Johns Hopkins, Anne Davids.

Maggie grabbed Derick a water bottle from her fridge and headed toward the dock.

Derick reached for the water. "Thanks," he said forcing a smile.

In the past few days white streaks had appeared in his long black hair. His rugged face was eroded by worry and sadness.

"You've become the ghost, Andrew Stanton, looking out to sea," she said.

"Like Andrew, I'll wait as long as it takes," he stated with resolve.

She flung her arms around his broad shoulders. "I'm so, so sorry. This is all my fault!"

"We talked about this last night. Enough of it," he said gravely. "It's the fault of some psychopath and has nothing to do with you."

"The worst part is that I never said thank you to Lin."

"Thank you for what?"

"Saving me. Getting me off the street. Giving me a home."

He exhaled. "You're kidding me. You two are impossible. *You* saved *her*."

"What?"

"That's what Lin told me. That you saved her. When she returned home from rehab that day and saw the mess that her ex-husband and his girlfriend had created while she was away, she was wanting to drink in the worst way. Then you showed up on her houseboat that night. Do you remember that?"

"How could I forget!" she said angrily. "Those drunks beat me up."

"She would never drink while you were there and disappoint you. She was amazed that you stayed as long as you did. Then, after a time, her desire to drink was gone. You saved her, Maggie. Never think otherwise." He patted her affectionately on the knee and raised the binoculars back to his eyes.

"Where did she think I was going to go? I had no place else to go. She was my last hope."

"Then let's just say you two saved each other and call it even." He sat up on the alert. "What the...?"

Maggie sprang to her feet and waved her arms. "Whoa! Up here!"

Olivia slogged through the marsh next to the Nolan beach, the hem of her long black dress damp with muddy sand. She hefted a bursting bouquet of flowers. "Your security system sucks," she called across the beach. "The press vans bottlenecked the main road, so I just drove down the dirt road, walked across your neighbor's beach, and here I am. I thought that the police were supposed to be keeping people out, including trespassers like me." She grinned ironically. "Slackers."

"Olivia, this is Derick," Maggie said by way of introduction.

Olivia squinted up into the sun. "I know Derick. I saw him at the Halloween party."

"Right," he said, recognizing her. "The bull's-eye girl."

"That'd be me. The lady at the florists put way too much water in this thing." With a groan, she lowered the bouquet into the sand.

Maggie jogged down the dock and dropped to the sand. The two friends embraced.

Olivia reached into a canvas bag slung over her shoulder. "Truant, here are the notes from Professor Tinkman's lecture, since you're clearly playing hooky. I brought you some cookies. "

Maggie stared longingly at them. "But I can't eat them. The police have advised me not to eat anything unless I prepare it myself."

Olivia nodded astutely. "Good. Good advice. At least they're doing *something* right." She opened the bag of cookies and enthusiastically crunched one down. "Then you can re-gift them back to me." She held the bag up to the edge of the dock. "Derick, do you want one?"

"No, thanks. I don't have much of an appetite." His view returned to the platform.

"Yeah, no shit." Olivia bent to lift the flowers. "These are from your friends in the dorm. The whole dorm contributed. That's how much we miss you."

"I've only been gone a day, but it seems a lot longer. I'm bored stiff here," Maggie said.

"By the way, Mythic Reptile is the coolest painting I've ever seen. Show me your studio here."

"Okay!" Maggie said, some animation returning to her voice. "I'll show you the sketch for a new work called Evolution."

*****

"What did the police ever do before computers?" Bill wondered aloud, searching a confidential database from the State of Minnesota.

"Or security cameras, or DNA testing?" Sandra responded, studying the website for Tate Network Solutions, Inc. in Cos Cob, Connecticut.

"Investigations took a painfully long time."

"Like this one," she said glumly.

"And before DNA testing, many innocent people were put behind bars."

"And still occasionally are. Anything yet?"

"No. You?"

"Yes. Jean Tate owns two computer stores, one in Cos Cob and one in Greenwich. They don't sell either PCs or Macs, but provide software upgrades and installations, computer repairs, and networking services for local businesses. She's the sole owner. She's also a member of the local Rotary Club and the Association of Women Business Owners of Southwest Connecticut, and her business sponsors a team for an annual breast cancer walk. Everything on the surface seems above board. Lily was seen on a camera in the Gripp Center around 2:00 p.m. Saturday so it wasn't her who nicked Edward Gripp's computer. Listen to this: Jean was in the Midwest and Cape Cod respectively when Darren O'Day and Edward Gripp's computers were either compromised or stolen. But during Edward Gripp's murder, Jean was at the Halloween party, and during June Perkins and Lindsey Nolan's murders, she was in Connecticut at work and at various social events at her country club with her husband, Evan. What have you got?"

She rolled her chair across the space between their two desks and leaned toward his laptop. The words he'd typed onto the search boxes were: drugs, teenage girls, and prostitutes. This led to a number of hits. One in particular caused him to break into a sweat.

It was an unsolved murder in a remote part of Minnesota, on a farm. A reclusive, middle-aged woman was found dead in her kitchen. Her body had been there at least two weeks before it was found by the sheriff. Her head had been staved in. A bloody shovel was later located under the ice of a pond. When the snow melted later that spring, her husband was located in a shallow grave in the woods. Toxicology reports revealed that he'd died of a lethal dose of poison some months earlier. The couple had been kind enough to employ two teenage girls that winter, the sheriff reported. The sheriff had had a run-in with the older girl, a ferocious Caucasian about fifteen or sixteen, named Bess. The silent African-American girl was significantly younger. He couldn't remember for sure, but the sheriff thought that her name was either Margie or Mary.

*****

Because of press vans and rubber-neckers on the shoulders of the road, it took Bill nearly a half an hour longer than it should have to make the drive from Falmouth to the Nolan estate in Woods Hole. He flashed his ID to a uniformed officer at the front gate, and the wrought iron gate swung open. He navigated the woods and the circular driveway, passed the beach house, and pulled into a spot next to the Jeep. On his way to the cottage, he awkwardly juggled a bag of Chinese food, a carton of orange juice, and a gallon of peppermint ice cream.

Maggie opened the door. "How can I trust that this food's not poisoned?" she wisecracked.

If she had any idea of the poor timing of that comment....

"Um... hi," he replied nervously. "Are you hungry?"

"Yeah. You?" She held the door open for him.

"A little bit." In truth, he was gripped by nausea.

She peered into the bag. "What is it?"

"Two choices. Cashew chicken and curried vegetables."

"Yum." She moved boxes of paints off the kitchen island and reached into a cupboard for plates and cups, then dug around until she found chopsticks. "Which do you want?" she asked, pulling out the food containers.

His stomach convulsed at the thought of food. The blander, the better. "Chicken, I guess."

She filled a plate for him, watching him doubtfully. She loaded her own plate and lifted chopsticks to her mouth. She hesitated and then threw the chopsticks onto her plate.

"What?!"

"What?" he asked, stunned.

"Shit! It's all over your face. Something's up. What is it? Are you ready to make an arrest yet?"

"Ur... No... I can't say anything."

"Are you all getting *anywhere* with this case? Lindsey's dead and I'm stuck here like a prisoner! Something's happened. It's all over your face."

He shoved his plate away. "I can't eat! Who am I kidding? The FBI's breathing down my neck. At any minute I'm going to be yanked off this case. There's too much conflicting evidence. And everyone has an alibi!"

"Someone's lying. Someone's alibi is bullshit."

He reached out for her forearm, an attempt to calm her down, but she jerked her arm away.

"Never, *ever* touch me, unless I say so!"

"We must talk!" he said hoarsely. "You must be completely honest with me. It's the only way I can help you. If I found the information, surely the FBI will find it also."

She looked warily at him. "What information?"

He inhaled deeply. "I know about Minnesota."

She gasped and jumped off the stool. His muscles tightened, readying to pursue, but she only snatched her cigarettes from the windowsill and fired one up. For minutes she circled the room like a caged animal, while smoke filled the room. Then she stopped and blew smoke through the screened door. It felt like a summer afternoon, it was that impossibly hot outside. He removed his tie and stuffed it in his pocket, then rolled up his sleeves and unbuttoned his collar in preparation for an exhausting conversation.

"I'm dead," she announced, gnawing frantically on her thumbnail. "I knew this would catch up with me. It was just a matter of time. And now it's here. I'm going to fry for four murders."

"Four?!" he choked.

"Two in Minnesota. Two here."

"I need to know everything that happened. I can't have any surprises. I need to be one step ahead of Agent Harris, if I'm to help you."

"There's no way to help," she said fatalistically. "Who would believe *me*?"

"What happened?"

"I forgot."

"That's not being helpful!"

She dropped onto the sofa and smoked silently for some time. "How much time do you have?" she asked bleakly.

"As long as it takes." He pulled a napkin off the kitchen island.

She slouched deeper into the cushions. "Bess and I...."

He sat cautiously next to her and squeezed the napkin around her thumb.

"What the hell are you doing?!"

"Your finger's bleeding. Who's Bess?"

"Another runaway I traveled with."

"From where? What's her last name?"

"Don't squeeze so hard! You're cutting off my circulation."

"Sorry, sorry!" He loosened his grip on her thumb. "Tell me about Bess. Where was she from? What's her last name?"

"I don't know. People don't run away from good places. She didn't talk about it. We met in Texas and traveled together for about two years. We usually headed south when winter approached, but one time we got delayed up north."

"Where?"

"In Wisconsin."

"Doing what?"

She stalled.

"Doing what, Maggie?" he insisted.

"We were messengers," she said obliquely.

"Delivering what?"

"Meth mainly. After we finished the job in Wisconsin, we were hitching across Minnesota when we met a couple at a rest stop." She stalled again.

"Who were they?"

She fidgeted. "This couple, Russ and Janine. We started talking. They offered us a warm meal and a place to sleep, which we were happy to accept. They fed us and offered us work on their farm. Things were okay at first. Bess was older and made the decisions. The plan was to work for a few weeks and make enough money to head south to Florida. So we worked during the day and at night we partied, and partied hard. Russ and Janine were smalltime dealers of all sorts of bad shit, and they'd invited friends over to party." She wiped perspiration from her forehead with the back of her hand.

"What?" he whispered.

"We'd party with men, really vile men. One disgusting redneck was the sheriff, Russ's cousin. Entertaining their friends was a way we could make additional money, Janine said—as long as they got a cut of it. Bess and I were completely fucked up by the drugs and went along with it, thinking we'd get money together to leave sooner. Then a blizzard hit that went on forever, and we were stuck in the middle of fucking nowhere." She smoked silently for a moment. "Bess was gorgeous. She didn't look fifteen. Russ was a sloppy drunk and obsessed with her. He wanted to fuck her all the time. So did the sheriff. He was infatuated also, and didn't want to share her with the other men. Russ and the sheriff would get shit-faced and fight over her." She fidgeted again. "Which left me with the other men.... I don't want talk about this.... I can't talk about this...."

"I'm... I'm getting the gist," he said, his throat dry. "Just tell me what happened with Bess."

"Bess had a temper, a really insane temper. And Janine was furious with Russ, and insanely jealous of Bess. She took her anger out on Bess. And Bess developed a crazy, murderous look. I was trapped in a house with insane people —three insane people! I was terrified all the time... by all of them. I didn't know what was going to happen from minute to minute, so I just kept my head low. Finally Bess had enough. One night we made a break for it and eventually found the highway. But that fucker of a sheriff picked us up and returned us to them! After that Bess and I were trapped and watched all the time. Then Russ became sick, and one day he died. The rat poison in the barn was missing. Bess or Janine killed him! I don't know which one. The three of us dragged his body into a forest and dug a grave through snow and frozen ground with shovels and pickaxes. It took forever while we froze, and Janine was nuts, sobbing hysterically... over the death of her baby brother. Russ was her brother, not her husband!

"That was the last straw for Bess. She told Janine that we were leaving. Janine lunged at Bess with a broken bottle. But Bess was quicker and lifted a snow shovel...." She lit another cigarette off the first, the bloody napkin still dangling from her thumb.

"What?" he asked uneasily.

A tortured expression distorted her face.

"What, Maggie?"

"Bess lopped off half of her head!" She took a few more drags. "Every night I pray to my Higher Power for amnesia, but the image doesn't go away."

"Then what?"

"What do you think? There were brains, blood all over.... We panicked. Put on every layer of clothing we could find... tarps and horse blankets from the barn... scrambled toward the river... any direction to avoid the highway and the sheriff." She struggled to calm herself, to slow her breathing. "A snowstorm covered our tracks... we only traveled at night so we wouldn't be spotted. We hopped a train... then trucks, and finally made it down south. We sold Russ's drugs on the way to make money. But I was terrified of Bess after that. She was changed. She had this look, a look I can't describe."

"That's why you asked me that question when we first met. About how a murderer might look?" he asked. It made sense now.

She nodded.

"Where's Bess now? Do you know?"

She sniffled into the napkin. "She died of a heroin overdose outside of Nashville. I buried her in the forest where we were camping out. At least she's out of her misery. But I had the horrible luck to survive."

"How did you end up in New England?"

"I hitched a ride north with two surfers, but the assholes robbed me, stole all of my stuff and dumped me on the side of a highway in Rhode Island. They left me like a bag of trash! I ended up at a crack house in Providence. The next thing I remember was waking up in a detox in Newport. A few days later I was moved over to the rehab. The first thing I did was rifle my roommate's drawers, searching for money and cigarettes. My roommate walked in while I was robbing her."

He leaned forward, his elbows on his knees, engrossed. "What did she do?"

"I was astounded. This sickly woman, shaking with DTs, stood there and watched as I went through her drawers. I don't remember exactly what she said, but it was something to the effect of 'You smell like a putrefying piece of shit. If you take a shower this very minute, I'll buy you some cigarettes'." Maggie pressed her shirt into her eyes. "And now that woman's somewhere on the bottom of Buzzards Bay."

Chapter 17

Much of the next morning was wasted in the captain's office, listening to Agent Harris drone on about his "intellectual crisis." It was astonishing to witness, but the FBI agent had the capacity for self-doubt. The Avenging Angel Theory was on shaky ground, ready to be shoved forever after into the chasm of Dunderheaded Police Work, and replaced with the equally ludicrous Jilted Lover Theory. Sandra looked at Bill and rolled her eyes in frustration. Precious time was ticking away.

"As with my Avenging Angel Theory, there are two proposed murderers," Agent Harris expounded, "the murderer of Edward Gripp and June Perkins as before, but now a totally new murderer enters the picture—the Jilted Lover, a woman irate at Lindsey Nolan for having sex with her husband."

Throughout the ensuing, tedious monologue, the famous Nolan photos were spread across the captain's desk. Harris stared unabashedly at the more titillating of the two: Nolan napping topless on her boat, the arm of the handsome baseball player, Rob Jenkins, slung across her long, tan waist. Sandra glanced at the photo as well, and wondered if adding a Zumba class to her exercise regime might tighten up her waistline in time for the wedding.

"The Gripp-Perkins murderer is clearly male," the agent pontificated, quoting statistics and winding up with "ninety percent of violent crimes are committed by men. The murderer of Nolan is clearly female, due to the indirect method of attack, characteristic of females." His prurient gaze returned to the photos. "The Newbury College murders and the Nolan murder are unrelated. It's just coincidence that they both occurred in Woods Hole at the same time."

While he maundered on, Sandra scanned her captain's office, his autographed photo of Bill Belichick, the Larry Bird and Bobby Orr bobble-heads, and finally a family photo taken at his eldest daughter's wedding. The daughter's gown was too frilly, she decided. And no way would Lenny ever wear a lime green tux. She checked her watch again. Too much of the morning was being lost. Plus, it was Bill's conversation with Maggie the evening before that she was dying to hear about.

The strategy meeting in the captain's office finally over, the two detectives went back to their office and closed the door. Bill leaned forward and related his conversation with Maggie.

After absorbing the lurid details, Sandra shook her head. "Talk about Avenging Angels."

"Yes, but at a huge cost," he whispered. "Imagine carrying that baggage around with you. It's haunted her for nearly ten years."

She leaned back in her chair. "The good news is that there are two less scumbags on this planet. What are you going to do with this information?"

"Absolutely nothing. Or... what do you think I should do?" he asked in afterthought.

"Absolutely nothing. There's no relevancy to this case, and the girls were both minors. It would clog up our investigation with too many variables... child abuse, child endangerment, unlawful sex with minors, drug trafficking, unlawful imprisonment, self-defense, manslaughter, and on and on. Besides, both perps are dead. Case closed." She stood and grabbed her jacket. "I'm going to talk to Owen Tucker. I want to find out more about the Lighthouse String Ensemble."

He turned toward his laptop. "I'm going to look through the tape from the Gripp Center once again. Something about it's bothering me, but I can't figure out what it is."

"Why am I taking this jacket?" she asked herself, draping it back over her chair. "It's going to be stifling today."

*****

Ltate: thinking about you every min. r u ok?

Mmay: life sucks... all of it.

Ltate: coming to classes 2day?

Mmay: no, too depressed. will b bored out of mind at cottage all day

Ltate: is going to be near 90 2day. sunbathe somewhere?

Mmay: yes!

Ltate: or one last dive for lobsters? weather is 2 amazing

Mmay: can't. have to be home b 4 dark. am treated like 10 yr old here. life sucks!

Ltate: dive early pm and cook lobster at ur cottage?

Mmay: yes. ill escape this prison when Geo takes nap

The Bends

*****

Owen Tucker lived down a small side road near Taft Park in the village of Woods Hole. He was the organist at the Episcopal church, taught music lessons throughout the week to schoolchildren, and on Tuesday evenings was the musical director for the Lighthouse String Ensemble.

Sandra could barely keep a straight face as the old man who welcomed her into his living room. He had an impressively long comb-over, his pants were pulled nearly to his chest to cover a potbelly, and he wore a conch shell bolo in lieu of a tie. With fluttering hands, he shooed his wife into the kitchen with instructions to make them a pot of tea. The tall, knobby wife with blue-purple hair had been a blue heron in a prior life, Sandra suspected.

"Yes," Tucker explained with grandfatherly affection, "I know Lily quite well. She's been with our group for the past two years. She plays first violin," he added, as if revealing a fact of great importance. "Our fall concert in two weeks is featuring pieces by Bach." At the word Bach, his hand swept with dramatic flair over the top of his head. He handed Sandra a concert program from the piano. "Perhaps you can attend?" he suggested with an enthusiastic smile.

"I'll check my calendar," she said politely, tucking the paper into a pocket. "And you practice every Tuesday night?"

"Yes, Tuesday evenings. Except in the summer months, June, July and August, when we don't meet at all. Too many people are on vacation."

"And recently you've had longer practices."

"Correct again. In preparation for the concert we've been meeting from seven to ten."

"Has Lily been there every Tuesday?"

"Oh, yes," Tucker answered.

*****

Bill closed his office door to block out the glares from Agent Harris. It was time to hunker down and scroll methodically through the footage, starting at eight a.m. on the morning of the Halloween party. No more distractions. The case needed closure. Now that the cast of characters was familiar to him something—anything—relevant and previously overlooked might stand out.

Around eight a.m. on October 14th, there was the usual bustle of students coming into the Gripp building for classes, including Maggie, Kyle and Lily, all carrying book bags or back packs. After morning classes, Kyle, Kristin and Curt left the building, heading toward the dorm around eleven. Fifteen minutes later, Maggie and Lily returned to the dorm as well. By noon the Gripp Center had been cleared of most students, as they'd migrated to the cafeteria in the dormitory building for lunch.

The maintenance staff appeared in the library and reception area of the Gripp building shortly after noon and set up tables, chairs, and a sound system. Around 2:00 p.m., Lily made a brief appearance in the Gripp building, headed toward the studios, and exited the building only five minutes later. A number of unfamiliar students lingered around the Gripp building throughout the afternoon, taping up Halloween decorations around the entryway. The Food Services staff showed up around four.

Bill scrolled back to the early morning when Maggie, Lily, and Kyle entered together. Maggie carried a large, frayed jean bag, Kyle an orange and blue backpack, and Lily a high-end slim leather computer case. Odd. The bag that Lily carried at 2:00 into and out of the arts center had been Maggie's frayed jean bag. Upon exiting the building, the jean bag had changed its form: no longer droopy, it was inflated and bulbous. Bill's heart raced. It contained the Nolan dive helmet! And Maggie was certainly napping soundly in her dorm room, perhaps drugged by sleeping pills and chamomile tea—oblivious to the events around her.

Bill quickly switched to the footage of the dorm. Lily entered the dorm around 2:23 p.m. with the jean bag, but it was again flattened and apparently empty. Somewhere, outside, the helmet had been stashed. In the woods? The trunk of Lily's Mustang?

Maggie left the dorm around 4:30 p.m., on her way to meet Tory V. at the Old Salt Diner.

Lily, Kyle and Amy, in Halloween costumes, left the dorm at 7:13 p.m. Lily wore elegant, black high-heeled boots that extended well above her knees. Amy wore bright red sneakers, and Kyle, sandals. Bill was overheating and loosened his tie. He switched back to camera footage of the Gripp Center. The three students joined the Halloween party at 7:15 p.m. He reviewed the footage from the party, but saw nothing new.

The group of students left the Halloween party together at 8:32 p.m. and entered the dorm at 8:34 p.m. Bill then focused on the camera footage from the side exit, next to Maggie's and Lily's room. At 8:57 Lily appeared on that footage. She'd removed her cat ears and tail, but she still wore a black shirt and black pants. Her feet were visible in the camera footage. She'd changed from the teetering high-heeled boots into pink bedroom slippers. She rushed outside, carrying a trashcan, and headed in the direction of the dumpster that was just out of camera range. At 8:58 p.m. she returned with an empty trashcan.

At 9:21 Lily made another run to the dumpster from the side door. Bill ripped off his tie, and undid the top buttons of his dress shirt. He swiped his energy drink can across his forehead and tried to slow his breathing. Lily was now wearing the black combat boots.

Lily did not show up again on the camera footage from the side door until 10:18, when she exited the dorm for a third and last run to the dumpster with the trashcan. She returned at 10:19. She was again wearing pink bedroom slippers.

There was a break in the pattern. When Lily exited the building at 9:21 p.m. for the second dumpster run, she did not return. Bill checked and re-checked the footage from the side entrance, front entrance, and back entrance by the patio and gazebo. No sign of Lily entering the building. Yet she exited the building at 10:18 for the last run to the dumpster. This meant two things. She'd returned to her room by the window sometime before 10:18, and she was unaccounted for an undetermined period of time from 9:21 to 10:18.

*****

"You're sure Lily was there every Tuesday?" Sandra pressed. Sometimes it was a good idea to check your assumptions and double check the data.

"Oh, yes." Owen Tucker smiled tenderly at the Blue Heron as she placed a tray with a floral teapot and two teacups onto a coffee table. Some interesting bauble being sold on the Shopping Channel drew her back to the TV in the kitchen, and Tucker returned his attention to his guest. "Every Tuesday. Earl Grey or Breakfast Blend, Detective?"

"Breakfast blend is fine. Have you noticed anything different about Lily recently?"

"No, nothing at all. She always arrives early and chats with the other members while she tunes her instrument. She's a very friendly, gregarious girl, and very dedicated. Though for a few practices recently she's had to leave early."

Tucker bent forward and whispered, "Just between you and me, it has caused a bit of friction with Tyler Goldman, who's second violin. He says that if Lily can't stay for the entire practice, then he should be moved to first violin. These types of professional jealousies occur all the time with musicians. Lily's better technically than Tyler so I haven't made the change, though he continues to pester me about it."

"How early has she been leaving?" Sandra asked, her vocal cords tightening. "How many times?"

"About an hour early. Maybe around 8:45. She had a conflicting event at the art college on Tuesday evenings this semester. Academics come first, I always tell my student musicians! Academics first."

Sandra's teacup rattled against its saucer. She stood abruptly, thanked Tucker for his hospitality, and hustled from his house. As she ducked into the police sedan, her smartphone rang from her pocket. It was Bill. Her lungs heaved as she lifted the phone to her lips.

There was no greeting, no collegial small talk. They blurted in unison, "It's Lily."

*****

Sex with John Sanders was a tremendous disappointment. The whole ordeal was cloddish, and I'm frankly baffled by what June saw in him, especially as she was so expert in certain techniques. His aftershave was cloying and he had coffee-breath. But no one was as bad as my bald, overweight Honors Chemistry teacher in high school. A B+ in chemistry would never do. I'm still trying to repress those horrible Friday afternoons in the stockroom where the glassware, analytical balances, and chemicals were stored.

Sex is nothing more than a means to an end. Still, the huffing and puffing on the sofa paid off—thanks for the pointers, June—because he called an emergency meeting with the Awards Committee that same afternoon. Here's their email:

"In light of the ongoing search for Lindsey Nolan [whose tissues are now being digested by the hydrolytic enzymes in the digestive tracts of two Mako sharks, ha!] and out of respect for the Nolan family and friends from the campus community, the Awards Committee unanimously voted to postpone judging and the announcement of the Windsor Award for two weeks."

Thank you, John Sanders! I'm aware of the email's content because I watched the committee compose it from my seat in MY tunnel, that I share with no one. How dare that old peeper not put in a word on my behalf about the Windsor! Old fucking perv! The postponement allows me time behind the office walls to gauge the inclinations of the judges, so I can act accordingly. With June gone, one less vote will be cast for Maggie. With June gone, needy John Sanders will be putty in my hands.

And the weather turned. More amazingly good luck. My plan of action suddenly changed. I watched the Woods Hole-Falmouth weather report from my laptop and pumped my fist into the air. Thank you, global warming! It's October and Cape Cod's having a glorious heat wave.

We're on a different boat today. It's significantly smaller than the Jack Rackham, which still sits at the NKDT dock surrounded by yellow crime scene tape. The Just For Today (Lindsey Nolan was once a lush) doesn't have staterooms with beds, a head, or a galley like the Jack Rackham. This is a garish banana boat with purple and orange glittery flames like the ones that race down the intercostal waterway in re-runs of Miami Vice or Heat Wave. I was spot-on in suggesting a dive. I know my roommate's addictions so well: nicotine, junk food, and scuba diving.

*****

Two unmarked cars screeched into the student parking lot at Newbury College. Bill and Sandra jumped out and dashed toward the dorm. Dean Shoemacher and a young police officer paced frantically at the front entrance.

"The police are at the girls' room!" the dean exclaimed.

Bill and Sandra tore down the hall.

"No one's here," a uniformed policeman said, hefting an assault rifle.

"Olivia!" Bill gasped to Sandra.

They scrambled up the staircase. Olivia's door was cracked. He pushed open the door and found her scribbling across a sketchpad. "Have you seen Lily?"

His panic registered immediately and Olivia jumped to her feet. "She was hauling her dive equipment down to the dock. Why?" She paused. "Oh... my... God..."

The detectives sprinted down the hall and the stairs. "Call headquarters!" Bill shouted to the policeman in the hallway. "Tell them to get a boat out to Spire Rock... with divers. ASAP!" He tore from the building. "We need a boat!" he called to Shoemacher. "Do you have a boat?"

"Ted Blanchard's work skiff is at the beach!" sputtered the red-faced dean. "But I'm not sure how fast it is."

"Anything will do," Bill yelled over his shoulder. "Tell him to meet us at the beach. Now!"

*****

How do I hate thee? Let me count the ways. I hate thee to the depth and breadth and height My soul can reach...

I hate the shirt Maggie's wearing. It's from the Vinland Viking Museum. It's one you might see on an eight-year old. On the front is a Viking ship, and across the back the phrase, "Cape Cod is for Vikings." Her intent is to rub in my face the fact that a fabulous job with Jessie McCabe awaits her upon graduation. Another brilliant idea: now that I've met Jessie McCabe, I wonder if she'd hire me as her art assistant if for some reason Maggie won't be able to accept the job. My advanced dive certifications should certainly impress her.

I hate it that Maggie's surrounded by interesting people. My dad, Evan, is a bore who watches the Knicks and files people's tax returns, while Derick Briggs is a stud who looks and talks like Rhett Butler and drives a Ducati. My mom networks computers and plays golf at the club, while

The Bends

Lindsey Nolan wins MacArthur Awards and Nobel Prizes, and hangs out with cool lesbian marine biologists. Life is so unfair! Maggie has had a great life of galas with celebrities, painting, and scuba diving. And if I don't act, she will win the Windsor Award. Mythic Reptiles is a ridiculous title for a painting, and the writhing snakes and lizards give me nightmares.

Today Maggie's more surly and withdrawn than usual, so I search the satellite radio for something cheerful. Spire Rock rears out of the water in the distance. I find a station that's playing Lady Gaga, Beyoncé, and Kelly Clarkson. Chick bonding music, I say to Maggie. She smiles but her mind's elsewhere.

I unzip my dive bag and swallow down two more extra strength aspirin. I'm careful not to reveal Edward Gripp's laptop that's wrapped in a towel. Maggie sees me swallow the aspirin and asks if I'm okay. Just a slight headache, I say. I'll take two more painkillers before the police arrive, and later some sucker of a doctor will prescribe me codeine. Better living through chemistry! I've rehearsed my story many times. Somehow I have to give myself a black eye and break my nose. This is going to hurt! But Mom will no doubt find the best plastic surgeon in New York City to reset it. I'm still pissed that she lifted Edward Gripp's laptop. What an idiotic thing to do! When I told her that Edward would be off in Boston for the weekend with a new girlfriend, I thought that she would just copy his hard-drive, like she did with Darren O'Day, not steal the whole frickin' computer.

"I was going to volunteer my computer skills to locate the laptop for him," she said. "He would be forever indebted to us for retrieving his stolen laptop, Lily. What terrible luck that he was killed!" Now she wants me to dispose of the laptop in Buzzards Bay.

When I asked why she didn't just toss it in the Mianus River, she told me, "Lily, saltwater has a better corrosive effect on metals. I've read about corrosion on the Internet."

I huff in frustration. Another in a long list of Mom's chores for me. Back to my story for the police. "I was taken completely by surprise," I'll tell the two doltish detectives. "I was putting on my dive equipment when out of nowhere she struck me in the face... I jumped in the water to get away... but she pursued... it was self-defense... by-the-grace-of-God (always smart to play the God card), I made it back to the boat and called for help."

*****

Ted Blanchard yanked a green tarp off the work skiff. Bill eyed the boat with a sense of dread. It was no more than flimsy pieces of sheet metal, two bench seats and an old engine. His knowledge of boats was minimal, but this boat, he realized, was constructed for slowly meandering through marshes and coastal rivers, not bucking across the open ocean.

Even Blanchard looked doubtfully at the boat as he dragged it across the sand. "It hasn't been used for months," he said gruffly, "so we'll see what happens." He pushed the boat into the shallows and swung his long, lanky leg over its side. He tilted the engine backward so that the propeller dipped into the water and squeezed the bulb to prime the engine. He muttered quietly in a grim prayer as he reached for the red starter button. The engine immediately rumbled to life.

"Um... small miracle," he said with surprise. He tossed the detectives orange flotation jackets. "Get in."

The Bends

Bill and Sandra waded in their suits through the water, climbed over the side, and huddled side by side on the front bench seat. Sandra gave Bill a reassuring pat on the forearm, but his eyes were already squeezed shut, his face in his hands. Ted Blanchard turned the outboard seaward and drove the throttle forward, while Bill's stomach lurched into his throat.

*****

We perform our usual pre-dive rituals as the Just For Today *rocks quietly in the shadow of a bird-speckled cliff. Maggie kneels on the dive platform and fills a cooler with salt water. I stand on the other side of the transom and receive the cooler from her and place it on the deck. She assumes erroneously that the cooler will later hold lobsters.*

"Let's also get lobsters for Derick, the McLeods, Ava and Danny," she suggests.

"That means we'll need seven," I respond. Maggie's an imbecile who can't do math. "That's going to take some time, so we might need to go a little deeper." Deep is good. Deep is lethal.

She shrugs indifferently. It's one of her more annoying mannerisms. "The visibility's great today," she concedes.

"I got a sun tan on the way out here. Who'd have thunk it, a tan in October. I can't wait to see your cottage and your new work," I prattle on, making mindless chitchat.

*"*Evolution *is only a sketch right now, but it'll give you an idea of what I'm trying to do."*

Maggie actually takes her work seriously. I smile and nod, as if I'm interested. She heads toward the NK dive helmets. So cool! I love those things.

"Use this one," she suggests. "I'll wear the heavier one with the weird canister thing that Lin was working on." The mention of Lindsey silences her for a few minutes. Our ritual continues solemnly, affixing the regulators to tanks, strapping our tanks onto our buoyance compensator vests, lugging on our weight belts, checking the seams at our dive booties and gloves where cold water invariably leaks in.

We're finally ready to go. I stand on the dive platform, my black fins flapping impatiently over the edge, while Maggie leans over the transom and attaches my regulator to a connector on my dive helmet. She then lifts her helmet onto her head, secures the watertight seal around her neck, and motions for me to attach her regulator to the connector on her helmet. Lindsey Nolan has done something peculiar to that regulator. In addition to the air hose attaching the regulator to the helmet, there's also a thick black wire, or tube, I can't tell which.

Maggie hands me a net and a plastic bag of bones that she pulled off of Mrs. McLeod's leftover chicken. The dive ritual continues. I'll miss our dives together, the lobster tail and white wine dinner parties on the Jack Rackham with Maggie and Kyle, but I castigate myself for my moment of weakness, of melancholic nostalgia. Get over it, I tell myself, there's an important job to do. I smile at Maggie. She awaits my usual line with an expectant smirk. I yell gleefully toward the green depths, "Fried chicken, lobsters! Come and get it!"

Somewhere amidst her sadness, Maggie musters a small laugh, and I splash into the shimmering water.

*****

Sandra nudged Bill and he glanced sickly upward. A jagged rock showed through the haze. Despite the sun and blue skies, Spire Rock was a diabolic place, fuzzy and jittery in the heat. The small skiff seemed to sense it too, for the motor briefly faltered as it eased forward. The rock's profile was suggestive of a ghost shrouded in a black cloak with a pointy hood. The treacherous edges and spikes rendered the rock insurmountable. The sharp ledges were white with feathers, bird droppings, and sea salt. But no other boat was in sight.

"What if they're not here?" Bill said miserably, squinting in the harsh light. "What if I've told the police boats to go to the wrong location? Maggie could be dead by now!"

"Where else would they go for lobsters?" Sandra asked.

He balled his maroon ball cap in his hands. "I have no clue."

Blanchard turned the boat around a corner of the rock. The motor suddenly idled in neutral. Sandra unsnapped her flotation vest and whipped the Glock from her shoulder holster.

Under a black cliff on the backside of the spire, an orange and purple banana boat glistened in the sunlight.

"It's Nolan's love boat," she whispered.

Bill nodded. A photo of this same boat had lain on the captain's desk that very morning, the bikini-clad Nolan and a Scandinavian Interpol officer poised for a kiss. "This boat just cannot stay out of trouble."

*****

"The bigger ones are over there, I bet." I point downward to a dastardly razor-edged outcropping. "We've picked over this area before."

Maggie's helmet tilts toward the surface. "Did you hear something?"

My heart surges at the question. An intruder? An unexpected variable in my carefully devised scheme? "Shh!" We float motionless by the slippery rock face. "It sounds like a small motor."

Maggie gazes upward. "But I can't see anything."

"We're too deep. Maybe it's the same thug who dumped the body?" I scan the sandy bottom just feet below us. "I don't see that body."

"It's hard to tell if we're in the same place."

"A bottom current could have moved it."

Maggie shrugs an annoying "no comment."

An intruder is an aggravating deviation from the game plan, and my mind scrambles to reorder the actions of the next few minutes. I'll have to direct my overwrought dialogue at the intruder: "I was attacked! Please go get the police!" I'll be too distraught to do anything but sob and cling to my stuff in the boat. If I can convince the intruder to seek help, I'll have time to lodge Edward Gripp's laptop in some dark crevice, only to be seen ever after by the stalked eyes of a curious lobster. Chore done, Mom. If the intruder will not leave, I'll just have to improvise.

But the first order of business is Maggie.

"Let's forget about him," I say cheerfully, "and get us some dinner!"

Maggie frowns through the transparent facemask. "It's daylight this time. There's no way they're not going to see the boat. If that asshole messes with the boat in any way—"

"They won't," I reassure her. "It's probably some decrepit retiree on a fishing trip. Let's check that crevice there," I point. "I bet there're big ones there."

Maggie's helmet shakes obstinately in the negative. "I want to go up and check that the boat's alright. And see who's there, and tell them that we're diving and to leave the boat alone. Come on." She turns to climb the wall.

Thank you, Maggie! Your air hose is now within reach. I reach for my dive knife.

*****

Bill tumbled over the transom onto the deck of the *Just For Today*. Knees wobbling, he struggled to get his sea legs. The deck was lined with long nylon seats, dotted with cup holders. It was an ostentatious party boat. Music played from two speakers at the helm, an old tune by Alanis Morrisette. Nolan's boat provided a more solid foundation than the skiff, and the slithering sensation in his belly subsided. Sandra ducked briefly into the small cabin, while Blanchard secured the lines of the skiff onto the banana boat.

Sandra reappeared from the dark space. "Nothing in there but a V-berth and a small head. The dive equipment's gone." She leaned fearlessly over the gunwale and scanned the water. "I don't see bubbles. They must be very deep, or they're somewhere else."

Bill rigidly clung to a cleat while she searched the dive bags. From a black US Divers bag, she pulled out an iPod with headphones, a Viking museum T-shirt (she had the exact same one, but in an X-large), shorts, a thread-worn towel, and a plastic bag containing a pack of Marlboro lights and a lighter. The pink and blue dive bag contained two water bottles, a sleeveless sweatshirt, purple running shorts, and two neatly folded towels. The bottom towel was unusually heavy.

Sandra unfolded the towel and held up a gray laptop. "Someone's taking out the trash for Mom."

*****

I slice effortlessly through the plastic of Maggie's air hose with my dive knife, severing the lifeline of oxygen from her tank to her helmet. Air bubbles explode around her head. Her hesitation seems endless. Then "Fuck!" shouts into my ears from the speakers. She labors to turn in my direction, but the new helmet is heavy and it takes her a moment. The eruption of bubbles frightens her and her face contorts. At her shoulder, in her peripheral vision, she spots it: her air hose flailing and dancing like a decapitated snake. There's a sudden reckoning as air escapes into the water instead of replenishing her helmet. Then her confusion gives way to a wide-eyed glare. For a moment she says nothing as more air evacuates from her helmet and air tube. Her breathing's labored, yet her eyes boil into mine. There's something she recognizes in my face, unnerving me. My life is a film, fast-forwarding in front of her eyes; she sees and knows all.

The lobster net drops from her hand and she grasps my wrist. Her two thumbs dig deep between the bones of my wrist. "Bitch!" I scream at her. My dive knife falls away, hitting the bottom with a sandy poof. No matter, I was never intending to hack or stab. Cutting equals blood and blood equals sharks. Scrawny Maggie's no match for my powerful hands and feet. My knee finds her belly and she heaves forward. Groans of pain waft through my speaker. A swipe of her hand dislodges the helmet's seal at my neck and cold water swirls around my head. How dare she strike back! Fury courses through my blood like lava. My hand slams her helmet back into the razor-edged rock. Her eyes are round in terror, her breaths ragged from a lack of oxygen. With another blow I strike her belly. The butt of her hand thrusts upward, knocking my helmet off, silencing her curses and cries in my ears. I kick her, this time in the ribs, and grasp both sides of her helmet. I pound her helmet again and again on the rock, but it doesn't crack. My helmet hangs down my back, bouncing on my tank to the rhythm of my rage. The oxygen in her helmet is now depleted and her face is a tan-blue. My pounding persists, unrelenting. Finally her eyes roll and close, and her furious, silent tirade ceases. Her limbs go limp, and I release my death grip on her helmet. Maggie drops to the bottom, lost in a cloud of sand.

My lungs are a cauldron of burning gas and blood. I twist and strain to retrieve my helmet, but it dangles too far down my back and out of reach. Saltwater singes my eyes and I grope blindly for the closest ledge. I kick off my fins and place my feet on the slippery shelf. I crouch and launch myself upward, blazing like a rocket toward light and air.

****

Images waft through Maggie's dying mind, memories sputter forward. Mother, a beautiful ebony woman, stands between the knees of a wiry, blond cowboy. He presses his mouth into her belly and she shoves him away with a strident laugh. A bottle smashes. A hot wind passes through the scorched trailer, a rip of fabric, escaping footsteps. For hours, maybe days, there is nothing but silence and hunger. Then a flashlight beam slashes the darkness. A parole officer creeps forward, her boots heavy with desert sand. She gasps to an unseen partner outside, "There's a child in here!"

A string of low clicks sound within the helmet, and a trickle of air caresses Maggie's cheek. Her eyelids twitch.

The grizzled man is fat and greasy like the griddle where he cooks the girls' breakfasts. He won't stop bothering me, the orphan cries to the counselor. Why doesn't the counselor listen? Or believe her? Sleep eludes the frail girl for weeks. Something—anything—has to be done. Only one option is left. Her few possessions fit easily into a plastic Hello Kitty backpack that had been donated to the girls' home. On Route 17 north of Phoenix a truck finally stops and she climbs in. "Headin' north toward Black Canyon City," the driver says. She shrugs a whatever. Direction doesn't matter to her.

The next stream of air hits her cheek like an arctic blast; Maggie's eyelids flutter. A metallic female voice sounds in her ear: "Respiratory rate too slow. Breathe deeply. Respiratory rate too slow." She dreamily opens her eyes. The place beyond the window is a peaceful olive green. It's the green forest near Nashville.

"Bess, wake up... C'mon, wake up. If we leave now, we might make Alabama by tonight. Bess?" She shudders and gulps air. That's no window... no forest! Other sensations percolate into her consciousness, a throbbing belly and head, coldness at her feet and neck. "Respiratory rate stabilizing," the voice says. "Follow the prompts. Two decompression stops required. At my command, follow the prompts."

The past few minutes cascade in Maggie's consciousness and she looks frantically around her. The tank anchors her to the bottom, and she struggles onto all fours. Lily's dive knife peeks from the sand, so she stretches for it and wiggles it into her weight belt. Lily might try anything when she approaches the surface. If the boat is even still there....

"Follow the prompts," the voice in the helmet insists once again. "Two decompression stops required. At my command, stop at the required decompression stops."

"Whatever you say, Lin," Maggie whispers, as she climbs the slick rock wall.

Chapter 18

Bill glanced at his balcony. Maggie had dumped the snow from the two plastic chairs into the parking lot below and sat blowing smoke rings into the cold January air. He slid the screen lid from Hercule Poirot's terrarium and knocked some crickets from a paper bag into the dried leaves in the snake's lair. The garter snake moved with furtive interest toward the bugs. Now all of the herps had had their dinner. Bill, too, was full. He dropped the empty pizza boxes into a recycling bin in the kitchenette, and looked once again at Maggie. That woman had an appetite.

He leapt over the back of his sofa and landed on the cushions on his back. He aimed his clicker at the TV. Yes—a Celtics-Knicks game! After a minute or two, he realized that it was impossible to focus on the game. Six points had just been scored and he had no memory of who had made the baskets. The mall rapist case was confounding him and Sandra. It had to be an employee who knew the mall hours and back corridors behind the stores very well, and especially the placement of the security cameras. Somehow the rapist always bypassed the cameras so they were of no help, unlike the essential role they'd played in the Edward Gripp case.

Something felt very wrong about the security guards, especially the bellicose one who drove the blue Segway.

Waterproof cameras hidden along the ledges of Spire Rock had proved essential in identifying the New York City drug dealers from the *Misty One.* The men had been captured attaching plastic bags of a designer drug, a highly addictive hallucinogen, to hooks hammered into the rocks above the high water mark. Also captured by the cameras were the drug pickups by the landscaper, Frankie MacDonald, and Lisa Caffrey's brother, Lester.

His view drifted to Maggie's black combat boots and pink socks strewn on the carpet. What was she wearing on the snowy balcony? he worried, peering over the back of the sofa. His L. L. Bean boots were on her sockless feet and his down coat was slung over her shoulders. At work next week his coat would be permeated by cigarette smoke and lavender perfume. Her scent would linger while she would be long gone, embarking with Jessie McCabe from San Diego, destination French Polynesia on the research vessel, *Lindsey N.*

God bless, Lindsey N., wherever she was. The NKDT dive helmet was a miraculous invention and had saved Maggie's life. As a last minute modification Lindsey Nolan had constructed an extra tube of some indestructible metal-rubber fiber that was part of an airflow backup system activated when the diver's respiratory rate dropped too low. The helmet, Sara Kauni had explained to him at the reception at the Montaque Galley, had oxygen and carbon dioxide sensors, and another sensor that detected respiratory rate. Additionally, it monitored depth, pressure, and dive duration, so that the tiny computer could determine the necessary decompression stops to inform the diver on where and how long to wait before resurfacing.

That October afternoon on the *Just For Today* a stream of green bubbles had appeared next to the cliff. Seconds later, the yellow high vis helmet broke the surface and a dazed, exhausted face stared from behind the facemask. Moved by uncontainable relief and joy, he'd released his grasp from the cleat and jumped onto the dive platform, wildly shouting and waving his arms. Terror melted from Maggie's face and was replaced by sobs of relief. She splashed toward the boat. He and Sandra each grabbed a shoulder of the wetsuit and lifted Maggie's light body through the air and onto the boat. She tore at the neck seal and tugged the helmet off her head. She halted, spotting the body on the deck.

Lily Tate had surfaced minutes before Maggie, bursting from the water, her arms flailing. Moans of pain garbled her accusations... lunatic... attack... savage! They'd pulled her aboard and for an interval she crawled across the deck, hissing and frothing like a rabid dog. Then she'd shrieked and collapsed, limbs convulsing, brain seizing. Nitrogen bubbles in her joints made her movements agonizing. As the coroner's report later attested, two large embolisms had lodged in the arteries of her brainstem and massive hemorrhaging had ensued. Tracy Blane determined the cause of death as decompression sickness, aka Caisson's disease, aka "the bends."

While Evan Tate silently mourned his daughter at the mortuary, his wife's Corvette screeched into the parking lot of the administration cottage at Newbury College and skidded into a spot once reserved for Edward Gripp. Jean Tate dashed into the dean's office, slamming her fists on Charles Shoemacher's desk.

"The Nolan family framed my daughter... the college has lax security measures... the Admissions Office does not thoroughly screen applicants!"

As she snarled a threat of lawsuits, the police entered Shoemacher's office. The charges against Mrs. Tate were lengthy. Upon posting bail and returning to Cos Cob, she found press vans massing around her home. The police had already removed computers from her home office. Mrs. Tate's computer was found to contain an astonishing array of information: the president of her country club's side businesses in the Caribbean, a member of her golf team's affair with the tennis pro, falsified school budgets by Lily's high school principal, photos of her next-door neighbor cross dressing when his wife traveled abroad, among others.

Upon finding her lovely executive home in Polo Springs cordoned off by yellow tape, Jean had wailed to Evan, "What will the neighbors think! And the women in my golf league?"

The humiliation was too much to bear. In the middle of the night she slipped from her house and climbed over the guardrail of the Mianus River Bridge. Jean had one last thought as she flung herself outward... the faculty at Newbury College had never recognized the full potential of her exceptionally talented daughter, Lily.

*****

On a chilly night some months before, in mid-October, *Talisman*, a transoceanic motorsailer, had floated silently in the shadow of a black cliff. The pirate on deck gazed upward. The jagged spire of rock that loomed over his boat bore no resemblance to his intended destination of tropical trees and lush vegetation. The only inhabitants of the pinnacle were seabirds that nestled along the narrow ledges and invertebrates clinging precariously to a slick rock wall below the surface. The seclusion of the island was what drew the pirate to this particular destination, as there was a body to attend to.

Talisman had lain hidden in the boathouse of his partner, the inside man at MIT, while provisions for the long voyage were secretly loaded. As night fell, the pirate had made a break for the open ocean. Upon crossing Buzzards Bay, a small red blink caught his peripheral vision. He crossed the helm and stared out a port window. Yes, it was definitely a flashing light of some kind. *An omen*, his wise grandmother would say. *Watch for omens, as they reveal all.* His first impulse was to steer away from it and continue the dash to the ocean, but some inexplicable force drew him to it, like a moth to a flame. *Watch for omens, my beautiful boy.* The old woman's advice had served him well over the years. Close calls had been many, but somehow *Talisman* always slipped through.

A thin veil of mist covered the water, and he stared into the darkness. He cautiously maneuvered the boat next to the blinking light and turned off the engine. He bent over the gunwale and cursed aloud in his native tongue. He leapt fleetly across the deck for a boat hook and nudged the source of the red light along the hull toward the transom.

It was a body in an orange flotation vest. A small light was affixed to the vest between the shoulder blades. If the person were dead he would simply push it away from his boat and be on his way. *Talisman* was already two days behind schedule, and a small storm was brewing north of Bermuda. The last thing he needed was to talk to the Coast Guard or local authorities about a corpse. Was this body a portent of a smooth voyage or of disaster breaking with every wave? He considered the body for a moment longer. The person had climbed onto some jetsam and curled into a fetal position, hands tucked into armpits to preserve warmth. He reached over the transom and moved a string of wet hair from the neck. There was still a pulse, though it was slow and faint. What to do? He could veer quickly into shore and dump the body on the beach, but too many beach houses lined the coast and *Talisman* would surely be spotted. Worse, the person would die of exposure during the night. Unsure of what compelled him, he grabbed the flotation vest at the shoulders and dragged the body over the gunwale. Anyone on shore with binoculars might be watching his actions. He hopped back into the captain's chair, restarted the engine, and headed out to that sharp rock that projected from the waters between the Vineyard and Elizabeth Islands.

Under the shadow of the cliff, the pirate dropped anchor. He pulled the person—a woman—from her wet clothes. Despite the ice-blue skin, her body was exquisite. He dressed her in a pair of dry pants and a wool shirt, then rolled her in a blanket. He lifted the blanket-woman-cocoon onto a sofa in the salon, and pulled up the anchor. Whoever she was, she'd delayed his mission by a half an hour. *Talisman* headed straight into the Atlantic, avoiding all shipping lanes.

Now, almost three months later, the pirate secured the gun in his holster. There were drug smugglers hiding in this remote chain of islands. There'd been a run-in here once before. He searched the boat for his unscheduled passenger. She had to be watched continuously. She was in one of her moods again, and thankfully hadn't spoken to him in two days. She was at her usual place at the transom, gazing northwestward toward the United States as if transmitting some invisible signal through the hot air of the tropics toward icy Cape Cod.

"I'm grateful that you picked me up. Truly I am. But I have three children, a husband, a family relying on me," she'd whined endlessly over the past few weeks. "They'll be missing me, thinking I'm dead!"

I have two wives, a number of mistresses, five children in three different countries and certainly many more that I don't know about, he thought to inform her. But it was best to remain silent about his business.

"You must drop me at the closest port," she'd demanded, stomping around the deck. "I don't care what contraband you're smuggling. I won't say anything to the police. I promise. Just drop me onshore so I can get home!"

For the first few weeks of the voyage, his strategy had been to remain mute and non-communicative, as if her language was incomprehensible to him. But she hadn't fallen for it.

"I know you understand me perfectly," she had said. "You were off the coast of Massachusetts for whatever reason, and the instruction labels on this boat are all in English." She'd stomped around some more and then muttered hotly under her breath, "You probably have a fucking business degree from Harvard."

He'd suppressed a burst of laughter. Harvard... please. His degree was from Oxford.

The most disconcerting thing about his passenger was that she'd forcibly removed the navigation system from the helm. He found her one morning tinkering with the wiring as if trying to rig some communication system. The unit was now securely locked in his cabin, but it was a source of recurrent concern whenever she wandered nonchalantly by his cabin door, no doubt envisioning how the lock might be disengaged.

He had no clue as to her name or identity, nor would she tell him when he finally decided to speak. Her response was always the same. "I'm a mother whose family is missing me." He could certainly activate the Internet and search for a missing woman around Buzzards Bay, but there was something mysteriously compelling about not knowing. And it was wise to keep his cyber footprint to a minimum. He finally gave up asking. Besides, what a disappointment it would be to discover that she was merely the trophy wife of a dentist or shoe salesman who'd fallen from a party boat after having too many margaritas. But the woman didn't drink alcohol, even after repeated offers of his superb Cuban rum. And that didn't explain why she was wearing a flotation vest. If she was a trophy wife, she had some level of intelligence.

In addition to her attempt to sabotage the navigation system, she'd walked with lithe confidence toward the prow, despite the rough seas that day, and peered at the boat registration. She had sniped, "Who the hell are you kidding? That registration's bogus." Another time he had to wave her away with his pistol when she tried to infiltrate the engine room.

Most astounding of all was that his passenger took a knife and two forks to construct a primitive sextant. After studying the position of the sun on the horizon and shadows across the deck, she scrawled mathematical formulae across the galley's white table—there was no paper on board—and predicted *Talisman*'s location to within a tenth of a degree of their actual location calculated by the GPS locked away in his cabin. This navigational information had caused her consternation, and she'd informed him in her off-putting American manner that, "This boat only holds four hundred gallons of fuel. I've seen one just like it at the Boston Boat Show. We'll run out of fuel before reaching Bermuda."

"We're not going to Bermuda," he'd said casually, walking away. But she was right about the fuel. It was time to switch over to quantal cells.

Installing the sun panels with the quantal cells had induced her to clamber across the roof and gaze underneath at the wiring. For days she barraged him with tedious questions about the technology—all of which he ignored. Finally she asked to unscrew one of the panels to look at the circuitry. This seemed a harmless enough request and might shut her up for a while, he'd decided at the time. She proceeded to scrawl more equations on the galley table for days, though their meaning was unintelligible to him. He was an entrepreneur and revolutionary, not a physicist or mathematician, as his passenger apparently was.

Then the storm hit. He and the woman screamed commands at each other throughout the night as *Talisman* was lashed by monster winds and waves. Had he not had a second mate who understood boats and who adroitly constructed a sea anchor as hurricane gales blew, *Talisman* would surely have been lost in the raging seas. For this he was overwhelmingly grateful to his ingrate of a passenger. Yes, she was most definitely a blessing and a curse rolled into one lovely package.

Now *Talisman* was anchored in the aqua shallows of a remote island, and the nameless woman was gazing northwestward again. She stood barefoot in her only pair of panties and one of his white undershirts, her long hair tied off her neck with his shoelace. The tropics became her. Her skin was now as brown as the islanders'. Her hair was streaked white-blonde from the sun, and her eyes were light green like palm fronds.

He stepped onto the deck. "Beautiful," he confessed in his exotic accent.

After days of silence, Her Highness deigned to speak to him. "Yes," she agreed. "This island's very beautiful. Maybe I can have a swim?"

"Why not?" he said pleasantly.

He watched her climb over the transom and down a dive ladder. She hovered, in his snorkel and mask, over a lush fringe reef. One day he would have to release her at some port city with an American embassy. But only after the delivery of the quantal cells was made, which would finally restore the balance of nations and free third world countries from the yoke of the superpowers. Besides, the woman—despite the prickly temperament—was an omen, a very good omen. Amazing luck this nameless woman had, finding that white surfboard to crawl upon and save herself from freezing in Buzzards Bay.

THE END

An excerpt from Leah Devlin's new mystery, *Vital Spark*, the first book in the Chesapeake Tugboat Murders.

The Upper Chesapeake
June 2017

"Once upon a time there was a tugboat..." was how every story her grandfather ever told her started. Next came his breathless pause, "... named..."

She waited expectantly, gazing up into his eyes overhung with bushy eyebrows. Gulls' nests, he called them.

"... named..." he'd teasingly repeat.

"What, Papa?" asked the squirming five-year-old.

"... the *Old Gray Mare*." On another day, "... *the Crabby Crab*" or "... *the Gimpy Gull*."

But more often than not his story started with, "Once upon a time there was a tugboat named... the *Vital Spark*."

That revealed, she could settle into the old sofa that had long given up and bowed into the floorboards. Then would unwind his tale of perilous adventures on the waters of the Chesapeake, starring a courageous grandfather named Randy—never was a person more aptly named—and his equally courageous granddaughter, Alex, master and mate of some tugboat, usually named the *Vital Spark*.

North of Chestertown Alex spotted a gas station and pulled over. She stepped out of her car and removed her suit jacket. It was ridiculous to have bought a suit to interview for a job in which she'd be wearing oilskins, a bathing suit, or a pair of waders. But the suit had paid off, and so had the haircut, cut just to her shoulders. A shorter haircut would make her look "mature and professional," Richard had told her at the start of the job hunt.

At the interview itself, she'd been able to reply an honest "Yes" to all questions. Yes about operating small boats, scuba diving certifications, statistical analysis, writing technical reports for funding agencies, conducting water monitoring tests... all of the predictable questions. Yes, yes, yes. And yes, she knew about invertebrate, fish, and bird species in the Delmarva region. She'd grown up on the Chesapeake, after all.

She pressed Randy's number on her smartphone and listened to it ring. No answer; no surprise. He had an aversion to technology and used it as little as possible.

"Papa," she said to his voicemail, "I'll be there very soon, before dinner. I have a surprise."

Over a dinner of crab cakes at the Dockside Café, she'd tell him her wonderful news. Old Ben would certainly join them, as she'd sent him a text with orders not to tell Papa of her surprise. She and Ben were co-conspirators in all sorts of surprises for her grandfather. Alice and Harry Hoffman, who owned the café, would be there. And hopefully Alan and Jacob. All the usual suspects.

She'd landed the job and would be moving back to River Glen!

No more sporadic contract work. No more part-time teaching at the community college. Finally, a full-time job with benefits! So what if, according to the man who'd interviewed her, the tiny marine station was very isolated, just a desk and a computer that sometimes worked, a rickety dock, and some salt water tanks. It was pretty much a one-man operation, he'd said. It all sounded fine to her. Things had ended with Richard, without so much as a whimper, since there wasn't much passion there in the first place, so no strings tied her to Washington, DC. Best yet, the marine station was just a few miles from her grandfather's house where she'd grown up.

Her gas tank full, she climbed back into her car and headed up 213 North.

Randy would be easy to find, as his world was circumscribed within a quarter-mile circle surrounding his house and dock. Either he'd be listening to CDs on the porch with Old Ben, pulling crab traps from the mouth of river, or be at Harlow's Pub, awaiting some bleached blonde divorcée from the marina to drop into the bar stool next to his.

Some time, many years ago, she had stopped keeping a tally of her grandfather's women. His first wife, her biological grandmother, had departed long before Alex was born. Her presence in the small village had been as transient as a wind sweeping across the bay. Wife Number Two was a music teacher at the elementary school. Alex had liked Number Two because she came with a piano. Number Three had worked in the public affairs office for the Baltimore Ravens, so for the year-and-a-half she'd lived with them, Alex got free NFL apparel. Randy's tastes then shifted toward the exotic: the Romanian gypsy, the Somali painter, and the Australian wanna-be-rock star. By the time Alex was in junior high, she'd come to regard the assorted wives as temporary lodgers. Six wives were apparently Randy's limit; after that it was easier and less costly to date the women in Harlow's. Besides, the younger ones could be accessed immediately by the marvel of texting, his sole impetus for the purchase of a smartphone. By the time, she'd left for college, she'd simply lost count of all of her grandfather's assorted flames and flings.

Alex's wristwatch, a birthday gift from Richard, vibrated on her wrist. "As a favor, I entered in all your important appointments. Since you're late for everything," he'd said when presenting the gift at the posh restaurant on M Street.

The Bends

Okay, she'd concede that she had punctuality issues. But Randy was partially to blame for that. Who grew up in a house without clocks?

"You can keep time by watching the tides," Randy had told her. That method worked fine when one was at the water's edge, but proved problematic inland. And he'd caused her to miss an entire year of elementary school because on the spur of the moment he'd decided to home school her. When school officials finally appeared at the house, asking her whereabouts, they found that she'd missed an entire year of math and social studies, but was the only fourth grader in the state of Maryland to have read the entirety of *Moby Dick.* No more home schooling, the school officials had insisted; they made her repeat fourth grade. And she was late to school so many times in eighth grade—it was so much more fun pulling crab traps in the morning with Randy and Ben than waiting for the school bus—that she had to repeat that year as well. When she finally entered the ninth grade, two years older and more developed than the other girls, the boys were relentlessly annoying. Worse, everyone assumed her to be like her notoriously amorous grandfather. That whole year was just plain awkward.

According her buzzing smartwatch, she was supposed to meet Richard at the gym in thirty minutes. Hot Yoga for Couples. Eventually the complicated settings would have to be changed, but figuring which part of the screen to tap or swipe was too daunting a task. Even though they'd broken up months before, the watch still reminded her, many times a day, where she was to be were she still the girlfriend of Richard Wells, for he had programmed in her appointments six months out. The good news about the all-controlling watch and the all-controlling ex-boyfriend was that they'd gotten her to her interview on time. She finally had a job, and home was only minutes away.

She turned off the AC and unrolled the window. A blast of heat and humidity—the smells of Chesapeake country, steamy grass and brackish water, of youthful summers—enveloped her. She started down the hill toward the river, passing the bed & breakfast owned by the Dennistons, the seafood restaurant run by her gay friends, Alan and Jacob, and the marina owned forever by the Smyth family. She rattled over the bridge and turned down the river road, passing the Hoffmans' Dockside Café, then Harlow's Pub, Luna's Tarot Cards, and a boatyard. Through the trees she could glimpse the houses of the two inseparable friends, Ben Hancock and her grandfather. She passed Ben's cottage and pulled in at the driveway to Randy's house. How she loved the large porch, and the dock jutting out into the river! Tied to the cleats was the ever-faithful tugboat, the *Vital Spark*.

She parked next to Randy's pickup truck and stepped out of the car. She pulled her shirttails out of the constricting polyester suit pants and rolled up her sleeves. Randy's puppy spotted her, bounded off the porch and pinned her against the car door. Water Boy was a gift from Randy's last girlfriend, the dog groomer. The dog jumped up on her, licking her pants and nipping at her hands.

"Ouch, shit, down!" There was no collar with which to restrain him. "Sit, Water Boy! Sit!" He leapt up again, nipping at her hand. Dog obedience was a foreign concept to Randy. Maybe if she ignored the dog, he'd calm down. She pulled her duffel bag from the backseat, while he lifted his leg and peed on her tire. He accosted her once again and clamped onto to the cuff of her pants. By the time she'd dragged him to the porch, her hem was shredded and coated with drool. No matter. After today she'd never have to wear a stifling suit again. She had a job with benefits. All was perfect in the life of Alexandra Allaway.

"Papa!" she called, pushing through the door. She

dropped her bag on the U-shaped sofa. An Allman Brothers CD played in the kitchen. Odd—she'd never heard Randy listen to the Allman Brothers. His passion was for the British Invasion bands, the Who, the Stones, the Animals. Another strange thing... usually when he heard her car pull in, he would stride out the door—followed by a crazed dog—then he'd lift her off her feet and spin her around, the ritual culminating with a scotch-scented kiss on her cheek.

The house was unnervingly still.

Then she saw Randy's head over the back of his recliner. He was napping. During her last visit, when she'd brought Richard to meet him, a disastrous weekend all in all, Randy had appeared wan and tired. Richard had that effect on people. She tiptoed around his chair and put her hand on his shoulder.

"Papa?"

Her knees gave way. Thrust through Randy's faded Pink Floyd tee-shirt and chest, into his heart, was a bloody carving knife.

To be continued....

About The Author:
Leah Devlin

"Leah Devlin is a mystery writer and marine biologist who grew up in the Washington, DC area. *The Bottom Dwellers, Ægir's Curse* and *The Bends* comprise a trilogy of mystery-thrillers centered on the scientific village of Woods Hole, Massachusetts, where Leah was a scientist at the Marine Biological Laboratory for over ten summers. At the epicenter of the action is the brilliant yet disturbed Nobel laureate, Lindsey Nolan, as well as her colleagues and family.

Leah's upcoming mystery-thrillers, the Chesapeake Tugboat Murders, are set in the fictional village of River Glen, a site of a notorious 1680s pyrate massacre that attracts modern day treasure hunters and various unsavory characters to the village. The first novels in this series, *Vital Spark* and *Spider* are completed. Leah is presently writing the third in the series, *The Death of a Chrome Diva.*

Leah enjoys outdoor adventures of all kinds: motorcycle journeys along winding back roads, boating, diving, rock-climbing, skiing, and long-distance trekking. When not traveling, she divides her time between Philadelphia and her boat on the Chesapeake.

Please visit www.leahdevlin.com and Leah Devlin's Mystery-Thrillers on Facebook for her essays on characters and landscapes that appear in her novels, and photography from her travels and adventures."

THE BOTTOM DWELLERS

BY

LEAH DEVLIN

Bioengineer and Party Girl...

Lindsey Nolan has it all: inventions paying large dividends, a dream job in the scientific village of Woods Hole, Massachusetts, and a stable of eager playmates. But when Lindsey wakes up in rehab with no memory of how she got there, her world is turned upside down. Her roommate, an HIV-positive teenage prostitute named Maggie, is the most volatile patient on the ward. The facility is plagued by disturbing thefts. And another theft unfolds when her competitor, an engineer named Karen Battersby, discovers and steals Lindsey's astonishing new invention from her Woods Hole lab. Lindsey and Maggie must face the consequences of past transgressions if they hope to deal with present perils and ascend from the desolate world of the Bottom Dwellers.

PENMORE PRESS
www.penmorepress.com

ÆGIR'S CURSE

BY

LEAH DEVLIN

A thousand years ago, the Viking colony of Vinland was ravaged by a swift-moving plague ... a curse inflicted by the sea god Ægir. The last surviving Norseman set the encampment and his longboat ablaze to ensure that the disease would die with him and his brethren.

In present-day Norway, a distinguished professor is found murdered, his priceless map of Vinland missing. The ensuing investigation leads to the reclusive world of Lindsey Nolan, a scientist and recovering alcoholic who has been sober for five years. Lindsey reluctantly agrees to help the detective who's hunting the murderer, but she has a bigger problem on her hands: a mysterious disease that's spreading like wildfire through the population of Woods Hole. As she races against a rising body count to discover the source of the plague, disturbing events threaten her hard-won sobriety—and her life. Will Lindsey be the next victim of Ægir's curse?

Leah Devlin is rapidly establishing herself as a writer of modern day mystery-thrillers. This story is as tight as a piano wire. Life at a seaside town in New England is full of treacherous undercurrents and peril, as residents are threatened by a menace from a thousand years ago. Murder, romance and deceit are a potent mix in this gripping novel, which I didn't want to put down.—James Boschert, author of the Talon Series and *Force 12 in German Bight*

PENMORE PRESS
www.penmorepress.com

Force 12 in German Bight
by
James Boschert

Considering that oil and gas have been flowing from under the North Sea for the best part of half a century, it is perhaps surprising that more writers have not taken the uncompromising conditions that are experienced in this area -- which extends from the north of Scotland to the coasts of Norway and Germany – for the setting of a novel. James Boschert's latest redresses the balance.

The book takes its title from the name of an area regularly referred to in the legendary BBC Shipping Forecast, one which experiences some of the worst weather conditions around the British Isles. It is a fast-paced story which smacks of authenticity in every line. A world of hard men, hard liquor, hard drugs and cold-blooded murder. The reality of the setting and the characters, ex-military men from both sides of the Atlantic, crooked wheeler-dealers, and Danish detectives, male and female, are all in on the action.

This is not story telling akin to a latter day Bulldog Drummond, nor a James Bond, but simply a snortingly good yarn which will jangle the nerve ends, fill your nose with the smell of salt and diesel oil, your ears with the deafening sound of machinery aboard a monster pipe-dredging ship and, above all, make you remember never to underestimate the power of the sea.

–Roger Paine, former Commander, Royal Navy .

PENMORE PRESS
www.penmorepress.com

WILDFIRE IN THE DESERT

BY

BRUNO JAMBOR

Action Adventure, Crime, Mystery,
Southwest History

Highly entertaining, well researched
and original:

A Navy veteran returns home to his ancestral land to escape the pace of modern life. His nephew begs him to hide the drugs he is transporting to escape his pursuers.

An astronomer trying to find a replacement for his estranged wife finds solace in his work with the stars.

Police and the drug cartel try to recover the missing shipment, regardless of consequences, ready to sacrifice any opponent.

The antagonists crisscross the desert of Southern Arizona in a chess game where the loser will be eliminated.

Unexpected help comes from a famous missionary who blazed new paths through the same desert three centuries ago.

The climactic resolution will captivate readers of this thriller with deep spiritual undertones.

PENMORE PRESS
www.penmorepress.com

A Gathering of Vultures

Donald Michael Platt

Murder, mutilation, and carrion... in paradise?

"There shall the vultures also be gathered, every one with her mate." -ISAIAH 34:15

Professional ballroom dancers Terri and Rick Hamilton aspire to be world champions. Unfortunately, Terri's recurring back and health problems place that goal well out of reach. They travel to Terri's birthplace, Florianópolis, on the scenic island of Santa Catarina off the coast of Brazil to vacation and visit their best friends and mentors.

Along the picturesque beaches, dead penguins and eviscerated bodies wash up on the shores of paradise, and Antarctic blasts play counterpoint to the tropical storms that rock the island. The scenic wonder is home not only to urubús, a unique sub-species of the black vulture, but also to a clique of mysterious women who offer Terri perfect health and the promise of fame—at a terrible price.

Praise for "A Gathering of Vultures

PENMORE PRESS
www.penmorepress.com

THE MAN IN THE SPIDER WEB COAT
BY
PHILIP ACKMAN

Titus Buchanan, a professor who runs a think tank at Williams College, believes he's figured out how to stage a successful revolution. When the United Nations adopts a historic vote spelling the end of colonialism, Buchanan seizes the opportunity to test his theory. His laboratory will be the Splendid Islands, a collection of palm-fringed cays scattered across three quarters of a million square miles of the South Pacific. Its inhabitants will be his lab rats.

But complications arise. The Splendids belong to New Zealand, and New Zealand has no intention of giving them up. The United States has its own secret "space age" agenda for the islands. The Queen of England is bound to support New Zealand, but she doesn't want Britain to fall out with the Americans, who favor independence. Meanwhile, the islanders, gripped with revolutionary fever, have ideas about self-rule. Reverend Geoffrey Brown, originally recruited by Buchanan to run the revolution, joins forces with an unlikely crew of locals and sets out to match wits with powerful opponents.

PENMORE PRESS
www.penmorepress.com